INTO THE JAWS OF DEATH . . .

Mountain Chief closed in on Doctor Sitgreaves until they stood a yard apart, each erect and unyielding. The chief lifted his bare arm and pointed beyond the circle of grumbling warriors. "Go away," he said in muted English. "You go now."

"No," said the Doctor, astonishing Skye. "No we will stay awhile."

"Bloody fools!" Skye roared, thinking he'd have to kill the Quakers now to keep them from being tortured. It would come in seconds. Warriors dared themselves, chanted medicine songs, shouted insults, whipped up courage. A thick warrior loosed his lance, which sailed like an evil bolt of lightning, grazing Artemus's frock coat and upper arm.

Skye scarcely could keep track of events. Artemus bled and wept. Abby Sitgreaves wilted. Jawbone trembled and pawed, berserk at his side; Victoria's knife glinted; Dirk stared solemnly up at him. The chief bulled straight toward him and Skye prepared to cut the man's guts out . . .

Tor books by Richard S. Wheeler

RICHARD S. WHEELER

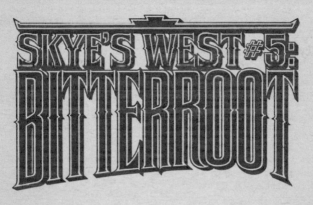

SKYE'S WEST #5: BITTERROOT

TOR

A TOM DOHERTY ASSOCIATES BOOK
NEW YORK

BITTERROOT

Copyright © 1991 by Richard S. Wheeler

A Tor Book
Published by Tom Doherty Associates, Inc.
49 West 24th Street
New York, N.Y. 10010

Cover art by Jim Warren

ISBN: 0-812-51305-3

First edition: August 1991

Printed in the United States of America

0 9 8 7 6 5 4 3 2 1

For Jeanne Williams

Chapter 1

Whenever Colonel Augustus Bullock summoned, Barnaby Skye hastened to the Fort Laramie sutler's shadowy office. The colonel was Skye's agent, and a summons often meant he'd found a client. That was why Skye kicked his evil horse, Jawbone, into a jog this bright mid-May day of 1853, down the bank of the Platte, past the stables, post hospital, and parade, to the cavernous store where the colonel waxed rich selling overpriced goods to soldiers and the hordes of settlers heading toward California.

Jawbone didn't think much of the fort or its soldiers, and he flattened his ears and peered about yellow-eyed, looking for handy targets for his hooves, but this day the parade lay deserted. Not for another month would the rush of emigrants heading to the gold fields of mythic California park their wagons and spill into the post.

Skye slid off Jawbone clumsily and left him untied at the hitch rail, where the animal would do sentry duty. He hastened through the double doors into a gloom thick enough to cut, making his way past bolts of canvas, barrels of oxshoes and horseshoes, sacks of flour, and tins of coal oil.

"You're one hundred ninety-seven in arrears, Mistuh Skye," Bullock greeted him. "Ah have to cut off credit."

Barnaby Skye lifted his black top hat and jammed it down again irritably. Was this what the colonel wanted to tell him?

"I'm hoping for a client with the summer's traffic, Augustus," he muttered.

Bullock stroked his white Vandyke disapprovingly. "Ah can't keep carrying you this way, Mistuh Skye."

The big guide sighed. The previous year he'd lost everything, his entire outfit, while guiding a party of New Englanders, and it had put him in the hole. This was as bad as the beaver days, he thought. In those days he was always in the hole to the fur company.

"Heah," said the colonel, handing Skye an envelope. "This came with the army express from Leavenworth this morning. I see it's from Culbertson."

Alexander Culbertson was an important man, head of the Upper Missouri Outfit for Pierre Chouteau's fur company. He divided his time between Fort Union and Fort Benton, far to the north on the Missouri River. But this letter had been posted in St. Louis and sent via military courier. Puzzled, Mister Skye tore at the heavy envelope and withdrew the note, penned in Culbertson's familiar bold stroke. It had been written May first, from Planters House, in St. Louis.

"My dear Barnaby," it began. *"Natawista and I will be going upriver on the* Robert Campbell *shortly. Also on board will be Dr. William Penn Sitgreaves, his wife Abigail, two sons, and two other gentlemen, all of them with the Society of Friends. They were going to make their way to Owen's Fort in the Bitterroot Valley on their own, but I prevailed on them to employ you at your usual rate, stressing the dangers of passage through*

that country without an experienced guide. They agreed, and if you are available they wish to have you meet them at Fort Union upon the arrival of the Campbell *on or around July 1. Doctor Sitgreaves is the founder of the Indian Aid Society and has closed his Philadelphia practice in order to bring medicine to the far tribes, and defend them with tracts. A remarkable man. My advice is, do it. Your obedient servant, Alec Culbertson.''*

Wordlessly, Mister Skye handed the letter to the sutler, who studied it.

"Well, suh, are you going to do it? You've time enough to get there."

"No."

"It's a fee."

"Greenhorns are dangerous. Get me killed."

"Ah'll outfit you."

Skye grinned. "You're protecting your investment."

The retired colonel paused and peered out the dirty window toward the Laramie mountains. "Ah'm not sure I'm protecting it. Society of Friends. Quakers, suh. Not ones to defend themselves with weapons. Pacifists, you know."

Skye didn't know. He'd never been back in the states. He'd been a British seaman until he'd jumped ship on the Columbia River at Fort Vancouver, long ago. "Tell me, Augustus."

"You should know about them. Persecuted in England, came to the New World in the seventeenth century. Persecuted here, too, until William Penn led them into what's now Pennsylvania, where they prospered. They practice a religion stripped of all ritual and formality. Not much of a clergy, either. Just themselves and God, suh. Quaker Meeting's mostly silence."

Skye pondered that, not liking it. "They won't take up arms—even to save themselves?"

"Not that I've heard of."

"You have any notion, Augustus, why they're going to John Owen's post?"

"I'm in the dark, Mistuh Skye. It couldn't be more out of the way. Maybe he knows John Owen. There's this, though: the tribes there, Salish, Kootenai, are peaceful. Father De Smet's work—before the Jesuits sold St. Mary's to Owen. That was eighteen and fifty, I believe."

"Bitterroot Valley's not that peaceful, Colonel. Blackfeet, Bannocks, maybe the Snakes now and then. . . . No. I'll pass this one up. I don't quite relish taking a party of pacifists across Blackfeet country."

"Well, why not go up there and find out?"

"Four hundred miles, just to see about a client who won't defend himself?"

"Your fee is five hundred dollars, suh. It'd clear the books with me."

"I'll wait. I usually pick up a client here."

The sutler sighed. "Mistuh Skye, suh. I've been holding out on you." He reached under his counter and withdrew a gleaming carbine of a type Barnaby Skye knew all about, and handed it to the guide. "It's a Hall-North breechloading carbine, suh. Cavalry model. First one in private hands. It failed to pass army inspection and was remanufactured to cure the defect. Uses paper cartridges. Work that breech mechanism, suh. You can reload in moments. Shoot it several times fastuh than that Hawken of yours. You take that, suh, and you can delivah a whole congregation of pacifists to hell if they want to go there."

Muttering, Barnaby Skye hefted the carbine, snapped the breech open, peered down the rifled barrel, slid imaginary cartridges in, snapped the breech closed, dry-fired, squinted down sights, squeezed the trigger, fingered paper cartridges, examined the .54-caliber balls in the cartridges, and discovered his palms were sweating.

"Haw! Har!" he said.

"Forty-three dollars. I'll add it to your account. You'll want two hundred cartridges. And a .54-caliber bullet mold. Some spare galena and caps. You can add whatever else you need to a total of four hundred. Give Culbertson your fee before you leave and have him credit my Chouteau and Company account in St. Louis with it."

"I haven't said I would. Pacifists'd get me scalped."

The sutler sighed. "Very well, then. Let me have the carbine."

But Skye's arms refused to hand it over. He wrestled with his arms, pushing on his massive biceps, commanding his burly forearms, insisting on the obedience of his thick fingers.

"I thought so, suh. I feared to show it to you, knowing it'd put you deeper in debt. It was an irresponsible act, showing this to you. Like giving spirits to a drunkard."

But Skye wasn't listening. He was, instead, waving the Hall-North about like a willow wand, discovering it weighed nothing, learning that it had magical properties. He was certain it could be used as a witching wand, a flute, a king's scepter.

"How fast does it reload?" he asked.

"About as fast as a platoon of Bug's Boys can jump you."

"What did you say it cost?"

"You weren't listening, suh. It'll cost you a trip to Fort Union and a summer of guiding a pacifist doctor and some greenhorns out to the Bitterroot Valley."

"Oh," said Mister Skye, aware that Bullock had been jawing at him for a minute or two. "Yes. I'll take the usual outfit, and add the jug. You know."

"I'll put my clerks to it, suh. Come back in a couple of hours. And oh, Skye—transfer Sitgreaves's payment to Culbertson before you leave Fort Union, eh?"

Something wicked burned in the colonel's rheumy eyes, and a faint mock lifted the corners of his mouth.

Then Mister Skye steered Jawbone back up the Platte, running like a dreadnought under canvas. He corralled his young wife Mary of the Shoshones, and his older wife Victoria of the Crows, dismantled the small lodge and loaded it on a lodgepole travois, stuffed their possessions into parfleches and loaded them into panniers, lifted his little son Dirk onto Jawbone's withers, and led his menagerie toward Fort Laramie.

Old Victoria glanced at him sharply but said nothing because he hadn't told her where they were going. He dreaded breaking the news—that they would be guiding a party of pacifists across the land of her Crow people's worst enemies, the fierce Blackfeet.

Back at the sutler's store, she watched sharply as Bullock's clerks handed Mister Skye sacks of sugar, coffee beans, and salt; trade gewgaws including ribbons and twists of tobacco and looking glasses; a crockery jug of spirits; and then something new—box after pasteboard box of paper cartridges. And then something stranger still: a shining, short-barreled carbine that Mister Skye slid triumphantly into the beaded elkskin sheath on Jawbone.

He knew Victoria wasn't disapproving, just curious. The disapproval would come later when she found out where this foray would take them. They took the military ferry across the swollen Platte and by evening were well away from Fort Laramie.

"Where are we going, Mister Skye?" asked beautiful Mary, as she played with little Dirk that evening before their lodge.

"Why, Fort Union, Mary, to pick up a party headed by a doctor. His wife, two sons, and two other gentlemen. I believe he's going to bring whitemen's medicine and perhaps religion to the Flatheads. He's the founder of something called the Indian Aid Society. So we'll head up the Missouri and over the passes to John Owen's place. He . . . ah . . . does not believe in taking up arms, not even to defend himself."

"Sonofabitch!" exclaimed Victoria. "When you don't say nothing, I know it's going to be bad."

Doctor William Penn Sitgreaves grew more and more quiet as the *Robert Campbell* approached Fort Union. That was a good sign. The calming of his spirit meant that he could accept what was to come with equanimity. At the beginning he had wondered about his courage and the courage of his party. But they all seemed eager to get on with it.

For weeks the paddle steamer had toiled its way up the mysterious flood called the Missouri, ever north and west, through utter wilderness. And each day, as the river packet fought its way north over sandbars and past desolate islands, the last outposts of civilization at Bellevue and Fort Leavenworth lay farther behind. There'd be no turning back. The river was a burning bridge.

The *Robert Campbell* drew five feet of water loaded, a foot more than most Missouri River boats, and that had slowed them. Doctor Sitgreaves had watched, fascinated, as its crew grasshoppered over the sandbars by lifting the boat on its own spars until it cleared the underwater obstacle. The *Campbell* carried three hundred tons of cargo, including the entire equipage of Doctor Sitgreaves and his party, and the whole annual resupply for the American Fur Company posts as well. Doctor Sitgreaves didn't entirely approve of the business conducted by Pierre Chouteau's giant fur company even though he was more or less a guest of the company on its chartered packet. It would ultimately ruin the western tribes, he thought. But that was why he had come. He intended to do something about it.

By a stroke of luck—or perhaps the Divine hand— he'd spent weeks on this very packet in the company of men who held the fate of the western tribes in their hands. In fact, a whole galaxy of distinguished people had come upriver this spring flood of 1853, including some Smithsonian paleontologists, Fielding Bradford Meek and Ferdinand Vandeveer Hayden. They'd debarked at Fort Pierre, far back in the Dakota country, to pry up dinosaur bones from the Dakota badlands.

Still, the ones who interested him more had remained on board. One of these was the new Indian Agent, Alfred J. Vaughan, who would begin negotiations with the northwestern tribes in pursuit of a peace treaty and reservations. The others were American Fur Company people, including Sitgreaves's gracious hosts, Alexander Culbertson, chief of operations for the Upper Missouri Outfit, and his Blood Indian wife, Natawista. Friends, perhaps—but soon, no doubt, antagonists. It troubled him that he might find it necessary to condemn such amiable men. But he would if he must, for right must prevail over might.

"Would thee prefer to talk with your gentlemen friends?" asked Abigail.

They sat in the women's lounge at the rear of the packet. It was permissible for the husbands or fathers or brothers of women to visit there by day, but not permissible for women to join them in the men's saloon evenings. At that hour, the women retired to their respective staterooms—cramped two-bunk affairs, or to the women's cabins adjacent to the women's lounge if they were single.

"I prefer to be with thee, Abby."

"Very well. I prefer to be bored in comfort. The odor of spirits and old cigars is too much for me."

"Perhaps I could find Natawista Culbertson—"

"She understands English but doesn't speak it. No, William Penn. If thee wishes to leave me, I will endure."

"Thee is kind, Abby." He rose gratefully, his afternoon duty done. "Until the dinner bell, then."

She nodded and reached for a darning needle and egg. A handsome woman, he thought. She wore, as always, a plain dress, except that hers had been sewn of richer stuff: a stiff black twill, finely needled, that wrought a spare elegance about her. Like his own. A worldly peccadillo, he knew. The Friends wore plain clothes, not necessarily black. But he liked black. He smiled, adjusted his thick black broadcloth suit coat and waistcoat, and retreated, feeling the steady hum of the twin steam pistons as they muscled the giant side wheels against the stream.

His announcement had been something of a shock, and not even the year's preparation for all this had entirely dissipated it. But he supposed the change would do her good. A Friend ought not to be too far gone in luxury. Her shining Walnut Street home had been the domain of two ancient maids and an English cook who boiled everything, leaving her free to devote herself to her Inner Light and to gossip.

"Thee will cure evil and sickness both," she had said when he'd told her how their life would change. "And perhaps cure me as well." There had been an edge to her voice.

He worked his way forward through the men's saloon, which lay gaudily between banks of staterooms. By night it became the social center of the packet. By day, passengers tended to stay outside in clement weather, endlessly fascinated by the unfolding panorama of the green river and the life on its banks. These things did not particularly excite Doctor Sitgreaves except during those moments when his mind hounded something he saw on shore, the way it did when he had a medical dilemma. He'd spent time at the rail when they'd come upon the first buffalo up above Bellevue somewhere. The beasts fascinated everyone, and quite a few of the ruffians who had bought deck passage had banged away at them. As a matter of medical curiosity, he'd observed which shots took effect and which hadn't. But mostly, the doctor had whiled away the trip indoors.

He let his portly self through the beveled glass doors at the head of the saloon and out upon the roofed boiler deck, the favorite resort of most passengers. Sure enough, Vaughan, Culbertson, and Mrs. Culbertson sat in deck chairs on the shadier side, in lively conversation, while Sitgreaves's wiry older son, Artemus, sat quietly, looking angry. The others of his party, his old debating friend Diogenes Fall, wrinkled and balding, and round-faced Freeman Price, whose brown hair had been slicked into a pompadour with goose grease, absorbed these strange sights serenely. Freeman's affectation was common enough among young bachelors, the doctor thought, but not a way for a Plain Person to embellish himself. Only Junius, his seventeen-year-old boy and forever the independent spirit, had scorned the shade in favor of his usual post at the prow of the packet, as if he could hurry the river by just watching it. Sitgreaves often wondered whether Junius would remain a Friend. Artemus would, but he'd be a dour one. Something was bothering the young man.

"Ah, Major Culbertson, may I join thee?"

Alexander Culbertson hooked an empty chair with his boot and dragged it closer.

"Last hours, Doctor Sitgreaves. We'll make Fort Union before dark," Culbertson said as the doctor eased his formidable bulk into the deck chair.

"That's why I seek thee. Tell me more, if thee will, about this Skye."

"He'll want you to address him as *Mister* Skye, Doctor. He's a former British seaman. A man of the mountains. A man high in American Fur for many years. The title Mister means something or other to him, and he'll want that courtesy. You'll find him rough in appearance, dressed in the way of the mountains: shoulder-length hair, a calico shirt, fringed britches, and ah, breechclout. Square-toed boots on the trail, moccasins in camp. Smooth-shaven, obscure blue eyes, but a nose! Ah, doctor, what a beak! It's been smashed a few times. A misshapen, enormous mountain—a ridge down his face that parts it the way Moses parted the Red Sea."

"Very well, I can accommodate all that, though it'll upset Abby. But could thee tell me about his ways, his manners? Is he a . . . civilized gentleman?"

Culbertson laughed. "Civilized? In an odd way. But as I told you, he's the best of all. He'll get you through if any mortal can. He'll want you to heed his advice—always—because your lives may depend on it."

William Penn Sitgreaves smiled gently. "We listen to our inner spirit and must act upon it, for it's light from above. I'm sure, Major Culbertson, that our peaceful intent will be plain to the Indians. Quite plain. It'll be upon our faces, I think. I don't want this fellow to go about brandishing weapons. We're here to help the tribes. We intend to alter Indian policy—transform the way civilized people treat these unfortunates. He can speak to them, I trust?"

Indian Agent Vaughan frowned and eyed the doctor sharply.

"Knows some of the tongues," Culbertson explained, "and uses signs for the rest. The hand signs are a poor way of talking, though. They don't get much across."

"Does thee know whether he speaks Blackfeet?"

Natawista Culbertson shook her head.

"Nope. In fact, there's some old grudges there, between Skye—one of his wives is Crow—and the Piegans, ah, the southernmost Blackfeet."

"One of his wives, did thee say?"

"He's got two. Victoria of the Crow, and Mary of the Snakes. Both as tough as he is. Women warriors. Like having a little army, them and that Jawbone—the meanest horse that ever got raised in captivity. A famous outlaw nag. He's butchered a whole passel of young bucks that gave him a whirl. They'll git you there, Doctor. It's like having a troop of cavalry with you."

William Penn Sitgreaves sighed slowly. "Major Culbertson," he said gently. "Would thee know of any other competent fellow who'd take us to Owen's Fort?"

Chapter 2

Major Culbertson introduced them on the boiler deck and then excused himself. He had to oversee the off-loading of the annual resupply and the shelving of the trade goods, he explained.

Below, on the main deck, sweating rivermen hoisted a mountain cargo from the hold and swung it ashore from spars. And on the riverbank, a vast crowd of Blackfeet, Cree, and Assiniboin gaped at the *Robert Campbell* and the treasure erupting from its belly.

"My dear Skye, it's a pleasure to meet thee at last," said William Penn Sitgreaves.

Mister Skye beheld a portly man dressed in black, his blue eyes bright and curious, his brown hair silvering.

"Doctor Sitgreaves," Skye rumbled. "A pleasure, I'm sure. And it's Mister Skye, mate."

"Ah! Forgive me! Alec mentioned it. Mister Skye, then. He had splendid things to say of thee. But we need to come to some agreements—I'm sure thee'll agree."

Barnaby Skye couldn't help but stare, and so did Mary and Victoria, for none of them had seen mortals accoutered such as these. Even without eyeing her, he knew Victoria was glaring at a woman who was dressed in black, as if life were a perpetual funeral. Handsome people, actually. The cut of Abigail Sitgreaves's black broadcloth spoke of wealth. She had not adorned herself with a necklace or jewels, other than a gold wedding band around her finger, but the severity of her costume only emphasized the oval beauty of her pale, and slightly amused, face. Her curiosity about the Skyes was obvious.

The sons, Skye observed, were polite gentlefolk, stamped by their parents, except that the older one, Artemus, seemed bored and unhappy. Under twenty, Skye guessed, and with a sullen quality about him. The younger one, Junius, looked to be fifteen and seemed much happier in this strange new world. The rest, including the two other gentlemen, Diogenes Fall and Freeman Price, appeared never to have been outdoors. Mister Skye frowned. It'd be hard enough to guide pacifists safely; even harder to guide indoor people, obviously bookish, who were so soft that sleeping on the ground would be an ordeal.

"Doctor Sitgreaves," Skye continued. "I think we need to powwow. I must ask some questions before . . . we decide matters. You see, sir, I don't always accept an offer—"

"Why, I had the very same thought, Mister Skye. Thee and thy ladies must sit down here and we'll talk. Perhaps we can find a boy to bring us tea."

That suited Mister Skye fine. They settled into deck chairs where they could watch the hubbub below. He was already concluding that the best thing would be to decline their offer.

"Thee must understand, first of all, that Friends trust in the Inner Light for guidance, and not at all in arms.

We could not engage a guide who might use a firearm upon other mortals.''

That settled it. ''Doctor Sitgreaves, I fear you'll run into grave trouble. The tribesmen here . . . Well, you'll lose your livestock and perhaps more—your lives . . .''

''Ah! We understand perfectly, and place our trust in Providence. I really wish to engage you for two purposes: one is to communicate with these tribesmen, and the other is to steer us to Owen's Post. And, of course, to hunt.''

''Sonofabitch,'' muttered Victoria.

That evoked an astonished halt in the conversation, and then it proceeded again, as smoothly as if Victoria didn't exist.

''If thee'll convey our purposes to visiting tribesmen, sir,'' explained Diogenes Fall, ''we will tell them of the Indian Aid Society, and dissuade them of any hostile impulses.''

Deepening alarm crabbed at Barnaby Skye. ''You don't exactly sit down and take tea with a bunch of Bug's Boys come just before dawn to snatch the horses, sir.''

''Bug's Boys?''

''Blackfeet. Devil's Boys, as the trappers called them.''

''Extraordinary. No mortal is the Devil's child, Mister Skye, but God's.''

''You might think otherwise if you've seen a friend scalped, tortured, mutilated—'' He stopped suddenly.

The doctor's blue eyes kindled brightly. The man had a powerful gaze, so strong that Skye could barely meet it, and all the more disconcerting because utter kindness radiated from him. ''We hear of these things. But thee must be aware that the Friends have found another way. Is it not a spiritual truth that if thee would return good for evil, thee would win allies and friends?''

Mister Skye was about to object strenuously, but Doctor Sitgreaves raised his hand. ''Ah, Mister Skye.

Perhaps we cannot come to terms, in which case we'll proceed alone to Owen's Fort. We'll do nicely, I'm sure. But I've scarcely said a word of our purposes here—the reason we've uprooted ourselves from Philadelphia.''

Mister Skye settled back in his chair to listen, but he'd already made up his mind. He'd wasted his time—and maybe a year's income—coming clear up here from Fort Laramie. But he couldn't resist those bright blue eyes, and a gaze that conveyed utter innocence, the directness of a child, the honesty of a saint, and, almost, the clarity of a madman. In truth, Skye confessed to himself, Dr. William Penn Sitgreaves was one of the most extraordinary men he'd encountered.

''Ah, Mister Skye. We Friends have, from the beginning, sought to heal the world. It is not our prideful doing, but our heeding of the inner voice. Thee may know we seek to end the abominable institution of slavery. Our dear friends Lucretia and James Mott have been much involved with it. She founded the Philadelphia Female Anti-Slavery Society. But thee perhaps do not know of our burning concern for our Indian brethren, and our stout opposition to the injustices done by whites to these good people for many decades. I took my inspiration from Lucretia and founded the Indian Aid Society. We Friends do things like that.

''After years of successful practice, I retired recently—in comfortable circumstances—to do something about all this. The federal Indian removal policy that pushed these people from their ancient homelands and deposited them ruthlessly in unknown wastes such as the Indian Territory north of Texas—why, sir, it seared my soul, and the souls of my brethren. I founded the Indian Aid Society to put a stop to it—to give voice to the suffering redman, to change policy, to reserve a fair portion of this continent for their use in perpetuity, to halt the invasion of land-grabbers, to awaken the Congress and people to the humanity and needs of our native peoples.''

Mister Skye found himself admiring the man and his passion, even if this gentle soul, both innocent and worldly, was as out of place here as a dolphin.

"But thee will understand it is not enough to reside in comfort and write tracts. We needed more than abstractions to meet the objections of, ah, frontiersmen, whose views, ah, are not in accord with ours. And here I discovered that strange confluence of career and ideal, for I discerned within myself a burning desire to practice my healing profession upon those red men who lack our sciences. I have with me, for instance, Jenner's vaccine for the pox. I wish to make some small amend for the scourge brought upon these tribes by the fur company boats.

"I made inquiry and learned about John Owen's post in the Bitterroot: how it'd once been St. Mary's Mission, founded by that estimable man, Father De Smet; how it lay in an idyllic mountain valley, home of the Salish people, industrious and friendly and admirable in all respects. How Owen's Post had, thanks to Jesuit industry, gardens and orchards, a dairy herd, poultry, sheep and swine, a gristmill and other amenities of civilization. I wrote him at once."

"What'd Owen say?"

"I never heard back—a natural hazard of correspondence to an isolated outpost—but we'll proceed anyway, for it's in me that we'll be warmly welcomed. And there, among friendly tribesmen who'll be recruited to spread outward among the other northwestern tribes, we'll bring medicine and study Indian ways. We'll prepare burning tracts, based on actual experience and expert knowledge. We'll employ the gifted Flatheads to build us a home near John Owen's own, and there we'll do the work that burns within our breast."

This amazing speech stirred turmoil in Barnaby Skye. "Why the Bitterroot?" he asked. "It's isolated. You'll be weeks away from the Oregon Trail; even farther from Salt Lake. You can't even get your tracts out to the world. Any fur post would be better; your patients would come to you in a steady stream."

"Thee has a point, but one we have weighed, Mister Skye. We might indeed have settled at Fort Benton or Fort Union, and indeed, we would have been thrown into contact with the people we seek to help. But you see, we have . . . doubts about the fur companies. In some respects they help the tribesmen—I need scarcely elaborate. But they're also an abominable influence, Mister Skye, doing a dark and dirty trade in spirits, demoralizing the tribes, and rendering them dependent on manufactured goods—metal things. They'll ruin the tribes. No. We could not rub shoulders with that commerce. We prefer Owen's Post, isolated as it is."

"He trades in furs, same as the Chouteau interests."

"The world's an imperfect place, Mister Skye. He also farms. Raises stock and poultry. His is the better place for us."

Skye stared down upon the main deck, where rivermen still toiled in the late afternoon sun. He had the peculiar sense of pulling himself out of Sitgreaves' unreal universe and into a concrete one while he watched the stevedores at their work.

"I imagine old John'd welcome you kindly, should you get there, Doctor. And I imagine you'd prosper there, doing about what you imagine, what with these gentlemen, your wife, and sons, to share the work. But getting there's another matter. These gentlemen with you are . . . city-bred."

"Indeed!" said Sitgreaves. "That older one talking to my boy is Diogenes Fall, a Latin scholar at Philadelphia Normal. An idealist, a man of soul. A burning conscience."

"Idealism won't harness mules, plow ground, or swing a scythe, Doctor."

Sitgreaves looked amused. "No, but it'll turn the world upside down. Now the other, the younger over there, is Freeman Price. A bookkeeper. He came for

the adventure and considers it a tour, Friends fashion.
The way a soldier serves for an enlistment. Oh, I suppose they'll try thee at first with their city ways. But
they're salty men, sir.''

Barnaby Skye wanted more than salt in any man he
guided. This wasn't country for Latin scholars and
bookkeepers. He sighed restlessly, not concealing anything from the doctor.

The doctor's eyes sparked light, a sensation that
seemed almost eerie to Skye. ''Well, my dear Mister
Skye. Thee has heard me out, interviewed me, so to
speak. Now I require of thee that I learn of thy ways.
Thee can begin, sir, by explaining thy choice of that
extraordinary top hat; and thee can continue by telling
me about that necklace of bear claws—grizzly, I suppose. And I shall wish to know thy beliefs, the things
that govern thee—would thee take a life? And I wish to
learn about these thy wives—lovely women, are they
not, Abby? And finally, sir, whether thee could abide
by the Commandments?''

Much to Mister Skye's astonishment, he found himself offering his life history to Doctor Sitgreaves, as
well as an account of his marriages. But even more
astonishing, he found himself tempted by Sitgreaves's
terms. He could do it, actually. His medicine would do
it for him. The terror he and Jawbone excited in the
tribesmen would do it. His legendary warrior wives
would do it. If need be, a shot intended to miss its
target would do it. He could deliver the Friends without
taking life.

''I reckon I could do that, mate.''

''Does thee include thy whole party?''

Skye considered. ''I imagine so. It's not a long trip.
We don't often run into trouble. And arms are a last
resort anyway.''

Victoria stared at him aghast.

''We hold thee to thy word, then. I'll draw a draft

for thee in the morning. God spare thee a good rest, thee and thine.''

''We'll leave at dawn, mate. I don't think they'll even unload your truck until then. Company freight first.''

Barnaby Skye peered down upon the chaos below, where armies of rivermen and engagés were unloading and carting tons of supplies that would provision three Chouteau and Company posts for an entire year. Later they'd load the returns, the entire mountain of baled buffalo robes the fur company had collected in the past year, a fortune even larger than the one that had come upriver in the belly of the *Robert Campbell*.

''Very well. We'll see thee on the levee at daybreak, Mister Skye.''

Victoria felt as if the marrow in her bones had frozen. Not in her wildest imaginings had she thought Mister Skye would take people such as these. Unarmed! She couldn't fathom what possessed him, and she peered anxiously at her man, to see if he had been witched. But he seemed serene enough as they trudged back toward Fort Union amidst a throng of tribesmen— Cree, Assiniboin, and Blackfeet—waiting for trade to open in the morning.

She trotted along beside him, wondering what he'd do when the time came, as it often did, when he and his wives would need to defend the ones they guided. His burly body had been fashioned for war, she thought, and it bore the scars and furrows of countless battles. His war medicine radiated from him as they made their way through the throngs; indeed, the hateful enemies of her people—Cree and Assiniboin—gave him wide berth, their eyes contemplative on him as he passed. They knew him well, and whispered of him around their campfires. The black topper that sat rakishly on his head had been pierced by several balls, and yet none had struck him. The bear-claw necklace radiated its own medicine. His new Hall-North carbine

shone malevolently in the orange sunset light, a deadly
wand resting lightly in the crook of his arm.

They all knew him for a warrior, him and his warrior
women, and his warrior horse, the terrible blue roan.
And they never suspected that Mister Skye had just bargained to forgo his warrior skills for an entire journey—
and not only his skills, but those of Mary and Victoria,
and his horse. Victoria knew the Sixth Commandment
and considered it amazing, at least when applied to
the laws of other nations: Thou shalt not kill. She felt
trapped. She thought wildly of leaving him here, with
these strange white men, and sliding back to her people
on the Yellowstone. But she knew she wouldn't. She
was Mister Skye's woman, from now unto death—which
might come soon.

Unless—A disturbing thought struck her. Unless these
Quaker people possessed some sort of medicine she
couldn't fathom, big medicine, powerful, terrifying
medicine that would strike dead anyone who harmed
them. Strike them dead, or mad, or sick. Was that it?
Did these ones who dressed in black have some sort of
secret power over all the things of the earth, power over
Mister Skye to make him weak? She didn't know, but
she feared witch medicine above all else, evil medicine
that stole the spirit of a victim, so that he was himself
no more.

An apricot twilight lay over the fort as they entered,
gilding the western side of the cottonwood stockade
surrounding the yard. The Skyes would be on their own
tonight, she knew. Everyone from their great man, Alec
Culbertson, to the engagés and clerks, would toil all
night, working in torchlight, dragging whitemen's riches
from the fireboat, shelving goods, keeping records with
the talking signs on the pages, not stopping until the
great task was done. And in the morning they'd be too
busy to see the Skyes and their clients off. They would
all be dressed in frock coats, and they'd go out among
the chiefs to give them gaudy gifts and make windy

speeches. Then they'd run up the company flag and fire the mountain howitzer, and trading would begin. But by then, she knew, the Skyes and the strange ones would be long gone. And she'd be glad. She never did like this sprawling fort, so far away from the home of her mountain Crow people.

They wended their way through reefs of crates and bales, heaped and scattered across the yard, and reached their own small lodge which they had erected beside Jawbone's pen at the rear. Culbertson always gave his former employee, Mister Skye, the courtesy of the post, and the Skyes had always made camp right in the yard. Victoria never liked it there, surrounded by ancient gray cottonwood poles, side by side, rising sixteen feet above them like prison walls.

Jawbone whickered his greetings and paced back and forth in his narrow confines, indignant at being caged. Mister Skye trotted to him at once and let the ugly yellow-eyed beast butt him in the chest and snort and bite playfully. She watched it all dourly in the thickening dark, knowing that this weapon, too, the great vicious medicine horse, would be set aside this trip.

Later, in the noisy dark, company men worked clamorously around the gates and trading room. The Skyes slipped to the kitchen and ate good buffalo loin in an onion stew. But Victoria could stand it no more.

"Goddam it, Mister Skye. Why do you do this?"

Her man turned to her serenely. "Easy trip. There won't be trouble, and if there is, we'll palaver some, hand out a few twists of tobacco, and be on our way."

"It's like being naked."

"We won't see a soul. Everyone's trading this time of year."

"I don't like them. They got witch medicine."

"Old lady, Doctor Sitgreaves has the brightest, kindest face a man can see."

"He's got crazy-fire in his eyes. They're all living in

the Other-Side Land. Maybe not the doctor, but them other ones, the wild-eyes one called Fall.''

Mister Skye laughed easily. "It's not even a long trip. And I think if it blows cold, they'll change their bloody minds in a hurry. Meanwhile, we got a nice fee coming, and we'll visit your people on the way back.''

"If we're alive.''

Skye bellowed happily, but nothing was funny to Victoria, or Mary either. Mary sat inside the lodge, undressing their chunky little boy, but she was listening, Victoria knew. She felt afraid. Not just afraid, but more. She felt terror creep through her body, through her bone marrow, and lurk in her skull.

"Medicine witches," she said. "They fixed you.''

She felt his alert gaze on her, across the darkness. "No, Victoria. They practice a radical form of Christianity, seeking to change the world. They'd like to be beacons, signal fires, a city set on a hill, to all men.''

"Witches," she said. "Are they shamans? Medicine men?''

"Like ministers or priests? No. They have none. I'm told their services are mostly silence. Sometimes some one or another stands up and says something. Something they're inspired to say. But no, no priests, no ministers. Unless maybe they're their own ministers. Why don't you ask them?''

She glared at him. "I've never fought you, Mister Skye. Hardly ever, anyway. But I don't think you should—''

"I've agreed, Victoria. I gave my word.''

"What happens if the Siksika come?" She spat out the name of her enemies. "Will you shoot? You gonna let us die?''

He sighed, not liking the question, she knew. "I'd try trading. Smoking the pipe. But I'd hate to go back on my word.''

"Have these Friends got medicine? Big medicine, so

Siksika fall dead? So dogs crawl away, tail between their legs?''

"No, no medicine like that. They're like sheep."

"I don't understand this!" she cried. "Sheep. Sheep need shepherds to keep wolves away!"

"We'll deliver them safely to John Owen," he said easily, sliding his thick arm around her bony shoulders.

She loved the touch of him, the strength of him, the warrior power she felt, nestled securely in the circle of his safety, and grieved at this strange turn of events. She knew, suddenly, that death would stalk them and strike, and strike again.

Chapter 3

Abigail Sitgreaves faced the future with considerable dread, although she did her best to conceal it from William Penn. This would be her last night in the stateroom, and she clung to it quietly. What passed for a stateroom on a Missouri River packet was a narrow cubicle with bunk beds and barely room to store valises or turn around. William Penn had taken the upper bunk, and it struck her as unseemly that his portly carcass rested each night directly above her. Still, the tawdry compartment was something familiar and civilized, something she could comprehend. From its door, opening on the men's saloon, she could find her way to the dining areas, or the privy closets aft of the giant paddlewheels, or the women's saloon, comforts all.

But tomorrow would begin a life so radically removed from her experience as a Philadelphia gentlewoman that she could scarcely grasp it. No matter that William Penn had purchased an elegant cotton-duck wall tent and camp cots for the two of them and a second wall tent for her sons, Diogenes Fall, and Freeman

Price. She couldn't imagine ever being comfortable, or feeling safe or at peace, on this mad journey. She'd tried hard to accept all this, but she couldn't. And now she lived a double life, a proper Friend and wife in her exterior parts—and a carping critic and cynic within. He had no idea of her true state of mind.

Were it not for the strange illumination God given surely that she saw in William Penn's eyes whenever he talked of helping the western tribes, and hearing their complaints, and bringing his formidable surgery and medicine to them, she would have gently begged off and stayed within the beloved confines of her solid red brick home on Walnut Street, surrounded by every comfort of civilization, not least of which was the utter security of person in the City of Brotherly Love. She yearned momentarily for that, and had an unruly impulse to stay aboard the *Robert Campbell* on its downriver voyage. But she hoped she might be made of sterner stuff. It was, she thought, within the power of Quaker women to rule over themselves.

He'd never asked her whether she wished to come, never worried about her fears and comforts, but had supposed from the beginning that she shared his own white-lit passion to uplift these benighted tribesmen. She didn't. Her soul yearned for nothing more than the comforts of sly gossip with her sewing circle, and mending his black stockings over her ivory darning egg. When he'd told her they'd be traveling into the far West to help the noble savage, her immediate thought had been that boys will be boys. William Penn was really an overgrown boy. But she had only smiled and said, "Wherever thee goes, there shall I go." He hadn't asked his sons either, and in Artemus, at least, she saw a rebellious spirit beneath his quiet obedience. William Penn didn't even suspect it.

He seemed cooped up here, dutifully entertaining her in the long June evening, something itching in him like a tick in his broad buttocks. The rest had fled the confining ship and vanished into the hubbub on the flats surrounding Fort Union. None of them wished to impose on the traders of Fort Union at a time when they were desperately busy unloading and stocking the mountain of trade goods steadily belching from the cavernous hold of the packet. She knew, though, that soon he'd grow weary of her knitting, which she did with evil intent, her needles clattering furiously to annoy him. She was manufacturing long woolen stockings, bright crimson and wholly un-Quakerish, which she intended to wear to bed, wherever they ended up. Perhaps crimson bootees would terrify redskins.

"Let's take the air," he said. "Thee would enjoy a stroll. We'll see the Indians."

She didn't reply, but instead found her tasseled shawl of pearl-gray wool, as protection against the evening, and drew it over her black dress. Then she tied her gray bonnet under her chin, feeling half curious and half afraid.

"The others are long gone," he added. "I hope our sons conduct themselves with dignity."

"They'd be incapable of doing otherwise," she said drily.

She took his comforting arm as he steered her down the companionway to the main deck, past sweating men wrestling strange crates, down the long stage, and then upon solid earth, which felt odd beneath her black-shod feet. He led her up a steep bank to the flat and to the vast array of conical lodges in which wild men lived. A thousand Indians, maybe more, were awaiting the opening of trade, she knew. And several hundred of them stood right there, silently watching the unloading, studying the fireboat in the golden evening light. She eyed them demurely, enjoying their near nakedness, though she was careful to avert her gaze, as she did in art galleries and museums. She had become very good at it, knowing how to study something to the keen edge without seeming to. Everywhere bronzed lean men, as finely muscled as a running horse, stood watching, along with bare-armed women and naked little boys, and tawny girls in tiny skirts. They titillated her, and evoked a queer feeling in her.

She smiled bravely at them. These were the very people who'd excited the compassion of William Penn, so she owed them smiles and her benevolent pleasure in their company. Doctor Sitgreaves didn't attempt to speak to any, though they stared at him boldly, as if transfixed. Instead, he doffed his black felt topper and smiled, an act that repeatedly drew sharp gazes and muttering, and she remembered that amazing Mister Skye wore a similar hat.

"They're a handsome, strong, curious people," Doctor Sitgreaves said serenely. "I haven't the foggiest idea of their affiliation."

"I don't think they have affiliations, dear," she said.

She clutched his arm a little tighter. Their gazes had settled on her, even more than on Doctor Sitgreaves, and she wondered if she were the first white woman they'd ever seen. How strange the fur men must have seemed to these people, she thought, coming up the river without white women.

"Thee are an attraction," he said to her.

"I should hope so."

He laughed gently. "To me especially."

William Penn pushed through the throng like Moses parting the Red Sea, intent on a walk among the lodges. But with each step they acquired an entourage of adults and children and wheeling mutts. Shy women, some dressed in plain calicoes or unadorned doeskin, pressed close, smiling, saying things she couldn't even guess at, sometimes touching the stiff black fabric, or examining the finely wrought seams, the work of a splendid Pennsylvania dressmaker whose tiny stitches welded one piece of fabric into its neighbor in smooth lines. One chunky child, a boy, wished to see what she wore on her feet, and flattened himself just ahead, waiting for a glimpse of foot leather. They *were* seeing their first white woman, she supposed.

"See how they welcome us," said William Penn, and she knew his startling eyes and sinless gaze had attracted their own attention. "I'd love to speak with them—tell them of our purposes, and of the services we'll offer them all. Ah, if only Mister Skye were here to translate."

Some of the males wore gaudy plumage she took to be festival dress in honor of tomorrow's ceremonies: corrugated necklaces of white bone that hung like washboards down their lean chests; small pouches worn on a thong around their necks, containing she couldn't imagine what; blue-black hair without the faintest curl, which they wore either loose about the shoulders, or braided. She caught scents new to her, of smoke and leather, of sagebrush and other things too subtle and unfamiliar to name.

"Does thee speak English?" William Penn asked a headman, one who wore two notched eagle feathers in his hair.

The man grunted something unintelligible.

"We must make it our first business to learn their tongues," he said to her. "Thee and I must persuade the Skyes to teach us the Crow and Shoshone; and Mister Skye shall be my mentor for the sign language."

They wandered among lodges now, with their retinue trotting politely behind. She grasped something of how they lived in these conical houses of skin, some of them gaudily painted by their proud owners with scenes of hunting and war, or sun and lightning and rain, or moon and stars. She could see into many of the lodges because their sides were rolled up a way to permit the summer breezes to flow through. Within she glimpsed dark buffalo robes, a few blankets, a backrest or two made of reed, and rawhide boxes and portfolios that apparently held household items or food.

On William Penn Sitgreaves's arm she felt no fear,

though had she been alone here, she would have been alarmed.

They emerged at last upon a small cleared area, devoid of any lodges except one larger lodge, gaudily painted in earth colors. Before it two war lances had been thrust into the dusty soil, each lance adorned with eagle feathers, crimson-stained rawhide grips, and odd bits of black hair that looked almost human. Not far away, the silvery west wall of the great fur post caught the dying sun.

A tall man emerged from the lodge, and his look chilled Abigail. He wore only a breechclout and a bonnet of eagle feathers. Great puckered scars deformed his powerful torso, twisting around ribs and out upon the small of his back, as well as his left cheek. From his neck hung a horrifying necklace of dessicated human fingers, blackened by sun and age. His thick sensual lips curled downward, as if they had been molded into a pout before birth; but his jet eyes, as opaque as obsidian, were what finally pinioned her mind—and emotions. His eyes struck her and William Penn like thrust lances, something palpably willful in them, and yet she could see nothing of his soul, nor did she have any inkling what sort of man this scarred leader might be.

"You come?" the man said in English.

"Ah! Thee speaks English, my friend," said William Penn Sitgreaves joyously. "I'd been hoping for just this. Whom do I have the honor of addressing?"

The headman paused, not grasping his words. "You speak Engleesh?" he asked.

"I do. I am William Penn Sitgreaves, and this is my wife Abigail. We are Friends. And thee?"

The headman seemed puzzled, but at last said, "Pakap-otokan. Bad Head. I am Kainah. A chief of the Kainah."

She had never heard of that tribe, and apparently William Penn hadn't either.

"Blackfeet," Bad Head said. "Some whitemen say Blood people. Why are you here?"

"Ah!" said William Penn, a great fire kindling in him that suffused his face. "We—some Friends and I—have come to help the Indian people of the west. I am a doctor, ah, a practitioner of medicine, ah, a surgeon. I've come to heal all who are in need, to the best of my abilities. Including you and your Kainah people, Bad Head. And we have come to learn about all the tribes, and carry your messages and goodwill back to the fathers in Washington City."

"You wear the victory robes. Have you won a great battle?"

That utterly puzzled her but William Penn was up to it. "Ah, our black clothing. Yes, the mark of victory among thy people. Thee paint thyselves black after a great victory. Indeed. With us, Bad Head, black represents another kind of victory, the triumph of the Spirit of God within us. Not all of us wear black, but we prefer it."

"Mighty big battle," said Bad Head, surveying the blackness of their clothing, head to toe. "Are you blackrobes, like De Smet? He was a friend of the Kainah."

"No, not priests. But we're going to Father De Smet's old mission, which is now Owen's Post, in the Bitterroot, my friend. And there, among the Flatheads—Salish—we'll begin our work."

A thundercloud spread across the visage of the chief, an expression so terrible that it sent a chill racing through Abigail. She tugged at William Penn, desperately wishing to retreat. "Salish. You take your whiteman medicine to our enemies. Dogs. Cowards. We kill Salish. There—"he pointed at some black pelts dangling from the leftward lance. "Salish scalps. Why do you go there? To give your medicine to the enemies of the Kainah, the Piegan, the Siksika?"

"But, my friend, it's for all the Indian people. For thee also."

"They would lie in wait for us. No. You must not go there. You will make medicine for us. Not the Salish dogs."

William Penn drew himself up thoughtfully. "We have come to help all tribesmen. Yours, Crow, Flathead, Assiniboin, Cree, Sioux, Gros Ventre, Kootenai—"

Bad Head snarled something at William Penn and without a word whirled into his lodge. A terror crept through her. They waited in a quiet that stretched tautly into the dusk, but the interview had ended.

"I think we'd best return to the packet, Abby. I didn't handle that well. Thee must not be afraid. We need the Skyes to explain these things, and tomorrow we'll have them." He looked so calm, his eyes so brightly kind and blue.

"I wonder if they play whist," she said.

He laughed.

Tomorrow they'll have the Skyes, she thought, faintly curious about the bizarre guide and his wives. But she wished now that William Penn hadn't imposed such—conditions—on Mister Skye, who looked like he knew how to use that shining weapon in his hands.

At that latitude, at that time of year, dawn rosed the northeastern skies early. But the Quakers were as good as their word, Mister Skye thought, spotting them assembled with their outfit on the levee beside the slumbering steamboat. Sometime in the night, the rivermen had gotten around to unloading it.

"Sonofabitch!" exclaimed Victoria as they approached, and Mister Skye knew at once what she alluded to. Percherons, giant draft horses half again larger than anything Victoria had ever seen. An enormous black stallion with a roman nose stood harnessed to a two-seat buggy that looked like a toy behind the animal. And a pair of gray Percheron mares, massive and high, stood in harness before a wagon with bows and an osnaburg sheet over it. The fourth horse, a sleek bay saddler, stood tied to the wagon.

But Victoria had started to hoot. It wasn't the giant draft horses that excited her, apparently, but the sight of these Quakers, or at least the gentlemen. Mister Skye understood that swiftly, too: each of them except the Sitgreaves sons wore a black topper like his own, albeit pristine.

"Big Medicine," howled Victoria, and the Quakers peered at her, not comprehending.

"Thee are here," said Doctor Sitgreaves. "Does thee approve of our outfit?"

Mrs. Sitgreaves sat in the lushly quilted leather front seat of the black-lacquered buggy, and in the rear seat sat Freeman Price and Diogenes Fall, each of them accoutred in Quakerly attire. Back on the wagon, Artemus Sitgreaves held the lines running to the giant mares, while young Junius, dressed less formally, stood beside the leggy saddler, ready to ride.

"First draft horses I've seen out here, mate. They're fine."

"Look at them hooves," muttered Victoria. "Look at the size of them. They gonna leave tracks. Horses get stole by everyone sees them."

"We hoped not, Mrs. Skye. We hoped they'd be too large to excite the soul of a passing warrior."

"Ha! Horse like that, they'll try anything."

"A Percheron stallion and two mares. We'll breed Percherons at Fort Owen, and teach the Flatheads plowing. We have the implements in the wagon. Does thee see anything amiss? Surely two of these formidable creatures can draw the wagon, and one can pull our buggy."

"No, mate, they're fine."

But Jawbone didn't like the giants. He laid back his ears and clacked his teeth evilly, and sidled toward the mares intending to commit mayhem with his incisors, and Mister Skye failed to check the battered blue roan with his knee.

"Thy horse is not happy with the mares. Nor with the stallion either, Mister Skye. He's some animal, your horse. Here, I'll hold him for you—"

"Stop!" bawled Skye.

Doctor Sitgreaves was puzzled. "Does he kick, sir?"

"No, he kills."

Doctor Sitgreaves peered thoughtfully at Jawbone, registering the evil yellow eyes, narrow-set in an ugly face; the battered, puckered flesh, rough-haired along wounds; the gaunt, sinewy frame; the lashing tail; and the way Jawbone tracked every step and movement of the doctor.

"Thee has a dangerous horse, Mister Skye. We will be careful."

"Best you do, mates. After a while he'll get to know you, but until then—he'd as soon butcher you."

"Oh dear," said Abigail.

"He's not been much around stallions," Mister Skye added. "Especially ones twice his weight. I'll have to take measures at first."

Jawbone shrieked, a wicked howl of rage that shattered the dawn peace. The Quakers recoiled. Mister Skye felt Jawbone shiver beneath him and gather himself for a murderous assault, his fear and hatred of the black stallion palpable.

"Easy, mate," he murmured, running his meaty hand up Jawbone's neck under the mane. He felt Jawbone calm slightly, but Jawbone's eyes tracked every move of every Quaker.

"All right, mates. My Victoria will usually be ahead of us, scouting and hunting, finding trouble before it finds us. I'll sometimes be ahead, sometimes leading our procession. Behind me, it'll be Mary first, driving our pack mules, our travois, and taking care of our son, there. Dirk. Behind them, Doctor, you'll follow with your buggy, and after that, the wagon." He turned to Junius. "You've a saddler there, no doubt looking forward to the hunt. I see you have a carbine sheathed. But I'd just as soon you followed behind the wagon, checking constantly behind you. Your brother, there, can't see much from his wagon seat."

Junius smiled. "And what will I see if I peer behind—the devil chasing us?"

The lad meant it for humor but it didn't seat that way.

"The bloody devil indeed, lad, and if you see him, you'd better pray."

"Now, now, thee dramatizes, I'm sure, Mister Skye," chaffed Doctor Sitgreaves.

But Barnaby Skye wasn't laughing. "You've imposed conditions on me that imperil you all, mate. You'd better trust in medicine if you don't trust in my other skills."

"Them medicine hats, Mister Skye," muttered Victoria, grinning hugely. "Three Mister Skyes this time, yes? Damn sonsofbitches Siksika, they turn to tallow."

She and Mary giggled. The Quakers looked affronted.

"Let's get," he muttered. "I'd like to sail clear of here before these people hyar"—he waved his hand at the hundreds of silent lodges—"see those draft horses and take notions."

They started at once, in perfect order, the draft animals tugging the carriage and wagon as if they were feathers, up the Missouri along a well-known trace that would take them west.

But they didn't escape the slumbering city at the foot of Fort Union. At first a few, and then a hundred silent warriors wrapped in blankets emerged from lodges to gape at the Quakers in black top hats and the awesome horses that stepped smartly along on hooves the size of dinner plates. And among them stood Bad Head, staring intently at the strange parade.

Chapter 4

William Penn Sitgreaves squandered a perfect morning on the centering of his spirit and the achievement of a sublime calm within his breast. A spanking west wind filtered away all the heat that the bright July sun incubated in his black frock coat, and he found himself utterly comfortable in the dry western air. In every direction the open land tumbled off to unseen horizons beyond the lip of the world, fostering a liberty in him he'd never experienced in busy Philadelphia.

He contemplated his new life with joy. Beside him sat his lovely Abigail, as much alive to the profound emptiness of the land as he. Behind him, his splendid colleagues Freeman Price and Diogenes Fall sat in comfort, absorbing the sights as they traversed a vague trace that took them farther away from the Missouri bottoms and out upon a flat bench land. And behind the carriage, his solemn son Artemus drove the lumbering supply wagon, handling the mares easily. The dutiful older son kept his own counsel, and Sitgreaves could never quite fathom what lay behind his sad eyes.

He saw nothing of Mister Skye's older wife, Victoria. She'd swiftly trotted ahead and disappeared, but he understood her mission as that of a forward observer, a sort of cat's whisker, seeing what lay ahead. And a hunter as well. She'd be ever on the lookout for buffalo and other game. As for Skye himself, the guide often appeared at the head of the procession, sharing a thought with his younger wife, and then wheeling off on that awful horse that fulminated hate from its eyes like a creature demonic. Just what Skye did all day William Penn couldn't fathom. Other clients, he knew, engaged Skye to protect them by whatever means was needful; but he didn't want that sort of violent protection. It'd be a scandal to murder Indians in the process of taking medicine and alliance to them.

"What does thee make of the Skyes now?" Abigail asked him, a small tart smile forming across her mouth. "We might better have employed a translator," he replied. "The trace seems clear enough. We scarcely need a guide, at least on this leg of the trip. It's their language we lack. With it, we can present ourselves and our purposes to them."

In fact he was regretting the costly five-hundred-dollar fee he'd agreed to; five hundred that might better have gone into medicines, or the printing of tracts. He'd given it to Skye that dawn and Skye had taken it into Fort Union and given it to Major Culbertson. It hadn't been a wise move, hiring these fierce people. All around him, the sunlit land lay benign. He knew indeed that sometimes it erupted into bloody conflict, especially when redmen fought redmen. But his own Inner Light had led him to an understanding of all this: apart from a few perverse mortals, the mad dogs of the universe, most men of any condition sought not war and blood, but friendship and advantage. A few words, and good intentions made plain, and trust in a merciful Providence who'd asked men to keep the Commandment for good and sufficient reason—all these were better proof against evil than all the world's Skyes.

"It's peaceful," she said, "for now."

He turned, wondering why he'd not heard from Fall and Price, and found them both dozing, sprawled across the seat, lulled by the monotonous clopping of those pie-plate hooves. Very well, then. They had begun this journey upon a somnolent, uneventful morning that would be the first of twenty-five or thirty such July days. He saw nothing alive in the slashed plains save for a circling crow off in the western haze.

They nooned at a cold freshet that ran from nowhere to nowhere, in a crease of prairie where a few cottonwoods nestled under the arching horizon. A picnic place, he thought. Crossing the high plains had more the aspect of a picnic outing than a trek across an alien land. He didn't miss trees, though he was used to canopies of them, bright with summer leaf, back east. Rather, he discovered in the vast reaches a freedom of the eye, a chance for the spirit to pierce into the future and see possibility unfenced. He loved this tan and green and brown world unfenced. Not a single barrier, other than natural ones, prevented him from progressing along any vector he chose, on any point of the compass. And yet, subtle as it was, the land herded them from water to water, on ground the most level, on a course that rounded mountains and avoided chasms. Even where no fences existed, man lacked perfect liberty. A lesson, he supposed.

Mister Skye had signaled the nooning from a ridge beyond the freshet. He sat Jawbone up there, looking like a pagan god, half wild and half civilized in his yellow calico shirt, his buckskin britches with great fringes hanging from them, and that odd silk hat perched cockeyed on his graying hair. Mary drew her pony up in a copse of cottonwoods and halted her packmules there, letting them all water noisily at the freshet. The

Friends likewise watered their beasts, and wandered along the tiny creek, stretching limbs.

Only after a considerable pause did Skye turn that wolfish roan horse downslope and join them. Victoria never appeared at all.

"We're making good time, mate. Those draft animals of yours come along right smartly."

"They pleasure me," William Penn replied. "I canvassed the country long and hard for them."

"You have no spares," Skye said abruptly. "Best unharness them and let them graze a little. And watch close. We'll give them a rest for an hour or two."

"Thee will cost us time, Mister Skye. I'm eager to be on our way."

"We'll take care of what we have," Skye replied. "You've no spares."

William Penn saw to it, of course, asking his sons to unharness the giants and let them graze. He recognized in Skye a man who knew what he was doing, and he would heed the guide in all ways. He regretted that he hadn't bought a fourth Percheron as a spare, to be rotated while the others got their rest in turn. They might have made faster time that way. But he'd done the best he could back there on Walnut Street.

Something in Skye's expression showed approval, William Penn decided. "Thee has had clients less willing to let you advise them, I imagine, Mister Skye. But you'll find me a perfect student of your ways. I'd no more resist thee here than I'd trust thee to do my surgery."

Barnaby Skye laughed easily. "We've hardly begun, sir. You'll come to resist all my deviling ways in time."

"I've seen not a soul all morning, Mister Skye. Are we passing through a land uninhabited by any tribes?"

"Nay, that's not it. This is Assiniboin country, except when Crees and Blackfeet come through, or Gros Ventres or maybe Sarsi or Sioux or Crow or Hidatsa."

"I see not a sign of them. We travel a road of sorts.

I've been watching. For horse sign, for discarded things, for campsites. Nothing, sir. Nothing but grass that crawls thinly over hills that stretch to the end of the world."

"Like the Pacific, mate. Like the northern seas. No, you'll not likely see them now. They'll be trading now that the forts are loading up. They'll push their robes through the windows, and collect powder and ball, caps and rifles, knives and hoop iron for arrowheads, hatchets and axes. After that, armed to the teeth, why, it'll be horse-raiding time, war time, migrating village time, buffalo hunting time, and maybe the time to buccaneer our horses. Those Percherons are like a merchant ship to pirates, Doctor."

"Thee will let me deal with them, I trust, Mister Skye. I need only to have you translate my words to them."

"Peaceful don't always do it, Doctor."

William Penn Sitgreaves drew himself up quietly. "I will not permit what God forbids. If worse comes to worse, sir, and we are slaughtered, or our whole wealth is taken from us and we are dead or ruined, we will still be faithful to the will of God."

Skye lifted that battered hat and screwed it down again warily. "I reckon we'll slip you through. I'm fixin' to hide us like a ghost ship over the horizon if we see some village or a painted-up party coming."

"Thee misunderstands, Mister Skye. We don't wish to hide, or flee, or circumvent. Should thee or thy ladies discover a village or a mounted party, let us go to them at once. I wish to begin my work."

"Your work?"

"Of course. I'm a physician. And while I cannot heal but a fraction of the woes of man, I can do what I can do. I have with me, for instance, some serum—smallpox vaccine—to give them. And I have quantities of the Peruvian bark, cinchona, that makes quinine for the ague. And I have large quantities of foxglove—

digitalis, sir—for the weakness of the heart and the dropsy. And a whole dental kit to pull rotten teeth. Thee needs only to tell them of our purposes, Mister Skye, to win us friends.''

Skye stared at him. ''I think you'd best let me decide that. Some villages aren't ones to go into. Depends on the bloody chief, like a good king or bad king. You'd endanger your party, endanger Mrs. Sitgreaves in— several ways. Torture, mate. They do that to anyone who's not one of themselves . . . and count it a blessing. Stick pitch-pine splinters into the body—the whole body, mate—and then ignite them. Cut off fingers, joint by joint—''

Sitgreaves waved his hand impatiently. ''I'm aware of that. I've studied upon it. Read cases in the medical journals. I confess to a risk, though I'd call it faithless in me.''

''Then give me leeway, mate. There's time, in a gale, that you sail close-reefed.''

Abigail had spread a picnic from a wicker basket filled with treasures she'd gotten from the ship's steward, and they all sat down in lush grass to eat. But William Penn noticed that Skye's obscure gaze never ceased to patrol the ridges above them.

These people dumfounded Victoria. She'd slowly gotten used to the idea that no client of Mister Skye's was a bit like any other one, and that white people were utterly unpredictable. But here were some who dressed in somber black, who would not defend themselves with arms, and who had a look about them of childlike innocence. Doctor Sitgreaves's bright blue eyes revealed no guile at all, but only amiable curiosity and a vast delight in the entire universe. She'd never seen eyes like that.

She didn't dislike them, exactly, but they bothered her, and she spent the whole day pondering them and their strange ways. Mad, maybe. She thought they might all be witches. In which case, she would stay far away from them. She would watch them sharply for the signs.

If she was dumfounded by these odd people, she was even more dumfounded by Mister Skye's agreement to guide them to Owen's Fort without the safety of his war medicine—his and Victoria's and Mary's war medicine. Had he lost his senses? Had these people witched him, too? She vowed to watch her man as sharply as she studied the others and warn him if she must.

They made good time behind her, with those giant horses drawing the carriage and wagon along as if they were nothing. She knew they'd make the Big Muddy that night, so she rode ahead until she reached the low, wide valley that streaked greenly under the brooding prairie, and selected a campsite near the river in a grassy park close to dense cottonwoods. He would find her there; it had been a resort of theirs several times.

She splashed her ribby mare across the torpid river and up the far bank, wanting to see what lay westward. That, too, had been a part of her duties when they traveled. She'd been Mister Skye's eyes and ears and nose, roaming like a spirit animal right and left, forward and down, peering from ridges, examining horizons, seeing without being seen. Now she took extra care: if these strange people truly would not defend themselves, then it seemed up to her to make sure no war parties were near.

She saw nothing. In the late light, under a horizontal sun, the prairies shimmered and slumbered. Distant antelope stood undisturbed. A hawk cruised over low ridges, unalarmed. Not even a wolf or coyote footed lightly over golden grasses. Satisfied, she turned the weary pony into a shallow coulee that would keep her below the skyline, and rode back to the river.

She found them making camp just where she knew they would be, and rode in silently. They'd erected two wall tents, prim and rectangular, one for Doctor and

Mrs. Sitgreaves, the other for the four men. Nearby, Mary had raised her lodgepoles and was tugging their small lodge cover over them while young Dirk watched silently. A quiet camp, Victoria observed, as she pulled the pad saddle off her mare and rubbed the matted, damp hair underneath.

She haltered her mare with her buffalo-hair bridle and then picketed it on lush grass. Mister Skye was enjoying his evening romp with Jawbone, and she watched amiably as Jawbone butted him, nipped at his calico shirt, whickered and shrieked and glared yellow-eyed at these strangers, whom he did not yet trust. Mister Skye, in turn, curried and muttered, tugged on Jawbone's battered ears, and examined hooves and pasterns and all the scars in the animal's ugly hide.

"This here's the quietest camp I've ever seen, Mister Skye."

"They're quiet people, Victoria."

"Buffalo people, waiting to give themselves to those who take."

"They'd like that, giving themselves, I suppose."

That puzzled her even more. In fact, Mister Skye puzzled her too. She fled to the lodge where she and Mary could gossip in her Crow tongue about these crazy people while they cooked the last of the beans and bacon they'd gotten from the *Robert Campbell*. Mary had mastered Crow when she'd become Skye's second wife, and Victoria had grudgingly learned a little Shoshone— very little.

Furtively, Victoria watched Mister Skye wander over to the Quakers, who were currying the giant slobbering horses.

"Graze them on pickets out yonder until it's dark, mates, and then peg them closer to your tents. There's many a warrior who'd like a big horse. And tonight we'll divide into four watches."

"Watches, Mister Skye?" asked the doctor.

"Watches, mate. Later, when Jawbone gets to know

you well, he'll serve as a watch well enough. But now we'll all do two-hour watches.''

"Against what?''

"Horse-stealing party.''

"And if they came, what would we do?''

"Shoot, mate.''

From across the camp Diogenes Fall protested. "But Mister Skye, that's quite against our principles. It'd be a scandal. A rejection of the Light.'' Victoria thought he looked like a raven with a death-face, babbling over there.

Skye looked pensive. "I didn't say kill, mate. A few shots'll be enough.''

Victoria listened, astonished.

William Penn Sitgreaves smiled amiably, his bright gaze biting happily into Skye. "No, my dear Mister Skye. Thee doesn't understand our ways. The threat of death is the same as shooting to kill. Thee must not. And we will trust ourselves and our horses to the Divine Will. There'll be no watch.''

"Sonofabitch!'' bawled Victoria. "I'll watch then.''

"Thee is kind, but there's no need, Mrs. Skye.''

Abigail Sitgreaves rose from a camp chair and came to her, smiling. "Thee are kind to look after us. I'll sleep better for it, Mrs. Skye, no matter what he says.'' The woman clasped her soft hands around Victoria's hardened ones while Victoria gaped at her.

"Goddam,'' she muttered.

Mrs. Sitgreaves looked half affronted, half amused.

They were all watching—the Sitgreaves sons, Junius and the unhappy Artemus, who paused in their currying of the Percherons; and Freeman Price as well, who stopped pulling camp supplies from the hulking covered wagon.

"We'll have a watch,'' replied Mister Skye. "Two hours each, and choose your time among yourselves. If you have trouble, wake me.''

"Mister Skye,'' said the doctor patiently. "No. If it

should be the will of Divine Providence that we lose our horses, then who are we to resist? Perhaps the tribesmen who take them have greater need than we do. We will trust.''

Mister Skye lifted his silk top hat, obviously puzzled, and screwed it down again over a scraggle of damp hair. Victoria waited sharp-nerved, wondering whether her man would surrender to this madness. He started to speak once, and then again, and finally turned away, troubled. Why on earth didn't he speak up? Always, for the protection of his clients, he set the rules for traveling through alien land.

''Mister Skye—'' It was Doctor Sitgreaves from across the camp. ''We, my people and I, wish to master the tongues of the tribesmen. We can scarcely bring medicine to them unless we can communicate. We want thee and thy ladies to begin with the Crow and Snake tongues, if thee would, this evening around our fires. And my son Junius wishes to learn the hand signs.''

Victoria glared at them. She would not teach crazy people, too cowardly and dishonorable to defend themselves, one word of Absaroka. Not a word. It'd be like giving good buffalo tongue to dogs.

''I reckon we could do that, mates. Might help your mission some,'' said Skye. ''And make an evening fly by, if you're not too tired.''

Astonished, Victoria padded after her man as he headed toward the riverbank to wash.

''Why do you agree to this?'' she hissed in Absaroka, knowing the strange ones wouldn't understand. ''They're witched. They've witched you, too. We're going to get ourselves killed!''

He grinned. ''We'll be fine, Victoria. I reckon we can hide and duck our way clear to Owen's Fort. And never see a Blackfoot.''

She spat. ''You're witched. They witched you.''

''Kind of a game, a challenge,'' he muttered. ''Slip four, five hundred miles and never be seen.''

"We'll leave a trail. They come, they see hoofprints the size of—of war shields, and they come fast."

He laughed. "Reckon you're right. Maybe we'll out-fox them."

"You make it fun! But it's my scalp! And yours and Mary's and Dirk's!"

Mister Skye laughed lustily, bawling at the twilight like a happy wolf.

"And I'm not going to teach them Absaroka words!" she cried.

"Reckon I will, old lady. They're good sorts, once you get used to their notions."

"Sonofabitch!" she yelled, and stomped back to their unlit lodge. "Teach them to shoot."

Chapter 5

Junius Sitgreaves loved to hunt. For all of his seventeen years city life had trussed him up, and he'd spent his days in the quietude of a Quaker family while his young blood ran hot and strong. But now, as the small caravan toiled over the somnolent broken prairies, something inside of him loosened and he became a different person, one neither he nor his family ever dreamed existed.

Each morning of that monotonous journey he wolfed down breakfast and then fetched his tall American saddler and settled his saddle on it. Then he collected his Pennsylvania long rifle and powder horn and clambered aboard, as eager as an eagle chick to leave the nest. The long rifle was a cumbersome weapon to carry horseback, so he laid it across his lap while he rode.

He'd ceased worrying about getting lost, or losing contact. They were progressing up the Milk River, threading along an endless valley thick with cottonwoods in places, and easy to spot from the surrounding hilltops. He wasn't much of a hunter, and rarely returned with meat, though he spotted an occasional antelope or mule deer on his day-long adventures.

His parents said nothing, and he'd been glad of that. He feared they'd admonish him with reminders of the way of Friends. But they'd eyed him quizzically, observing the bloom of his tanned face and body, and let him go, keeping their worries to themselves.

But more than once Mister Skye had paused in the morning chores to speak to him gently. "Be careful, Junius," he said. "We haven't had a bit of trouble so far, but things are never what they seem here. If you see Indians, return to us at once. Don't hunt. Don't try to negotiate. Don't even try to use some of those hand signs I've been teaching you. That horse looks like it'll outrun most Indian ponies, so use it. Let me handle it if they follow you."

Junius nodded impatiently. He'd not seen an Indian since they'd rolled out of Fort Union, and he rather wished he would. "I will keep thy warnings in mind," he said amiably, and kicked the gelding, not wanting to listen to more admonitions. He had, after all, a Friends upbringing and a belief that his own good intentions would be plain to Indians, and more—that one who trusted in Divine Providence would be duly protected.

But he felt the stare of their strange, uncouth guide upon his back as he rode from camp. Most mornings he left the wide valley of the Milk altogether, steered his powerful horse up the grassy bluffs and out upon a sea of grass that stretched mysteriously beyond the horizons. He'd never experienced anything like this. He rode beyond the sight of God and man. Not literally beyond the eye of God, he knew, but it seemed that way, and he found it intoxicating. He'd never been drunk, and had scarcely tasted spirits, but he knew drunkenness had to be something like this giddy joy he felt as he sucked air into young lungs.

Wilderness! He understood its fascination and attraction even without verbalizing the ideas. He felt a lover's covetousness of this empty land, where he could do anything he chose. He could dismount and lie in the grass and watch puffball clouds. He could heel his gelding into a fine gallop. He could stop and study dusty tracks. He could rein up and watch a soaring eagle fold in its wings and plummet like a meteor toward its prey, its feathers fanning into a great kite just as it pounced.

He stalked antelope, but even as he eased toward them they broke into a swift lope and vanished. He hunted for deer and rarely saw one. But most of all he ached to find the king of the prairies, the black buffalo. Each day he rode out wanting to find the magical beasts. Mister Skye's wife Victoria hunted them too, but he wanted to find them first, bring home a delicious tongue just to show that he could best her. On board the *Robert Campbell* he'd queried frontiersmen about the buffalo, and he'd picked up a goodly knowledge. He knew to stay upwind because they could smell him. He knew to crawl the last distance and then lie prone, resting his rifle on shooting sticks for accuracy. He knew to spot the sentinel cow and shoot her first if he could. He knew to aim for a spot the size of a hat just behind the shoulder, too.

And Mister Skye had added something else: "If you find the buffler, mate, take a long look around before you shoot. It's likely the Indians have found them too, and are fixing to hunt themselves. Most of the ole coons I know that went under—they got to banging at the buffler and plumb forgot to see who's in the neighborhood."

It wasn't Junius, but his father who had replied: "Surely, Mister Skye, they wouldn't have evil designs upon a stray hunter. They might take his meat, I imagine."

"They might," said Mister Skye thoughtfully.

It didn't really matter, because day after day through the heat of July, Junius saw neither buffalo nor Indians. He roamed like a half-grown wolf all day, and then cut back toward the distant valley of the Milk, which wound north of some great mountains and badlands that had made wagon travel along the Missouri impossible. Pulled by the great Percherons, the caravan routinely made good time, and when he rode down into the lush valley of the river, he hunted for wheel tracks, parallel shining lines of crushed grass, indented dust or mud, as unnatural and obvious as could be in this vast wilderness. If he found them he knew he must ride ahead. If he didn't find them, he knew he must turn back.

He rarely discharged his piece, but sometimes he heard a distant boom, coy on the breeze, illusory, and then he knew that Skye's squaw had shot their dinner. She rarely failed to bring in something every day or two, and there always seemed enough venison or antelope to feed them all. She ranged ahead, usually up the river valley, so he ranged off to the side, usually out upon the plains. He saw nothing. In fact, the trip had been so uneventful that he wondered whether his father had been wise to engage the expensive guide and his squaws. It amused him faintly, a man with two squaws. Mister Skye had been helpful about organizing camp and seeing to details, and of course would be helpful if they had to talk with tribesmen, but beyond that, the man seemed a costly luxury. His parents were learning a few Crow and Shoshone words at Skye's campfire each evening. Their guide seemed overly cautious and Junius wondered whether all those years in the wilderness had addled the man a little.

One afternoon, Junius followed a nameless creek ever southward toward a distant blue hump that Mister Skye had called the Little Rockies—mountains that obviously didn't deserve the name, in Junius's estimation. There he spotted the thing his eyes had ached for weeks to see. Before him, in a dished grassy valley, a herd of buffalo languished. He estimated eighty. Some slumbered; some grazed. Some calves had gathered into a nursery, surrounded by bulls and older animals. And sure enough, even as Junius studied the quiet tableau, he spotted a gray wolf, constant stalking companion of any herd, watching from a ridge.

The hot wind eddied up from the south so they wouldn't smell him. He eased his horse around, hoping not to be seen, and retreated to the creek where he tied the mount tightly to a stout chokecherry limb. He gathered his hunting things, the tied-together shooting sticks that would rest in an X on the earth; his powder horn, and his possibles. And then he stalked the black beasts just as he had been told, patiently on hands and knees, over the low ridge and down the long slope into range, pausing a moment when a rattler slithered away. He felt thirsty; the effort and hot sun had dehydrated him faster than he dreamed possible. Nonetheless, he'd soon be carrying a huge tongue back to his people. The thought excited him.

The animals didn't pay him any attention as he furtively crawled within range and set up his shooting sticks and rested his long rifle in the notch. He did everything exactly as he'd been instructed, noting a sentry cow just to the left of the herd. Every few moments she peered about, sometimes straight at him, but then resumed her placid grazing. She faced him, though, and wouldn't be a good target. He chose, instead, a young cow that stood broadside less than two hundred yards distant. She would do. He rejoiced. How they'd welcome him that evening! Even his quiet mother, whose interest in hunting was nil, would gently praise him.

He added fine powder to what was in his pan, cocked his piece, and aimed. Slowly the pressure of his trigger finger increased, until at last the flint in the lock snapped across the frizzen, sending a hail of sparks into the pan, igniting the powder there, which in turn ignited the powder in the barrel, through the touchhole. The rifle boomed, spewing a cloud of blue smoke. His ears rang.

He studied the cow, supposing he'd missed. It stood

stock-still. He thought he ought to reload and began digging for a ball and a patch, but then the cow walked forward several steps, shuddered, and sank to the earth, pawing the ground unhappily. One shot! He exulted. He put the ball and patch back into his kit, waited a moment while the cow died—he'd been warned about that—and then stood. Let the rest run, he thought; he didn't need them. And indeed, as he stood, they were all scrambling to their feet, rolling up onto four legs, snorting, and breaking into an astonishing gallop—straight toward him.

He hadn't expected that at all. They were supposed to run away from him. He stood up and shouted, waved his empty rifle at them, bawled at them—he'd rarely shouted before and it seemed an alien thing to do with Quaker vocal cords—and somehow diverted them to his left, a rumbling river of shaggy animals, red-eyed and snorting, like monsters from under the earth. But they thundered by, so near each animal was an individual to be reckoned with, even the blatting calves which ran close to their slobbering mothers. But they passed, and Junius peered outward upon a black sprawling lump, the cow he'd killed. And something else: two Indian warriors, wearing only breechclouts, their flesh coppery, their fine muscles rippling. Each carried a short bow with a nocked arrow in it. And the arrows were aimed at him.

Dread boiled through him, riding the tips of the arrows that pointed relentlessly at his chest. These two wore paint of some sort, greasy black and white and yellow smears, daubed in chevrons upon their arms. He knew that was supposed to mean something but he wasn't sure what.

He stood frozen, wildly calculating his chances of running back to his horse, his swift horse. Both warriors halted a few yards from him, surveying him carefully with eyes of agate that revealed nothing. Both were taller than he, much taller than he'd imagined Indians would be. He hadn't the faintest notion of their tribe. One had terrible scars coiling over his stocky torso, the puckered marks of war and battle. He had massive cheekbones, and graying straight hair worn in two braids. A notched eagle feather poked from his hair. The other, tall and thin with washboard ribs, seemed much younger, not much older than himself.

Junius found himself dreading the burly older giant, whose gaze skewered him as if he were just another buffalo. Never in his brief life had he experienced the kind of terror that climbed up his throat now, making the cartilage of his windpipe ache. He felt sweat river from his body, and knew it didn't come from the boiling sun. He knew also that he'd never really thought of death before, not as anything more than an abstraction the elders talked about at Meeting. He remembered then. He swallowed his gorge and closed his eyes a moment, shutting out the world so he might center on the Spirit, the Spirit of God he'd been so halfhearted about in all the Quaker gatherings he'd been brought to, since infancy.

Have mercy on me thy servant.

When he dared to peer at the terrible reality he faced, he felt better, as if something peaceful would soon gentle the clawing fright that convulsed him.

"Would thee speak English?"

They ignored him. The younger one picked up his long rifle and examined it carefully, especially the burl maple stock, glowing in well-oiled beauty. That one grunted and motioned at Junius, who understood at once. Shakily, Junius lifted his powder-horn strap and handed the powder to the younger warrior. The rest of his kit followed, his possibles and the skinning knife he'd been about to use on the buffalo cow, which lay quietly, flies gathering around its bloody wound.

The older warrior examined the knife, drawing his finger lightly along the keen Sheffield blade. Then he said something in a sharp tone, and Junius couldn't fathom what the warrior wanted. The older one repeated himself impatiently, but Junius didn't know what to do.

"I am a friend," he babbled. "My family and our guide—Mister Skye—are nearby. Coming—"

He saw something change in the warrior's face, something subtle and cold and even more frightening.

"We've engaged Mister Skye," he continued shakily. He pointed in the general direction of the Milk River.

The older one gestured violently, the knife arcing close to Junius. But Junius didn't have an inkling what to do.

The younger one stepped forward and tugged on Junius's shirt, a white collarless one. They wanted the shirt. Fumbling crazily, dismayed at how unruly his own fingers had become, he undid it at the cuffs and down its front, and stripped it from his torso, noting how pale his flesh looked compared to the rich umber of these warriors.

The younger one took it and tried it on. His arms were too long for the sleeves. He wrestled it off, saying something or other to the older one in a language with clattering sounds in it Junius had never heard before.

He smiled shakily. "Would thee follow me, now? I'll take thee to my father who brings medicine to thee, and more than that: a voice for you among—"

He couldn't believe his eyes. The older one was lifting his bow. Junius bolted, his legs driven by some wild terror. He had to reach his horse. He lurched away with giant bounds, the contracting muscles of his young legs speeding him.

The arrow struck his back just under his right shoulder blade, piercing through to his right lung and popping bloody from his chest, a giant hammer shoving him forward. He staggered, his legs refusing to stop, feeling his body convulse and then buckle under him, until he tumbled to the earth. He landed facedown, the hoop-iron arrow point burying itself in clay and hurting crazily as he landed on it. He clawed clay, unable to make his body obey him, feeling white heat rise from him.

A moment later they squatted beside him, studying him. He saw that they were studying him. He couldn't speak because his lungs didn't pump air, but he groaned. Was this death? But he'd barely started life! And he came as a friend! And he'd done them no harm! He felt his heart rise into a frenzied patter, felt wetness leak from his chest and black nausea rush up from his belly. But he didn't die. The hurt came in a rush, pain scorching out from his chest up his neck to his eyes and skull.

I am Junius Sitgreaves, he thought.

He saw them looking at him, hovering over him. The older one stared and then reached for Junius's wavy brown hair. Junius felt the warrior grasp it and tug, lifting up his whole head and twisting his neck so that it almost broke. He saw something glint and then felt the bite of steel on his skull, a ludicrous feeling, like a moving bee sting over his forehead and above his ears, and down around the back, twisting his head almost off, and then over the other ear again. And then he felt a violent yank, a sucking sensation and a pop, and something had left him. And still he lived.

Mister Skye had settled them once again at one of his peculiar campsites, Doctor Sitgreaves noticed. The guide rarely camped on the bank of the Milk River, even though such places abounded with good wood and grass. He chose, instead, to camp away from the river and its traffic, often in small spring-fed gulches cut into the bluffs—places where a campfire could not be seen from any direction. The doctor admired the guide's caution even while supposing it was a bit overdone. For weeks they'd seen nothing. Not a single Indian. And Skye himself had said they likely wouldn't because it was the trading season.

The doctor really didn't mind. These higher, drier camps meant fewer mosquitoes, for one thing. The infernal droning insects had been especially hard on Abby, who'd lost sleep because of them. He'd rigged netting for her but it barely slowed the vicious things down.

They made camp easily now, a little before dusk so they could erect the wall tents, gather wood and water, and perform other chores in the last light of a summer's day. By some miracle the older Mrs. Skye emerged wraithlike from some coulee or gulch about this time of day, often with an antelope or a portion of a mule deer behind her. He admired a horse that would calmly accept such a bloody burden. Junius usually arrived in camp earlier, wolf-hungry, having worked up an enormous appetite in his daily roaming. This evening, though, he hadn't yet arrived. But he would soon. No matter how vast the country—and it was more enormous than he'd ever imagined any land could be— returning to the valley of the Milk was nothing more than a matter of following any watercourse downward until it tumbled into the broad trough of the river. Junius would come along, perhaps after he'd finished butchering meat somewhere.

All about him his colleagues hummed through their evening chores. His good son Artemus had taken the chore of seeing to the horses each evening, watering them, staking them on lush grasses, currying them, hunting for harness sores and splints and heated pasterns and sand cracks in hooves. He dutifully cleaned the frogs of their giant feet. The Percherons bloomed, even after weeks of pulling the carriage and wagon along over bare traces. But something in the young man troubled Doctor Sitgreaves. Anger, perhaps. Whatever it was, his son bottled it so tightly inside that no one knew what passed through his mind.

The others, the estimable Freeman Price and Diogenes Fall, shed their black suit coats and began chef's duties, sawing up a rear quarter of a doe that had been silently handed to them by Victoria. Abby had displayed a vast ineptitude when it came to camp cooking, managing meat on a spit, or dealing with open fires, and had taken to waiting out her dinner in her tent, questioning the Divine Mind about mosquitoes. It was a great theological question: Why had God made mosquitoes? Doctor Sitgreaves himself had debated the matter.

Over at the Skyes' lodge the guide frolicked with that vicious blue roan, butting heads, muttering, while it glared yellow-eyed at them all and squealed. Skye's horse had been the great novelty of this trip, its conduct so malevolent that Doctor Sitgreaves thought it was possessed by Beelzebub. They built much tinier fires before their lodge each night but somehow the two women managed to roast their meat better than the Friends did, even while roughhousing with young Dirk or washing and cooking strange greens they harvested each day from the river flats.

They ate. They cleaned mess ware. Stars emerged and hung over them. The day narrowed to a blue line on the northwestern horizon. And Junius did not come. Worried at last, the doctor ambled to the Skyes' camp, seeking Victoria.

"Did thee see my son today?"

She shook her head crossly, but peered sharply at him. None of the Skyes had noticed the absence.

Mister Skye heard it and stared into the gloom, a look on his battered face that sent a chill through the doctor. The guide said nothing, but in a moment he'd thrown his pad over Jawbone and ridden into the night.

Chapter 6

Finding Junius in a couple hundred square miles of broken plains would be hard, especially at night. But Mister Skye had never been one to find excuses. He had a few things in his favor, including the boy's big gelding, which would very likely whinny if it heard another horse. Still, the task seemed daunting. Mister Skye didn't even know which bank of the Milk River to ride. If the boy had been injured or immobilized, the chances were slim of ever seeing him again. But if the boy had simply missed the wagon tracks, perhaps arriving after dusk back in the valley, why then they'd connect in the morning.

He rode Jawbone through a powerful dark, down the valley of the Milk, making out groves of cottonwoods by the evanescent light of stars. The night was pleasant and not a cloud darkened the dome of heaven. Typical weather. But a thundershower could wipe out both wagon tracks and those of Junius's horse, and that would make the reunion all the more difficult.

Every little while he stopped, feeling Jawbone chafe

at the command, and spoke out into the darkness: "Junius. Junius, boy, we're missing you."

And only the night answered back.

He weighed the possibility of Indian trouble, and considered it unlikely. But he knew, out of a lifetime of experience in the wilderness, that the unlikely could be the likely. They hadn't cut a track in weeks but that meant little. Blackfeet patrolled here, with ancient antagonisms toward Yankee whites that went back to a bloody skirmish with Lewis and Clark.

The boy might have met them with Quaker gentleness only to have them strip him of his horse and flintlock and leave him on foot. Or worse. But the worse didn't seem likely in a friendly night with a prodigious scatter of stars smiling above.

"Junius, boy. Junius, are you here?"

But his talking into the hollow silence netted him nothing but the occasional startle of an animal in the dark.

Thus he rode for perhaps three hours, Jawbone sullen under him, not liking the extra labor. Mister Skye recollected what he could of the day, but it had been one identical to the others this quiet trip: a benign day under a benign sky, with the Sitgreaveses' Percherons hauling the carriage and wagon along at a smart pace, the world as peaceful as the souls of these unusual people. He could not think of a thing out of the ordinary. Nor had Victoria or Mary seen or heard anything to set this day apart. Victoria, especially, had been the party's eyes and ears with her cunning gifts of reconnaissance and a way of roaming far ahead, following draws so subtle no one noticed them, peering like a gopher over shallow ridges, studying the flight of birds, edging wraithlike across flats in a way that never caught the eye of man or animal. No one else he knew, male or female, had gifts like that. No one else could return each evening with the future mapped in her head, even a knowledge of where game would be.

"Junius, boy. We're missing you. Holler if you can, boy."

He waited impatiently and rode on, finally cutting toward the distant bluffs. He'd return to camp riding along the tops of them.

A coyote barked, and he listened carefully. Some barking was fun, merriment in the night. Other barking signaled food. He listened for the food yelp, the bitch summoning pups, but that was not what he heard.

He turned back, wearing the north star on his right shoulder, the black valley of the Milk an inky ocean off to his left somewhere. The serene night seemed alive with menace.

"Junius! We're missing you, boy."

They'd always done that in the mountains, hunting down lost trappers in the midst of hopelessness, and sometimes it had paid off. He'd found trappers half dead of thirst or starvation, lying with a broken leg in places without shade. Sometimes they'd been too late, but most mountain men he'd known had made the effort, if not because of any love for their fellows, then at least because they expected the same treatment.

Strange people, these Quakers. He did not dismiss their stern pacifism as some might. They took their faith in the goodness of God to radical lengths, and took the commandment against killing as an absolute, beyond traditional Hebrew or Christian interpretation. It seemed a great dare to Mister Skye, but he couldn't find anything against it. Not even common sense made a case against it. He'd seen and heard of cases where self-defense cost a man his life; such a man would have been better off greeting menace with smiles.

And yet . . . the tribes loved bravery more than anything else. Let a captive warrior defy odds, defy death, defy torture, laugh at his captors, and they might release him, or at least kill him swiftly. How did that fit with Quaker attitudes? It made no difference, he realized. Theirs was an obedience to a commandment—at least as they perceived it—that made no allowance for common sense or the creeds of Plains warriors. He sighed. Victoria had it right. Big medicine.

Even if they all perished.

"Junius! Junius! If you hear me, holler. If you can't speak, clap your hands."

Something scurried away.

The moon bulged over an eastern ridge, the proverbial city on the hill, and with it came the perception of distances and an openness found only on unfenced prairie. He reckoned the time as not far from dawn and knew he'd fight tiredness the coming day.

No Junius. He'd hold them there a day or two. The horses could rest. They could ride out tomorrow and search. And he could begin the painful task of letting them know about odds, death, accident, disease—and eternal separation.

He didn't know how to approach that topic. He himself wouldn't grieve the boy. Not yet. He'd seen too many astonishments during a long life in the wilderness. And he'd heard of others, like old Hugh Glass, hurt and left for dead, crawling hundreds of miles to safety after being abandoned by young Gabe—Jim Bridger. No, it wouldn't do to pronounce premature doom. But a bad feeling crabbed at his innards, and he sensed he wouldn't see Junius alive.

When he reckoned he'd gotten back to camp, which nestled on a bench in a side coulee, he turned Jawbone down the shallow grade toward the Milk. He'd reckoned wrong. He sat the horse quietly in the bottoms, unsure where the camp lay, and finally released the single rope rein and let the wily horse do it. Jawbone snorted angrily, wheeled sharply around, enjoying the chance to unseat his master, and lifted into an easy jog back down the river. A few minutes later the horse trotted into camp, snorting and glaring at the Percherons who pulled hard on their picket lines, terrorized by the evil apparition.

No one was sleeping. They huddled around orange coals, watching him return alone and reading the answers to their questions. Abigail had drawn her gray shawl about her and sat on the grass. Doctor Sitgreaves paced. Artemus stood waiting. The other two, wrapped in blankets, sat staring.

Since he had no more news than they could read from the sight of him, he unsaddled Jawbone and rubbed the animal's back, roughing up the roan hair so it'd dry. Jawbone snorted, butted Skye, and wandered off to roll and shake and eat a belated meal.

"What would thee suggest?" asked Doctor Sitgreaves.

"Waiting, mate. Boy's probably holed up somewhere. Missed the wagon tracks. We'll try again when we have light."

"He came to harm," said Abigail.

"He could."

"What are the possibilities, Mister Skye? I have a complete surgery and pharmacy with me—"

"I reckon you know them as well as I do, Doctor."

"It'd be a comfort if thee would—"

"Of course, mate. He could of got lost. Horse injured. Bucked or fell off. Junius injured. Junius sick— bad water maybe. Snakebit. Horse got loose and he couldn't catch it. Got back to the Milk too late to pick up the wagon trail. Killed game and spent too long butchering . . ."

"Does thee think it is any of these?"

"No, mate, I can't say as I do."

"We'll stay here and search," the doctor said. "We'll trust and meditate and welcome the Spirit."

"Junius must come home," said Abigail tautly.

"I'd suggest you sleep now—we're not going anywhere in the morning, and you can rest."

Doctor Sitgreaves sighed. "The Divine Will imposes a price on those who love it most."

Skye watched them clamber to their feet and trudge, brokenly, to their tents, and the night grew still.

Victoria and Mary and Dirk waited before their lodge.

"Siksika," hissed Victoria.

"I fear it may be," he said.

"It is so. I know. I smelled buffalo today but I couldn't find them. On the wind. Siksika came. The boy's dead."

"It sometimes plays out better, Victoria."

"No—not with crazy people like these. They got big medicine or no medicine at all."

She slid through the darkness to him and wrapped her bony arms around his burly body, squeezing him, and he felt her tears dampening his calico shirt.

"Goddam, I just know," she said. "Why'd we take crazy people like this? Crazy people!"

In the first graying, William Penn Sitgreaves thought the day would be overcast but it was a trick of the light, or a trick of his soul, which was clouded. He peered about him, first at Abby on her camp cot pretending to sleep, and then out upon the silent camp, wanting evidence that Junius had come in after all. He peered at the great horses on their picket lines, thinking he saw the saddler there, and knew he hadn't and was deluding himself. Skye's horse stood malevolently near the lodge, watching the dawn with an evil eye. Indeed, watching Doctor Sitgreaves as he peered from his tent. The blue horse made him feel unworthy and citified, a peculiar feeling for a horse to evoke in a mortal.

He dressed wearily and emerged into the world from which he'd been protected by a fragile layer of cloth, which suddenly seemed no protection at all. Skye had gotten up and was roughhousing with that horse, and Victoria Skye was saddling her own nondescript mare.

"I'm going with thee," he said.

The guide looked skeptical. "Nothing to ride. Not those draft animals. Split you in two."

"I hope thee will offer me Mary's mount."

Skye sighed, peered at his own lodge where nothing stirred, and settled his battered hat on his head. "I think this is something my wives and I'd best tackle, mate."

"Thy mule, then? I'm a doctor, you know. I thought I'd take my bag—"

Skye nodded. "Mary's pony. I'll square it with her."

"Perhaps Artemus could come on a mule—"

"No," said Skye so brusquely that it startled the doctor. "I'd rather not have to look after—I'd rather not have city people . . . Ah, Doctor, we'll need good men in camp to take care of Mrs. Sitgreaves, and—your friends. And Mary, too."

A few minutes later and without any breakfast, they splashed across the river, having a bad time on a soft bottom that sucked at hooves. The doctor rode Mary's horse and carried as much of a medical kit with him as he could behind the cantle. Wordlessly Skye turned them downstream and led them into a shadowed bottomland dotted with cottonwoods. The man reminded him of one of his medical professors, Sitgreaves thought—the one who sliced open cadavers taken from the dead house and handed human parts to students, shouting at them to learn, learn, learn.

About the time the sky blued and a hint of the approaching sun stalked the earth, Skye paused, sitting quietly on that abominable horse. "We're clear of trees now, mate. We'll spread out. I want you closest to the river bank; I'll be in the middle, and Victoria'll ride wide—and we'll stay in sight of each other at all times. I'd just as soon do this silently so look for a wave of my hand if I want you. Or signal me with a kerchief if you find something. And look sharp."

All morning they rode. Victoria, off somewhere to Sitgreaves's right, was barely visible to him, but he glimpsed Mister Skye frequently a half mile or so distant. The immensity of the area they were searching appalled him. The land seemed limitless, stretching beyond human imagination. How could they find an injured youth in this? The smallest hollow could hide him. And yet—nature offered its clues, he thought unhappily. A circling column of raptors would be one. A carnival of wolves or coyotes would be another.

He knew they were dealing in improbabilities. And he had to face the likelihood that Junius was either dead or gravely injured. These things oppressed him beyond any strength he could summon, any comfort he could draw from centering himself on the Divine Light that had been the refuge of Friends always. He bounced on Mary's mare, a portly man who hadn't been on a saddler for decades, and felt it in every muscle and bone. But the physician in him remained, and the curious observer, so that William Penn Sitgreaves studied everything around him as he rode, his keen eyes missing nothing.

Riding closest to the river turned out to be the hardest, he discovered. He had to circumnavigate acres of brush, cut around sloughs, push through cottonwood and willow flats, all the while studying every dark lump, fallen tree, odd wrinkle of the earth. Several times he turned the mare toward some peculiarity that attracted him, only to discover that nature mocked him. And yet, these were occasions when he felt relief; when he could hope that Junius was hale and hearty somewhere, somewhere . . .

He steered the mare up a slope and discovered Skye waving at him far off to the south. Had they found Junius? He turned the mare and kicked her into a trot, feeling every jolt of that painful gait jar him, but he never slowed until he'd reached the guide.

"Victoria's flaggin' over on the bluff, mate."

They put their horses into a canter and Doctor Sitgreaves clung to the saddle, frightened by the gait, frightened by what lay ahead. On the ridge, the wiry

Crow woman awaited them, hunched lightly over her pony. They climbed a long grassy slope, the horses laboring under them, and emerged out upon a broken plain, with the shadows of puffball clouds scraping over the hills and coulees.

She glanced at him sharply, something hostile in her black eyes that he felt instantly. She disapproved of him, he knew, no doubt found his beliefs utterly alien.

Wordlessly she led them into a shallow basin rimmed by grassy slopes. Animals had been here. Buffalo, he supposed, from the abundant and still-green sign. On a distant slope he saw the ruin of a carcass, bright bone and dark hide, and a small army of crows at work. But it was not toward the carcass she was leading them, but toward something else that wrenched at his heart.

Skye glanced at him sharply. He fought back the horror rising in him, because the thing ahead was human, and bloody. He knew who it would be and what it would be long before his eyes verified it. And he felt faint with the grief welling through him, and with the things he would have to do—telling Abby and Artemus. A hurt washed through him, a sense of betrayal. God had let him down. He wrestled with it, commanded it to leave his face. He did not want the Skyes to see the naked doubting that had come upon him.

They rode up to the boy in the midst of an unearthly quiet. The wind had ceased. Junius wore no shirt—and no hair. He lay on his belly, an arrow protruding from his back. His arms sprawled out ahead of him, and the earth had been furrowed where his spasming fingers had clawed it as he died. The yellowish bone of his skull lay obscenely naked to the sun. Green-bellied flies swarmed and feasted. The flesh had a gray cast, a color Doctor Sitgreaves was all too familiar with.

"Junius," he said. "Junius." He clambered slowly off the skittish mare, landing painfully on unsteady legs, and walked toward his son, knowing he would perform a ritual medical act out of habit rather than trust the evidence of his senses.

"Easy, mate," said Skye, quietly.

"Siksika!" hissed Victoria, a shocking hatred exploding in a single word.

He wondered how she knew, or whether she was guessing. He settled himself beside the body, grateful for his medical experience. He felt an arm. Cold, save for a small warmth of the sun. Flies whirled about him. He sought a pulse at the wrist, knowing beforehand but needing to do it. He stood shakily and walked to the mare, dug out a stethoscope, and laid the horn of the tiny trumpet over Junius's heart, and heard only his own pulse. He dreaded turning the boy over, not wanting to see the lingering terror in the boy's eyes. He'd been running from his killers; the arrow had pierced his back at about the fourth or fifth true rib.

Slowly, he turned Junius, not wanting to. The boy's open brown eyes stared lifelessly at the sky. The arrow point projected from his right breast near the sternum, and was brown with his blood. The long, narrow point had been honed from flat iron, and was cunningly anchored to the shaft with sinew.

He stood at last, a heaviness in him that he couldn't cope with, and stared at Mister Skye, who stood nearby.

"I'd like to take him back and bury him at the camp," he said. "If thee would."

"Victoria's horse will carry Junius. She can ride behind me on Jawbone."

"Siksika!" she said, her gaze fierce upon the endless places where land and sky conjoined.

"Would thee tell me about that?"

"Arrers. Each tribe makes it arrers different," Skye said. "The color bands dyed on the shafts. The choice of wood for the shafts. The marks cut into the wood. The fletching—feathers. And each warrior adds his own mark, too. Saves arguments about who shot what."

Sitgreaves shuddered. "We'll leave the arrow here, then."

"I want it, mate. It can tell me who." Skye pulled his belt knife from its sheath and knelt over the boy, sawing through the shaft close to his chest. In a moment he'd freed the point. Then he turned Junius over again and tugged. But the body didn't yield the arrow, and clung to the instrument of its own doom. Skye yanked harder, finally extracted the slick arrow, and handed it to Victoria.

Doctor Sitgreaves slumped beside his saddle horse, concealing his ravenous hurt, letting the guide do the rest. He watched them lift Junius—how ghastly his skull looked—over the nervous horse and tie him there, sprawled stiffly over the saddle, his rigid arms and legs poking outward. He watched Victoria study the area, hunting for things known only to herself, the shape of a hoofprint, perhaps. She disappeared over a ridge a while and returned with a small bit of information.

"He tied his horse on a juniper back there. Lots of prints. Shod hoof. Goddam Siksika took it."

"Which Blackfeet?" he asked, wondering why he asked.

"Piegan," she replied crossly.

They began the noonday journey back to camp. Doctor Sitgreaves didn't know what he could say to comfort Abby. Didn't know whether Abby would blame him—this trip to help the Indians had cost his son his life at the hands of Indians. They all might want to give up, go back. He didn't. He wanted to go on. In fact, he wanted this terrible trial to confirm them in their work. He thought of Junius who had possessed the joy of the young, just beginning his voyage. It seemed so cruel, so wrong. And yet, who was a Friend to question the Divine?

They'd go on to the Bitterroot. He'd insist on it, and pay evil with good, for it was dawning in him that this terrible sacrifice, this murder, would be the foundation of everything he wished to achieve among the western tribes. He knew, then, that once they'd completed their hard duties at camp, he would request something of Skye, and if Skye refused he'd do it anyway, but on his own. And he knew Skye would be appalled at the very thought.

Chapter 7

When they rode quietly back into camp that afternoon, Victoria seethed with curiosity. What would the Friends do next? Would they go home? Would they quit?

They'd ridden across a sunny afternoon, burdened with death and withdrawn into themselves. Doctor Sitgreaves had turned to granite, and she couldn't imagine what passed through his mind. He hid everything behind that stony face until she wondered if he had been born without feelings, if whitemen had no grief in them. Where was his hurt? She'd tried to put it all together, over and over: they'd come to help Indian people of all tribes; but they would not even defend themselves; now one of them had been killed by Siksika. Why didn't he rage against them? Why didn't he vow to avenge his son's murder? Was he a man without bravery, without glory, that he should permit this to go unpunished? More and more he simply disgusted her, he with his sheep-ways and his choked-down grief.

As they rode into camp the others stared solemnly, absorbing the terrible sight without crying out, and that puzzled her too. Didn't they care about Junius? The white woman stared, gasped, her hand flying to her mouth, and groaned.

"Junius, oh Junius," she said, taking it all in, absorbing the sight of the boy's bloodied naked skull. Then she fled to her tent, a strange hurt on her face that she was trying to disown, as if grief was sinful.

Victoria slid off Jawbone as Mister Skye checked the restless horse. She took the rein of her own burdened pony from Doctor Sitgreaves, who dismounted shakily and peered gently into the haunted faces of the rest, his son Artemus, Diogenes, Freeman, and finally Mary.

"Please tell us, Father," said the doctor's remaining son.

"We will share it in Meeting. Thee must find a shovel now."

Artemus and the other whitemen sprang to their wagon and extracted two spades while the doctor and Mister Skye untied the dangling body and slid it gently to earth.

"Please bring me Junius's blanket and some cord, Mister Fall," said the doctor.

Within a few minutes, Mister Skye and William Penn Sitgreaves had wrapped the body in the blue blanket, covering the sightless eyes and naked head first.

"Junius," the doctor said. "Why did it have to be thee? My last-born. My bright light." He reached gently down and touched the boy's cold hand. Then they completed the shrouding.

Artemus knelt beside the body, saying nothing but revealing something angry all the same. The sight of the blanketed bundle seemed all too much, and he shuddered. "It didn't have to happen," he said.

Victoria marveled at the silence in all of this, and wondered if these strange people were numb inside, without rage toward the killers of their son, without— what? Without feeling? Didn't these Friends care?

Wouldn't they weep, or cry out, or seek revenge? What was the matter with them?

Doctor Sitgreaves stood, brushed dirt and grass off his dark pants and stared at the landscape, peering first at the distant bluffs and then focusing closer as if to memorize this place. Victoria saw something in his face, like a man seeing a medicine vision, a man communing with something alive and mysterious within himself, something that could bring bright light to his eyes even in a moment like this. She realized he was making medicine, seeing high and grand and sacred visions beyond her own seeing.

She unconsciously slid over to Mister Skye, and felt his brawny arm slide around her, and wondered why her man didn't take charge, command that things be done according to whitemen's ways. It puzzled her. Mister Skye had remained as silent as the Quakers, and as unobtrusive as a watchful buck at the edge of a woods. If these whitemen were practicing their religion, it was something they did inside themselves.

Doctor Sitgreaves directed his portly frame toward a grassy shelf back from the river, commanding the sun and wind, the rain and snow, unhindered by weeping trees. He nodded to his colleagues, and they all walked there, the doctor leading them like a great black plow horse to a spot he had selected. He paused and nodded.

Artemus jammed his pointed spade into the turf and found it resistant, the roots of the bunchgrasses impeding him. Diogenes Fall stabbed clay with the other spade, only to feel the instrument spring back in his hands. He looked about despairingly, and Mister Skye took the shovel from him and rammed it into the tan clay. It proved to be a hard place, the earth skinning thin over the shelf rock, and Mister Skye beckoned them back to the thick earth of the bottoms, to a place as open as the other but less noble. In an hour, they'd cut through three feet of moist clay and gouged a grave barely as long and wide as the boy himself.

And all the while the Friends watched silently, drawn into private worlds as high and distant as snowy peaks, and so removed from this earthy place that they frightened Victoria, and excited suspicions in her that she was viewing long-dead spirits.

When Mister Skye's shovel bit into wetness he withdrew it and stopped digging. The earth's own tears would fall upon Junius, she thought uneasily. She preferred a scaffold in the fashion of her people, and a body given to Sun.

Doctor Sitgreaves nodded. "If thee would help us now, Mister Skye, I will bring Abby."

Doctor Sitgreaves set off for the distant tent, with Mister Skye beside him, and presently they returned, the doctor with Abby clutching his arm, and Mister Skye carrying the shrouded blue burden that lay stiff in his arms. Mrs. Sitgreaves looked composed. Too composed, Victoria thought. A woman of the Absarokas would have cut off her hair, or chopped a finger at a joint, or carried a warrior's possessions to place beside him on the scaffold for his journey through the spirit world.

"If thee would, Mister Skye," the doctor said.

What sort of request was that? If thee would. Victoria could make nothing of it, and yet Mister Skye seemed to know just what to do without instruction. He lowered the body into the hole, settling it there, and then stood back.

She dreaded whitemen's burials, into the earth where the under-earth spirits reigned. She waited for Doctor Sitgreaves to say something. Whitemen always said things, or read from the Black Book, and made great prayers, or recited a psalm, or the Father prayer they all knew from memory. But not these. They stood like black posts on the green meadow, as mute as trees.

And then, to Victoria's astonishment, Abigail Sitgreaves spoke. "Thee are in the bosom of God, Junius, even now beholding us below, less fortunate than thee.

We miss thee, our son and brother and friend, and we yearn for the reunion.''

Something luminous lit her face as she spoke, as if this mother were gripped by something spiritual that had brought the words to her lips. The gentle force of it subdued Victoria and puzzled her deeply. She resolved to ask Mister Skye of these mysteries later. Was this a different kind of love?

A silence pervaded the waning day again, shattered only by the cawing of crows at a distant rookery. And then, just as mysteriously, the older son, Artemus, spoke up, as if hidden by some unseen force, like a marionette on strings she had once seen. ''Junius, thee were torn from us. Thee had no choice but to come, and to die. Butchered and scalped.'' The young man stared around defiantly.

He didn't sound like the rest. He had hate in him. He was the only one of the Friends who seemed angry. She glanced at Mister Skye and found his face as blank as those of the others. His graying hair lifted in the breezes as he clutched his battered top hat at his waist. She glanced at Mary, golden-skinned in the late sun, and found puzzlement deep in the young woman's bright eyes.

''Junius, I envy thee thy safety now,'' said Diogenes Fall. ''My young friend, I shall redouble my efforts to help thy tormentors.''

''Thee live on forever, Junius, in the work we do,'' said Freeman Price.

After that Doctor Sitgreaves recited the Father prayer she'd heard so often, and she felt faintly surprised by this familiar ritual after experiencing such a strange one. He lifted those guileless eyes toward the fading blue of the skies, and even smiled as he glorified the foreverness of God, and it affected her strangely, this peacefulness that seemed even to contain joy at death. Big Medicine, she thought, half afraid, half awed. Except for Artemus. That one had no Quaker medicine.

Sitgreaves nodded, and again Mister Skye seemed to know what to do. He lifted a shovelful of clay and settled it into the hole, letting it tumble heavily onto the blue blanket. In a short time the grave was full and mounded over, and covered with rock lifted from a nearby outcrop.

"You want a marker, mate?"

"The body without spirit is nothing, Mister Skye. It is not important."

"Just as well," said Mister Skye. Victoria knew he referred to grave robbers, both two-footed and four-footed.

The doctor peered at his guides expectantly, his gaze surveying first Mister Skye, then Victoria, and finally Mary and Dirk, but he said nothing for a moment. Then he exchanged glances with his wife, who still clung to his arm, and his son and friends.

"We have something to ask of thee, Mister Skye. If thee would do it, we'd be grateful, but if thee would not, we understand, and we will attempt it ourselves."

Mister Skye nodded, obviously curious.

"Take us to the village of the ones who killed our son. We had expected to begin our work at Fort Owen, but we are called to begin here, now."

Siksika! A wild dread flared through her. Piegan, the whites called them. Pikuni, they called themselves. Killers. Torturers. Warriors who loved bravery and death. Who'd vowed at every Sun Dance to kill Mister Skye if they could, and his women and his horse for good measure.

Victoria peered at her man, not at all fearful. He would never do such a mad thing. He would argue them out of it, offer to take them back to Fort Union, or ahead to Owen's Fort.

He ran a stubby hand through his long hair, his eyes on each of his clients, measuring, and all the while a dread welled up in her and finally burst.

"Goddam!" she exploded.

Doctor Sitgreaves peered at her with those flaming sapphire eyes, a smile building on his face. She couldn't meet that gaze, and peered westward into the dying sunlight.

"I guess we could do that, mates. If we can track 'em down. They might be far away."

"Sonofabitch!" she snapped, gaping at these madmen and her husband, who would kill her for sure.

Harmony did not rule the Skye lodge that night. In the wavering light of a tiny fire, Mister Skye propped his chunky two-year-old boy in his lap and taught him whiteman things. Dirk listened solemnly, repeating his alphabet and numbers, forming the strange words his father insisted he learn, and studying his father from bright brown eyes. He knew his mother's Shoshone tongue, and his other mother's Absaroka tongue better, and his mothers' words made him laugh while his father's turned him solemn.

"Let me go," Dirk said.

Mister Skye rumbled his amusement and let the child crawl toward his wickerwork cradle and robes.

Victoria remained silent, seething actually, her dour gaze telling Mister Skye everything about her mood. He understood. Victoria had lost brothers and nephews, uncles and friends to the Blackfeet, and hated them with the fine, keen hatred honed out of tribal legend over many generations. And now he would lead her right into one of their villages—if they could find it— and subject them all to mortal danger. If she didn't voice her objections out loud, she made them abundantly clear anyway with the way she banged things around. Only Victoria could make a brass kettle rebuke him.

His glorious Mary of the Shoshone had suffered less from the Blackfeet, but nonetheless her people counted the dreaded northern tribe enemies as well, and the Blackfeet worked their own incessant war upon the weaker Snake people. She watched solemnly as he toyed with her son, their son, his only heir. There were many among the Blackfeet who itched to kill them all—Mister Skye, who'd led the Crows against them; his two wives; the terrible medicine horse Skye rode—and Dirk. If they ever caught Dirk they wouldn't adopt him the way tribes usually did with the small children of their enemies. No. Not this sole man-child of Skye. They'd grasp him by his small ankles and dash his brains out upon the nearest tree, and count it a great victory.

Mary's somber glances and sighs told him she was thinking of this but keeping her thoughts to herself, as Victoria did. He was, he thought, less than popular with his wives this night. But he reckoned they'd go along. A visit to a Piegan village wouldn't be so dangerous as all that, not under the peace sign of a twist of tobacco. Not with these Quaker clients looking as harmless as magpies. Maybe too harmless, he thought, something stirring at the back of his mind. The Plains tribes admired and respected only the strong. The weak were prey.

"Why must we do this, Mister Skye?" Mary asked at last, looking up from her work. She was resoling a summer moccasin. "They'll do something"—she spoke guardedly, lest Dirk understand—"we don't want."

"Peaceful visit. Smoke the pipe. Let Sitgreaves have his talk. Piegans treated Father De Smet right kindly."

"In every Piegan village are warriors who—won't obey the chiefs," she replied with guarded words.

"We hired on to help our clients, Mary."

She turned away angrily and slid out the oval lodge door into the night.

"You could say no, dammit. Too dangerous," Victoria muttered.

"They got their rudder set, old woman. You figure out where the village is?"

She refused to reply, but he knew she knew. When they'd found Junius, she'd ridden off a way, following

the tracks of two unshod ponies, along with the tracks
of the shod horse that Junius had ridden.

"I imagine I can find it," he added against her silence. "Not so hard."

Even in this endless land, which could conceal a hundred villages anywhere, he knew how to lower the odds.
The nomadic villages all came to rest at water. One
tracked down villages by following creeks. But tomorrow she would pick up the trail without another word
of protest, out of some ancient love of her man, and
they would all tag along behind her hunched figure as
she led them toward doom. It had always been like that,
her love transcending even her own sense of preserva-
tion.

He'd have to talk with Sitgreaves, of course. There
were ways to enter hostile villages, and showing fear
wasn't one of them. He also wanted them all to understand the risks—whether or not they felt the embrace of
Divine Providence.

"Why do they go to the village of the ones that killed
their son? I don't understand, dammit."

Mister Skye laughed. For Victoria, that was temper-
ate talk. In her own mind she must seethe with it all.

"Medicine."

She glanced at him from raptor eyes. "They got no
medicine."

He winked. She muttered her way back to silence,
and he knew they'd not discuss it again. Whitemen remained mysterious to his wives, and none were more
mysterious than these silent Quakers.

They were mysterious to him, too, but at least he
fathomed their purposes: paying evil with good, making friends and allies of their tormentors, and trusting
in the utter goodness of God. Odd how they didn't refer
much to God. They used the abstractions, Providence,
the Divine Will, the Light. To Skye, it sounded about
like believing in gravity.

"Big medicine," he said, settling himself in his

robes. He wondered how big it was, and whether Quaker medicine would protect him and his family and Jawbone, and whether he was making a fool mistake—the kind of mistake that led to the grave.

But the next dawn, when a dew whitened the grasses of the bottoms, Victoria led them back the way they'd come, with the carriage and wagon cutting wheel-lines through the wet grass. He'd studied each white face that dawn and found it composed, except for a grief in Abigail's eyes. Then he'd warned them. Sitgreaves had listened and nodded. And then they'd left, as quiet as ever, like ghost ships sailing through uncharted seas.

Even as he knew she would, Victoria picked up the faint trail of hoofprints and led them north across arched prairie, where no creature made a home and all sensate animals hurried to wherever the hospitality of nature beckoned. He'd never known prairie more lonely or grave.

They nooned at an alkali spring, saying nothing. Doctor Sitgreaves surveyed this foreboding world calmly, and the rest withdrew deep into themselves. The faint trail, Skye knew, cut an angle toward Lodge Creek. Far off to the south the Bearpaws humped up in the blue summer haze. No one ate. He confessed to himself that he couldn't eat, not with the dread that torsioned his body and clamped his belly. He knew he felt fear, lots of fear. He knew he might violate his promise to these people, and shoot to kill. The fast-loading carbine gleamed in his quilled sheath, a comfort worth more than prayers.

They topped a squat ridge and halted to let the horses blow. Even the Percherons had winded themselves dragging the carriage and wagon up the mile-long slope. Before them, the faint trail steered relentlessly down toward a dark streak that looked like a fissure in the earth. Lodge Creek, a favorite haunt of the Piegans in summer. And there on the horizon was an elusive skein of smoke.

"North by northwest. Are you sure, mates?"

William Penn Sitgreaves eyed him kindly. "We are eager, Mister Skye. Now we begin."

Skye sighed, and felt in his possibles for a twist of tobacco, the diplomat's ensign out on these wastes. He knew approximately what would happen—what was likely happening even now. The village wolf society, responsible for the protection of the people, would find them shortly, feeling their presence the way a bug's antennae would, and escort them in—alive or dead, but probably alive if all went well, and the village wasn't under the spell of some shaman's unpredictable medicine.

Victoria looked sharply at him and motioned them forward, and the little Quaker entourage rattled uneasily down a shorter grade toward the distant streak of cottonwoods. And almost as he'd predicted, horsemen boiled toward them, not one but a dozen, and more. Twenty, he guessed, as he eyed the clot of riders uneasily.

He halted his party and waited unhappily, his carbine sheathed. Victoria's face had become sandstone, and he could read her angry thoughts as they played across her like lightning flashes.

Too late now to retreat, he knew. Too late. He felt himself the fool. Then they rode up, proud amberfleshed warriors, wearing their summer garb, which was almost nothing, breechclouts, moccasins, medicine bundles, and a few necklaces of bear claws or things more ominous. All of them sat tall, lithe in their pad saddles, radiating a rippling power as they subdued their ponies and stared from hard eyes set in razored faces. He knew it was coming then, the recognition, and they did not disappoint him. Their fierce gazes raked his scarred face, his familiar top hat, his women, the sinewy battered roan under him, the glinting carbine in its sheath, the knife and revolver at his belt. Then, after surveying their bitter enemy, they studied the Quakers, mildly curious, astonished by the black suits such as traders sometimes wore; at Abigail, the first white woman they'd seen.

A headman kicked his wild-eyed pony close, and Mister Skye didn't like the looks of him, or the war scars that puckered his honeyed flesh and announced his prowess to the world.

Skye lifted his tobacco twist and made the swift hand signs for peace, for a council. The warrior nodded, did not introduce himself, and motioned them violently to follow him. They did, nervously eyeing one giant whose lance trip was lowered toward them as they began the endless ride toward the mysterious village ahead.

Chapter 8

Whatever his private feelings about his father, Artemus Sitgreaves tried hard to be a Friend as they rode into the village. Around their little party rode twenty, then thirty, stern warriors, some with feather-decked lances lowered ominously, as if these visitors weren't visitors at all, but captives. It frightened Artemus. None of the other Friends seemed to be afraid, and he felt ashamed of his own terror.

He showed them all he wasn't afraid with broad smiles, letting his gaze rest benignly upon these fierce savages who swarmed about them as they reached the outskirts of the nomadic town. Piegan, his father had whispered to him. The southernmost Blackfeet, fierce enemies of Americans and all the Plains tribes; bitter at the devastation smallpox had wrought among them; brutal beyond description. Their legendary bloodiness made him dizzy, but he took it for the trial it was.

But trusting Divine Providence here was the lesser trial, he knew. The greater one was to love the ones who'd murdered Junius. He hoped, feverishly, he might

discover who they were so he might forgive them their
fiendish act and turn enemies to friends. Maybe even
Friends. He would listen quietly to their complaints, the
wrongs done them by fur traders, by whites, by soldiers, and by trappers, and then he'd write a book in
such clear, pellucid prose, such transparent logic, that
he and his brethren would transform Indian policy in
Washington City. At least that's what his father and the
Friends wanted him to do. Use his gifts. He had a way
with words that Junius had lacked.

These thoughts made him giddy, as he imagined wine
would make him giddy, as he steered his covered wagon
into the village. The savages gaped at his paired Percherons, clapping hands to mouths at the sight of horses
half again larger than their largest Spanish mustangs,
horses whose powerful muscled shoulders pushed into
their collars and dragged the heavy wagon along effortlessly. How they stared! He flipped the lines lazily, and
his giants lifted their gait slightly, their platterlike feet
rising and sinking. Brown children squealed; young men
eyed the gray giants thoughtfully, seeing unheard-of
power; squaws pointed and exclaimed. All this he discerned as he steered his giants easily along the corridor
between tawny lodges.

He'd never been in a village before—other than the
lodges around Fort Union—but knew from the books
his father required him to read just what to expect, and
here it all was. Yapping dogs, buffalo meat cut into thin
strips and curing on racks, medicine tripods from which
dangled trophies of black human hair. He eyed them
carefully, dreading to find one fresh scalp with Junius's
chestnut brown. But he saw nothing of that sort.

Ahead in the carriage his mother looked stiff and
fearful, but the Spirit had never caught her soul as com-
pletely as some Friends. He knew he had the same fear
in himself. A boy of ten or twelve paced beside his
wagon, staring, daring himself to do something with his
child's bow. And then the youth sprang lightly, a blur

of brown, and landed beside Artemus, menace in his brown eyes. Artemus felt his heart lurch, but he smiled at the youth, who didn't smile. Then he handed the lines of the Percherons to the boy, who grabbed them, letting his bow clatter to the floorboard, and proudly took command of the giants. Artemus laughed.

"Thee are a bold one!" he said, and the boy gazed at him solemnly, saying nothing.

No sooner had the boy assumed triumphant control of the horses than a giant warrior, trotting along beside the wagon, leapt upward and settled in the seat beside the boy, wresting the lines from him. It shocked Artemus. This one, a burly giant with graying hair encased in a headband made of rattlesnake skin, peered at Artemus from ebony eyes that glowed like the coals of hell, radiating hatred and contempt. Artemus shrank back under the hammer of that glare. The warrior reached over with a muscled arm and smacked Artemus hard on the back, dislodging him from his plank seat. It hurt. Artemus slid back into his seat aching at the shoulder.

Counting coup! He knew that. This one had counted coup, the way tribesmen did with enemies. A lump formed in his throat. The warrior stood then, swaying easily with the rhythm of the wagon, shouting to the massing people watching the procession. Artemus didn't understand a word of it but he knew the gestures, and he knew the tone of voice. This scarred giant—Artemus discovered the warrior lacked three fingers of his left hand and bore a cruel puckered slash down his left forearm—was claiming the wagon, the Percherons, the contents inside, and maybe Artemus himself.

But surely—but this was utterly unthinkable. Fear bled away his resolve, especially when he came under the malignant scrutiny of the warrior, who examined Artemus's soft flesh, his black suit, his slender hands, and saw no force in Artemus at all. A terror built in

Artemus that he couldn't contain, not even by centering himself on the Divine Spirit, and he shivered.

Ahead, the carriage containing his father and mother and Fall and Price continued unmolested, though the Piegans crowded so close that passage became difficult and the Percheron drawing them flinched and twitched.

Mister Skye turned back, studying the warrior on Artemus's wagon, and drew up Jawbone to wait. Artemus's pulse exploded into a wild panic running through his veins. He felt utterly split down the middle of his soul, wanting Skye to rescue him and all their possessions from the razor-faced warrior beside him by force of arms if necessary—war, power, prowess—but also wanting the Divine Spirit to resolve all this in tranquillity. He ached with terror and love, with dread and hope, with the knowledge of severe tribulation and the ecstasy of the testing.

"Thee are a powerful man," he said to the warrior. "But thee will comprehend a greater power."

For an answer, the warrior slapped him, a blow so brutal it catapulted him clear off his seat, and he felt himself tumbling to earth in the midst of the pressing crowd. He landed on his shoulder and felt pain claw down his back. But he smiled at those who dodged him, and stood up. They laughed, these savages, and one of the squaws, a toothless crone with braided gray hair, whacked him, sending him tumbling to the dirt again. After that they pummeled him, laughing, kicking, drubbing him, all of them counting coup.

Until Mister Skye rode in on the terrible medicine horse. And then they fled, knowing the medicine power of the murderous yellow-eyed animal and the burly whiteman who rode it. The Piegan women and boys who'd pummeled Artemus screamed away, seeing Jawbone with his ears laid back, his teeth clicking manically, his mouth snapping, biting air, his legs trembling, ready to erupt in murder.

"Get up, boy."

Artemus did, brushing his black clothing shakily.

"Catch up with your wagon and get aboard. I'll be right beside you."

"But—but—he'll kill me."

"Do it, boy."

"My faith is in Providence. The Spirit will descend ''

"I hope it will, boy. Meanwhile get going."

Something terrible in Skye's voice compelled obedience. Artemus trotted ahead, hating himself for it, hating Skye, his fragile spiritual kingdom usurped. And yet he couldn't resist Skye, and he threaded through silent Piegans until he caught up with the wagon. Just behind, Jawbone plowed through the crowd, parting it.

From his seat, the warrior peered down at Artemus, mocking. He said something Artemus couldn't understand, but it evoked a titter among the scurrying onlookers. Then Mister Skye pulled up beside, and the warrior's face locked into deadly readiness.

The guide's meaty fingers described a circle and slashes, and then Skye waited, while Jawbone kept pace.

The warrior sat stone-faced, doing nothing.

Skye smiled, his obscure gaze never leaving the warrior. The crowd turned quiet. Artemus felt a chill.

Jawbone shrieked, a weird, shrill squeal that pierced to the bone.

"Thee promised my father not to use deadly force," Artemus managed to say.

"I invited him to count coup on me, boy."

Time hung suspended, and still the caravan rattled through the village, past tan lodges, picketed ponies, and smoldering cookfires. By now, the Friends in the carriage ahead had discovered the affray and were watching. All but Doctor Sitgreaves, who continued to steer the carriage behind Mary and Victoria up front.

"Artemus, you'd best get away from Jawbone. He sometimes forgets who's friends and who's not. You climb on up there and take the lines. I reckon the warrior'll give them to you if you're right smart about it. You show any fear, though, and I can't rightly say what kind of bloody mess we'll be in.''

Skye was asking him to clamber up beside that savage who'd knocked him off!

"Climb on, Artemus. If you don't, you may lose everything. Do you follow me? Everything.''

"Thee has threatened deadly force.''

"No, I'm doing it your way.''

"My way is friendship and peace.''

"That takes courage, boy. Get up there. Take the lines. Count coup—hit him a bloody good smack on the head or arm.''

"I want to reconcile—''

The warrior snapped the lines, and the Percherons quickened their pace. Jawbone shrieked.

"Go!'' rumbled Skye with such steel that Artemus dumbly trotted ahead, stepped lithely on the iron stirrup just forward of the front wheel, and swung upward to the bench, too astonished with himself to ponder what he'd done.

Beside him, the giant watched malevolently.

"Do it, Artemus,'' Skye rumbled.

Artemus lifted his hand—a hand that had never struck another mortal—and smacked it on the warrior's head, deranging the headband and knocking his two notched coup feathers askew. The warrior snarled, started to knock Artemus off, and froze. Skye had edged Jawbone close and stood in his stirrups, ready to spring, his top hat perched rakishly. The warrior slowly abandoned the lines, letting them drop rather than handing them to Artemus, and slid off the wagon seat on the far side, landing lightly on his feet. Artemus grabbed the lines.

"No one's dead yet, boy.''

"Thee used force all the same.''

"You got your wagon and horses back, boy. And everything your folks possess.''

"Thee did not rely on the Spirit. Thee took my testing from me," he protested. But inside, he didn't mind at all.

Skye laughed shortly. "It's not over yet, boy. If you want a testing, you just may get it. When they strip us, tie us to trees, and start the slow torture. Cut off fingers joint by joint. Jab pine slivers into us and fire them. You want that testing, boy, you just may bloody well get it. Meanwhile, I'll have to do some fast talking with the chief, whoever he is."

Artemus's pulse slowed. He felt better with the horses in his possession and the wagon under him, and no savage claiming anything—yet. He sighed, unable to cope with the turmoil of his soul, and unable to acknowledge the fragile safety Skye had wrought with the brute force of his own legend.

Ahead, at last, the Friends halted before a larger lodge, lavishly decorated with carmine and umber drawings of horses and war. Before it, feather-bedecked lances stabbed the earth, the breeze whirling the eagle feathers crazily about, testing their magic. Victoria reined up, her face frozen into a glare, and Mary, with Dirk before her, halted also, along with the Skyes' pack animals.

Artemus swiftly recovered his aplomb. The chief's lodge. Safety. A council. Reconciliation. A flood of joy released in him, as if he'd weathered a stormy passage, and the sight of the squat, bowlegged chief with the imperious face radiating contempt didn't really faze Artemus at all.

Headmen gathered beside the chief, and along with them a freckled half-breed who seemed to be important in the band. Not a face among them showed the slightest sign of friendliness. They peered at Skye as he rode up, and at the dread horse they knew all too well, and at the carbine stock peeking from its sheath, and the weapons at his waist. Jawbone made his own space, glaring at them with laid-back ears and vicious darts of his head, as if deciding whom to murder first. A horde of Blackfeet warriors pressed into a circle, effectively capturing these visitors, and en masse fully able to murder them all with weapons at hand, most of which were wicked-looking lances tipped with whitemen's iron. But not yet.

His father handed the reins to Diogenes Fall and clambered slowly from the carriage, his manner amiable and dignified. The fresh breeze caught the lapels of his frock coat and toyed with his hair, but the man beneath seemed as solid as a brick wall. Indeed, Artemus took courage from his father's quiet dignity and erect, unafraid demeanor. The scowling chief eyed William Penn Sitgreaves, and the doctor peered back unsmiling and uncowed.

"Would thee introduce us, Mister Skye?" he asked.

The guide chose to address the half-breed. "French or English?" he asked.

"McDonnell," the breed replied. "My mother and wife are Pikuni. My father was with American Fur— before your day."

Skye smiled, even if McDonnell didn't. In all other appearances, the breed had taken the ways of these people, and would be loyal to them.

"And who is our host, Mister McDonnell?"

"Mountain Chief."

Some fleeting caution flashed across Skye's face, and Artemus supposed this chief had a reputation unsavory in some way. It filled him with dread again.

"These people are on their way to Owen's Fort in the Bitterroot, Mister McDonnell. They are Doctor and Mrs. Sitgreaves, of Philadelphia, their son Artemus on the wagon yonder, and the other two gentlemen are Mister Fall and Mister Price."

He waited until McDonnell translated for the headmen.

"They're members of the Society of Friends, Mister McDonnell, coming this long distance to bring medicine to the western tribes, and to give the western tribes a strong voice with the fathers and chiefs in Washington City.''

The breed translated again and triggered a harsh, brief debate among the headmen.

''Why do they go to the Salish, our enemies?'' asked the translator. ''Mountain Chief wishes to know. If they go to the Salish to help the enemies of the People, we will be unhappy.''

A chill ran through Artemus. His mother winced. But William Penn Sitgreaves lifted a gentle hand. ''Tell our esteemed chief that we favor no tribe over another. All are welcome to my surgery. We will hear all the chiefs and carry their word and requests back to the white people in the east. We go to Owen's Post because it is a good place for whitemen to live; a place for us to plow our fields and plant our gardens and orchards. We come in friendship and have many gifts for the Blackfeet, words of the One Above and things of man.''

Artemus discerned a fine Quaker logic threading his father's address, and found the tone of his father's voice comforting. He could see his father's amiable dignity having its effect on these hard-eyed men.

But McDonnell's translation seemed only to confuse and excite the headmen, who argued heatedly.

''Mountain Chief wants to know if Doctor Sitgreaves is a blackrobe, like De Smet.''

''No, I assure you I am not, though I believe in the priesthood of all believers,'' Sitgreaves replied.

That only puzzled them the more, and elicited a torrent of Blackfeet words that had harsh consonants in them, like hail rattling a roof. ''What is the medicine? Why will he give it to the Salish first?''

His father thought a moment. ''I can heal wounds. I have a live smallpox vaccine. It can prevent smallpox, which has devastated thy people. Surely they know of the inoculation. It's been done here many times. I will vaccinate Mountain Chief first of all, and the little scratch will keep him from ever dying of the big disease.''

McDonnell eyed Doctor Sitgreaves uneasily, and conveyed the message to Mountain Chief, and once again a fierce debate ensued. ''Mountain Chief says you must prove your medicine on someone else. He will give you an Absaroka slave first. If the slave woman dies, then he will know.''

''It takes many days, Mister McDonnell. And we wish to be on our way.''

Mister Skye intervened. ''We come for a smoke, mate. We brought a twist of tobacco for the chief. Lots more, too.''

Artemus knew what happened next would be crucial, because the ritual smoke would be the sign of welcome and peace. If it was refused, he knew they'd be considered aliens, prisoners, and in mortal danger.

McDonnell translated for Skye, and they all waited. Mountain Chief surveyed his guests one by one, his eye harsh upon the Skyes, contemplative while examining Jawbone. In the end, he said nothing at all, a bad sign.

''Mister McDonnell,'' said Doctor Sitgreaves boldly, ''we believe that in this village are two hunters who took the life of my youngest son. I would like to meet them.''

''There's no one like that here!'' the breed snapped, and then translated swiftly for the headmen.

''I believe they are here,'' Sitgreaves continued, ''and we've come to offer forgiveness and reconciliation, though our own hearts overflow with grief.''

McDonnell stared.

''They can't grasp that, mate. Forget it. Beyond their way of lookin' at things. They'd bloody well think you crazy. Let it rest, all of you.''

''Thy counsel is welcome, Mister Skye, but I'll go where the Light leads me—leads us, even if to the final testing.'' He turned to the breed. ''Mister McDonnell, we adhere to the belief that God will protect us if we fully follow his will. We have no arms and will not use them on mortals. We come defenseless as lambs. We have come to repay evil with good. Somewhere in this throng are those who took my son. They have his scalp, and his saddle horse. Thee must learn that we will not avenge our loss, but rejoice that his death will bond us to thee now. Neither do I wish to take the horse back. We have ridden here to cleanse our own souls, and give our peace to those who took Junius from us.''

Artemus rejoiced. Skye frowned. The breed shook his head.

''I can't say nothing like that,'' McDonnell muttered. ''I can't say it.''

''Does thee mean they won't understand?''

''I guess. It ain't how Injuns think.''

''Try it, anyway. Just translate what I said.''

''Like to have a smoke, mate. This'll take some long talkin', I think,'' Skye murmured.

The half-breed looked up at him. ''Skye, they already figgered what to do with you and your women and the brat. They got you at last, and every warrior in the village's itchin' to begin, and thinkin' how to do it mean, and repay you for every Blackfeet scalp you ever took. You aren't going to get to smoke. You aren't going to see tomorrow. It's the others, these wagon people, they don't know what to do with.''

Chapter 9

Mister Skye knew he was doomed. Not just doomed, but destined to suffer the most painful torture they could devise, and it would begin only minutes ahead. The knowledge of what they'd do, and how it would reduce him to a screaming madman, broke sweat from him and loosed a turmoil in his gut.

And his own torture would be only the beginning. They'd slow-kill Victoria and Mary, too—and because they hated anything connected with Skye, they'd torture the boy, the little innocent two-year-old boy whose crime had been to have the wrong father. And Jawbone.

Victoria would take it and take it, hard woman that she was. They'd tie her to a tree, chop off fingers joint by joint, and burn her flesh, and she'd only glare. But Mary, beautiful Mary—he knew she'd scream, and feel pain a thousand times more, and suffer a terror beyond description. She'd be forced to watch her son's torture and death, and because she would not be stoic, they'd slow it all down and make it worse. And Jawbone. They'd pump arrows into him, avoiding the vital areas,

inflicting mad hurt until he bled to death, berserk. And
then they'd all file past and count coup on the medicine
horse and enemy of the Blackfeet.

He peered at Victoria and saw the knowing in her
eyes. But in Mary's eyes he read only terror as she
clutched Dirk to her. Poor Mary, doomed to suffer the
most because her terror would delight these Piegans and
they'd enjoy every bit of hurt they could squeeze out of
her. A despair swept through him: the end. He'd leave
nothing behind. His only child, Dirk, dead. His wives,
dead. And even Jawbone. He'd planned for years what
he'd do with the horse when he grew old. He'd take the
gaunt old warrior up high into the Pryor Mountains in
the heart of Absaroka country and release him among
the wild herd there, release his old friend to spend his
last days as free as ever a horse lived out its days; release him to sire a few more colts, and let that crazy
blood that made Jawbone a terror and a legend flow in
the veins of his get.

Victoria stared at him unblinking, saying something
to him without the slightest movement of a facial muscle. He got her message and stared back unblinking.
They had made a compact. She'd been angry with him
for coming here, for guiding these strange whitemen,
for accepting their pacifist terms. But that anger had
dissolved, he knew, in the face of this. They had to die
well. He finally lifted his battered top hat and ran a
hand through his matted hair, the ancient signal among
them to watch and wait.

He peered harshly about him, as he always did in
desperate circumstances, looking for chances, for surprise, for ways. He saw none. Several hundred Piegans
swarmed around them, in effect imprisoning them.
Many were warriors, armed with lances or knives. Even
the women had butcher knives in hand, as eager for the
coming sport as the men. He dreaded the Piegan women
most. They were expert torturers. At the last, one of

them would saw off his genitals and stuff them in his mouth while he yet lived to know it.

But that would not happen. He could no longer choose to live, but he could choose how to die. On a signal from him, his wives and Jawbone and he himself could begin a hopeless war that would end in their own butchery. It would be better than a day and a night and another day of torture. Better than Mary watching them bash the brains of Dirk. He'd made himself and his wives and his medicine horse a legend; they would die a legend. But the Piegans could thwart even that if they caught and hog-tied them, trussed them up for the long torture, before they could act.

As always, Jawbone commanded space, and no Piegan edged closer than ten or fifteen feet, but crowds pressed close around his wives and their ponies, close enough to grab them in an instant. A danger.

"Victoria," he said. "Come hold Jawbone. Mary, you too."

Victoria understood. Mary didn't. Jawbone didn't need holding. But Victoria harshly yanked at Mary, who dismounted, carrying Dirk, and walked closer to Skye. Victoria grasped the ugly horse's simple hackamore, while the evil-eyed horse watched her madly, his ears flattened back upon his skull.

Skye felt a moment's relief. Jawbone gave them a bit of room, enough time to slide knives from sheaths and ready themselves to fight the final battle. At last, Mary's troubled brown doe-eyes revealed some understanding, and he knew they were as ready as they'd ever be.

He'd quite forgotten the Quakers as his mind had whirled through the possibilities, but now he turned toward William Penn Sitgreaves, who was still remonstrating with the breed, Mr. McDonnell, for not translating. A vast rage swept him. Their folly had become his doom. Their pacifism had brought the whole party to this—had killed him, his wives, his son, his dreams. He loathed the man and his sheeplike colleagues, and knew he'd violate his appalling vow: to keep himself and his family from endless torture, he'd take life, all he could take, with Mountain Chief and the headmen the first to taste his bowie knife. He wondered what Sitgreaves would think of that. Condemn Skye, no doubt, not fathoming what Skye would do, or why.

"Thee must tell the chiefs," Sitgreaves droned on.

"I'll sign-talk," Skye rasped, in a searing voice that triggered surprise among the Friends.

From Jawbone's back, Skye began flashing signs, a poor language, the worst language, with no finger symbols for half of what he wanted to say. His gaze locked with the embered gaze of Mountain Chief, seeing murder in it. But it didn't matter. He flashed the peace sign, the smoke sign. He pointed at Sitgreaves and made a medicine sign, and a shaman sign. He made the sign for alliance, for friend. He made the help sign, the sickness sign, and the help sign again. He paused, and signed in succession help, against, whiteman, chiefs, grandfathers.

That at last drew Mountain Chief's gaze toward Sitgreaves, and the gazes of the other headmen also. McDonnell said something to them in their own tongue, and Skye had no notion what McDonnell said. But McDonnell was allied to them, even as he was one of the Crow, allied by marriage. Skye continued making signs, as furiously as his fingers and hands and arms could move, buying precious fleeting moments, buying whatever signs could buy. Seconds. He made the Salish sign, then Piegan sign, and signed the other tribes Sitgreaves hoped to help. He made the signs for food and corn. He made the sign for gifts.

"Give Mountain Chief a gift, mate. Now."

The tone of Skye's voice, with all the violence bristling in its timbre, startled Sitgreaves, but he nodded, and Artemus dug into a crate back at the wagon, and then walked forward with an armload of things. Sitgreaves handed Mountain Chief a hand mirror, but the chief did not accept it—a bad sign. Helplessly, the doctor set it on the ground and added bright ribbons, a good Sheffield knife, black twists of tobacco, a skein of blue beads, a string of hawk bells. The chief eyed the growing pile with opaque contempt, and his expression told Skye that with the slightest wave of his hand his people could pillage the entire wagon, so these gifts meant nothing. Nothing.

"Stop the giving, Doctor," Skye snapped.

Sitgreaves turned around to stare at him, with eyes so innocent and bright they looked like the summer day. "Have thee explained why we came? About Junius?"

It startled Skye. The poor fool was still thinking about his fool mission here, a victim of his unworkable theology. And yet . . .

"I will try that."

He again addressed Mountain Chief, whose malevolent gaze had turned into a sneer. The chief understood Skye's terror perfectly even if it eluded the Quakers.

He began making signs again, this time for death, son—he pointed at Sitgreaves—horse, stealing, scalp. And then he signed the words that surprised the chief. First peace, then friendship, then One Above. Good payment. Bring the ones who killed the son. Then, since there was no exact sign for forgiveness or reconciliation, or anything abstractly religious, he signed honor, good, friendship. And big spirit.

The chief looked puzzled. He frowned, and peered at the Quakers curiously, studying them all, their dark suits, their odd serenity, their lack of arms, their obvious inability to make war. He talked with his headmen, and finally with McDonnell.

"They don't understand nothing," the translator said. "Like I said before, Skye. They don't care about them. They care about you. They got you now. Just a few days ago, big shaman of theirs says they'll catch you at last. They'll have their fun, if you know what I mean."

"Thee must tell them," protested Sitgreaves. "They mustn't treat our guides badly. We hired them. We insisted they come here. You tell Mountain Chief I am unhappy."

McDonnell shrugged and translated. Skye watched the doctor, a tight rage building in him, a hatred of the man's innocence.

"The chief says, You're unhappy? What are you going to do about it? Have you war medicine? How you going to keep his people from it? You got such big medicine, maybe you should strike him dead right now to prove it."

Sitgreaves thought about it, and shook his head. "Thee will see. We did not come to strike chiefs dead. Thee must tell him we come to give life, not death; that the One Above watches, and we have all taken his Spirit into us. We are sheep, but we have a Shepherd."

Skye laughed crazily. Jawbone clacked his teeth and snapped at flies and murdered Piegans inside his horse mind.

The chief's hands slashed and bobbed. What did the medicine man say?

Skye turned to McDonnell. "You tell him. I can't."

McDonnell talked, the chief nodded, and Skye sensed the squaw man was putting his own coloration on it.

Plainly, Mountain Chief was puzzled. He stepped out from his lodge toward the Percheron harnessed to the carriage, wanting to examine the giant horse. From within the buggy, Abby Sitgreaves watched with unalloyed fear in her face while Fall and Price sat behind her, stiff and dour. The chief surveyed the other two Percherons, running his powerful hand along their necks and withers while Artemus smiled sickly.

"Thee may not have them," Doctor Sitgreaves said firmly, trusting McDonnell to translate. "Thee are an honorable man, my chief." He waited while Mountain Chief listened to McDonnell, frowning. "I understand that among all the tribes guests are honored and their possessions are never touched. Isn't that the law of thy people?''

Skye watched, astounded by the man's firm demeanor. Didn't Sitgreaves have any notion of his helplessness here, unarmed among warriors who prized strength above all else? But there was Sitgreaves, his rectangular face a model of calm dignity, dealing with a murderous chief as an equal.

Mountain Chief listened impassively, revealing nothing in his opaque, glittering eyes.

"I will do this," continued Sitgreaves. "These are mares. The one drawing my carriage is a stallion. We have bred them. At Owen's Post we intend to use them to plow our fields and help us plant and cultivate, as well as draw us about the country, and take us out to heal and help the Indians. But thee, Mountain Chief, may buy our foals next fall, upon their weaning. I will not give them to thee but I will sell them for robes at a fair price.''

Skye listened, astonished. Didn't the doctor know he and his people were a hairbreadth from being butchered? Still, Mountain Chief listened to McDonnell's translation, his sharp gaze shifting from the translator to the doctor.

At last Mountain Chief turned toward his headmen, who gestured and shouted at him. But he cut them off with an imperious wave of his hand. Power resided in that hand. It throttled the clamor with an authority that Skye had rarely seen before in white or Indian. The young chief possessed something in his stocky frame and demeanor that few men possessed, a natural authority that other men obeyed without wondering why they obeyed.

And Doctor Sitgreaves had somehow made himself the chief's equal. A grudging respect built in Skye, for Sitgreaves had the natural power of his patrician class, while Skye's own power resided solely in the terror he fostered in the minds of others. Skye somehow knew what he possessed was shoddy compared to the fine steel of Doctor Sitgreaves's will.

Mountain Chief closed in on Doctor Sitgreaves until they stood a yard apart, each erect and unyielding, like horned buffalo bulls ready to fight. Except that Sitgreaves had no horns. The chief lifted his bare arm and pointed south, toward the Milk. "Go away," he said in muted English. "You go now."

"No," said the doctor, astonishing Skye. "No. We will stay a while."

The chief was taken aback. "Go now." He turned to the translator and rattled something. McDonnell said, "He says he's kept you from harm; some wanted to torture you, take your horses and things. Now you must go. Skye stays. They want you gone first."

"First?"

"It ain't for your eyes."

"What isn't?"

"They got some settling up to do."

"And what will that be?"

McDonnell turned silent.

The doctor addressed Skye. "What will they do with thee, Mister Skye?"

"Get out while you can, Sitgreaves," Skye snarled. "Get your bloody wagons out."

The doctor's bright gaze surveyed the scene, rested on the Skye family crowded close to Jawbone, noted the space around the fierce horse; observed the predatory gaze of scores of warriors, who eyed the Skyes with ill-concealed lust of some sort; studied the lowered lances imprisoning the Skyes, and the hawkish eagerness in the shamans; and finally settled on the Skyes themselves, at the haunted look in Mary's face, at Victoria clutching the Green River knife at her belt, and at Skye's grave demeanor.

He faced the chief. "They will come with us." McDonnell didn't need to translate.

The chief said nothing.

"Mister Skye," said the doctor, "I will make way with the buggy, and Artemus will follow. And thee'll follow behind."

"Go," roared Skye.

Doctor Sitgreaves settled himself in his carriage and snapped the lines. The big Percheron lifted into a walk, and the sullen crowd gave way. Artemus brought his mares to life, and the wagon rumbled behind the carriage. And behind them the Piegan crowd closed, sealing the Skyes once again. The only thing that kept scores of warriors from flooding in was Jawbone's murderous glare, his laid-back ears, his clicking teeth. Skye's heart hammered. Dying time now. He slid carefully off the mad horse, a signal to the animal that he would soon unloose it with a word, and stood tautly beside Mary and Victoria and Dirk.

The carriage halted. The bloody fool doctor wasn't fleeing. Skye saw the Quakers consult briefly—Sitgreaves, his wife, the men—and cursed them roundly. He couldn't help fools. He couldn't keep sheep from wolves. Incredulously he watched them string their way through the pressing mob, firmly elbowing Piegan women aside and then pushing warriors apart to enter into Jawbone's barren circle.

"Get out!" Skye roared. "Goddamn ye bloody fools!"

"Thee takes God's name in vain, Mister Skye."

They pushed through, these black-suited men, black-dressed woman, naked but for their firm wills, and arrayed themselves around the Skyes, clasping hands and forming a trembling barrier of black against the blood-lusting mob.

"Stand back, mates," Skye muttered, enraged. "Jawbone'll murder you. Go!"

But they stood, leaking tears, arms locked, an odd little circle around the Skyes.

The chief shouted at them in a tongue they didn't know.

"Mister McDonnell," said Doctor Sitgreaves. "Their

fate is our fate. We hired the Skyes on our terms, and we will share their fate, whatever it may be. Thee will tell this to Mountain Chief.''

"Bloody fools," Skye roared. "Bloody fools."

Sitgreaves turned to him and pinioned him with that bright gaze, the blue eyes transfixing him. "Where the Spirit leads us, we will follow. We asked thee to come here; we asked thee to avoid bloodshed; we will join thee now."

Skye hated and loved the man, cursed and wept.

Off beyond the lethal crowd, young warriors leapt aboard the carriage and the wagon and drove them off, prizes of war. Skye watched the vehicles disappear behind lodges, cursing Sitgreaves, cursing his God. Around him the mob seethed now, blood-lust boiling through them, excitement, joy. They'd kill the black-suits after all, along with the Skyes. Count many coups this fine day, take a few scalps, and tear the Skyes to pieces, until nothing remained even for dogs to eat

"Bloody fools!" Skye roared, thinking he'd have to kill the Quakers now to keep them from being tortured. It would come in seconds, as soon as the Piegans nerved themselves to face Jawbone's murderous hoofs. War-riors dared themselves, chanted medicine songs, shouted insults, whipped up courage. A thick warrior reared back and loosed his lance, which sailed like an evil bolt of lightning, grazing Artemus's frock coat and upper arm and clattering beyond. Artemus cried and clutched his reddening sleeve.

Jawbone screeched, a shriek so eerie and bloodcur-dling it paralyzed them all at the ragged edge.

Mountain Chief roared and bulled through his war-riors into the naked circle. Warriors with lance arms poised to throw halted under the chief's thunder.

Skye scarcely could keep track of events. Artemus bled and wept. Abby Sitgreaves wilted. Jawbone trembled and pawed, berserk at his side; Victoria's knife glinted; Dirk stared so solemnly up at him. The chief bulled straight toward him, and Skye prepared to cut the man's guts out—and would have, but for that paralyzing wave of the arm above them, a thrust of hand that halted men on the brink of butchery.

In powerful, harsh cadences, the chief shouted commands that warriors reluctantly followed, lowering lances, axes, war clubs, knives, buffalo-hide shields, and drawn bows. But some seemed reluctant, plainly wrestling with their own wild lusts. Skye watched one in particular, whose gaze burned into him. He'd seen that look before, too many times. Skye glared back, knife in hand, daring the warrior. The challenged one faded into the mob.

Then a nasal command from the chief drew McDonnell into the circle, and the chief snapped something at the translator.

"The black-clothes people are very brave, big medicine. He will send you away, now. He says the black-clothes people must not make bad medicine against his village."

Skye could scarcely believe it. But with his own eyes he witnessed the Percherons and wagon and carriage being driven straight toward him by several warriors crowding the seats of each.

"We are not brave, Mister McDonnell," said the doctor. "We were filled with terror, even as thee would be. We thank Mountain Chief and will ask Divine Providence for his blessings upon this village. And, Mister McDonnell, tell him we will not go just yet. We wish him to bring to us those who took the life of our Junius. We have unfinished business with them."

Skye, his body still quaking and sweat-streaked, gaped.

Chapter 10

A dread suffused Abigail Sitgreaves. She did not want to meet the murderers of Junius. She didn't want to peer into their wild faces. She didn't want them examining her, or looking into her soul. She didn't want to conceal the hurt—and dread—she felt. She didn't want to reconcile herself to them even if that was the way of the Friends. She didn't want her own weakness tested this way.

An anger swept through her. William Penn was subjecting her to this. She peered into his face and found those innocent eyes peering back, schoolboy's eyes, she thought, not the eyes of a man. She'd hardly ever been angry with him before—not until this trip. And yet he had relentlessly asked for this, without the slightest consideration of her feelings, and she felt a wash of bitterness toward him, and guilt because it was darkness, not light.

But it was happening, as surely as the sun shone. Mountain Chief had commanded something, and headmen had spread out through the throng, while Piegans gathered quietly around, obviously filled with curiosity. The Skyes, looking shaken, scarcely noticed or cared, and were an island unto themselves.

"Thee test me," she said to her husband. "Have thee no care?"

"We're all tested. This is a great moment, Abby. The greatest moment. Everything we do depends on this."

An awful silence descended on them. Not a soul spoke or moved. Even the wind seemed to cease, birds halted in mid-flight, and the clouds loitered, paralyzed above. Raptly, the Piegans studied these strange people, and she felt a thousand gazes probing her, and wished not to be the cynosure of such attention.

"Mister McDonnell," said William Penn, "I will need thy services."

Reluctantly, and with an air of not wanting to be associated with these people, the scraggle-bearded squawman slid out from among the headmen and into Jawbone's naked circle. The horse, cued by the quiet, stood in malevolent peace, a rear leg cocked.

Abigail felt William Penn's strong arm slide around her shoulder, and she drew comfort from it. The pressure of his fingers about her arm quieted her roiling soul. Thus it had been from the first, when he'd courted her in her parents' parlor. Both families were Friends. She'd had her heart set on a neighboring young man, a clerk of court but not a Friend, and it had occasioned grave objections from her parents. To marry outside was to be disowned by the Meeting. She could not bring herself to let that happen, even when a freer life tugged at her. And then he'd introduced himself at the Monthly Meeting, on a First Day, and she'd been galvanized by the sweetness of his gaze. How could the male nature ever be so sweet?

They'd married, exchanging vows before the Committee of Oversight which acted as witnesses, to the pleasure of both sets of parents. He'd undertaken a worldly profession, but Friends would tolerate it so long as he kept first things first—which he had. It was she who hadn't. She'd borne three boys and two girls, the fruit of their rare joining . . . but typhus and summer complaint had taken all but Junius and Artemus in infancy. And now she had lost free-spirited Junius . . .

The crowd parted slightly. Two men, young and old, erupted from it, and Abby beheld the warriors who'd taken the life of her son. They stared sullenly from opaque eyes, not wanting to be there any more than she wanted to see them. Her pulse quickened and a shiver ran through her. Killers! One was stocky and graying, as arrogant as a hanging judge; the other seemed much younger, lean and cunning, with eyes that darted furtively. Both wore breechclouts and moccasins and medicine pouches.

Abigail saw the older one in her mind's eye drawing the bow, loosing an arrow, running the scalping knife around her boy's skull, laughing at his conquest. Now the Piegans herded tighter, until Jawbone screeched his warnings. Not a villager wanted to miss an event so amazing. She found scant comfort in William Penn's grip.

"Mister McDonnell, tell them I mean them no harm, and would like their names," her husband said quietly.

"I know their names. Bad Belly—he's the older. And Quick Otter."

"If thee would tell them that I mean them no harm— "

"Why should I? They ain't gonna understand anyway," the squawman muttered, but he did say something in the Blackfeet tongue.

"Tell them that we seek reconciliation. We wish to become friends, even though they have grieved us mortally."

"Look, Sitgreaves, there's no words. No idea like that. Reconciliation. I ain't about to make some fool of myself."

"If thee would—"

"I ain't some slave of yourn, making myself look bad in my own village."

"Why, we will reward thee handsomely, Mister McDonnell, for services rendered."

"Like what?" The squawman turned crafty.

"Name thy price for translating everything as best as you can, until they truly do grasp our intent."

The scruffy man shrugged. "No way these people's gonna swallow this crazy talk."

The chief and headman watching this intently, their attention on each speaker, and Abigail wondered how much they grasped.

"Very well, I'll ask our guide to use sign language— "

"Rifle. I'll take a rifle."

"We've none now—they took Junius's hunting weapon. But we'll give thee powder and shot, as much as we have."

The squawman grinned malevolently.

"Say it true, McDonnell," Skye rumbled from the side. "We understand a parcel of the tongue, even if we don't use it."

"Mind your business, Skye," McDonnell snarled, looking trapped. Abby intuited that McDonnell had no intention of conveying William Penn's thoughts to his tribal friends.

William Penn waited peacefully and then began again, a great earnestness rising from him. "Tell Bad Belly and Quick Otter that we come in peace and we forgive them, please. That we wish to be friends—isn't the term bury the hatchet, Mister McDonnell?—and give them our esteem."

McDonnell laughed, and then, catching Skye's steady, murderous glare, shrank back, and began addressing the two warriors, pausing and stumbling now and then. Abby sensed he was trying.

Some in the crowd exclaimed. The warriors stood

impassively, revealing nothing, staring at the whitemen as if they were mad.

"Tell them, please, that we Friends think nothing of war honors. We are people who don't fight, ever, because we have a better way. Tell them, if thee would, that to make our point we will kneel before them and they can count coup on each of us."

McDonnell laughed crazily. "Yer plumb mad, Sitgreaves. That's like makin' yourself dirt before them."

"Please do as I say—and now."

A wild turmoil built in Abigail. Would she have to do this ghastly thing, let murderers of Junius hit her over the head while she knelt before them? She rebelled.

"William Penn, I can't—"

But his innocent smile stopped her for a moment.

"Don't thee care about Junius?" she cried. "Don't thee miss him as I do? His boyhood gone? His soft voice? His—his affection for his mother? Have thee no mercy?"

"This is thy test, Abby."

She couldn't keep tears from welling, and couldn't contain the shame and anger boiling through her. She pulled free of his arm, knowing how they all stared, how every one in the whole village studied every tear. She wanted to scream, scream at them all, scream at William Penn. She wanted to leave!

"Sonofabitch," muttered Victoria.

"Say it, McDonnell." Skye's menace transfixed the translator, who began at once, stumbling with concepts that either didn't translate at all or were wildly improbable to the Piegan way of thinking. Headmen gasped. Women averted their eyes and turned sideways, not wanting to see mad ones. Mountain Chief's eyes glittered, and he seemed on the brink of rescinding the safe-conduct that perilously protected them. Bewilderment stole into the faces of Bad Belly and Quick Otter. At last, the older one, Bad Belly, spoke to the translator, and she could fathom the man's thoughts from his mockery.

"He says he don't count coup on dogs, only brave men. He says if you want peace, you got to count coup on him, and he ain't going to let you."

William Penn pondered, and sighed. "It was a poor suggestion. Tell him I spoke poorly, sir. Tell him I wish to have a peace smoke with him, and that I wish to help his people with my medicine—I am a physician—and with my support. I will be their voice with the grandfathers in Washington City."

"He ain't gonna get that, either, Sitgreaves. They don't know about takin' back words. They think before they talk, and don't take nothing back. Hardly ever."

"If thee would—"

McDonnell shrugged and made a gesture even Abby could read. It said to his friends, *I must do this nonsense*. Still, he bumbled his way along, keeping an uneasy eye on Skye, who listened intently, and all the while the villagers gaped. Some held their mouths to hide giggles. They weren't rude, Abby knew; they just couldn't take William Penn seriously. She felt humiliated. She couldn't take William Penn seriously either.

"Tell them, Mister McDonnell, that we pay evil with good. They'll understand that. And we lose no pride, no self-esteem, giving ourselves away for the sake of love and peace."

"They ain't getting any of this, Sitgreaves. I can't say it none. How about you get the powder and shot and get outa here whiles you can get?"

"If thee would."

McDonnell tried, and met the same astonishment. Plainly, William Penn was getting nowhere. The two warriors stared back impassively. A strange, ludicrous mood settled over the whole village.

"Mate, we'd better bloody well get out. They're not grasping any of it. You'll do better with the Salish . . ."

William Penn sagged, defeated. "Very well, Mister Skye. Artemus, we have things to give these people now."

Her older son—thank God he lived—dug into the wagon and emerged with a sack. William Penn took it, and walked slowly toward the two warriors, who stood sternly erect. He handed each a twist of black tobacco, and then a hand mirror, which, he'd discovered, they prized here.

"I forgive thee," he said to Bad Belly. "I forgive thee," he said to Quick Otter.

And then he approached the chief and gave him the same gifts, in addition to what had been laid before him earlier, and spoke the same words, and did the same with the headman and one scowling medicine man who wore a buffalo-horn bonnet. And then, with half a dozen mirrors and a few twists left, he bestowed the mirrors on the children and the twists on warriors, repeating the same incantation while they stared at him solemnly, making nothing of it.

He'd failed. None of them brought a gift in return. Neither had they smoked the peace calumet. Neither had the warriors returned the horse stolen from Junius. Not a one of them grasped his purpose or the gracious meaning of his Friends message. Still, his whole ludicrous performance may have bought her life, Abigail thought. She trembled, half in lingering terror, half in a rage against her boy-husband. She wanted just one thing: to flee from here now, this instant, and go just as far as they could go.

"Gimme my powder and shot, Sitgreaves," said McDonnell.

They made camp on the Milk River again, in the last possible light, and across the thin sheet of water, as if its flow would protect them from the prowling Piegans. They were all hungry but Victoria hadn't made meat. She'd try to find greens when the horned moon rose.

All that afternoon, she'd stayed with the little caravan, willing its Percherons along, needing distance—hills, creeks, valleys, grass, rock, and earth spirits—between herself and the Piegans. Never had she come so close to dying. Never had Mister Skye come so close. She rode beside the wagon instead of roaming, knowing she'd shoot on sight any Blackfeet no matter what her man had promised.

Madness. She'd peered back at the Quakers many times through the afternoon, seeing the madness. Now she knew. She saw it in their eyes. The doctor's bright eyes were those of a child, innocent of guile. No grown man could possess such eyes. They were taking crazy people to Owen's Post. The sky spirits mocked; the under-earth spirits clutched the souls of these strange ones. They frightened her. Worse, she hated them, with a keen, hard hatred that burned hot inside. She made up her mind: if they endangered her man again, or herself or Mary or Dirk or Jawbone, she'd kill them if she had to. Even if their ghosts haunted her afterward, as all mad spirits did. Crazy people. There they rode, across the land of the Piegans and Bloods and Atsina, without a weapon among them.

Witches. They all were medicine witches, and they'd witched Skye, made him do strange things, like going into that village to be murdered. Her man had taken leave of his senses. Hadn't he spent a lifetime in the mountains, as stealthy as a cat, as wily as a wild stallion? Hadn't he learned all there was to know about surviving, avoiding trouble, only to let these mad ones witch him into foolishness?

She spat.

They'd crossed a hard-bottom ford late in the day, and her man had settled them here in a crease of land that would hide their fires. She'd dourly ridden a wide circle, scouting, but found only clean wind. All the evil spirits crouched in her own camp now, not out beyond the horizon.

She'd never seen her man so haggard. So silent. A single hour that day had devastated his health, and he looked ancient. He failed to play with Jawbone or scratch his ears. Instead, he lowered himself to earth and peered vacantly at nothing.

She knew the Quaker witch medicine had rescued them. She worried that in her mind, over and over, reliving the moment when those people formed a human chain around the Skyes and smiled at the Piegans. Mad creatures. Yet it saved them. She'd be dying now, suffering pains beyond imagining. And her man—she refused to even think about what his fate might have been. It affected her man now as he sat there almost stupefied. She knew what he was thinking. All his days in the mountains he'd made himself strong, and now the very weakness of these clients had saved him. The world had turned over, and sky was down and earth was up, and weak had become strong. She worried that he might get up and go to the packsaddle and withdraw the jug. Sometimes he was like this when he went for the fire spirits. But he didn't. He hunched on the earth, looking vacant and gray.

Over on the naked flat where the Friends had pitched their tents, they sat in the bunchgrass facing each other and saying nothing as night settled. She eyed them malevolently, knowing what they were doing. They did this strange thing once in a while and called it a Meeting. They had Meetings every seven suns, just like the whitemen who went to church on Sundays back at Fort Laramie. Only these people didn't listen and sing and pray; instead, they sat silently facing each other, looking half asleep. Once in a while someone of them rose and spoke to the rest, but mostly they just sat quietly.

Strange ones. They even had their own way of counting suns and moons. Their days were First Day, Second Day, and so on. The months were First Month, Second Month, and so on. Mister Skye had told her that they thought the other names whitemen used, like Sunday, or March, were pagan, so they made their own names. Big medicine. She preferred Sunday, the day named for Sun, and couldn't imagine any sane person objecting to that. All this business about pagan words made her cross, and she refused to learn any more. All whitemen were odd, but these especially.

She eyed them malevolently, sitting there with blank faces, as if they'd turned their thoughts into some kind of inner well they could peer into and find sweet water at the bottom. She watched them exactly as she stalked a cunning elk, studied them in the deepening darkness, with nothing but the creak of crickets disturbing the silence. She closed her eyes and listened to them breathe, and heard them think. Blind ones, not even aware of what lurked out beyond this little camp.

"Sonofabitch!" she exclaimed.

She stood and glared. Over at the lodge, Mary hugged Dirk and made no effort to find a meal. Mister Skye sat on the grass, staring at stars, dumfounded. Jawbone cropped buffalo grass, his ears laid back distrustfully. She was the only one with any sense, she thought. And she was going to share her wisdom with the mad ones.

She stomped over to the Friends and stood at the edge of their circle.

The doctor looked up at her. "Would thee join us, Victoria? We are seeking the light."

"Goddam," she snarled. "You almost got us killed. And you too. Tortured. I don't like you."

They all peered up at her, their pasty faces gray in the starlight, and she felt raw loathing overflow in her.

"We were put to the test, and triumphed," said Diogenes Fall in a way intended to make her small.

"You goddam crazies. I'm telling you this: I don't care what my man promises. Next time, I'll do whatever I want. Maybe I'll shoot. I ain't gonna rescue you, either. I'll save us. I ain't gonna let you make bad medicine on my man, and Mary, and—"

"Thee are free to leave us," Doctor Sitgreaves said. "We'll find our way to the Bitterroot."

It startled her. "Maybe so, maybe so," she muttered.

"Did thee die? Did thee suffer? Did we lose a soul?" asked that older one, Fall.

"Crazy-medicine," she retorted. That explained everything.

It seemed to puzzle them, so she elaborated. "Anyone makes bad medicine among my people, the Absaroka, we drive them away and beat the drums and blow on whistles to frighten bad spirits. Maybe we paint signs too. Maybe we kill, if medicine's bad enough. We kill a bad Hidatsa woman once. And afterward we have good sweats to clean ourselves, and go to a different place to live, and burn sweet grass and sage to make bad medicine stay away. And if the bad-medicine ones come back, they are not of the People and we make war on them."

Doctor Sitgreaves smiled gently. "We will show thee other ways, Victoria. Would thee sit quietly and join us now? We've found our refuge this evening, beneath these glowing stars. The Divine Will."

She was having none of that, and snarled.

"But everything ended well," Freeman Price persisted. "Would thee chastise us—indeed chastise the Divine Will—for sparing us, for leading us to triumph over the flesh?"

"Ha!" she cried, half confused. "I didn't see no goddam Piegan saying yes, yes, we got Big Peace Medicine here. They're afraid of crazies, always treat crazies careful because crazies have medicine. You got crazy-medicine. That's all. Me, I am no crazy. I wish you'd go away. But as long as I got to care for you, hunt meat—you don't even have a rifle to make meat—as long as I do that, and my family, I'll do it my way."

"Thee has blessed us," said the woman. Even her,

crazy, Victoria thought angrily. She'd privately thought Abigail was the only sensible one.

She knew Mister Skye and Mary had heard every word. But she didn't care. She meant Skye to hear too, because he was halfway gone mad himself.

"Goddam," she snapped, and wheeled away. She had an overpowering need to build a tiny medicine fire, find sweet grass and sage leaves, and bathe herself and all the Skyes in the cleansing smoke.

Some sort of emotion she couldn't identify seethed in her, and it made her cross. As much as she wanted to hate those crazy ones, she couldn't manage it. They were unfailingly kind, and that only made her all the angrier. If they were bad-tempered and vicious and liars and arrogant, then she could get her teeth into something. But they weren't. They were as soft as goose down and harmless as sparrows. Except for what they believed. That could easily kill her and all she loved. How strange was the power of belief! She marveled that these Friends had more power than warriors with lances and bows and clubs.

She found Mister Skye grinning at her, and his smile—the first sign of life in him ever since the village—pierced her.

"Well, old lady," he said amiably, "you've got quite a tongue for someone in the guiding business."

She rewarded him with a long, desperate hug.

Chapter 11

Mary didn't sleep that night. No one in Mister Skye's lodge slept much. The events of the day haunted them. Her man had been ashen and subdued, a gray showing under the ruddy brown of his flesh. Several times in that long night, both Skye and Victoria had slid outside and studied the night.

Mary knew why. Among Mountain Chief's band were dozens of young warriors itching to try their hand against their greatest foe, Mister Skye. Young ones, with the recklessness and optimism of youth, daring themselves to ignore their chief's stern prohibition and skulk out into the night after the ones they'd come so close to butchering.

Mary feared them too, and listened sharply to every night sound, a shift of the wind, a coyote howl—which may or may not have been the laughter of the skulking four-foot. There was always Jawbone of course, at his sentry post as usual, but even he seemed restless, perhaps sensing Mister Skye's wariness. Once the horse snorted just outside the thin skin of the lodge cover, lifting all three of them from their robes. But always, it had been nothing. Nothing.

Later, not long before dawn, he'd come to her and she'd welcomed him with her arms. But they hadn't made love. They'd clung nakedly, drawing strength from each other, both of them astonished to be alive, to see another sunrise. He'd gathered their sleepy son to them and placed the boy between them, protecting the child of their loins with their own bodies. And then Victoria had joined them too, nestling up to Mister Skye's back, and they renewed life together after they were all certain they'd lost it.

But Mountain Chief's authority held, and no young warriors pounced on them that night. At the last they dozed fitfully, the terror never far from their minds. It would be a moon before the last of it drained from her spirit, she knew. Even as the blackness grayed into murky light, her man slid out into it to study the hill-tops, because this hour was a favorite for murder.

They continued that day up the Milk River, traversing an endless waste under a sky that reached beyond the farthest horizons. Not a tree marked the broken prairies beyond the river valley. Victoria had glared at the Quakers and ridden off to make meat and note the smallest flight of a sparrow and the passage of every hare. Mary knew the Crow woman would stay away all day, wanting nothing more to do with Mister Skye's clients.

And so it had been. It had been a long time since rain had blessed the earth mother, and the passing carriage and wagon lifted golden dust that left a haze marking their passage, and silted over the quiet travelers. Her man stayed away from the Quakers too, and rode alone on Jawbone, sometimes visible to her, but mostly not. She knew he needed aloneness, like some wild thing, he and the horse together, restoring himself to the winds and waters. But in the middle of the day she found him waiting in a box-elder grove that lined a nameless creek at its confluence with the river. The rippling shade seemed welcome.

They nooned there in the coolness, letting the friendly Percherons graze the bottoms. An eerie quiet pervaded the nooning. The Friends said nothing; neither Mister Skye nor Victoria wanted to. And her man peered dourly at his clients from time to time. She didn't ask him his thoughts.

She watched her boy wobble through grasses as high as his waist, stretching his chunky legs after long confinement on her horse. He'd come to the awkward age when he was too heavy and long for a cradle board but too young and small to care for himself. Sometimes she carried him on the saddle before her; other times she slid him into a shawl and pinned him over her shoulders with it, until her back ached with his weight. Neither was very good, because she needed both hands free to look after the pack horses, steer her own mare, and—if necessary—meet danger with her rifle.

Some women of her people, and other Plains tribes, carried children that age on their travois, and kept them from falling off and vanishing from sight by making a cage of willow withes lashed with rawhide. She'd done that sometimes too, setting Dirk on their lodge cover and constructing the framework. But neither she nor the boy were ever very happy that way, and he soon complained. She had a basket crib for him, with a sleeping bag made of an old blanket and a leather outer liner, and she could pin him into that and hang it from a packmule—until he grew restless. But mostly, she made do, shifting from one thing to another, and getting along.

She loved him dearly, this only child of Mister Skye. He was a half-child of her People, and half whiteman. His golden flesh was like her own, but his red hair came from Skye's people. Dirk's bright brown eyes were Indian eyes, but his cheekbones were like Skye's. He'd been a silent child, but often he talked her Snake tongue

quietly with her, and that was his natural tongue. But
Mister Skye spent time teaching him English, too, and
he spoke those words solemnly and carefully. She didn't
really like his name, Dirk, but Skye had said it was a
fine English name across the big waters. She yearned
to give him a Shoshone name, and secretly thought of
many. But some day they'd visit her people and she'd
let a certain medicine man who'd smiled at her in her
girlhood name the boy and make him one of her people. For now, though, he was Dirk. The short hard
sound of it didn't please her much.

The boy, who wore whitemen's britches, toddled farther through the box-elder glade and then vanished
from her sight, and she picked herself up and sprang
after him before he got into trouble at the languid
creek. She pushed through thick brush, hearing him
laugh, and then found him in a private glade beside the
creek. And beheld Abigail Sitgreaves there beside
the water, her face wet.

"Oh!" exclaimed the doctor's wife, swiftly brushing
back the wetness and turning her face away. "Thee surprised me."

Mary started to back off. She wanted only to recover
her son, who'd sat down beside Abigail in the lush grass.
But the woman stretched her arm toward the chunky
child and touched his shoulder, something haunted in
her face.

"He's a good child. I've watched him with thee, day
after day. He could be a trial at that age."

"I will go away if you want me to."

Mrs. Sitgreaves shook her head. She dug into her
sleeve, extracted a rumpled white handkerchief, and
dabbed at her eyes and cheeks. "Thee must not tell
anyone," she whispered.

"Tell anyone?" It puzzled Mary.

"I'm fine. I'm fine."

Mary considered that curiously. She pitied the
woman. "If I lose Dirk, maybe I wail many days and

cut off my hair. Maybe I do more than that—make a hurt in my flesh so the world knows of the hurt in my spirit."

"I'm fine. Thee must not mention—oh, you see, we thank and bless our God for everything, and we let ourselves be filled with Inner Light because . . ." She stopped, and dabbed at her cheeks again. "I've always had trouble accepting . . ." she added.

"Don't you cry?"

She shook her head. "No. It is a bitterness against God. It's—darkness, not light."

"But didn't you love Junius?"

Mrs. Sitgreaves sobbed at that, a great spasm within her that subsided swiftly. "Only one left now. I gave the world so many but the Divine Will did not spare them."

"You can cry all you want. I'll sit and watch for others. Maybe you should do what you feel. We do what we feel." The whole thing bewildered Mary. She couldn't fathom this law against grieving; she couldn't imagine a religion that said that everything that ever happened was done by the One Above, and everything that happened was good. Was the death of Junius good? She knew better than that. The First Maker was tricky, and one had to be careful. And anyway, demon-spirits lived everywhere, especially in water and under the earth, and made bad things happen. The more she peered at Mrs. Sitgreaves, wanting to weep when she was supposed to be smiling with something called an Inner Light, the more dismayed Mary became. White-men were odd, but these Quakers were worse than that.

"Oh, I wouldn't do that. But I needed a moment alone. I'm a bit of a—I don't know what."

Mary corralled Dirk before he splashed into the brook and the child laughed as she clung to his britches. Abigail watched, some sadness etching her face. Mary didn't know what to say to such a strange one, so she said nothing. Maybe just sitting with her would lift her spirits.

"I dreaded coming. I really just wanted to stay on Walnut Street—that's our home. That's all I wanted, to pass my days with Doctor Sitgreaves. Thee should know he was a great physician there, much loved and trusted, and his surgeries were the hope of so many. Daring, yes, daring. He even cut into the abdominal cavity—the stomach, once, to remove a diseased organ called, I think, the vermiform appendix, and the poor man lived. Of course he was only an iceman and it was little noticed. Doctor Sitgreaves insisted on washing. He always said that a good soapy scrubbing would prevent the fevers . . . I didn't want to come, but they said this was a great work, and we should all rejoice. I confessed my selfish doubts in Meeting."

Mary listened, bewildered at this sudden onrush of words, little of which she understood. It shocked her that she knew so few words of the whitemen, just the ones Mister Skye used a lot.

"They begged me to examine my soul. Was I resisting the Divine Will? I suppose I was, really. Their Light told them that the Indians"—she turned to Mary—"that thee needed help, just the way the poor black slaves need us. Our people help the slaves and fight against slavery. We all do, the Friends. It simply took hold in William Penn like a flame, helping the redmen, smallpox vaccine and a great Witness, and I knew from the joy in him that the Divine Will had spoken. But I—I preferred my comforts. Such a hard trip. To nowhere. I buried my happiness the day we left. What'll I do there at Owen's Post but pine for all that was taken from me? Shall I go to the lending library when I wish? So I'll bury myself. Thee couldn't understand that. I have no Light within me, really."

Mary heard a bustle beyond the brush and knew the Percherons were being harnessed and the nooning had come to an end. She hated to leave this cool bower and face the glaring day again.

"Say, I got a need," she said, an idea sudden upon her. "This boy of mine, he's got me tied up. Could you mind him? I mean, take him in the buggy with you?"

Mrs. Sitgreaves stared at the child. "A little savage boy?"

Mary winced. "I need to look around more. I need to keep an eye out for greens and berries. For meat. Sometimes I can make meat, but not with Dirk hanging on my back. I can maybe make us safer, watch better, if I didn't have to watch him."

"But I couldn't. I don't know what he does."

Mary peered at her, amazed. "He'll take care of himself."

The doctor's wife looked dubious. "I suppose I can manage. It'd give me something to—it'd keep me from thinking."

Mary smiled. She liked the woman who wrestled with things in her mind.

That night Jawbone's low snorting just outside the lodge cover lifted Mister Skye right out of his robes, and his women as well. Skye listened, gauging the horse's clamor. Not men. When men approached in the night, Jawbone shrieked like a loon, squealed like a throat-cut pig. No. This woofing and snorting meant something else, and Skye dreaded it worse than he dreaded a party of horse thieves.

He fumbled for his camp moccasins in the inky lodge and clambered toward the door flap, feeling about for his carbine. Outside, Jawbone's mad woofing and snorting crescendoed. He peered out into a night so thick it seemed like tar coating the earth. Not a star showed. The moon went to bed early these nights.

He fumbled into the night, waiting cautiously for his eyes to adjust, to pick up landmarks, to sense movement even if he couldn't see it. He knew it'd be nothing small. Jawbone rarely bothered to trumpet the presence of wolves, and he ignored deer and elk altogether. He edged around the lodge toward the horse, hoping to get a sense of direction from the scarred old brute. Jawbone's ears would be cocked and his nose would point along the right vector. Off to the left one of the Percherons squealed, and the others joined in.

Victoria slid by him, racing to the horses to catch picket lines before they all thundered off.

A night breeze eddied and on it came the rank smell, and he knew. Sweat blossomed on his forehead with the knowing. He found no comfort in the carbine; a load nestled in its chamber, but only one. The rest lay in a saddlebag. The weapon was worse than useless, especially when not a soul among his clients had a rifle. He crept ahead warily, knowing the night could explode into blood, into a kind of war that didn't respect women or the weak. Behind him, Jawbone minced along, snorting, shuffling feet in mad delight. No other horse on earth, he supposed, walked toward terror.

Ahead lay the vague forms of the two wall tents and the higher rectangle of the wagon, with its gray osnaburg sheeting over its bows. All three huddled together, and he wished they didn't. Something crashed in the vicinity of the wagon, and he heard muted thumps and a clatter. Near the wagon something woofed and snorted close to the ground. Jawbone screeched, and clacked his teeth and muttered.

"Mister Skye, is that thee?" The doctor's voice. Skye turned, discerning the man standing before his wall tent in a white nightshirt. The others were erupting from the second tent.

"Back inside, mates. If ye have food in there, throw it out, as far as you can."

"What is it, Mister Skye?"

"Old Ephriam, mates. Belay yourselves now. You're in more trouble than you know."

"Old Ephriam?"

"A mountain term. A bear."

"A black bear?"

Skye sighed. "I don't know, and hope we never know." But he knew. This one up in the wagon, pawing away the truck in there to get at the staples—dried fruits probably—would be one of the sovereign lord kings or queens of the wilderness. Most likely a grizzly sow. That low woofing around the wagon wheels sounded like a cub. He could scarcely imagine a worse situation, five unarmed greenhorns including a woman, none of them doing what he knew Mary was doing behind him, climbing the nearest tree with Dirk in her arms, after dragging their parfleches with jerky and pemmican away from the lodge, an offering of the weak to the bear-gods.

"He's up in the wagon!" Freeman Price's voice. "I'll chase him off."

"Get into your tent!" Skye bawled. "Play dead." The thought of one of those grizzly paws, each claw three or four inches long and hooked murderously, slashing at Price filled him with utter dread.

"Thee needn't speak in those tones, Mister Skye. I'm aware of the danger and prepared to run."

"Lie down!" snapped Skye. "Griz run two, three times faster than you."

"Thee must heed our guide, Freeman." The doctor's voice.

A racket rent the night—the whine of cloth ripping. The bear was slashing up the wagon sheet. The wagon creaked under its weight. Crates crashed. Skye could see nothing, its vast brown bulk utterly invisible. Silence settled then, and he knew the sow was observing them, listening to their talk, fixing the vectors in her head, like a great man-o'-war heaving to, her cannon broadside.

Another woof and a snort, and Skye knew the sow and cub were talking; maybe she was telling it to get away.

"They're stealing our food!" said Price. "Stop them, Mister Skye."

Jawbone snarled.

Skye sighed. "If you don't lie down, stir up your coals if you've got wood. Don't go hunting for wood. When you've got a burning stick, a firebrand, you've got a little something, mate."

"Would thee shoot it, Mister Skye?" The doctor's voice.

"No. It'd just enrage her. I've seen a grizzly take ten, twelve balls, and then start murdering anything that moved."

"Mister Skye, I'm going to drive her off with rocks. Lots of river cobbles—"

"Price!" Skye roared. "Get into your tent!"

He heard, instead, the thunk of cobbles. One caught the sheeting, another banged off the wagon bed. One evoked a sharp woof, and a thundering moan.

"Avast, mate!" Skye roared, and then remembered where he was. "Stop!"

Jawbone squealed, some unearthly whine that raised the hair on his head.

Off at the wall tent, a fire suddenly flared, a small light wavering yellow. Not a one of them had heeded him. Every man stood there. Every one stood in mortal danger.

As swiftly as the fire rose, the darkness receded, and the whole tableau came clear. The cub skulked, its eyes shining orange, near the wagon. It darted toward the tents and wheeled sideways into the night.

Far away, he heard the bleating of the picketed horses, and hoped Victoria could keep them from a twenty-mile stampede.

"Into your tents!" roared Skye. The doctor reluctantly acceded, and Artemus obeyed along with Diogenes Fall. But young Price pitched pebbles.

She came at him like a giant cannonball, a whirl of darkness out of darkness, impossibly fast. The cub woofed and scampered away. A thunder erupted from her. Price, slow-witted, turned toward the tent.

Jawbone exploded, his shriek deafening. Skye lifted his carbine, too late. Horse and bear and man all converged into his buckhorn sight. The sow wheeled and reared up on her legs, towering eight or nine feet, her great forearms swinging like sharpened scythes. The horse snarled, snapped at air, his teeth mashing like rifle shots. Skye stood aghast. He'd never seen a horse attack a bear. Horses ran.

"Jawbone. Come!" he roared. Too late. The manic animal had gone berserk again, and wheeled now, bringing his murderous rear hooves around, like a volley from a line-of-battle ship.

Jawbone missed. The sow ducked and whacked at him with her butchering paws, deadly toothed catapults that could rake his flesh to ribbons.

He howled, like some suicidal kaffir, and plunged in again.

"Jawbone!" he cried, his words lost. For once, his horse disobeyed.

The stallion whirled, his deadly fore hoofs arcing past her, and then his rear hoofs. One connected. He heard a thud, a roar, and something like a whine. But she spun on her rear legs and plunged, her deadly claws lashing down, and Jawbone screeched, pain lacerating the night. Jawbone screamed his hurt like a child sobbing, and folded away, while the grizzly paused. Jawbone limped, staggered, stumbled away, shrieking, the sound so ghastly that Skye clapped his hands to his ears to keep that noise out of his soul, and shut his eyes, because he couldn't look at the solid red sheet of blood rivering down his right shoulder.

Jawbone sobbed, teetering shakily, refusing to move even as the sow edged closer, smelling blood and meat. Hot flesh.

"Go!" he cried, panicked. "Go!"

But the medicine horse didn't. It stood sobbing,

sheeting blood that collected under its belly and dripped into the clay.

He lifted his carbine, not knowing whether to shoot Jawbone or shoot the bear, a sob of his own choking him. His pulse raced and his arms trembled and he couldn't aim. The sow paused, respecting Jawbone's hoofs, circling, waiting, daring herself to spring and clamp her massive jaws into Jawbone's throat.

He steadied himself and aimed for her heart, just back of her forelegs. A head shot might kill, but his arms weren't obeying. The carbine bucked, a sharp crack in the night, and jolted his shoulder. The sow whirled, nipped at the wound, digging at her flesh with her snout, licking and nipping the entry hole, ignoring Jawbone. Then, slowly, angrily, snapping at her side, she hastened toward her cub out in the darkness.

Jawbone sobbed. Mister Skye groaned, a sinking dread flooding him. Slowly, the Friends emerged from their tents in nightclothes, and gaped. He wanted to shoot them, shoot Price, and might have if his carbine had been loaded. Instead, he turned away to hide his tears from them.

Chapter 12

Doctor Sitgreaves had never heard a sound like that from a horse. Jawbone sobbed, the groaning in the stallion's throat almost human. His head hung low, as if lifting it would be a burden beyond what flesh could bear.

The doctor surveyed the clawed withers with a practiced eye, noting the gout of blood. There wouldn't be much time. He peered around fearfully, worried about the bear, and then made his barefoot way toward the wagon and the chaos of crates, pasteboard boxes, kegs and implements scattered around it by the sow. He hunted a certain brown pigskin valise which contained his surgical kit, and finally located it in deep shadow, behind a fore wheel.

"Artemus, build the fire. I must have light."

The youth slowly emerged from his own paralysis, and began heaping sticks onto the wavering blaze.

"Mister Skye, if thee would?"

The guide turned toward the doctor, a wetness on his

cheeks, not registering. Jawbone's sobbing seemed to stupefy the man. He stared at the doctor, in a trance.

"Mister Skye. I must suture quickly. Before he loses too much blood. You must hold him. Hold him tight."

Skye stared, comprehension coming to him slowly. "Aye, mate," he said with a gentleness the doctor had never heard in the man's voice.

Mrs. Skye, back from collecting the Percherons, trotted into the circle of light, saw Jawbone, and gasped. "Aiee, ah," she said, her mouth forming aborted words. Then she glanced sharply at Skye and ran off to their lodge. A halter. Maybe she'd be able to control the animal.

"Hurry!" cried the doctor, rummaging in his valise for curved surgical needles and silk thread.

Skye came alive in a rush, his face hawkish again. He lumbered toward the stricken horse intending to steady it, but Jawbone lifted his head, flattened his ears back, and snapped at Skye.

"Whoa, mate."

Skye stepped forward again, and this time Jawbone shrieked and sprang at him, the eerie howl erupting from his throat. He butted Skye, sending him cartwheeling backward, and then reared up to strike him with those vicious hoofs. Skye rolled and the hoofs struck earth where he had been.

Jawbone shrieked now, circled, limping gruesomely, daring anyone to approach him, bleeding red rivers down his withers, down his right foreleg, down his belly.

Skye sprang up, shocked, and Jawbone flattened back and catapulted toward him, staggering, his jaws wide, ready to bite a lethal piece out of him.

"Whoa, whoa!"

The doctor detected terror in Skye, and agony.

Victoria raced back with a halter, muttering, cursing, blaspheming again, tears welling in her gaunt face. It struck the doctor how much a part of the Skye family that evil horse was, how its wound was their wound. Its terror and hate, turned against Mister Skye, lacerated something tender inside the man.

"Thee must hurry, Mister Skye."

The guide turned toward Doctor Sitgreaves, a grief on his face he didn't try to hide. The horse faced him, his hellish yellow eyes wild with pain, daring Skye or any other fragile mortal to come within murdering distance. Around the circle of light, the rest watched, astonished by this spectacle. Only Mary didn't appear, but her soft sobbing lifted from within the Skye lodge.

Victoria handed Skye a halter tied to a long, braided rawhide line. Skye didn't move. Instead, he peered directly into the shadowed face of the tormented animal and began speaking quietly, urgently, like a man talking to his lifelong confidante, like a father to a son.

"Aye, lad, ye hurt bad, and if we don't stop the bleeding, ye'll go to the ground and never get up. Jawbone, lad, we've got to sew you up. You've got to live. You'll hurt some, the needle and thread pulling you together.

"Remember me, Jawbone. I pulled you from your ma, and wiped you before you knew you'd been born, and raised you up, and taught you to be a medicine horse, and forget fear, and forget running, and fight when I said it, and go when I said it, and come when I said it . . .

"Trust me, lad. Trust me now, if you ever trusted me. Come. Save your life. Come to me, Jawbone."

The horse lifted his head and shrieked again, a sound to roll the dead over, and then coughed back into strangled sobbing. Terrible tremors shook through his flesh, spraying blood like red rain.

Skye's face turned grim again. Doctor Sitgreaves had never seen a face so anguished—not even in his practice, when he bore grievous news to loved ones.

"We love you, boy. We'll sew you up, and then, if we must, we'll put you out with the wild ones, high up in the sweet meadows where you came into the world. Where the brooks run cold and the west winds whistle and you can touch the sky. Whoa up, boy.''

They stared at each other. Skye silent, the horse sobbing out pain with each breath.

''Come.''

Jawbone's ears lifted. He stepped forward and stopped, pinioned by the pain. He stepped again.

''Goddam,'' muttered Victoria.

''Come.''

''Thee should go to him, Mister Skye.''

Skye's gaze never wavered. ''He's got to come, mate.''

The doctor understood, somehow. Coming to Skye meant submission again. A flood of relief swept him: he was dreading trying to suture the wounds of a berserk horse who could kill him with one kick.

Then, in a rush, the horse hobbled the last few steps and lowered his head for Skye's halter. The guide slid it on swiftly, and the animal stood, trembling.

''Go ahead, Doctor.''

Sitgreaves found himself terrified to approach, and it took all the will he could muster to do it. He studied the wounds. Four long curved slashes furrowed flesh from the apex of the withers down the right shoulder, each gouged an inch or more into the animal's muscle by those lethal claws. Each trench rivered blood, pulsing out of the horse steadily with every beat of its great heart.

Tentatively, he placed a hand on the area, and the horse twitched and trembled but stood still. Dealing with this massive multiple injury bewildered him. He dug for clamps, found some, and decided against controlling the bleeders. Too many, too little time, too dark to find them. Victoria materialized beside him and he thought of something better.

''Madam, please press the wounds together, a hand on either side of them, as hard as he'll tolerate.''

She did, muttering. Her pressure pushed the edges of the gouting slashes together. The horse shuddered and shrieked, deafening him. He leapt back.

Swiftly, Doctor Sitgreaves threaded a needle, having trouble in the wavery yellow light and black shadow, his urgency driving the silk thread true.

Swiftly the doctor jabbed flesh, pausing for a reaction, but he got none. The wild pain of the wounds masked his needling. He put four stitches into the worst wound—enough to draw it together for a moment. And then he tacked the second gash, and the third and fourth, wanting all four pinched together before he began to close a gash.

"Keep pressing if thee would," he said to her as he found more silk and glided it into his needle. Once the horse winced, frightening him, but mostly he was able to stitch unhindered, the wounded side of the horse turned toward the firelight. The bleeding slowed. Endlessly he stitched, his arms and fingers aching, his nightshirt soaked with black blood in the orange light. Artemus kept the fire high, and started another to one side to lessen shadow, but still the work strained the doctor's eyes. Every shiver of the horse, every wild snort or shriek terrorized him and he jerked back, afraid of those killer hoofs. All sense of time deserted him, but he knew he'd end up putting more stitches into flesh than he ever had before, sewing together canyons of muscle that ran two feet long.

"Easy, boy," muttered Mister Skye, in a voice that hinted of self-possession again.

The bleeding almost stopped, but a pool of browning blood stained the clay beneath him. The horse weakened, his head sagging low. The doctor paused to listen to the horse's heart with his stethoscopic horn. It raced, shallow and fast. He didn't know how it should pulse but he knew it labored desperately now.

"Artemus, if thee would—find a bucket of water. The horse needs liquids."

The youth hunted around through the chaos left by the sow, and finally located a bucket and trotted toward the Milk River, obviously fearful of the bear. But a moment later he returned with a splashing load, and handed it to Skye. The horse stuck its nose in but wouldn't drink.

Not until close to the end of the suturing did he release Victoria. All the while she'd pressed the horse's flesh together, muttering, singing songs to her own gods. He finished at last and stood back, surveying his work, feeling some pride in it. Neat stitches drew the raw edges of the wounds tight together, forming low ridges where great gouges had canyoned the muscle. If the horse hadn't lost too much blood he might survive. He doubted the horse would be usable again but he didn't know. This was not his profession.

He peered toward the shredded wagon, where Fall and Price were sorting through chaos, salvaging all they could and restoring precious things to their customary place within. Tomorrow they'd sew up the wagon sheet and try to make it rainproof.

"I am almost done, Mister Skye," he said wearily, his shoulders aching. His own muscles trembled at the burden he'd put upon them. "He needs liquids. Would thee fetch some salt?"

Victoria dashed off while he dug in his bag for a bowl and his syringe. When she returned with the canister of table salt, he swiftly mixed a saline solution in the bowl and filled his syringe with it. This he injected into Jawbone's rectum, and then repeated the procedure until he had injected a gallon or so. In mortals that was a classic procedure for hemorrhage and shock.

"See whether he'll lick salt from thy hand, Mister Skye."

The guide poured a little and tried it, but the horse ignored the offering. Gently, Skye pried open its mouth and dribbled the salt on its tongue. The weary animal slavered and swallowed.

"If thee would, for a while, give him all he'll take. I'm done now, Mister Skye. I have nought other remedy. I hope he weathers it."

Something joyous crept into Skye's face. The doctor had seen the look before, but never in a man. He'd seen that look in the faces of women he'd assisted in childbirth, at the moment they could gaze upon their newborn child. He packed his bag, affecting not to notice an expression like that in a man like that.

At the last he used the bucket of water to wash his needle and his hands. Skye's sense of relief came too soon, but the doctor said nothing. Those wounds would putrefy. They might mortify and kill the horse. He had no remedy for that, but perhaps a poultice would help keep flies and vermin off, which seemed to help in human cases. He had some adhesive plasters and salves. But that could wait. The critical problem now was loss of blood, and for that he could do little but inject more saline solution. That and total rest. He wondered how this might delay them.

Skye tugged gently at the horse's halter, speaking softly to the strange animal, but the horse seemed too weary to move. Then, at last, the horse took a step, and then another out into the darkness, to the gravelly shore of the Milk. They all followed, subdued and respectful, having witnessed the steel bond between this man and this beast.

There, in a dim light of a quarter moon, wobbling in the water, Jawbone lowered his head slowly, drunkenly, into the wetness and drank.

All the rest of that silent night, Mister Skye, Victoria, and Mary kept vigil beside Jawbone. They sat crosslegged in the grass, watching the giant roan. Jawbone stood on three legs, but cocked his right foreleg to take weight off that shoulder. He stood braced, refusing to go down, his head hanging low, his eyes closed, too weary to do anything except keep himself up.

Mister Skye knew that if he went down, he'd likely not get up. Once in a while, Skye rose stiffly, padded over to the horse and held its head between his palms, rubbing his rough, stubby fingers along his neck, under the mane.

"You got to hang on, boy. You got to live. You got to make blood and get strong," he whispered. "You're a medicine horse; no old grizzly sow will do you . . ."

And thus he coaxed and cajoled, letting his words sink into the ears of the shocked and bled-out animal.

Twice more he injected saline solution into Jawbone's rectum with the syringe Sitgreaves had left him. And at dawn, with gray light transforming the world, Jawbone perked up, lifted his head, and stared evilly at his solemn attendants, and Skye knew he'd live.

"Aiee!" cried Victoria, a small smile on her gaunt face. "He'll live."

"Sitgreaves saved him."

Victoria glared. "Jawbone's own medicine saved him. He's a spirit-horse."

But Skye knew Doctor Sitgreaves's skills had done it. The doctor had brilliantly tacked all four gouges together, slowing the bleeding before suturing any gash tight. Skye knew neither he nor Victoria could have done that. And neither he nor his wives had known anything about saline solutions. "I reckon I'll thank him when he gets up," he said.

Victoria muttered. The memory of their desperate moments in the Piegan village scorched her mind. He knew she'd never trust or like these clients again.

But he calculated they were even, in a way. Sitgreaves had saved the horse. Sitgreaves was a mountain, and Skye knew it was a long way up to that summit.

The day quickened, and still they sat beside Jawbone, watching the sun stretch its loins and illumine the western slopes. It'd be another cloudless, hot July day. The kind of day that would brown the bunchgrass and bake the clay.

They were not far from the confluence of the Big Sandy, which they would follow on down to Fort Benton, back on the Missouri. Skye reckoned they'd come about halfway to Owen's Fort in the Bitterroot. This would be a good enough place to hole up, let Jawbone heal, and let the Percherons recover after a long haul. A good enough place, but no more than that, he thought uneasily, aware they were on important Indian routes and likely to encounter trouble at any moment. And yet it'd have to do. Jawbone couldn't move, and wouldn't for several days. And it occurred to him that it'd be weeks, maybe months before he could be ridden—if ever. Fortunately, the gashes didn't run where his saddle pad would rest, except at the withers. He wondered if Jawbone would scar up and gall there under the chafing of the pad, and whether that'd be the end.

And still Jawbone stood, braced, legs locked, head drooping, eyes shut, green-bellied flies crawling and humming along his raw wounds. The day turned golden and the skies azure, but none of them rose, and no one stirred around the wall tents. The night had taken its toll of sleep.

Victoria peered around crossly, muttering "I go look," she said. She stretched and headed for her picketed mare. The wary old woman trusted nothing, and now she'd ride a wide loop up on the river bluffs, looking for signs of trouble on any horizon.

But if trouble came, they'd have to deal with it here, he knew. Right here.

The Quakers stirred at last, emerging one by one from their wall tents to stare at Jawbone, who stood like a gray statue in the young sun. Their curiosity irked Skye, though he couldn't say why. They were all Peeping Toms.

He'd have to deal with them, he knew. They'd not tolerate much delay, eager as they were to reach Fort Owen and settle before cold overtook them. He had no idea how long it would take before Jawbone could walk.

He knew it'd be a long time before he'd ride, but that he could live with. He could walk himself, or sit on the freighter with Artemus while Jawbone followed along.

But Doctor Sitgreaves said nothing of that after he'd finished his morning toilet at the river. He studied Jawbone a while, nodding, looking vaguely pleased.

"Our patient lives," he said.

"He's hanging on, mate, thanks to you. I'm right thankful. I'd be pleased to pay—"

"Would thee hold him, Mister Skye? I'd like to apply a salve I think will keep the flies off and balm the flesh."

Skye held the quivering animal while the doctor gingerly applied his dressing.

"Doctor Sitgreaves," Skye rumbled. "I'm thinking maybe my ladies should take you on to Fort Benton while I stay here with Jawbone. No need for me to hold you up. It'll take a while—weeks maybe—before this horse can travel."

The doctor's bright eyes peered at Skye, absorbing that.

"I suppose you'll want another outfit to guide you to Fort Owen. I reckon we're about halfway there, and I can draw a draft for half of my fees. Plenty of good men at the fur post to get you through. The company can spare one."

The doctor frowned.

"Mate, my women are better on the trail than I am. They'll get you where you're going."

In truth, Skye rather wanted to end it. These pacifists and the conditions they imposed on him and his women had become a liability. They'd brought his whole family to the ragged edge back in that Piegan camp.

"I've been pondering it. We are not ones, Mister Skye, to make great decisions lightly. Would thee object if we tarried here a day or two? I thought we'd rest the draft horses and mend ourselves, and await illumination."

"This isn't a safe place, mate. You should know that."

"Our safety is not in our hands, Mister Skye. But we've come to understand thy safety may be."

"I was aiming to hide." He pointed toward the south river bluff, a half-mile distant. "Back there. As far off the trail as I can get. Just as soon as Jawbone can walk."

"Let's wait and see, Mister Skye. We've repairs to make. The bear's work. And if thee are uncomfortable with us, perhaps we can make some new arrangements."

Chapter 13

For two sunny days they tarried on the bank of the Milk, waiting for Jawbone to recover. But the horse didn't come around. He sagged into his braced legs, his head low, ignoring the world. He'd lost too much blood to bounce back easily.

The Skyes were plainly worried, trapped there on a great prairie avenue and unable to hide. Mister Skye had tried to coax the horse into a grassy coulee off to the south, but Jawbone remained too weak to walk more than a few paces. He didn't eat and didn't even care much about water.

At least the Percherons profited. They grazed the good bunchgrass all day, their bodies fleshing out after the long haul from Fort Union. Diogenes Fall mused on the legendary relationship between man and horse as he and his colleagues waited restlessly. He'd had a classical education, including Latin and Greek, and was given to long thoughts. At Fort Owen, once they settled, he would be the pamphleteer for the Indian Aid Society because of his keen way with words and his skill at embellishing tracts and speeches with gracious figures of speech that would command the respect of readers.

Each of them would have a primary duty. His was to be the compelling voice of the society, steadfastly and lovingly making a public case for Indian welfare, even as Doctor Sitgreaves would be the administrator and physician, bringing healing and immunity to the pox to the northwestern tribes. It had all been worked out long ago, in the whiteness of the Divine Light.

He abhorred idleness, and the long wait turned tedious. Camping was a discomfort at best, something to be endured by his aging carcass. Each evening he bore the ache of muscle and the creak of groaning bone gracefully because it was all for a noble cause. But the physical discomforts of life on the hard ground in a wall tent were nothing compared to the spiritual deprivations. He had a few books along, Caesar's *Commentaries* among them, and he took to studying the great military mind with relish, if only because he could argue with the emperor from Friends principles. Thus he passed the hours on a boulder in the shade of a cottonwood, gazingly idly from his text to the blue hump of the Bearpaw Mountains to the south, or to the swift passage of a hawk or eagle. He did not dislike the wild, though aspects of it left him uneasy.

But ah, how the subject of man and horse intrigued him. Indeed, they halted here to heal a horse—a unique horse, ugly as it was, that carried a unique man, ugly as he was. Fall toyed with the notion that Skye was a wilderness knight, and discarded it. Knights lived by codes. The only organizing principle that Fall could discern in Skye's behavior was a will to survive at any price. No, not a knight, though the union of warlike man and battle horse did seem extraordinary.

Skye himself approached the restless Friends that second afternoon, just as Fall's colleagues were about to approach Skye, having felt the need to bring this

lengthening delay to some sort of resolution. As usual,
the older squaw had ridden out to hunt and to keep a
weather-eye on the whole area, while the younger one
kept house—kept lodge, Fall thought, amused—and
cared for the breed boy.

Skye lifted that battered silk hat and screwed it down
again, concealing several puckered scars lacing his
skull. Just what that emblematic hat meant to Skye's
inner man, Fall couldn't fathom, but he found meaning
in symbols, and the silk hat was the ensign of a gentleman. That fit. The man insisted on being called Mister.
Gentle status had either been a lifelong goal or else he'd
fallen from that perch long ago. *Sic itur ad astra*, such
is the way to the stars. Fall congratulated himself for
his shrewd observation.

"The longer we stay here, the more trouble we beg,"
Skye began without preamble. "I don't think my horse'll
be able to travel for a week or so, and even then only
for short distances." He sighed. "My ladies will take
you to Fort Benton in the morning. You'll find a guide
there easily enough. I'll stay here with the horse—can't
abandon him. Not this one. You'll do fine." He dug
into a pocket in his red calico shirt and withdrew a
paper. "We've come half the distance by my reckoning,
mates. I'm returning half of the five-hundred fee I
charged you, two-fifty, draft on my account with my
agent, Bullock. And you'll have the services of my
wives for another hundred miles or so."

He paused, waiting. None of the Friends responded
at first. Fall knew that Sitgreaves would have preferred
a Meeting first to discover the Divine Will. Still, Fall
thought, this made sense. The rough guide had been
fair. He'd shown concern about his clients and their
need to hasten on. A clawing by a grizzly bear was,
simply, one of those acts of God that parties to a contract could do nothing about.

"Thee are most generous, Mister Skye. We've been
entertaining some thoughts on the matter, though we

might have been persuaded to tarry another day for the sake of thy horse—and ours. The Percherons are prospering nicely.'' Sitgreaves turned to the other Friends. ''Have thee any counsel?''

No one had much to add. Artemus and Freeman were itching to be off. Abigail looked forward to Fort Benton and a modicum of comfort and perhaps even some female society there. Fall suggested that their mission be ever at the front of their life. *Dum vivimus, vivamus,* while we live, let us live, he concluded.

''Very well then, Mister Skye. We'll leave in the morning,'' said the doctor, his voice expressing sorrow.

Victoria showed up late in the day, bringing two quarters of a slain mule-deer doe. She stared unhappily at Jawbone and listened to the news. She peered sharply at the Friends, said nothing, and vanished in the lodge. Fall sensed she didn't approve of them but he also sensed they would be in good hands the rest of the way to Benton. Better hands than Skye's, he ventured.

As always, he slept restlessly when he eased his bones onto hard clay instead of a mattress, and thus he sat up swiftly when the night rhythms exploded into muted thunder. But the rest slept on, unaware of any change. He pulled aside his blanket, crept to the door flap, and peered into the night, seeing nothing. Something had changed subtly. The crickets didn't chirp. But in the surly glow of a reluctant moon, he saw Skye and his wives slide out of their lodge and peer around, first at the inert form of Jawbone, and then off into the blackness.

''Goddam,'' muttered Victoria. Fall always winced when he heard her blaspheme in such a way. The woman, wearing a white shift of some sort, slipped into the night.

Fall watched from his tent door. In a while she trotted back and spoke sharply to Skye and the younger squaw, and then all three vanished in the direction where the horses had been picketed.

Alarmed, Fall groped for his britches and boots, dressed, and stepped into the night, to find the Skyes returning.

"Gone," muttered Skye.

"Would thee mind explaining?"

"Horse raid."

"The horses are gone?"

"Run off. Those Percherons were always a temptation, mate. Made some warriors dream big dreams, capturing animals like that."

"Warriors from the Piegan village?"

"Likely, mate. I suppose we've been watched."

Fall had read about horse stealing, the great sport of Plains warriors, but reading had been abstract and this was real. "But how will we—how will we—move our wagon?"

Skye seemed testy. "You won't," he snapped.

"But surely we can recover—"

"How?"

"They took yours too?"

"Jawbone's here. And a lot of help he is." Then something softened in Skye. "He's our night guard. But the last couple of nights he's hardly turned an ear. I'd ride after them, the way I usually go for the bloody thieves, but . . ." He ran a stubby hand through his unkempt hair.

"But surely the Percherons won't move fast, Mister Skye. What good are they to warriors?"

"Honors. Big horse, big honors. Pull a whole lodge, eighteen poles and cover."

"But won't the Percherons fall back? They're drays, after all, Mister Skye."

Skye sighed, said nothing, and turned into his lodge. In a moment he emerged again, fully dressed and carrying his carbine and a possibles bag.

"I'll walk them down, mate. You tell the Friends I'll be back when I get back."

He turned and hugged Victoria first, and Mary, lingering with each, whispering things to them. It touched Fall to see such tenderness in a man so atavistic. Then Skye padded over to the mute horse, which stood in its usual trance, and whispered things into Jawbone's ear, as if the beast could understand English. Then Skye trotted into the starlit void.

Fall retreated unhappily to his wall tent, pondering the twists of fate so that he could fashion wisdom and philosophy. They'd come to enlighten redmen, and now had been thwarted by redmen unless Skye miraculously returned with the three Percherons and his own horses and mules. The Friends would get replacements, of course, from Fort Benton, but that wasn't the point. Fall knew, for a certainty, that these tribesmen were simply avenging all the ill-treatment Indians had received everywhere at the hands of whites. He prided himself on understanding the views of the oppressed and abused, and delighted that he had fathomed the motives of those who had stolen the horses. In a way, the Friends deserved it. They too were whites, after all. And the horse thieves had no way of knowing the Friends differed from other whites and had come into the wilderness to be the Voice of Redmen.

Yes, he thought, the Indians had expressed themselves by stealing their horses. It was a just punishment. He dreamed, idly, of having enough money to give horses by the hundred, the thousand, to the tribes to compensate them for all the wrongs done to them. He dreamed of agitating Congress for such a bill; of shepherding the legislation past the House and Senate; of seeing President Franklin Pierce sign it into law. He dreamed of a tax, a special tax, equal to a tenth of the income of the land, a tithe, really, set aside to compensate the redmen of all tribes. It filled him with a strange holy joy to think of it, a sense of rightness. *Finis coronat opus*, he thought. The end crowns the work.

Skye had vanished into the night. Diogenes Fall

frowned at that. The guide might steal them back, steal those horses from the redmen who'd just acquired them. It troubled him to think of it. He hoped, secretly, that Skye would not find them, would not wrest them from the rightful new owners. And yet . . . if perchance Skye would return not only with the horses but with the redmen who took them, Fall might have a chance to meet them, shake their hands, express his esteem. Redmen were incomparably superior to whitemen, more soulful, more ethical.

He sighed, knowing the limits of fantasy. Tomorrow they could send one of the squaws to Benton and instruct her to buy some drays there. Skye had said it was only sixty miles.

Mister Skye walked out to the pasture where the horses had been picketed, hoping for a clue. But even as he reached the place, a hundred yards from the Milk River, he knew the futility of it. Behind him the night closed, curtaining the camp. Before him the meadow lay in deep obscurity.

He'd tracked stolen horses at night once before, but on Jawbone, relying on the horse's uncanny way of scenting out a trail, trotting toward the fleeing herd along some vector known only to the medicine horse. Now, in the deep silence, Mister Skye understood he would have to wait for daylight. And by the time he could see the signs of passage, the stolen horses would be far away and increasing their lead unless the horse thieves tarried along the way.

Even so, Skye circled the perimeter of the meadow, along a cottonwood grove on one side, the formidable river on another. His sole hope was to discover a missed horse, and the chances of that were minimal. Horses were gregarious and stayed together. Only Jawbone, trained from his first day of life to stay with Skye, resisted the instinct.

Still he walked, hoping for a vector, some clue that

would narrow down his choices. The horse thieves could, actually, have headed any point on the compass. But if they were from the Piegan village where he'd narrowly escaped with his life, they'd be traveling northeast, across the Milk. That village, if it was still in the same place, would be forty or fifty miles away.

As he walked, he puzzled through the problem. He'd have to find the village and steal the horses back, outwitting a heavy guard. Indeed, the Percherons would likely be picketed right at the lodges of the triumphant warriors. To be caught was to die a brutal death.

Nothing moved. A black pancake of cloud obscured the moon, plunging the night into gloom, and Skye wasn't at all sure he could find his way back to the camp. A sense of helplessness overtook him. He'd experienced that before; anyone living in the wilderness had encountered that feeling many times. This time the feeling was multiplied and sharpened by the things the Quakers had insisted upon. He thought of them darkly, liking them as individuals yet dismayed by the beliefs and practices that had gotten them into this fix. If they had not visited that Piegan village, not displayed those Percherons and excited the lusts of fifty warriors well, it had happened.

He navigated what he believed to be a whole circle around the pasture, arriving once again at the riverbank, with only the soft gurgle of the water eddying around snags to orient him. He eased himself down upon the dewy grass, his thoughts as obscure as the night. He knew he had to come up with a plan but he had none.

He sighed. The truth of it was that this expedition of these Friends had come to an end here. Fort Benton might spare them a saddle horse or two, but not teams of drays, or oxen. In the morning he'd tell them that, plainly. And yet . . . even as he came to that decision, he doubted that it was the right one.

He fumbled his way back to camp in an inky blackness, arriving at his lodge by sheer mountain intuition. Beyond, like ghosts, stood the wall tents where the Friends slept the sleep of the innocent. He ducked into his own home, set his carbine near the door flap, and crawled into his robes, well aware that Mary and Victoria were awake. In a moment both of them crawled close to him and they shared, as they often did, a time of silent tenderness.

He didn't sleep and the July sun refused to rise, as if the globe had stopped spinning. A part of him didn't want to see the sun; he wanted to lie there forever. His mind simply went blank, refusing to form a plan, perhaps because these strange Friends would overrule it and propose something that would blister his soul. But dawn did come, slowly chipping the blackness away. Up in the smoke hole he saw gray, then white, then pale blue. He dreaded having to deal with those people. He'd lay out the options and they would make crazy decisions.

The confrontation came soon, before full light, while he lingered in his soft buffalo robes. He heard the sounds of life outside, and shortly Doctor Sitgreaves's voice addressed him.

"Mister Skye, we wish to speak with thee."

He pulled on a red calico shirt, belted up his fringed elkskin britches, jammed on his camp moccasins, and crawled out, discovering them all before him, solemn as crows.

"Mister Fall has told us of our difficulty," Sitgreaves said. "We slept through it."

Skye was relieved not to have to explain.

"We've counseled at a Meeting," the doctor said. "There are divine reasons for all things, and we sought to understand the reasons for this. We never expected to reach Owen's Fort without a testing."

Skye nodded, still clearing the cobwebs away. "You'd better go back east. Back to Philadelphia. We're on foot, mates. We can walk to Fort Benton, and you can arrange for a mackinaw or keelboat to float you back to Fort Union. And maybe on down the Missouri, if you hire a boatman or two from the company. Too late to catch a steamer.''

The doctor shook his head. ''We'll continue as before.''

Skye knew he had to try to explain even if these people wouldn't listen. ''Look, mates. Your dreams are in that wagon. All your medical equipment. Every scrap of paper you'll use to write your tracts. All the hardware for the house and offices you'll build. Your farming equipment—the plow and rake. Your seed. Your food, what's left of it. Your clothes. Your shoes and boots. Some furniture. Your library. Your spices. You can't replace these things at Fort Benton or Owen's Post.''

''We'll wait for succor, Mister Skye. Something will come along.''

Skye thought the doctor was demented. Everything in that wagon was as good as lost. ''First Blackfeet party rides by here'll plunder the outfit,'' he said roughly.

''We've decided to wait patiently.''

It irritated him. ''Well, while you're waiting, I'm going after those horses. Cold trail now. And I'll have to walk 'em down. I've walked down horse raiders before. Takes patience. They get careless sometimes. But if they make it back to their village, forget it.''

''That won't be necessary, Mister Skye. And we'd not want thee to employ violence.''

He didn't answer. He had no intention of waiting for the first war party that came along to plunder them and kill them all. He'd leave Jawbone with Victoria and Mary—back away from this river trail—and start walking. Sometimes you could steal the horses back. Or grab others.

"Do what you want," he said curtly. "I'm going to hunt down horses. Stay here forever if you want."

The Quakers eyed him unhappily.

"I'm going with you," said Victoria. "Two are better than one."

"But Jawbone—"

"Goddam!" she snarled.

She was right. Mary'd look after him. There was nothing anyone could do anyway but wait. Take him to water if he'd walk. Hide him in the woods maybe. Let Sitgreaves doctor the wounds.

"The Inner Light bids us to continue onward, Mister Skye. We'll await thee here, and then walk to Fort Benton if we must. Not a soul of us would turn back when the illumination is so clear."

"Cache your outfit while we're gone. You've got spades."

"We'll await thee and Victoria, Mister Skye."

Muttering, Victoria ducked into the lodge and reappeared with her old flintlock and powder horn. "Here!" she snapped, thrusting them at young Artemus. "Make meat."

The youth took the weapons.

Mary slid a hand into Skye's and pressed his tightly. "Jawbone is my brother and father and son, Mister Skye," she said, smiling. "See, he is better today. He looks at you."

Jawbone was looking at him, his head up, the glazed stare gone. The wounds had crusted over. Definite progress.

Skye ran a thick hand up his neck under the mane, and the great medicine horse whickered softy. Skye pressed back a terror that something would happen to Jawbone while he was away, that Jawbone was too vulnerable to leave here. "Get well, matey," he muttered roughly. Jawbone tormented him.

"God be with thee, Mister Skye," said Sitgreaves. "Don't count on anything."

An hour later he and Victoria, who'd armed herself with her bow and quiver, found the marks of passage leading south—a faint surprise—and followed them toward the Bearpaws.

Chapter 14

Under a brutal sun, they climbed the river bluffs and out upon a scorched plain. The signs of passage were clear enough: prints the size of platters cut into the cauterized clay, elongated oval mule prints, round prints from the Skye horses. And here and there the imprint of unshod hooves, ragged around the toes and heels. The occasional droppings had already browned in the brutal sun and whipping winds. All that, plus battered bunchgrass, made the trail as visible as a highway. It wandered aimlessly southward, veering around hills and avoiding drainages.

Mister Skye felt parched after scarcely an hour, and admired his sits-beside-him wife who walked lithely along, her knowing eyes studying distant horizons and nearby gulches rather than the signs of passage close at hand. When they'd topped the bluff, the camp was instantly walled from their sight, and it left Mister Skye uneasy. He half expected to find them all slaughtered, including Jawbone, and the wagon plundered when they returned. But he couldn't help that. He and Victoria would track horses and steal them back.

He liked walking with her, and knew the thoughts flowing through her mind even though neither of them spoke a word. She always saw things he didn't, and he swore she knew what lay in hidden gulches or beyond copses of cottonwoods or behind hills where she couldn't see. That uncanny knowing had saved them many times.

He felt burdened, with the sweaty carbine hot in his hand, the possibles bag weighting him, along with his holstered dragoon revolver, knife, bear-claw necklace, and heavy square-toed boots. He'd walked a piece in his life, but now, with age, it had grown harder and he felt pain with every step.

She was lucky, he thought, to have remained so slim that no great weight rested on her small moccasins. She chose the path, and kept below skylines and under ridges, like a wild creature fearing to be seen.

"You got any notion who they were? I can't get a feel for it, not with just some unshod prints."

"I don't know," she muttered. "It ain't right."

"Right?"

"Yeah. Where's their village?"

He shrugged. "Up in the Bearpaws. That'd be coolest."

He squinted at the shimmering peaks that rose a good twenty miles away. There'd be water there—not much, but some. The Bearpaws were prairie mountains, well east of the Rockies, tilted tables of grassland that surrendered to jack pine on the upper reaches. They'd always desolated his spirit through the years, instead of lifting it the way the Rockies did.

They struck a hidden gulch, invisible even from a few hundred yards' distance, and found green bottoms there, along with a thin line of small cottonwoods and brush, and a tiny silver creek angling northwest. The signs of passage led straight down a rocky escarpment to water.

Victoria froze as the gulch hove into view, and then sagged to earth, not wanting to be skylined. A place like that could conceal a whole village. Skye was parched for water but knew enough to wait and let his woman probe the place with her knowing eyes and ears. Around him, furnace winds eddied and sucked sweat from his baked flesh. In a moment she rose and padded downslope and into the coolness of the trees. The whole herd had watered there and then been pushed upstream, following a tortured crack in the earth that led toward the distant mountains.

Skye and Victoria drank and sat in merciful shade.

He'd hoped to find a moccasin print at the creek bank, but he found nothing. A good print might have told them the tribe.

"Something strange." She glared at him, as if it were his fault she couldn't figure all this out. "Horse spirits," she said. "Medicine horse."

She did that. Gibberish, almost. He had listened to her muttering over the long years, understanding little of it. It wasn't Crow she spoke, nor English, but her own language, which she withheld from lesser mortals like himself.

"Feel like a siesta," he said. In truth, the heat had drained him. But they wouldn't stop. Not if they hoped to catch up with the horse thieves before they reached the safety of their village.

She sat cross-legged in the grass, her doeskin skirt hiked high, her restless gaze peppering the bluffs.

"I'm thinkin' Assiniboin," he said, not really knowing why.

She snorted. She rarely used words when she was dismissing a notion out of hand. She had a withering snort that could reduce him to a schoolboy. He swore she could snort a man into a big dry. Which, in fact, was beginning to build in him. He thought, too late, of the crockery jug in his parfleche at camp, and worried that it'd be looted.

He lifted his top hat and let the dry breeze sweep away the sweat that had built up on his brow. He wondered why he wore it, especially in its battered condition, half stove in, twice perforated where a lead ball drilled from ear to ear. He'd forgotten his original reasons.

"We'll have to walk them to Fort Benton and then get shut of them," he said, knowing she'd pick up the new thread of his thoughts. "Probably have to carry her—those shoes of hers weren't made for walking." He referred to Abigail. "Nice enough people. Like 'em all. Even if they almost got us killed."

"Big medicine," she said. "Like a hundred rattles."

"Their faith is something," he said. "Waiting back there, expecting us to return with the horses, like they hadn't been stolen. And just hook them up and be on their way again."

She studied him. "Big medicine," she said. "They tell the world what to do. They act like there's no danger."

"It's hard to explain. I mean, you can find that in the Bible. That kind of faith. Some try it. Usually they end up in an asylum."

"What's asylum?"

"Place for mad people."

"Good madness," she said. "Big medicine. They either crazy fools or—" She left the rest of her thoughts unsaid, rising and stretching, her signal to be off again. She studied the various prints again, this time sharp in moist riverbank earth, and then trotted up the narrow gulch that twisted toward the mountains.

He followed. Now they had patches of shade and constant water, and the going wasn't so hard. The stolen horses had been driven straight up the gulch.

Mid-afternoon, she paused at a moist place and studied the tracks. "One. One thief," she announced triumphantly. "Only one unshod horse. I been looking for more. One warrior. He got rich. I think he's not Siksika. Someone else."

He didn't ask her how she surmised that. If only one warrior had done this, they could overwhelm him easily. The first stirrings of hope filled him.

By late afternoon he could barely put one boot before the other, but she trotted ahead. They'd been climbing steadily through foothill country. At one point the trail left the gulch and paralleled it over open slopes easy to traverse, slopes which commanded a vast and strategic view across the apocalypse of the north, clear back to the Milk and the invisible camp there.

"He was checkin' his back trail," he said.

She muttered again.

He laughed at her, and then bawled into the emptiness, roaring at wind while she glared.

They followed the trail until dusk, surrendering only when they feared they might lose it. He might have continued up the watercourse anyway on the principle that it was the only route, but in fact he hurt so much he could barely walk. He dreaded the swelling of his feet.

She had only pemmican in her small bag, and while it nourished, it never satisfied. She handed him a cylinder of the greasy trail food and he wolfed it down. This pemmican was rancid with age but that didn't stop him. Some squaws made delicious pemmican but hers had always been bitter. Probably her fiendish way of pounding unripe chokecherries into it, he thought. He wondered whether she would hunt roots or greens, but she didn't.

"We get the horses tomorrow," she said mysteriously. "Goddam, they're right, them Quakers."

He waited for her to explain this burst of knowing, but she said no more and he was damned if he'd ask her. But she grinned at him, muttering, rubbing it in. She acted like a girl who'd solved a puzzle.

"Like Jawbone," she said coyly.

Just that. Jawbone. He glared at her in the lavender light. Sometimes he wished he had a proper English bride, especially when this old savage began withholding things from him the way she was now.

But she just grinned, toothy and triumphant.

They had no robes but wouldn't need them if the heat held. He cleared a bed for himself, knowing how his comfort depended on removing pebbles and sticks and lumps of clay from the spot where he'd rest. Day faded, except for an eerie azure light far to the northwest, the hallmark of a prairie summer night. She kept grinning at him in the dusk, hoarding her secret, taunting him with it, but he resolutely concentrated on releasing his tortured muscles and watching the busy heavens. He spotted a shooting star streaking greenly down an infinite decline.

A distant trumpeting filled the silence, a whinny and an answering whinny, far above them in the mountains. It echoed softly down canyons and plains, lofted on the night breeze, a sound as haunting and lonely as any he'd ever heard from a horse. It sounded to him like a victory cry, like something Jawbone would bawl into the night, the cry of the lord of the mountain.

He heard it again, this edict of an equine emperor.

"Sonofabitch!" muttered Victoria.

Horses dotted the grassy plateau snugged between two roots of the mountains. Thirty, forty, she thought, dark dots far ahead. Even from where they stood at a bend of the little creek she could make out the three larger ones, the Percherons, half again the size of the others. She couldn't tell whether they still wore their halters and trailed picket lines but she hoped they did.

She felt grateful for the south wind that stripped their scent away. She glanced at her man beside her, who studied the distant herd, his gaze restless, darting to the ridges, to the pine-clad black mountains beyond the valley.

"Where's the village? Where's the thieves?" he muttered.

"Quiet!" she whispered, so vehemently that she startled him.

She studied the tableau again, looking for something, dreading what she knew she'd find. At this vast distance she had to focus on each horse one by one. But yes, there he was, on a slope above the herd. She studied the golden stallion as it stood surveying the world over which it was lord and master. Yes—Fire Horse. She'd never seen Fire Horse, and it sent a thrill through her. Fire Horse!

The great stallion resumed his grazing, walking leisurely through the endless pasture. Everything she'd ever heard about him was true. He glowed in the afternoon light like sun fire; he watched his world constantly; he ruled the lesser animals, mares mostly, on the slope below him.

"See the horses but I don't see the horse thieves," Mister Skye muttered.

She glared at him. Even whispering he spoke too loudly. "The thief ain't any goddam Injun," she whispered. "No lodge, no tribe. It's him." She pointed.

He followed the vector of her finger, and she saw him registering at last that a stallion had raided their camp on the Milk, a stallion that would have been chased off by Jawbone if Jawbone had not been gravely wounded.

"Haw!" he said, too loud.

She glared rebuke at him. "Fire Horse," she whispered.

She watched his face sober. Caution replaced the joy of discovery. Curiosity, too. He squinted, his pale eyes poorer than hers, focusing at last on the stallion. "Bloody well is," he muttered.

The legendary Fire Horse had never been seen by a whiteman before, she knew. But around the council fires of all the prairie tribes, warriors dreamed of Fire Horse, lusted for Fire Horse, told stories of seeing Fire Horse— only once. Because once he ran, herding his harem and children and whatever others he could sink his teeth into, he ran until they dropped, some vast distance away. The warriors kept their secret from whites, except for Mister Skye. Fire Horse had roamed the Bearpaws for so many winters that even the grandfathers spoke of him with awe. He shone like the sun and floated above mother earth when he ran. The Siksika called him Sun Horse because he shone like Sun; the Absaroka called him Fire Horse because he glowed like fire. The other tribes borrowed those names, Sun or Fire, but they all spun their medicine stories about the same horse.

No man had ever put a rope over his neck; few had ever gotten close enough to see any detail, but those who'd somehow crept near said that he was actually battered and scarred, his hide checkered by countless battles with other wild stallions who had challenged his lordly right to rule this world. They said he was actually a stocky horse, powerful rather than graceful, with a heavy curved nose—whites called that kind of nose Roman—that had a blaze down it. But it was the way Fire Horse stood, the way he ruled, the way he ran—with a gait as soft as rabbit fur—that riveted mortals. That and his vast mountain kingdom, which now included all of the Skye mares and mules and the giant Percherons. With some malevolent genius, he'd sneaked upon them, terrorized them, and herded them off to make slaves of them.

She stared, awed at this mystical giant. No other horse except for Jawbone had captured the imagination of so many. More than imagination: he'd become sacred, the medicine horse of Absaroka boys, and no doubt Siksika boys too. He carried fire and sun in him, and lived forever, the grandfather of all horses.

Mister Skye sighed. "Have a bloody time stealing

our horses back," he muttered. "I'd rather take on a whole hunting party."

She said nothing, looking for the lead mare. In flight, a band didn't follow the stallion but the lead mare, with the stallion herding from the rear, nipping rumps and defending the herd from whatever menaced it. She knew, coldly, that they'd have to kill that mare if they were to snatch away their own horses. And even then, the chances were slim.

They were simply too far away. A lead mare might graze at the edge of a herd. She'd peer around more than the others. She'd nose foals toward the center of the herd where wolves would have little chance of reaching them. But from where Victoria stood watching in the shade of cottonwood brush beside the creek, the horses looked alike.

She looked for the young Percheron stallion. He'd been stolen with the rest, herded away by Fire Horse. But the wild stallion would have driven the Percheron away, and he probably hovered nearby, staying close to his friends, the mares. But she didn't see him. The banished Percheron was her best chance.

She was better with horses than Skye, and he knew it, and let her make decisions. She eased back from the hill and down into the narrow bottoms, out of sight of the band. Then she nodded, and they stalked quietly upstream, avoiding sticks, keeping an eye peeled for a stray horse watering ahead. She found a cottonwood slope where they could leave the gulch, and crept up it, with Skye following. Near the edge of the trees they startled a rookery of crows, which leapt cawing into the blue void. They froze. Wisely, she sat down and waited and he joined her. She let Sun walk west a while, and then slid upslope again after signaling Skye to stay at the creek. The horses had drifted closer, eyeing the woods. The two Percheron mares grazed together, so close she ached to run out and grab their picket lines.

The Percheron stallion grazed well back from the herd, but still a part of it. He'd run if the herd ran, she knew.

Crouching, Victoria studied the rest, spotting her mares and mules. Only one mare still had a halter with a line trailing from it. So close! She forced down the impulse to stand softly, walk quietly out there and capture one of the big, dumb Percherons before the whole band vanished. Instead, she studied the wild mares, letting her gaze rest on each one, seeking the dominant one who would, by some mysterious common consent, lead them all away in the moment of trouble. She knew what she would have to do, and she hated it. She'd do it herself, too. She'd borrow Mister Skye's carbine. If she shot that mare, totally surprising them, the band would mill around, leaderless, and she'd dart out and collect the tame ones, the ones new to living in a band and least attuned to its ways.

She studied them, deciding at last that it would be one of two mustangs, both shaggy broom-tailed duns grazing a little to the left of the rest and back a way. Each one grazed a bit, then peered around, especially at the shaded copse where Victoria squatted not far from where the crows exploded into flight. She could not tell which was the leader. Maybe both. It happened sometimes. She had to pick the right one.

She slid back slowly, and then padded down into the creek gulch again, where Mister Skye waited, a quizzical look on his face. She said nothing but pointed at the carbine. He handed it to her, and several paper cartridges from his possibles as well, though they both knew she'd have one shot—just one. She nodded dourly, hating what she had to do, and slid upward again, taking her time while Sun marched into the far west. She felt a deep kinship with the mare. Was she not herself a lead mare and her man the great stallion?

By the time she arrived back in her shadowed bower beside the field, the band had shifted back, making the shot much more difficult. She could not follow across open ground without triggering instant flight. She would need shooting sticks. She crabbed back once again, found two sticks, wrapped them in the middle with a thong, and wriggled forward. She'd made no noise, and yet the whole band stared straight at her.

Gently, she spread the sticks, making an X, and planted her carbine in the crotch where it nestled solidly. She swung it toward the two dun mares, peering down the barrel through the pronged sights. On its shooting sticks, the barrel didn't waver at all. Now, which one? Both mares faced her and she didn't like that. She knew what she'd do. One or the other would return to grazing and then she'd shoot the one that still stared at her.

She waited angrily, utterly unmoving and silent and shadowed. Raw rage boiled through her, anger she couldn't understand. She hated both mares, hated them enough to murder them. She made herself hard and let the anger percolate, and kept one mare's breast squarely in her notched sights.

A wild squeal shattered the peace. A shriek, and a whinny, eerie with power and loneliness, racketing distrust and hate into the quiet. Too late, she saw Fire Horse explode into a gallop, veering westward toward the ridge, and with him the whole band, including the lumbering Percherons. Fire Horse didn't follow; he led. And the two dun mares bolted out of range, straight toward foals and yearlings, and nipped them along. Almost before she could grasp what had happened, the whole band had vanished over the grassy ridge.

They'd run for miles, because that was Fire Horse's way. She and Mister Skye might not get another chance.

Chapter 15

He knew what she was thinking: they'd never recover the horses. But he decided he would; he would not let a mustang—even a fabled one—defeat him. They drank at the creek, not knowing where the next water would be, and scaled its west bank and up a soft grade toward the ridge. The sun had already swung north of west, but he had no intention of making camp. The herd might not stop until it was miles away, and that meant more walking. He'd walk all night if he had to.

No one had ever stolen animals from Fire Horse. No one had even come close. Still . . . the thought of those lumbering Percherons heartened him. Those, at least, might fall behind the rest. But even as he thought it, he doubted it. Each Percheron was a mountain of endurance, and would catch up with the rest eventually—unless they could be cut off. As for his own mares and mules, he suspected he'd never possess them again.

Beside him, Victoria nocked an arrow in her small bow. She'd try to make meat because they had little pemmican left. Not enough for a chase that might last several days. He thought uneasily of Mary and the Quakers, camping for days right on an important Indian road. She said nothing, reading his mind without the redundant benefit of words.

They topped the ridge and beheld a new drainage, this one sere, with humped foothills rising in the southwest a few miles distant. A shadowy trail of broken bunchgrass and occasional sign marched before them, elusive because the horses had run far apart, in a mile-wide line, splintering into fragments.

Dusk was going to catch them somewhere in the middle of that dry pasture. He studied the far slopes for some sign of water, a copse of trees, a thin line of brush, a greened area—and saw none. He was already parched. But the sun didn't burn the way it had earlier. He peered into her face and saw acquiescence, and they hiked forward into a calf-high sea of buffalo grass, sere from the pummeling of the sun. It wasn't like riding Jawbone, this step-by-step progress.

As light faded the tracks grew elusive. These mustangs had gone their separate ways to meet ahead somewhere. At water. His legs ached and his back as well—he felt his age in his back, mostly—but he wouldn't stop. Some stubbornness carried him on into orange twilight, when the sky still scattered light though the earth hung in shadow. Victoria never spoke. She'd had no chance at game. By morning they'd be parched and hollow-bellied.

He wanted to blame the Quakers, but couldn't. Not for the grizzly that clawed Jawbone, and not for a camp-robbing wild stallion. He pushed himself through the evening, his muscles crying at him now, his need to halt becoming more and more urgent. Things skittered through the night. Off on a ridge a coyote chorus started, mocking him and his two-legged walking. No, he couldn't blame the Quakers. A heat began to build in him as he thought about the thief.

Fire Horse. It was just another mustang, this one a

little wilier and tougher than most. And almost as demented as Jawbone, he thought. A whiff of mare in
season—or maybe not in season—had done it. No one
had whipped Fire Horse but that didn't mean he couldn't
be whipped.

They stood at last at the base of the ridge they'd observed that afternoon, and he knew from the lay of the
dipper that it was around midnight. The coolness abated
his thirst but in the morning he'd be desperate. They'd
lost the tracks at dusk and the whole night's trek had
been a gamble. But a mustang didn't stray far from
water unless it had to. He sighed. A mile above was
the crest of the grassy shoulder, and at dawn they'd have
a fine view. He started up the long grade, feeling his
heart pump almost at once.

The moon rose orange, spraying cold light over the
slope, but still they pushed one foot ahead of the other.
A few hundred yards shy of the ridge, she tugged at
him.

"Sit," she said.

He did, thinking she needed a halt. Instead, she slid
her Green River knife from its belt sheath and began
slicing into a prickly pear. Now that he looked, he saw
a thick patch of them. Gingerly she peeled the flesh and
thorns away from the base of a lobe to get at the most
pulpy fiber within, muttering to herself as she often did
when doing something painful. She winced and sliced,
and eventually handed him a small lump with a bit of
moisture in it. He mashed it around in his mouth, ex-
tracting what bitter liquid he could, and subduing the
fiber into something edible. He could do that all night,
he thought, and not allay his thirst.

"We stay here," she said, and he didn't argue. He'd
imagined he'd spot the band in the moonlight from atop
the ridge, but in fact the sitting had become so seduc-
tive he didn't want to get up. She fed him more bits,
industriously cutting and peeling and cussing, sliding
bits into her own mouth as well. After an hour of that,

he thought he'd maybe ingested a cup of water; he needed a gallon. But it helped, and the fibrous pulp in his belly took an edge off his hunger.

He took off his boots and let his aching feet air.

"Sonofabitch!" she said, angrily.

He stuck a smelly foot into her lap and hoorawed softly, and she elaborately stood and settled down upwind.

She grew weary of defanging prickly-pear lobes and joints, and walked a spiral around the place where they sat—rattlesnake duty. She found none. He knew she wished she would; they'd eat raw snake meat if she had. He'd never tried it in spite of all his years in the mountains, and was halfway glad she didn't find one.

Neither of them slept, and when dawn pried away the blindness of the night he saw her face had grown haggard, and black circles bagged under her brown eyes. He supposed his own face looked much the same to her. His whole torso ached. He dreaded the day. But the dawn brought with it, twice over, a smouldering need to humble that bloody Fire Horse. War to the finish. No bloody horse would ever beat him. The horse would kill him or he'd kill the horse.

He stood, feverish and unslaked. She eyed him solemnly, reading the rank mood on his scarred face.

"Let's go," he said roughly. He gathered his possibles bag—why did it feel as if it was loaded with cobbles? They clambered up the last hundred yards of shoulder, crackling grass that awaited water angrily. Off to the north the earth lay low and troubled and obscure. They topped the ridge slowly, innate caution dictating their pace, and peered down upon another creek bisecting another north-south valley. Water.

And off to the north a couple of miles grazed the mustang band, mysteriously coalesced again. Two bands, actually, and he supposed the smaller number—with one of the dark Percherons in it—was a bachelor band, defeated stallions running with, but separate from, the harem of the dominant stallion. All of them grazing quietly, looking as tame as domestic saddle horses.

"I see all three Percherons," he whispered.

She glared at him. "Bad medicine."

"This time—I'll get him." He referred to Fire Horse. A redman's myth it might be, but an open wound for Skye.

"You leave him. Shoot the lead mare, dammit," she said in a voice so low he could barely hear.

"I'm going after him."

"He's Fire Horse."

"I don't care if he came down from heaven."

"His spirit gonna kill you."

"My spirit's gonna kill him."

Alarm clawed up her face. "We gonna get our horses. That's why we came. They follow the lead mare."

He didn't reply. He was going to kill that sonofabitch.

He surveyed the whole valley, letting his gaze rest on one animal after another as he'd learned to do when trying to make sense of distant things. The sun drove the shadows down. There were puffballs scudding above. He didn't see Fire Horse. Had the stallion gone after mares again? A faint disappointment took him.

He sighed and backed off the ridge until they were on its eastern slope again and could walk much closer to the wild ones without being detected.

"Fire Horse, you can't kill him. He's medicine, big medicine. You just make him mad as hell," she muttered. "Maybe count coup," she added mysteriously.

He paid no attention. He strode ahead, the madness in him whipping his tired flesh, oblivious of his thirst and hunger. A half hour later, he calculated, he'd be opposite them. He needed a gulch to crawl up now. The wind sliced out of the northwest so he had to stay east of the herd. He chose a notch in the shoulder and peered over it cautiously. A pair of magpies popped up nearby, streaking south. Victoria hissed. Magpies were her medicine helpers.

The herd had drifted back, and as a result he'd overshot. He cursed and backtracked half a mile along the eastern slope of the shoulder, fuming at the Fire Horse. He followed a brushy crease that took him straight to the hogback, and found himself peering right down on the band. Two bands. Harem mares and young stuff in one, and lesser stallions in the other. He exulted. He could pick out every Skye mare and mule as well as the Percherons, scarcely three hundred yards off.

"Them two dunes, the mares," she mumbled in a voice so low he strained to hear it.

He registered the mares in his mind and ignored them. A pair of gray sharks when he wanted the blue whale. He studied a brushy gulch that twisted close to the herd, good cover if he kept low and took his time. He edged toward it, abandoning Victoria, who chose to squat there, obdurate as granite.

He eased into the gulch, hunkering down, nicely hidden by chokecherry and buffalo berry. The day had turned busy, with cloud shadows plowing the broken land, gloomy patches leaping up slopes, jumping cliffs, and hushing the dancing grass. Good. Lots of movement, he thought. Whole world doing cartwheels.

He made a hundred yards—shooting range now—and felt the carbine grow thick and powerful in his hand, like the sceptre of God, with Judgment in its barrel. He eased his face above the brush, studying the peaceful herd. Still no Fire Horse. But he could grab three picket lines in sixty seconds—if he shot that bloody stud first.

He crept lower, waiting for a snake to slither by— bull snake, he thought—and catfooted along in small fluid bursts like a stalking lion. Ahead lay a fine break in the brush where he could hug the earth and wait for Fire Horse to be stupid. He crawled the last distance, making not the slightest sound.

A shriek startled him, exploding like a riverboat

whistle. Scarcely fifty yards away the golden horse screeched and raced around a soft hump, vanishing in an instant. Mister Skye had not even had the chance to lift his carbine. In another moment, while Skye collected his wits, the herd had swept south, up the creek toward the mountains, and didn't look likely to stop for a long time.

She saw the muskrat on the creek bank before it saw her, and sent an arrow through it. Food. She picked it up by its rat-tail and glided back to the place where she had left Skye sitting on a log and staring at the blank hillside. She'd found greens and breadroot, too, but it was too early for berries.

Swiftly she gutted the muskrat and gently peeled back the hide after cutting off its head. He did nothing but stare, his face expressionless, and she wondered about him. She found some tinder—soft fiber from under the bark of a dead branch—and struck sparks into it with her steel, and soon had a tiny fire whose smoke was dissipated by the overarching cottonwoods. In a bit she had pieces of the muskrat skewered on green wood and roasting over the flame.

He needed food, she thought. He'd drunk from the cool creek where they'd repaired after losing Fire Horse's band. He wanted to go on, but she'd crossly stopped him. They'd had nothing much to eat for a day, and she'd find something. It wouldn't be much of a meal but it'd bring her man back to her.

He intended to try again and she marveled at that, but it disturbed her, too. Didn't he know the medicine horse would win? He had become stubborn, filled with a strange madness that she saw in his unblinking eyes.

The smell of burnt meat drifted with the steady breeze as the tiny fire licked the brown flesh. She'd never tasted muskrat before, but it would help them.

She planned to talk to him but not until he had something in his belly and the mad-eye went away from his face. His medicine was no match for Fire Horse, and they should go back to the Quakers.

She fed him, and he gnawed at the tasteless meat on the stick and ate the roots she'd peeled and washed, and the mad-eye never went away from his face so she knew it was no use. She put out the fire with creek water while he rose, stretched, and stalked southward toward the Bearpaw Mountains and Fire Horse.

Neither had said a word and yet each knew the other's state of mind. She walked beside him, feeling the weariness in her calves, wanted to protect and feed him wherever his footsteps went. She'd never seen him quite like this, possessed by some spirit that was not his own.

The rushing creek—it plunged down foothills here—made a cool avenue through a boiling afternoon. Her man didn't bother to hunt for horse sign but continued steadily into the throat of the mountains, as if the magnetic needle of his mind pointed straight toward the vanished herd somewhere ahead. She muttered. Now the mustang band would be twice as wary. Skye knew that too, but it didn't stop him.

They camped that night at a pond where the creek tumbled several feet over a ridge of limestone. They'd not exchanged a word all day. He'd paused only to drink now and then, his face hard, his gaze upon some inner horizons. The valley had narrowed into a steep-sided vee, not natural horse country because the grass had given way to rocky slopes where silvery sagebrush grew. Still, he never paused, as if he had gotten inside the mind of Fire Horse and knew exactly where the stallion had led his band. She found little to feed him—some arrowroot, hard and tasteless, in a swampy bay of the pond. He'd chewed a few bites of the thick root and quit.

That night an evil wind robbed them of heat, and neither slept. They had no robes. He awoke demented, his eyes wild, his face drawn and stubbled with days of growth.

"Today," he said.

She had formed a plan of her own. What he intended to do was so terrible that she would not let it happen. Not that it would happen; Fire Horse had his own medicine-knowing. She examined herself and knew she cared more about Fire Horse than about the Quakers far below; cared more about the horse that walked the mountains than about her own mares and mules. It was good knowing, good to separate her loves and hates. She eyed her man as an adversary now, loving him, dreading him, planning to thwart him. He would be angry if he found out, but he might not: arrows went swift and silent toward their mark.

He found them in a verdant hanging valley, cloistered by rock, the grasses lush and watered, unlike the scorched prairies below. He and Victoria had clambered up an escarpment over which the creek tumbled angrily, and the noise masked their passage. Above lay an intimate meadow as sweet as Paradise, and the band lolled in it as if it had arrived at a sanctuary. She peered out upon the creatures, knowing their happiness. One horse rolled lazily, stood, and shook itself.

Mister Skye's eyes burned and she knew his gaze hunted not for the missing horses, but for Fire Horse. She saw the Percherons and her mares and mules, and the two dun mares she thought were the leaders, but she didn't see Fire Horse and that gladdened her. Two of the Percherons and one mare still dragged picket lines.

Beside her, Mister Skye took his time, settling slowly into the grasses deep in the shadow of some brush, waiting to pounce like a mountain lion. He looked fevered. She knew he wasn't seeing this idyllic place, or experiencing its coolness and the sweet pine-scented air that intoxicated her. Maybe the mountain spirit would alight on him, settle something in his soul, and he would become himself. Once in a while the breeze rolling down from the towering slopes brought with it the strong smell of horses, or coldness, or mountain flowers.

All afternoon he sat unmoving. The sky grayed as massive thunderheads built above them, and soon icy showers or hail would pelt them. She watched the heavens boil and darken from gray to indigo to black, and she thought the mountain spirit was angry at them. And still he sat, even as the first icy drops smacked around them, water lances probing his will. But he never moved.

In moments, the rain soaked her calico blouse and pelted into her doeskin skirt, raising goose bumps on her. The winds sliced and jabbed, freezing the blouse to her flesh. Rain dripped off the rim of Mister Skye's battered hat, flooded along his neck, dripped off his massive nose. He seemed not to notice.

The mustangs turned their rumps against the mountain and slumped with necks lowered, enduring the shower, letting the pelting rain river off them into the grass. They all looked black, soaked with water, and she rejoiced in their horse strength and wisdom. A blinding whiteness followed by a sharp crack of thunder scarcely disturbed them though it jolted her and filled her with dread. The angry mountain was crying out against Mister Skye and herself.

He lifted his carbine, aimed through a sheet of gray rain, and shot, and she scarcely knew what he shot at. He reloaded slowly, jamming a wet paper cartridge into the breech and a fresh cap over the wet nipple. Not far ahead, a rain-blackened horse staggered, and she saw a hole in its side just behind the forelegs, and the rain rivering the blood away. Then the horse died, and as it fell she knew, and something flew out of her and died along with the medicine horse.

The other horses scarcely noticed amidst the crackle of lightning and the roar of rain. The dying horse folded into the wet grasses, rolled partway, its legs spasming, and then slowly sank into nothingness.

The tears came unbidden, salty, mixing with the rain dripping down her face.

''Fire Horse,'' he said woodenly.

She acted intuitively, gliding up and out upon the darkened meadow. The wild horses edged back, peering around for Fire Horse. Her mares stood, knowing her. The mules stood. The Percherons grazed, uncaring. She walked past the dead medicine horse, not wanting to pause there at a place so evil, yet compelled to look at its rain-darkened body, laced and gashed and scarred. Fire Horse looked ordinary in death, head thrown backward and mouth open in a grin. His teeth were worn and broken. His dead eye beheld her and she shuddered, knowing his spirit had seen her. She fled.

The wild mares exploded up the valley and the rest followed, confused, through sheeting rain. The Percheron mares stood, heedless of wild alarms, but the mules and packhorses bolted with the rest. Victoria muttered and hastened through wet grass, feeling the sodden stalks soak her. Her mare stood, watching her, its picket rope hanging from the halter.

The mare accepted her weight and she felt its sopping back chill her own body. The leaderless wild ones, still confused by the storm, paused at the edge of light to look back at her. But she cut out Mary's mare and three mules easily, along with the Percheron mares. In a few minutes she'd cut out the young Percheron stallion from his band of brothers, while the wild ones, half-panicked, scrambled up slippery slopes, snorting. She had the Quaker horses but two of the Sky packhorses had vanished into the mist. It would have to do. She gathered three picket lines and hoped she could keep the rest of the recovered horses from escape.

She found her man out on the meadow, rain sluicing off him and dripping from the barrel of his carbine. He stood beside the dead stallion, his head bowed, gazing somberly at it, his face slowly darkening in the bad light.

"What did I do?" he asked.

Chapter 16

Mary wondered if Jawbone would ever recover. For days he had stood silently, his head low, ignoring the world. It didn't matter to him that flies paraded along his wounds, or that vicious deerflies bit, or that mosquitoes sucked his blood.

Each day she had led him to water, and he'd poked his nose in the flow of the river, drunk a little, and then stood listlessly on the bank, his eyes shut. He ate almost nothing though she'd tempted him with succulent bunchgrass. It was as if his spirit wasn't present, that Jawbone had fled up into the mountains leaving only his wounded body here for her to care for.

He'd been a part of the strange family composed of a Briton far from home, a Crow woman, a Snake woman, and a two-year-old child. She had never really known Jawbone well because the horse barely tolerated her. He accepted Victoria, but even after the winters she'd spent with them, he had always eyed her as someone he might have to bite or kick. She'd known that, and left the care of him to her man.

But now, as she waited tensely for Mister Skye and Victoria, she found time each day to go to Jawbone and speak to him in her Shoshone tongue. She wasn't able to express herself well in English. Victoria talked to Jawbone in her Absaroka tongue so she thought she could talk to the medicine horse in her Snake. Maybe, maybe, he would let her into his life.

The waiting time flew swiftly because she had so many burdens. But she always found time to face Jawbone and talk to him, and run her hand down his neck under his mane, feeling him shiver when her hand neared the lacerated shoulder. He was a brother, and in her tongue she called him Brother Horse and told him that she, Sister Woman, would watch over him, and that he must obey swiftly if trouble came. She meant to hide him in the cottonwoods if she had to. She didn't like being here on the Milk, on a trail the Siksika had worn into a wide dusty road.

She didn't even like leaving him while she gathered roots and greens and hunted with her bow and arrows. But she had to do these things. The Friend People were almost helpless without weapons. But at least the woman, Abigail, had come along on Mary's gathering trips. Mary made a stout digging stick for her with a sharpened end, fire-hardened, and a crotch at the other end that she could lean into to force the stick into the hard earth.

Abigail had made herself helpful in other ways, too.

"Would thee like me to care for Dirk while you gather your food, Mary?" she had asked the day Mister Skye and Victoria had left.

Mary was glad to turn over the solemn child to her, and Abigail had taught the boy English, which he knew the least well of the three tongues of his lodge. And whenever she returned with greens or roots the Friend woman had helped prepare them, peel and boil, until they had an acceptable stew to keep them nourished.

Mary had asked Doctor Sitgreaves to gather his men

and pull, if they could, the great wagon into the cottonwoods and take the white sheet off its bows to conceal
it, but he'd fixed her with those bright blue eyes filled
with infinite kindness and gently refused, as if he
wanted to be discovered.

She didn't understand that, or these people. But she
suspected Victoria had said it wisely: they had big medicine or they wouldn't be so reckless. Medicine or not,
she dreaded the arrival of a war party of painted Bloods
or Piegans or Gros Ventres who would laugh, kill the
Friends, and take everything—including Jawbone, who
would be the greatest of all prizes.

If they wouldn't conceal themselves or their wagon
and buggy and tents from the passing eye, she could.
Patiently, after Skye and Victoria had gone, she'd dismantled the lodge and dragged the cover to a grassy
park on an oxbow of the river, well hidden from the
trail. And then she carried the poles, two at a time, and
erected them there, a tripod first, followed by eight
more laid in the crotches. And finally she hoisted the
cover, a hard task that made sweat run. But at last she
had a place of refuge beside the river where Jawbone
could recover strength and become Medicine Brother
again, unseen by strangers.

By the third day of waiting, she began to worry about
her man and his sits-beside-him wife. Whenever the
Skyes separated she wondered if she'd ever see the others again. Their life had often been lonely and dangerous, without the protection of the villages of her people
or Victoria's, or Mister Skye's own people. But she'd
grown used to that and she knew what to do. If the
spirits of Mister Skye and Victoria were freed from their
bodies, she was to raise her son among her people, with
stories about his father so he might know his inheri-
tance; and she was to take Jawbone on his last lonely
trip up into the Pryor Mountains in Absaroka, and release him there to be with the wild ones until he grew

old and died. She would do these things. At any and all cost.

On that third day Jawbone became himself. She went to him at dawn and found him staring ember-eyed at her, head up, evil, the cruelty back in him. He looked gaunt but he looked more vicious than ever. He watched her, clacking his teeth at her, snorting and muttering. She felt the old dread, but made herself walk close while he studied her with laid-back ears and death in his yellow eyes.

But she had to do this thing. So she caught his loose picket line and he did not bull into her and bowl her over.

"I am glad you are better, Medicine Brother," she said. "Now you will eat and drink and heal. Soon Mister Skye and Victoria will return. They went to get the horses if they could—the Siksika dogs stole them from us. I am glad you are feeling better. Each day the Doctor Friend comes to put a salve on your wounds and see how he sewed them together with silk thread, but now I will not let him come close."

He whickered gently, and it surprised her. Hesitantly, she ran a hand under his mane, wondering whether he'd kill her. But he stood still, trembling, clacking those evil teeth. She felt a strange joy, as if she'd met her own brother for the first time.

"Now eat!" she cried.

He did, greedily, peering about him alertly, registering the familiar lodge, her son, and the flowing river.

She had four Shoshone brothers but never a Medicine Horse Brother, and it lifted her heart. When she found a moment she would find a quiet place and make a song about this brother.

That evening at dusk, when she and Dirk and the Friends shared a common pot of root stew and greens, she heard the sound of moving horses rising from the south. Swiftly she faded back into the cottonwoods with Dirk, going to get her long rifle. No matter that the

Friends didn't want to be defended with arms; she would do what she must.

But as she returned with the weapon and powder horn in hand she saw her man and Victoria, each riding a Skye mare, and a gladness swept through her. They drove horses and mules before them, including the great Percherons. Victory! She ran toward them, joyous, marveling that her family could steal the animals back from the Siksika and not be caught.

And the Friends rose too, exclaiming at the sight of their lost Percherons. But they didn't seem surprised; at least not the way Mary herself was surprised. She feared her man and Victoria would come back with nothing at all.

Swiftly, the Friends caught their great horses and examined them for injuries, finding none, rejoicing all the while. And as they did, Mary realized not all the Skye horses had returned: only the two black mules and the two mares. So some were lost after all. And yet it didn't matter: the parfleches could be stored in the Friends' wagon.

But something wasn't right. She peered into her man's eyes expecting to find joy in them, and found, instead, a darkness and pain that chilled her. A bad-medicine intuition came over her. She peered into Victoria's eyes as well and found bitterness there, her old face set like stone, unsmiling, angry, alien. Something bad had happened. She couldn't imagine what. She looked for wounds in them and the horses and found none—at least none in flesh. She shivered, not knowing, yet knowing.

Doctor Sitgreaves helped with the Percherons and then approached the Skyes, who still sat on the wiry mares.

"We thank thee," he said amiably, eyes bright as always. "Divine Providence has restored these drays to us. That was just how the Inner Light revealed to us."

Something thunderous passed across Skye's face,

something so terrible that Mary could see him wrestling to contain it. And when he did speak at last, in a voice low and biting which somehow carried across the dusky flats, he shocked her.

"Sitgreaves, don't ever mention Divine Providence around me again. Not ever. And when we get to Fort Benton we'll go our separate ways."

The savagery of his voice stunned them all. Sitgreaves looked bewildered, and exchanged glances with his astonished wife, and his son Artemus, and Fall and Price, all frozen at their tasks.

"Mister Skye," the doctor said gently. "We've offended thee somehow, to my regret. And perhaps thee has offended God, the Providence which has brought our valuable animals back to us. Can we make amends?"

"Not ever."

That answer too, barked out like cannon shot, astonished them all.

"Did thee negotiate with Indians for these?"

Skye stared, unmoving.

"Did thee kill—did thee resort to force, let me say?"

"I killed the owner."

Victoria wept.

"God have mercy on thee," said Sitgreaves. "And on the soul of the departed. We dreaded this. We came in fellowship. Would thee tell us about it? Truly, we would like to make peace with the grieving family."

"No."

It puzzled Mary. Victoria would not weep for a dead Siksika. In fact she'd likely have his scalp dangling from her saddle.

The older woman turned to Mary, and through the wetness of her gaze said two words: "Fire Horse."

And Mary wept too.

They toiled up Big Sandy Creek through a broiling heat, under a furnace sun that parched the prairies, turning the grasses and brush brown and gold. The midday heat had become so fierce that Mister Skye usually halted the caravan for several hours after the nooning, often under box elders along the aptly named river. The Friends had taken to spreading out blankets under the wagon or in the shade of the arching trees, and taking a siesta through the worst of it.

There'd been thundershowers up in the mountains, but no rains blessed the prairies. Often, of an afternoon, great thunderheads built up in the west, gray and black towers of cloud filled with the promise of coolness and wet, but they proved to be fickle. They would boil up overhead, bristling with lightning, rumbling and growling, stirring the air, only to betray the hopes of those frail mortals below, yearning for cool air to sweep down from the heights bearing cold water. Sometimes a few drops did fall, wicked with promise, only to stop after popping the dust a bit. But mostly the storm clouds whipped by, cheating them.

Mister Skye rode the wagon these days, handling the lines to the team of mares when Artemus wearied of the task. Jawbone walked alongside, but Skye didn't attempt to ride him. The horse showed signs of weariness after each stretch, and often lay down in the grass, something he rarely did before the grizzly had nearly killed him.

Everything was much the same but somehow things were different. Victoria still rode out each day, scouting ahead, peering over ridges, studying the land from lookouts, and finding game, which she either brought back on her unflagging mare or left hanging conspicuously on the trail. And yet, he knew, something lay between them and that something was Fire Horse. She'd grieved almost as a widow would. She'd stared at Skye in the evenings, seeing the murder in him. He saw it in himself. The wilds, the quarter of a century unchained from civilized restraint, had made him dangerous and atavistic. He couldn't imagine why he'd shot Fire Horse, but he had. And had felt a savage joy as he squeezed the trigger. She'd been right: shoot the lead mares. If he'd done that they probably would have recovered all their horses. But now he was forced to store some pack-saddles and parfleches in the wagon, and would have to bargain for horses in Fort Benton.

Her eyes accused him, and so did Mary's, and neither of his wives had forgiven him. He wondered if they ever would.

One noon, when they had paused on the Marias river, less than a day's travel from Benton, Doctor Sitgreaves drew him away from the rest and up the stream a bit, to a wooded place beside the bank.

"I have things to discuss with thee, Mister Skye," he said gently, his steady gaze suggesting that this encounter might be unpleasant.

Skye nodded.

"Tomorrow we'll be in Fort Benton, I gather. What of the future?"

"What of it?"

"Thee knows we are not satisfied, and I suspect we do not please thee, either."

Skye nodded, staring into a glaring brightness that made his eyes water.

"For our part, Mister Skye, we grieve that thee engaged in violence to return our horses to us. Perhaps thee felt it was necessary to take the life of a tribesman, but it saddens us, and embarrasses us also. We abhor such things. We ache for the man's family. Thee hasn't told us who he was, or what tribe, though we've asked thee often enough. You see, quite apart from this—this casual murder—you've put our mission in jeopardy. What will the ones we've come to help, to give voice to, think of this? We came to heal. My Hippocratic oath, Mister Skye, quite apart from my chosen mission, requires something . . . finer. No doubt thee felt thee had to. I understand that. It's the normal way of dealing with things here. But, sir, thee didn't have to. We'd have gladly forgotten the horses if it meant saving the life—''

"Fire Horse. Shot Fire Horse," Skye muttered.

"What tribe, Mister Skye? Our deepest need is to make amends. Not that we can give much except sympathy."

"No amends, mate. He was a stallion."

"Yes, yes, a powerful man. But what tribe, Mister Skye?"

Skye lifted his battered top hat, wishing he weren't being grilled by this earnest man who meant to help the world's unfortunates. "Mustang. Wild horse. He stole the mares while Jawbone was too sick to chase him off. Herded the mares and all the rest out of camp that night. Slick as bear grease."

"Are thee telling me, sir . . ." Sitgreaves stopped speaking, stared at the Marias river glinting in the harsh sun, and finally smiled. "A horse. Thee didn't take life after all. A wild horse. That makes things better, Mister Skye."

"No, it don't, mate. That was a medicine horse, known to all the tribes hereabouts; a mythic horse, worshiped by them. They thought it lived forever."

"Well, that's a heathen thing—"

"They've a right to it, mate. I may have lost my wives because of it. Don't know what took me."

"Well, at least thee kept thy word to us, Mister Skye. A horse isn't much. Not like killing a mortal."

"To them, mate, it's like killing a grandfather or a chief, or breaking the tribe's sacred medicine."

"Surely a horse—Mister Skye, are thee telling me that if word of this gets about, our mission is in worse trouble than if thee'd killed a tribesman?"

Skye nodded.

"Then, may we count on thee to keep it private?"

Skye shook his head. "Not the Indian way, mate. My wives will tell it. Not gossip. It's medicine talk, sacred talk."

The doctor stood and peered out upon the burning universe, unhappy. "And thee, Mister Skye?"

"I'm not sure what you're asking. If you mean how do I feel about the horse, I feel bad. It was a hard thing. He'd escaped us twice, taking the whole band with him. I was mad and I killed. I shouldn't have. I regret it. My wives are prayin' to his medicine spirit for forgiveness. Maybe that's a good idear."

Sitgreaves nodded warily but his gaze grew distant, as if he were separating himself from a murderer. "It cost thee," he said finally. "Thy women love thee."

Skye ignored him, feeling a roughness building in his mind. "If you mean how do I feel about continuing with you, I'll say I'd rather not. I don't fancy keeping myself in some kind of bond where I can't defend myself, when my life, or the lives of my women, or Jawbone, are at stake as they were in the Piegan village. We almost went under. And that was because I let myself be led into it. Against my common sense. Against all that I've learned in the mountains. You think maybe Divine Providence rescued us, but that wasn't it, mate. When you stepped between them and us and linked hands, they admired that. They like bravery. They honored you for it. Big medicine. That's all it was. It sure as hell wasn't any bloody rescue by God. So, yes, let's cut the knot at Fort Benton. I've offered to refund half. You thought that was fair enough."

Doctor Sitgreaves nodded and smiled, his eyes bright again. "I hope it's nothing personal, Mister Skye. We're fond of thee and thy wives and thy amazing horse. I hope it's nothing more than our ways that offend thee."

Skye smiled uneasily. "It's only that, mate. We all wish you success. Tribes here, they bloody well need a voice in Washington City, and a good surgeon, too."

"It's settled, then," said the doctor, proffering his hand. Mister Skye shook it.

Chapter 17

William Penn Sitgreaves first beheld Fort Benton from atop the yellow bluffs that rose to the north of a great flat along the Missouri. The starkness of the landscape caught his eye. The river ran in a deep trough, far below the level of the surrounding prairie. The post squatted close to the swift river and was surrounded by countless lodges of Indians who had come to trade. It had been fashioned of a tan adobe, though he could see a great deal of wood had gone into it. A gray bastion guarded the south and east palisades of the fort, and another bastion was rising at the northwest corner. The main gate opened to the south, upon the river. Not a tree graced the entire area except for a few on gravelly islands well downstream. But in the hazy southwest, the slopes of the Highwood Mountains were black with pine and he supposed the fort's firewood had to be floated from there.

He felt, intuitively, a strange isolation about this farthest outpost of the American Fur Company. Just a few miles upstream the great falls of the Missouri halted navigation. The post brooded in quiet isolation, a world unto itself, unaware and uncaring that Franklin Pierce had become president, that France had a new constitution and Louis Napoleon had declared himself Emperor, that war was brewing between Turkey and Russia. He had no sense at all that this place was a part of the United States; it seemed a nation unto itself.

"Oh, dear," said Abigail, which was as close as she ever came to expressing dismay.

He hoped their enterprise would not be too hard on her or drive her into a spiritual drought. Ahead of him, Mister Skye, riding Jawbone for the first time since the mauling, gave some sort of invisible command to the beast and the caravan followed down the grade toward the river flats. The doctor guided the young Percheron stallion down, and the carriage carrying himself and Abigail, Freeman Price and Diogenes Fall, proceeded. It pleased him that neither the horse nor the carriage were any the worse for wear.

Lodges crowded the flat, and the doctor surmised that trading was at its height just now, that the clumsy keelboats had just recently arrived with full bellies. But no boats were tied at the levee and he supposed they were now drifting downstream with the previous year's returns, the buffalo robes carefully graded and baled into tens for ease of handling the endless distance back to St. Louis.

These lodges would be Piegan and Blood, Cree and Assiniboin, possibly Gros Ventre, or any of the mountain tribes to the west, such as Kootenai or Flathead. Enemies, abiding by the neutrality of the fort. He could not really tell one tribesman from another although he knew an experienced mountaineer could separate them easily by their dress, the cut of their moccasins, the symbols painted on their bright lodges—even by the way the lodges were put together, the number of poles, the way the ears, or smokeflaps, were cut and supported.

One thing was plain to his discerning eye: as the

Skyes pierced through the trading village, a sudden silence surrounded them. Young warriors watched quietly, absorbing every detail; women paused; children slid to their mothers and hung on them; older boys drew mock bows and loosed mock arrows. And once an aged headman or chief of some sort emerged from a large, gaudy lodge, carrying some sort of feather-bedecked staff of office, and watched the passage of these Skyes with hard eyes. Plainly, not a soul among these Indians was a friend of the Skyes, and not a few of them looked like they would gladly murder the whole family. Sitgreaves counted himself blessed that he and these Skyes had come to a parting.

Within the crowded rectangle of the fort they found themselves in a different world, and Doctor Sitgreaves felt a sudden yearning for the amenities they'd left behind. Solid buildings baked in noonday sun; the high adobe walls of the post quietly spoke of security against wind and weather and the dangers of wildmen. A ramshackle barracks lined one side of the post while the chief factor's home, plus offices and guest quarters, filled another. And along the river wall was the trading room where orderly business was conducted day by day upon the schedule of clocks. He'd not seen a clock or kept time other than the passage of sun and moon for months. The remaining wall was devoted to a warehouse, redolent of new robes. Within, engagés sorted and graded the buffalo pelts and were loading them by tens into a stout robe press where they'd be compressed into a tight pack and baled.

From the trader's frame house—with real glass windows—a dark-haired thin man in a black frock coat whipped toward them, spotted Mister Skye, and hallooed the guide.

"Denig!" Skye bawled, embracing the man with a mountain hug and laughing heartily.

"Mister Skye!" the man exclaimed. "I nevah would have guessed. What brings ye, ye miserable coon?"

The guide turned to Doctor Sitgreaves, who emerged from the carriage along with the rest. "This gent is William Penn Sitgreaves, Doctor Sitgreaves. His lady, Abigail; his son, Artemus, yonder on the wagon seat; and these are Freeman Price, and Diogenes Fall. This here gent is Edwin Denig, a partner in American Fur, and a friend since he and I were pups here."

An Indian woman in brown calico approached shyly from the house, and Sitgreaves guessed at once that she was Denig's wife.

The trader wasted no time introducing her. "This is my lady, Deer Little Woman, of the Assiniboin," he said, and introduced them all to her. The man remembered names, Sitgreaves observed, getting them all correct the first time. A rare enough trait even back east.

"I am pleased," she said in obscurely accented English. She smiled, leisurely assessing each of her guests.

Skye got to the business immediately, even before Denig invited them in for tea. Maybe not tea, the doctor thought, eyeing the red capillaries in Denig's nose, which announced his long acquaintance with spirits.

"These folks are Friends from Philadelphia," Skye rumbled, his voice thundering oddly when confined within this walled place. "They're heading over to Owen's Post in the Bitterroot. Practice surgery there, and do some work with the tribes. They're looking for a guide, Edwin. We're—my ladies and I—we're heading south. We thought you'd probably spare a man or two, or find one easily enough."

The trader looked puzzled, glanced at the Quakers, noting their attire, black except for Abigail's severe gray. "You're not going to the Bitterroot?"

"Nay, we're heading south before the snow blows, mate."

Sitgreaves admired Skye's diplomatic way of saying things. He'd left it entirely to the doctor to make any explanations.

"It's a busy time—the keelboats came in only a week

ago—but we'd like to be of service, Doctor. I think we can spare a man. I have a fine one, a French-Canadian, Jean Gallant, my senior engagé here. We're having quite a summer—a German prince and his retinue came through, and a military party's coming in September. Governor Stevens of Washington Territory—Isaac Stevens. And Lieutenant James Doty, the Wisconsin governor's son. And a military escort. They'll treat with the Blackfeet chiefs. But more of that later, eh? Come in, if ye will. I'll have a man look after your animals—some plugs ye have there. Don't see those here.''

Denig shepherded them toward the house, but Skye detained the doctor as the rest clambered up the broad wooden steps.

"I have this for you, mate."

He handed a draft to the doctor. Sitgreaves read the even copperplate script, finding the note drawn on the account of Augustus Bullock, Skye's Fort Laramie agent, for the sum of two hundred and fifty dollars—half the guide's fee.

"Fair enough?"

"Very fair, Mister Skye. We've come better than halfway.''

"Gallant's a good man. He'll get you there.''

"I'm grateful for the counsel, Mister Skye—and grateful for the rest. Thee went out of thy way—''

"Nothing, mate. Just doing what we're used to.''

"Well, come along then. We'll all have tea—''

"No, mate. My ladies and I . . . we'll put up our outfit out here. See Denig later.''

"Thee're not saying good-bye, I trust?''

"Oh, no, we'll be around a bit. We'll bloody well see you off on the next leg.''

"But I wish thee'd join us. There's things thee can explain to Mister Denig far better than some Friends—greenhorns, I would say—can tell him.''

Skye hoorawed, an easy laugh rumbling through the fort yard. "You go on in there, mate, and meet a good man and a fine lady. Me, I'll be here, and wetting my whistle a little.''

Sitgreaves looked at the grinning guide and at his unsmiling wives, each standing solemnly a little way away, Mary holding her boy. Suddenly he felt loss, a terrible sinking feeling that swept away all comfort.

He swung uneasily toward the worn wooden steps and turned back again. None of them had moved. All the Skyes, and that impossible horse too, watched him.

''I'll miss thee. I hope thy horse will be—''

''Jawbone's coming fine, coming fine, mate.''

Only a few days earlier the doctor had pulled the silk sutures from the healing wounds while Skye soothed the menacing animal. He'd feared the horse would murder him as he tweezered out the thread. But Jawbone didn't even flatten his ears.

''Very well, then, Mister Skye. Victoria. Mary.''

The guide doffed that battered top hat, then settled it over unwashed hair.

The doctor stepped into the cool, civilized darkness of the trader's house and found them all in a parlor not much different from one he might find in Philadelphia.

''Have some tea, or something more spiritous, Doctor Sitgreaves, if ye will. And then, gents and Mrs. Sitgreaves, tell me it all, right from the beginning. We're starved for gossip here, ye know. I'm all ears. Tell me, how come ye to part with the Skyes?''

Abby Sitgreaves felt at home in any parlor, and this one, a thousand miles from any other, piqued her curiosity. She examined it discreetly, her face polite even if she permitted herself tiny edged opinions about everything.

The two teapots, for example, Haviland, one steaming, one quite cold. The trader, Denig, poured generously from the cold one into his demitasse, an amber tealike fluid to be sure, but about a hundred proof. He didn't fool her an instant, the old tosspot! She eyed the angular Deer Little Woman and speculated about her relationship with Denig. There were children. She heard them back in the house somewhere. What, exactly, was the implied contract between an Assiniboin woman of some fair beauty and an important trader for American Fur? She let her curiosity run to certain borders, and then stopped and smiled. Smiles were the wallpaper that covered cracks in the walls.

"But Doctor Sitgreaves," the trader was saying, "surely ye don't expect to impose such a condition on a guide?"

"It's a matter of principle," William Penn replied amiably.

"Well, sah, I know of no theologian who opposes self-defense. In fact, it's a Christian duty, sah, to prevent one's own murder."

It surprised her, this rude trader who sounded familiar with books and theology.

Her husband smiled, that bright, blue-eyed incandescent smile that captivated skeptics whenever the doctrines of the Friends were questioned. "We trust utterly in Divine Providence, Mister Denig. Utterly. Whatever trials befall us are all for the chastening and benefit of our souls, so we may arrive at the Inner Light."

"Admirable, admirable, sah, but not very practical. No wonder the Skyes, ah, decided to retreat. I'll fetch Gallant and you may ask him. But I'm not holding him to your principles, sah. You can't ask a man to give up his right to defend himself. It'll be up to him, eh?"

Denig swept out, leaving the Friends and Deer Little Woman sitting uneasily in the dark parlor. Abby occupied herself by surreptitiously studying the woman's clothing, discovering it rudely made with large stitches that puckered the brown calico print.

"Thee has a lovely dress, Mrs. Denig," she said.

"I made it. Mister Denig showed me the way," she said softly.

"Do thee suppose we'll have difficulty employing a guide?" asked Diogenes Fall.

"Why, we can proceed on our own, with a map. I'm not distressed about it, Diogenes," the doctor responded. "Perhaps it's best that we toil west independently, making acquaintance with our tribal friends as we go. I'll learn a bit of the sign language now, and we'll be set."

"Maybe you die," said Deer Little Woman cheerfully.

Denig reappeared, herding a bald man in buckskins who had morose eyes. The man looked exhausted and delicate. He eyed them all, his gaze settling at last on Abby, wandering over her intimately.

He was undressing her with his eyes, stitch by stitch! she thought, alarmed and curious. Such a thing was a novelty.

"This is Gallant, my best man. A senior man in the company. I've explained your purposes to him, at least a bit. If ye'd like to lay it out plain, he speaks perfect English."

Gallant smiled mournfully, looking like a put-upon dog.

"We wish to employ thee, Monsieur Gallant, to guide us to Owen's Post in the Bitterroot. Our society will settle there and begin to bring some small comforts to the surrounding tribes, including my surgery. Would thee be available?"

The man sighed. "I'd have to leave my dear Owl Woman behind, and that would be a torment, oui, a torment."

"I think Owl Woman will prosper," said Denig drily. "She always has, the other few hundred trips ye've made."

"Ah, my life is a series of ordeals. But tell me, what is this thing that Monsieur Denig says you will ask of me?"

William Penn, she knew, had a practical bent, and

now she saw it at work. "We're prepared to compensate thee abundantly, as well as pay American Fur for your services, Monsieur Gallant. Does that appeal to thee? Now as to conditions, we Friends are pacifist by principle, and we would require of thee that in all circumstances thee would abjure the force of arms."

"I don't know thees word, abjure."

"Renounce. Renounce on oath. Swear it."

Gallant peered about mournfully, his gaze lingering long on Abby, who felt it feather over her bosom and slide down her skirts.

"It's a hard thing," the man said at last. "So much reward. But monsieurs and madame, I treasure my scalp, oui? My very own bald fringe of hair riding over my floppy ears, oui? Now that is the tip of the iceberg. I treasure—beyond money, beyond love, beyond fair womanhood—I treasure my scalp and that which is attached to it, oui—my flesh."

"We understand, Mister Gallant, and thank thee for thy consideration," said William Penn amiably.

The man fled, and Abby regretted it. He'd mesmerized her. Much more interesting than that smelly old Skye. A true gentleman, too.

"Doctor Sitgreaves, I'll fetch some more and ye can interview them. But I fear—"

"I understand," William Penn said. "If we must, we'll proceed on our own."

Denig gaped at him and then the rest of the Friends. "I could simply put a man in your service, but I won't. I won't require any engagé of the company to forswear the use of arms, ye understand," he said roughly, and darted outside again to round up other prospects.

William Penn smiled. Freeman Price sipped tea. Artemus gazed out the window into the busy yard, looking angry.

Within an hour, William Penn had interviewed five other rough men who were herded in one by one. They looked strong and competent to Abby, some in leather, some in wool britches and calico shirts, most of them in floppy felt hats, all French-speaking and dark-bearded, and not a one as delicate as that delicious Gallant.

It came to nothing. As shadows snaked across the yard Denig ran out of candidates.

"I'm sorry," he said. "If ye'd bend a little on the question, I'd have ye a good guide."

He looked distressed, she thought. Deer Little Woman had long since vanished into the rear of the building, and the smell of cooking meat reached her nostrils.

"We've a room for ye and Mrs. Sitgreaves," Denig said, a bit wearily. "And the gentlemen may stay in the barracks, if they wish."

"Why, Denig, we'll be quite comfortable in our wall tents down near the river. We've no firewood, though, and not a stick's to be found. If thee would spare us some—"

"William Penn!" She was not about to let the luxury of a bed escape her. He turned, puzzled. "We will be pleasured if thee would show us to our room," she said sweetly. "Thee are most kind."

"Course, course," said Denig. "And join us for dinner. Meanwhile, the afternoon is yours. Perhaps ye'd enjoy a visit to the trading room."

Abigail soon found herself lying upon a real four-poster, with a real cotton-stuffed tick under her, and a real washbowl and pitcher of floral china on the stand beside her. The comfort of a real bed improved her thinking at once.

"William Penn," she said, watching him unhook his black high-top shoes to ventilate his feet and ease his bunions, "I wish thee would engage the Skyes again, if they will have us."

"I fear they wouldn't, Abby. Not as long as we insist upon—"

"But William Penn, why do we bind them? They're

not Friends. We might trust in Providence, but there's no need to insist on it when they don't hold to our beliefs. Is there?''

He smiled that boyish smile of his, which always annoyed her. ''There is, Abby. We can't permit people in our service to do what we would not do.''

''Thee're planning to go ahead without a guide. I know it. Not even a translator.''

''I'm thinking of employing an Indian youth. Surely Denig could find one that'd speak some English and knows where to go. He'd communicate with other tribesmen. A Blackfeet boy. Maybe a whole party of them.''

''Oh!'' she said, undirected worry building in her.

''Why should we employ whites, anyway?'' he pressed on. ''What a sublime expression of trust it'd be to place ourselves in the hands of those we've come to help.''

''Oh,'' she said helplessly, her wits deserting her. ''But what if their enemies attack them—and us? How will thee stop them? How will thee tell them—Does thee remember our Junius, killed by Indians only a few days ago? Does thee?''

''I grieve for him every day.''

''We need the Skyes.''

''We had the Skyes when Junius was taken from us.''

''But he was alone, hunting—''

He smiled gently, his eyes bright. ''Thee and I shall hold a Meeting and seek illumination.''

''I don't wish for illumination.''

''Abby—are thee well?''

''This is a real bed in a safe place,'' she said, annoyed at the boy-man sharing her room.

Chapter 18

That afternoon Diogenes Fall wandered out among the tribesmen camped near the fort. He could not speak with them and he didn't even know which tribes they were, but he felt a profound need to grasp the nature of their life. If he were to become the voice of these abused people back in Washington City, he must learn their ways and needs.

He supposed, actually, that these were Blackfeet, probably Piegan, the southernmost band and frequent visitors here at Benton. What struck him instantly was that these were handsome, tall people, save for a few who wore the cruel mark of the pox, which had carried off a third of them in the late 1830s. They were lean and muscular and well formed. The women were comely, as he put it delicately.

What struck him next was that the women toiled ceaselessly while the men idled, gossiped, smoked, and gambled in small groups, sometimes under a brush arbor erected of poles and branches lashed with rawhide. He watched women fleshing the hides of fresh-killed buffalo, or rubbing buffalo brains into them to tan them. Still others, working in pairs, softened a robe by running it back and forth through a crotch or around a smooth stump. He watched others bent under a heavy load of firewood, gathered some vast distance from the post because every stick anywhere near the fort had been snatched long before.

His observant eye noted that women had sewn the lodges together and made the clothing by tanning and sewing skins, or sewing trade cloth; women kept an eye on the scampering children while making moccasins from smoke-blackened lodge tops with a metal awl—a favorite trade item. He watched women returning with a bundle of roots and greens slung over their back in a shawl, and knew they'd walked far to collect the food, and had pried the roots from hard clay with a crude digging stick that took brutal pressure to pierce into the earth.

But the men simply congregated in groups wherever they could find shade, and talked and smoked. They watched him amiably, supposing him to be a trader, he thought, but saying nothing to him. He knew they would take his black frock coat as a mark of importance. White traders wore their frock coats on the day trade opened, a sign of celebration, even as the chiefs and headmen wore their finery to celebrate the occasion. He smiled at one and all, letting them know of his deepest empathy and compassion. He beamed especially at the oppressed women, and it gladdened him to remember that the Friends, Lucretia Mott for instance, had been at the forefront of woman emancipation. With his pen he would transform the world. He groped for the correct Latin for that but it eluded him.

He saw at once that time meant nothing; industry meant nothing; a day existed merely to be squandered according to whim. The men's task was to hunt and war. Perhaps they groomed their horses as well. He saw few ponies on this vast flat, and realized what little grass grew here had long ago vanished. The horses were being herded up above somewhere, beyond the yellow bluffs that demarked the river flat. He watched them smoke and play the stick game and talk, and thought that they would benefit from honest work. He meant to encourage them all to become plowmen and learn the value and pleasure of sweat. But as long as they had buffalo to prey upon they would remain indolent nomads. His own motto was *ora et labora*, pray and work. He intended to awaken these indolent men who were oblivious of their suffering women to the nobility of labor.

Satisfied at last, he meandered back to the fort, dodging around lodges, avoiding children, easing around women who stared up at him as he passed, meeting the hard gaze of old men who watched the passage of life from a place of honor before their lodges. He passed the tall gates of hand-sawed cottonwood plank into the somnolent yard. Everything about a fur post had a dream quality, as if schedules didn't exist and the world's work could be shrugged off to another day. But in the cool darkness of the trading room he found life at last: a senior trader at the small window, and two busy clerks in shirtsleeves. One fetched the required goods from shelves while the other sat on a high stool and recorded transactions in a leather-bound ledger with a nib pen.

The trading room was a wondrous place, even to his old eye. Here, so far from civilization, shelves groaned under a vast array of useful things: gleaming copper pots, iron kettles, blankets, mostly the color of natural wool but some brightly dyed in scarlets and azures; trays of shining steel knives, steel strikers, flints, hawk bells, hanks of beads, hoop iron or ready-made arrow points, awls, needles, axes, hatchets, a rack of shining trade muskets, some of them used and battered; sacks of coffee beans, barrels of sugar, hand mirrors, sacks of ball and shot, small one-pound bars of lead. And the bolts of trade cloth! Flannels in carmine and green and yellow; calicoes, ginghams, blue-striped bed ticking, duck canvas, and more fabrics he couldn't name. And much to his surprise, a shelf of black silk top hats very like Skye's. For stylish redmen, he supposed, a faint amusement building in him. The Friends set no value on style or clothing.

He stood entranced, absorbing the colors and glints of metal and the rich redolence of freshly manufactured goods.

The senior man, the one at the window, noticed him. "Ah, you're one of the Quakers. I'm Malcolm Clarke. Pull up a stool and watch if you'd like. I can't spare the time to explain—not at the peak of the season—but I think you'll see how it goes."

"I'll do that, Mister Clarke. I'm Diogenes Fall."

Even as he found a stool, a tribesman pushed a robe through the narrow trading window. Clarke spread it out, looking for flaws.

"Good robe," he said to Fall. "See, softly tanned. Piegans are good tanners. No scars. Good thick pelt. Winter robe. Summer hair is thinner and the robes bring less. Good color."

Clarke and the powerful warrior bartered in what Fall presumed was the Blackfeet tongue, and even as they were reaching an agreement a clerk dropped a cloth pouch of ready-made lead balls and a premeasured quantity of powder encased in a waxy paper. The warrior nodded, and the clerk recorded the transaction in the ledger.

"Sixty loads of powder and shot for one good robe. A common transaction, Mister Fall."

"What is a robe worth?"

"A good one? Over six dollars wholesale in New York City; around two dollars here."

Out of discretion Fall didn't ask what the powder and ball were worth, but knew that a few cents would have bought the sixty charges back east.

One by one the tribesmen filled the window, each with one or more buffalo robes. Clarke carefully examined each robe and then told the man how much credit he had. Fall discovered it took six to ten robes to get a trade rifle; a robe was worth three or four pounds of sugar, or two pounds of coffee; a robe traded for a hank of beads, or a yard of cloth, which the trader measured from the fingers of his stretched arm to his neck rather than by ruler. He discovered that the trade blankets came in various sizes and were marked by bars denoting weight, and that the blankets traded for one to four robes.

"The bars used to signify the beaver plews—pelts— it took, but now they don't signify much of anything," Clarke told him. "A three-point blanket doesn't necessarily weigh three pounds."

"That's a lot of robes for one small blanket, sir."

"Come from England. Witney makes them. Same ones used by Hudson's Bay."

A gaunt Indian woman shoved a robe through the window and Clarke spread it out on the shelving. Fall could see at once that this one was made from two halves of hide sewn together.

"A split. Not worth as much. Buffalo are so heavy a squaw can't turn one over to pull the hide off the underside; or sometimes part of a hide's been damaged, and they can only get a half hide from an animal. Sew the halves from two buffaloes together sometimes. We take them. People back east can't always afford a good carriage robe, and buy a split."

She got an awl, a striker, and some sugar for her split.

The more he watched, the more he believed that the Indians were taking a beating. The enormous labor that went into a fine-tanned buffalo robe fetched miserabl amounts of goods: a knife or two, a few trinkets, a sleazily measured pound of some staple or other, probably short-weighted. A vast indignation began to surge through him. These oppressed redmen were being cheated.

"These prices seem rather high, Mister Clarke," he ventured in a momentary lull in the trading.

"Average about nine times eastern prices."

Fall gaped.

"At that, the fur companies don't get rich at it. Most of the opposition companies collapse after a year or two."

"But surely thee could be more generous. Does thee know the toil that goes into just one robe?"

Clarke didn't answer. Another tribesman was pushing several robes through the window and the trader was busy again. Fall watched hawkishly, learning what he could. The trading room no longer seemed an enchanted place, an island of plenty in a wilderness, but a glittering trap where redmen came for necessities and were bilked by smooth-talking men who had a monopoly—almost a monopoly. Fort Campbell, off a way, did a trade for the opposition, Livingston and Fox. Yes! he thought, a monopoly. It was take-it-or-leave-it for the poor redmen.

Nine times eastern prices! He knew it cost a considerable sum to transport all these goods up the river, by steam to Fort Union, and keelboat here; and it cost the fur companies a similar sum to haul the robes over two thousand miles down the river. Even so, even so . . . he suspected he had witnessed a scoundrel trade, and only the surface of it at that.

The rest lay hidden because of the will of Congress, which had several times prohibited a trade in spirituous liquor in the Indian territories. True, he had seen nothing. Not a drop of spirits did he discover in the trading room. Not a drunken redman did he spot on his tour of the encampment. And yet, he'd heard, he'd heard. And he'd read a few indignant accounts, penned by reformers back east. Indian whiskey was nothing but raw alcohol mixed with river water, and flavored with tobacco, red peppers, or molasses to make it fiery, the reports said. And even though the Indian whiskey was around five-sixths water it corrupted tribe after tribe. A robe, the product of countless hours of toil, would barely buy a minor drunk.

Diogenes Fall felt the profound illumination of the Inner Light suffuse him. This afternoon in the trading room of Fort Benton had been the happenstance of Divine Providence. He knew what he'd soon be doing; he'd set his fiery pen to paper and shake the nation to its foundations. *O tempora! O mores!*

One thing about old Edwin, thought Mister Skye. This time of year, after the keelboats came in, he didn't spare the Scotch. Each year he'd had his own private barrel of it smuggled upriver past the puritanical captains of Leavenworth and the prim inspectors at Bellevue. Not even a thirty-gallon barrel of it lasted long in the Denig household, but it made the trader's summers and falls splendid. Usually the Denigs ran Fort Union, but for some reason Alec Culbertson, head of the Upper Missouri Outfit, had posted them here this season and was running Union himself.

At least, Skye thought, Denig didn't have anyone else to share the Scotch with this evening. None of the Friends across the table touched it though Doctor Sitgreaves allowed himself a glass of wine. Skye sipped the amber product of Scotland. Victoria and Mary glared at him every time he lifted the glass to his lips, and he responded by winking at them.

Deer Little Woman, freshly provisioned by the keelboats from civilization, had set a great feast so that the usual buffalo tongue and humpribs and fried boudins were accompanied by such exotica as pickles, crackers, and butter from the states.

This was, he knew, a sort of farewell dinner. He'd grown fond of the Friends at that, even though Victoria made withering comments about them in Crow, which he devoutly hoped Sitgreaves hadn't absorbed as yet. He himself was glad to be free of them even though it cut his income in half and left him badly in debt to Bullock. Civilized idealism didn't work here and it had almost cost their lives. He'd gladly take them the rest of the way, but not bound by any pacifist oath. Still, he furtively admired their bravery and faith. How could anyone help but like Doctor Sitgreaves, bright and merry and kind to all?

The meal had been oddly silent, but Denig had undertaken to keep the sputtering conversation alive between generous sips of Scotch. The Friends lived largely in silence, Skye remembered. But now Doctor Sitgreaves settled back in his chair and addressed him.

"Mister Skye, we've been unable to engage a guide. We may go on alone, or seek to employ an Indian youth. Could thee draw us a map?"

"I could draw you a map and it'd do you no good at all, mate."

The doctor eyed him quizzically.

"You can't tell one gulch from another. Map's just paper. You've got to get that carriage and wagon over the continental divide to go to Owen's Fort. There's no way to escape that, Doctor. Lots of passes, but only one I can think of that's not forested. That'd make a road. You could go over to the Blackfoot River and follow it to Clark's Fork. But the way's forested. If you go alone, mate, you'd best ditch the wagons—no road—and pack everything over there."

"Could thee explain the proper pass to an Indian guide, if we employ one?"

"I don't reckon I could. They've got their own names for places. And . . . Doctor, you won't be finding an Indian that goes along with those principles of yours."

"We're in the hands of Providence. Perhaps, Mister Denig, thee could direct us to a tribesman?"

"Well now, ye'll not have an easy time. The Blackfeet aren't likely to take ye over to their enemies, the

Salish. Kootenai over there, around Owen's place too. Maybe a Crow lad. Can you think of a proper lad, Victoria?''

"Sonofabitch," she muttered.

"She means, mates, she doesn't want to condemn one of her own people." Skye rather enjoyed the exchange and was curious to see just where principle would yield to practicality. "I'll take you there, but on my terms, Doctor Sitgreaves."

Victoria glared at him. Skye sipped a generous slug of the Scotch, which felt marvelous, a languid heat permeating his belly.

Sitgreaves laughed amiably. "The essence of Friends' religion, Mister Skye, is to let ourselves be guided by the Inner Light, Providence speaking to us directly. Thee will find me unyielding on some matters."

It was Skye's turn to laugh. The odd thing was that he knew, somehow, that the intractable Sitgreaves would arrive at Owen's Post along with his reluctant Abby, unhappy son, and colleagues, somehow, some way. His bright blue eyes mirrored his resolve.

"I think we should have a Meeting," said Freeman Price, which put an end to any discussion of how the Quakers would proceed.

Fall changed the subject. "I say, Mister Denig. I learned this afternoon that the prices of goods sold to tribesmen here average nine times what they are in the states. Is that so?"

Denig dabbed at his mouth, and toyed with his emptied glass of spirits. "Ah, Mister Fall. We operate thousands of miles from the sources of manufacture, which are largely in New England. The cost of bringing them is very high."

"But nine times! Surely that's more than a just profit, Mister Denig."

"There's a double risk, sir. The prices reflect the precarious nature of the business and the long waits for a return on investment. Every once in a while, Mister Fall, the entire annual supply of trade goods is lost in shipping. The boats sink. And every once in a while, the entire year's returns—the robes, baled in tens and stored in the steamboats or keelboats—is lost on the treacherous Missouri. The cost of the trade items here reflects that. It also reflects something else. Even now, our factors in St. Louis—Pierre Chouteau Jr. and his colleagues—are spending money gathering up next year's goods. The Witney blankets come clear from England, but the tribesmen will have no other. The robes and other pelts come down the river just once a year, sir—at least usually. Sometimes a keelboat or mackinaw takes some down. That's a long wait for a yield." He eyed the Friend amiably. "Does that satisfy your interest?"

"It seems high. You give the redmen a dollar or so of trade goods for the robes, and sell them for six, I take it. It seems to me to take undue advantage of a savage people."

Skye discerned a cutting quality to the remark, and wondered just how friendly Friends were to those they disapproved of.

But Denig was quick with a response. "Mister Fall," he began smoothly—Skye thought he'd dealt with this at table before—"let me hasten to say that the prices in the trading room apply to all. White trappers come in and deal on exactly the same terms as the Indians. If ye resupply before heading out, ye'll find the prices no different. Indeed, sir, while American Fur enjoys guests, such as yourselves, they do burden the company substantially each year. We make every concession we can, though. We've always given Father De Smet and his colleagues whatever he wishes at cost. We do what we can while trying to stay afloat. There's more still, sir. Some years the robes don't come in. The Indians can't find the herds. And those years we suffer grievous losses, with those shelves burdened with goods we can't trade.''

Skye thought the answer a reasonable one but Fall had mounted his charger and wouldn't be satisfied. ''And now they're all dependent on the companies. I fear for them, Mister Denig.''

''We fear for them too, Mister Fall. The thing ye speak of, sir, is a deepening tragedy that no one knows how to prevent. The things we trade have transformed their lives, Mister Fall. Imagine cutting meat and hide with chipped stone. Imagine making moccasins with bone awls. Imagine cooking with fired clay pots, not well suited to their roaming life, or cooking in temporary pots made of green hide. Do their women toil? Imagine how it was before, sir! Try gathering food with chipped flint. Try lighting a fire without a steel striker and flint. Try making an arrowhead from stone. Try dressing entirely in skins—no cloth at all. Try keeping warm only with robes, never a blanket. Eh?''

But Fall wasn't listening. ''The fur companies ought to tithe back a part of it for the betterment of these tribesmen,'' he said. ''Or there ought to be a tax on the republic. I hear Governor Stevens is en route here this very summer to begin a new skulduggery against them—more treaties, more reservations. Isn't that right? Isn't that the whole history of it? Fur traders first, making them dependent, and then the army not far behind, and the settlers. Sometime, sir, Divine Providence will scald us all for this. Maybe the next century.''

Fall stopped suddenly, leaving an odd quiet resonating around the table.

Sitgreaves filled it at last. ''Diogenes cares deeply,'' he said amiably. ''The light blooms in him. I wish we might all live with such ideals. But the world is the world. Mister Denig, would thee invite the tribesmen who are ailing in any way to my surgery? I'll heal as best I can while we wait for a guide. This is as good a place as any to begin our work.''

"I'll invite them to your surgery, doctor," the chief trader said.

Mister Skye drained the whiskey, and poured some more.

Chapter 19

Beauregard Clement had arrived in the mountains just after the beaver trade, and just ahead of the law. He'd operated a ferry across the Arkansas River near Pine Bluffs until 1841, when he'd suddenly abandoned it and fled west. In fact, large parties crossing in his flat-bottomed scow were safe enough but single travelers, on foot or horseback, weren't safe at all, especially at night. The evidence had been so easy to dispose of, and he always kept a few spare rocks on board to weight it down, not wanting it to wash ashore downstream somewhere. But he'd gotten into trouble selling a horse, and had fled one night just ahead of the sheriff, who had put a dozen missing-person stories together and had warrants enough to choke a horse.

Beau Clement had a face that radiated both guile and innocence, and a ready smile that softened the ferret-like plainness of his features. People trusted him uneasily, seeing a harmless blue-eyed man who somehow stirred faint reservations at the back of their mind. In the mountains he'd been a loner with a small outfit that suggested he did trapping for a living. He had a fast horse he kept well fed and shod, plus a gaggle of scrawny packhorses that toted a bevy of traps, a battered tent, assorted firearms, and the rest of his plunder. Each summer, when the shelves of the various fur posts were newly stocked, he'd ride in with enough robes and pelts to outfit himself for another year, and do some modest, careful drinking. He'd become a fixture at the fur posts along with others of his kind, wandering into Fort Hall one season, Fort Benton another, and Owen's Post still another. He always had robes to trade, and made tolerable company. He'd never learned to read or write but he read men and weather shrewdly and had a native intelligence that commanded the respect of his auditors.

He collected his robes, actually, by preying on solitary Indians, or small groups of them, often from ambush so that the victims were mortally wounded before they grasped they were in trouble. It'd been an easy living, and a safe one because he'd mastered the wilderness skills. He scalped each victim. He collected arrows and knew those of each tribe and band, and made each of his crimes look like the work of Indians— which greatly exacerbated the tensions between the bands. He knew himself to be the best tracker, stalker, eluder, food gatherer, deceiver, and predator among all the solitary whitemen—and he'd found dozens—roaming the unsettled Rockies. As a cover, since robes were often identifiable by tribe, he'd always bought a few trading trinkets and made it known he'd bargained for his peltries. And indeed he did bargain once in a while to help establish the legend that he was a trader.

And thus it was that he'd wandered into Fort Benton that July, knowing the shelves would be stocked and the traders eager to collect his robes. As he approached, he noted the forest of lodges: a band of Piegans, another of Bloods, and over east of the post a separate village of Crees, all provisioning themselves and having a summer saturnalia. And something else: several whitemen in black frock coats wandering about.

He rode into the post through the small gate—a whiteman's privilege—and discovered a lodge pitched in the yard, two Indian women and a boy before it, and in a small pen nearby a blue roan, yellow-eyed and ugly, watching him with malevolent interest. He'd never seen the horse but knew it at once, and knew who the women were and the owner of that horse. Every man of the western wilderness knew of Skye. From within the lodge came a strange rumble that rose and fell. The women ignored it, as if a grizzly roar from their own lodge were an ordinary thing.

He smiled, dismounted, and hitched his packhorses. Business first. He wandered into the trading room from the post yard and found the usual gorgeous array on the shelves, as well as traders and clerks, desperately busy. They knew him and acknowledged his presence with a nod.

"Well, Beau," said Malcolm Clarke, during a mid-afternoon lull, "in for some refreshments?"

"How be youse, Malcolm? A lean year this time. Crafty redskins beat me outa my trade goods. But I got a few. Fifty-seven prime robes, plus a pack-load of other stuff, elkhide, beaver plews, few otter."

"Enough for a party, eh, Beau?"

"Enough for a new outfit, anyhow. Your prices are so bad I cain't hardly get anything no more."

"You didn't do so pore," Clarke replied. He nodded at a clerk, who slipped into the yard and began toting bundled robes into the trading room. Clarke nodded to another clerk to watch the trading window, and dealt with Beau's peltries himself. A couple of hours later, Beau's robes had been examined, graded, and priced, his peltries looked at, the whole counted and credited, and Beau had collected some of his loot. He had enjoyed a privilege the tribesmen didn't have, the opportunity to wander through the trading room, pinching flannels, hefting firearms, studying flints, looking at the trade gewgaws. He always feigned great interest in trade items such as ribbons and mirrors, inquiring about prices and quality, and he always bought enough to make him seem to be an independent trader.

"I see Skye's here," he said to Clarke.

Clarke chuckled. "He's on one of his trips."

"Trips?"

"Crawled into his jug. He does that."

Beau laughed appreciatively. A clerk had brought him a jug from somewhere within the bowels of the post. It hadn't come from the trading room. "Who them whitemen in black suits?"

"Quakers from the city of Brotherly Love, Beau. The one, Sitgreaves, is a doctor. They're heading out to Owen's place."

"Skye guiding?"

"He quit. At least that's how it seems. Or maybe they quit him."

"How does that calculate?"

"Way I hear it from Denig, the Quakes are demanding something Skye isn't about to agree to, which is an oath not to defend themselves or the Friends by force of arms. I think old Skye nearly got his scalp lifted, and wants shut of them."

"I don't calculate it."

"Part of their religion. Pacifism. Trusting in the Good Lord."

"I trust in this," Beau said, rubbing the shiny new breechloader he'd just acquired. "Funny stuff. What're them folks doing out here?"

"Takin' medicine to the tribes, I hear. That and showing them some farming, and maybe making a pitch for them. The Friends are abolitionists, y'know."

"Nigger-lovers. Pukes. I never had no use for them. How come they're sitting around hyar?"

"Can't find a guide, Beau. They tried the whole lot. Denig, he won't impose that condition on any Company man, and they've plumb run out. Sitgreaves asked a few Piegan boys but they didn't cotton to it neither, and couldn't talk English anyway. So they're sittin' and waitin' and holding Meetings—their word for prayer services, Quaker-style—and the doc's patching up a few Piegans, those that let him.''

"That's plumb interesting. What do the Quakers have in that wagon?"

"Oh, I don't know. They resupplied here, mostly sugar and coffee. They got some farm tools, I know that. I think some hardware, nails, and the like. Good clothes. They dress plain but don't let it fool you. Did you see the draft horses? Three Percherons penned out there, breeding stallion and a pair of draft mares. Now that's something, in this country.''

"Is that so?" mused Beau Clement. "And old Skye backed out?''

"That's the word.''

"Think I'll mosey around, Malcolm.''

"You want to load your truck now? I can have a man help.''

"Naw. I'll hang around a whiles. Park it there in a pile if it don't bother youse none. And sell me a bait of grain for my saddle horse.''

Clarke nodded and entered the purchases in an account, debiting the amount against Clement's credit. Beau Clement wandered into the sunbaked yard, wanting to study matters a bit. He meandered over to the black carriage, admiring it, and then over to the Quaker wagon hulking near the small livestock pens. A big wagon, rightly the biggest that'd come into the northwest. He peered inside and made out a heavy load there, crates and barrels, a collection of trunks, a plow, spades, hoes, and rakes. Wealth. And there had to be money in there. Those Quakers, they had some put by.

He'd missed the Percherons when he'd ridden in, but now they commanded his attention. They stood taller than the local mustang stock and looked hardly the worse for wear after hauling the carriage and wagon from Fort Union. He wondered where he could sell them. The Oregon settlements. They'd command a fine price out there. But that was a long trip . . . Maybe Salt Lake.

Satisfied at last, he meandered toward Skye's women, who were busying themselves before the small lodge. The young eye-turning one was Mary, and he would have liked to mess with her but he thought he'd better be careful. The older one he knew was Victoria of the Crows, dour and flinty. He approached her. From behind, that blue roan screeched, a sound as bloodcurdling as Beau Clement had ever heard.

"I'm lookin' for Skye," he said to her.

"He ain't here."

"They told me—"

"You some friend of his?"

"Naw, not exactly. I allus wanted to meet him, though. And I got business."

"You got business?"

"Yeah. I want to find out about them Quakers, and how come ol' Skye, he quit 'em. I'm thinkin' maybe I could hire on with them folks, take 'em out to Owen's."

"Sonofabitch," she said. "No one with brains would do that. I'll tell you how it went."

A few minutes later he had the story, or as much of it as he needed to know, and he wondered how Skye could have been so dumb, almost getting himself and his women killed. The old mountain man must be slipping, he thought. That or he'd become too cocky, after all his years of good luck. Beau knew that he could do better, and that he'd take the job, and that his unique skills would serve him perfectly in a few days.

On the shady side of the fort, William Penn Sitgreaves erected his wall tent, gathered together his medical equipage, borrowed chairs from the trader, and opened for business. He'd sent two breeds through the villages announcing the services of the doctor, and hoped that he could do some good. He was prepared to perform simple surgeries, inoculate for smallpox, and pull a stray tooth or two.

A lifetime of practicing medicine had made him a worldly man in spite of his Quaker beliefs, and he suspected he would have a hard time overcoming fear and prejudice, or perhaps the hostility of tribal shamans. Some things, such as applying anesthesia, might meet with resistance. A dentist, William Thomas Green Morton, had been using ether since 1846 and had shown doctors how to administer it for surgery. Since then, chloroform and nitrous oxide, laughing gas, had been used, often against the opposition of clerics who argued that pain was God's chastening. The controversy had raged on both sides of the Atlantic until a British surgeon, Sir James Y. Simpson, observed that in Genesis God had "caused a deep sleep to fall upon Adam, and he slept," when Eve was created from the rib of Adam. That had quieted most of the clergy, but Doctor Sitgreaves knew that biblical citations wouldn't apply here among the tribes where shamans might have their own reasons to resist him. It had been Doctor Oliver Wendell Holmes who had named the process *anesthesia*, meaning insensibility, and it was just that quality—loss of sensibility—that Sitgreaves worried about. How would the tribesmen take this little death? With terror?

Still, the doctor was not one to worry about himself. He lived out his days with a zestful curiosity, amiably seeking ways to help the suffering, heal the sick, uplift the despairing. He had always been at the forefront of medicine, seeking better ways to heal and comfort, and he had counted it a trait of the Friends to relieve the world of its misery.

One of the breed boys, Henri, a son of a French trapper and a Piegan woman, returned with a powerful-looking young warrior in tow. And along with him, a dozen curious Piegans, mostly women. But in the party was a wizened old man heavily burdened with strange emblems, including a necklace of dessicated human ears, whom Sitgreaves took at once to be a shaman. A professional rival. The doctor sensed at once that this episode, wherever it might lead, could make or break his whole enterprise, at least among the Blackfeet. He surveyed them uneasily. The warrior eyed him from a face that hid pain from the world, a face any doctor had seen countless times in all species of humanity. The rest watched passively except for the medicine man, who studied Sitgreaves's equipage with malice. Scars of battle laced the warrior's arms and bronze torso, and Sitgreaves discovered the familiar sundance wounds on the warrior's breast.

"This here one, he got a bad tooth and it hurts," said Henri.

A toothache. Something Sitgreaves could do something about although there might be complications. "Tell him I can help him. I can pull his bad tooth without pain if he's willing to face the little sleep."

"The leetle sleep?"

"I'll put him to sleep for a little while and he'll feel nothing while I pull his tooth."

"How do you do that?"

"Thee'll see. Tell him it is safe, and he'll be made well. And he'll heal."

Henri explained all that to the warrior, who stared impassively at the doctor. The crowd watched raptly. At last the warrior spoke.

"He say he will think about it."

"At least let me see the tooth."

After a conference the warrior agreed to that, and sat down on the chair. Sitgreaves rummaged through his surgical apparatus and found a good pick.

"Would thee tell me his name?"

"Diving Otter. Of the Old Bull Clan, oui?"

"Tell Diving Otter to show me the tooth that hurts, please."

Diving Otter opened his mouth a little, not enough, and fingered an upper right molar. Sitgreaves lowered himself onto another chair and examined the stained tooth. It had been damaged somehow. Enamel had been chipped from the crown, exposing hard dentin, and that in turn had deteriorated. Sitgreaves knew that if he probed the dentin he'd pierce through to the pulpy tissue that contained blood vessels and nerve ends. He wiggled the tooth gently, finding it firmly anchored in its socket. The man grunted. It would be hard to pull out, and if his dental forceps didn't work he might have to chisel it free.

He paused quietly, letting the Inner Light guide him. He saw risks. If he failed he might drive away the ones he'd come to help. This big tooth would be hard to pull. It'd be bloody. It would hurt. But when had medicine been without risk?

"I'll pull it. Would thee tell him I'll have him breathe air that makes a little sleep, and that he must not be afraid?"

Diving Otter listened, and stood, and Doctor Sitgreaves thought he'd lost his patient. Instead, the warrior nodded to a woman who had followed him, and she laid a fine-tanned, reddish buffalo robe before him. The doctor frowned. He didn't want to be paid.

"He say, it is not enough and he send his woman for another."

"No! It's fine, fine. Too much. A great payment." He knew he must accept the robe. And he knew he would trade it for supplies to help his enterprise along. He lifted the robe, ran his hand through the glossy hair admiring its unusual color, and smiled, letting his bright eyes say what needed saying to the woman and her man. "Thee will be my passage into the hearts of the Blackfeet people," he said softly.

He found his black walnut box and opened it. Trapped

in velvet there, pinioned against breakage, was a glass globe with a vented stopper on top and a hardwood stem and porcelain mouthpiece that made it look rather like a familiar pipe. A sponge rested inside the globe. He lifted the stopper and withdrew the sponge. Next he unstoppered a ceramic flask of ether, or sweet vitriol, instantly sniffing the sweet dizzy odor, and poured it generously into the sponge. Then he thrust the sponge into the glass globe and stoppered it.

"If thee would, Henri, tell Diving Otter to hold the mouthpiece at his lips gently, and breath in the vapor, like tobacco smoke. He'll feel sleepy. He must not breathe through his nose. Tell him to trust in me, and in a little while he will return, and his bad tooth will be gone and his gum ready to heal."

Henri explained all that, and Diving Otter gazed at the doctor, his opaque eyes unblinking and aware, as if assessing his hangman. Doctor Sitgreaves met the Piegan's gaze with his own calm one. "Thee are a brave man," he said softly.

Around him, the Piegans pressed closely now, watching intently. The shaman frowned, his eyes unpeaceful.

"Tell them all will be well, and to wait and be patient. It will take a while for Diving Otter to come back."

Henri did. Sitgreaves slid the ceramic mouthpiece between the lips of Diving Otter, but the man didn't suck the gas at first. Instead, he gazed directly into the doctor's eyes and the doctor found a message in the gaze, a message that simultaneously and silently addressed fear, trust, willingness to die—and revenge. Then the warrior sucked. The effect plainly astonished him. He sucked again and again, smiling slightly as his lips pressed around the thick glass stem. His eyelids lowered.

Women gasped. This was a terrible thing they witnessed in the bright afternoon sun. Diving Otter sucked in the ether easily, his features relaxing, awareness retreating from his face. Then at last he slumped, no longer among the living. The shaman muttered. The crowd swelled as word flew magically back to the lodges. Doctor Sitgreaves eased Diving Otter to the hard earth. It would be much easier to extract the tooth from a prone patient. Behind him, he heard a fear-laden murmur and a soft sob from the warrior's woman. Some of the gathering Blackfeet made hissing sounds.

"If thee would, Henri, tell them to take heart. Soon Diving Otter will return."

But Henri's words did little to dispel the thundercloud of horror behind the doctor. Swiftly he pulled the largest and most powerful forceps from his surgery and clamped the tooth in its jaws. The warrior didn't respond. A rising murmur greeted this astonishing thing. Sitgreaves pried open the lax mouth with his free hand. The warrior breathed gently, his chest rising and falling as he sprawled on the clay. Sitgreaves wiggled the tooth, using the forceps as a lever. It didn't wiggle much. He felt sweat collect under his shirt as he kneeled beside his patient. He twisted and felt roots loosen deep in the skull, with small snaps of surrender. But the man's head twisted with the tooth. The doctor clamped the warrior's head, twisted his instrument hard and pulled, but the tooth didn't yield. He twisted again. Blood oozed around the loosened molar and collected in the man's throat. Sitgreaves lifted him, helped him swallow. The warrior moaned. Sitgreaves dosed him with ether again, and the warrior slid back into oblivion. The doctor felt weary and sweat-drenched. How could a molar suck so much energy from him? His heart raced, and he felt a tremor in his hands. He wished the warrior were on a surgical table where a man could work on him.

Sitgreaves tugged but still the tooth didn't yield. He feared he would need to start hammering, but when he rotated the tooth its roots loosened again. He yanked hard, lifting the warrior's head off the clay, and the bony socket surrendered this time. The tooth came. In the socket, blood gouted, catching in the warrior's throat. Swiftly, Doctor Sitgreaves lifted his head and propped him up, letting the gore drool from his lips. The crowd muttered behind him, witless with fear.

"Henri, if thee would. Tell them that dead men don't bleed."

"It is the little death they fear. You have taken him away."

He sighed. Let them wait. He peered into the swollen cavity, finding the bleeding less severe than it appeared, as he knew it would be. He packed rolled lint into the wound, letting it soak up blood. He washed his forceps and the pick and returned them to his kit. He handed the bad tooth to the squaw, who examined it as one might examine a pretty pebble. Others crowded around. The shaman studied it and the inert warrior.

He finished cleaning up and still the warrior lay unconscious—too long, he thought. Perhaps redmen needed less of the gas. He eyed his patient warily and checked the pulse, which remained rapid and small. Did people of color respond differently to ether? He'd never read of such a thing. He forced a smile.

A whiteman smiled back. Doctor Sitgreaves hadn't noticed him before. The man was a trapper, from the look of his skin garments, his unkempt hair and beard. Not a prepossessing man, the doctor thought. The man had a rodent face and a gaze that hid rather than revealed the inner spirit.

"If youse doctorin' I got me a carbuncle needs lancing."

"I'd be glad to help, sir. If there's no rush, perhaps I can help my Indian patients first."

Around them, the Piegans gazed sullenly at the inert form of their friend and clan brother.

"I'm Clement. Beauregard Clement. I trade a little for plews and robes. Been in the mountains almost since I was birthed. Know them like the back of my hand, I reckon. Missoura. Arkansas. I got me whelped there, but that was the last they saw o' me.''

''Thee knows the mountains?''

''Shore do. Guided some.''

''Are thee familiar with the Friends?''

''I can't rightly say as I am, but I heerd about ye from my old friend Victoria, Missus Skye.''

Something joyous built up in William Penn Sitgreaves. ''Thee may be our salvation, Mister Clement.''

''Call me Beau.''

That was when Diving Otter came around at last, and something dark bled away from the gathered crowd. Swiftly, the doctor plucked the red-soaked wadding from the man's mouth. The warrior moaned, thrashed, opened his eyes, recognized the world and sat up, feeling his inflamed cheek. In a few more minutes he was smiling hugely from swollen lips, and Piegans were peppering him with questions. Diving Otter responded, giggling occasionally.

''I reckon you set right smart with the redskins, Doc,'' said Clement.

''We came to help them, Mister Clement.''

''Call me Beau. Youse just call me Beau now.''

The shaman glared at them both, and then spun away.

Chapter 20

Doctor Sitgreaves examined Diving Otter carefully. The bleeding had stopped. Except for a swollen red gum, the Piegan warrior was better off than before, and the source of his pain rested in the palm of his wife.

"Henri, let them know I'm ready for the next, please."

The boy addressed the shy multitude, but found no patients.

"Are they afraid of the little death, Henri? Tell them it's only for pain, and goes away."

The youth said things in the Blackfeet tongue, but no other Piegan stepped forward.

"Tell them this, then. I've come here to bring healing to them anytime they need me. We've come to help all the peoples of the plains and mountains. We'll be at Owen's Fort."

Henri translated, and the gathered crowd stared back. The doctor knew what angered them: he would bring his friendship and medicine to enemies of these people. It couldn't be helped. He wanted to make it clear that he would not be a partisan.

At last, one heavyset Piegan—a headman, Sitgreaves thought—addressed the youth, and Henri translated: "He wants you to stay here, Fort Benton, and help the People. He wants to know why you go to Owen's Post, to the Salish and Kootenai."

The doctor picked his words carefully. "To help them. Just as I helped thee. To start a farm in that fertile valley. To start a school to teach our ways. That will be my home. But I will come to these people. I will make many trips to the Blackfeet people."

The answer seemed to satisfy the headman and the others as well. But he could induce no more of them to sample his medical skills, and he realized the anesthesia had been a terror and sensation among them. Maybe, after observing Diving Otter a while, they'd be less afraid.

"They say you take the spirit away from Diving Otter and keep it," Henri said.

"Tell them that many whitemen opposed the little sleep, especially the clergy—the shamans. They said that God meant to impose pain on us, to chasten us. But Friends believe the One Above is kinder than that, and doesn't inflict pain. Tell them that if thee can, Henri."

Henri looked dubious but made a stab at it, and all Doctor Sitgreaves could tell was that the Piegans were listening and not objecting. Even so, none stepped forward.

"Well then, Henri. Tell them I'll vaccinate for smallpox. Once I do this, they will never have the disease. I'll make a small scratch in their arm and put a weaker disease in it, one called cowpox. It won't hurt them. I'll do it to myself first if they want. Once I do it to them, they'll be safe all their lives from smallpox."

He waited while Henri tried to translate all that. Smallpox had devastated the tribes—killed a third of the

Blackfeet in the late 1830s—and they dreaded it, and hated whitemen for bringing it to them. The shaman glared at him imperiously, an expression laden with raw hatred. He returned the gaze calmly.

"They afraid," Henri said.

"How about thee?"

The youth shrugged, and stepped forward, much too nonchalant. Dr. Sitgreaves selected a spot on the youth's bronzed upper arm and scratched it gently with a surgical scalpel until it bled. Then he rubbed a drop of Jenner's vaccine—hoping the serum was still potent after all these weeks—into the wound.

"That's all there is to it, Henri. Thee may be mildly sick, but that's unlikely."

The boy suddenly looked afraid. "I'm going to get it!"

"No. Not smallpox. Thee are safe from it all thy life now."

"Maybe you kill me."

Sitgreaves smiled. "I would not do that to thee. Please ask the rest to step forward. I can make them safe."

But none came. The women shrank back. The shaman didn't budge. The children hid behind their mothers' calico skirts.

"How about this little one?" the doctor asked, pointing to a wee girl. The girl's mother grabbed her instantly and dragged her back.

He said nothing, but removed his frock coat and rolled up his own sleeve, baring his upper left arm. There he scratched his own flesh, and daubed the wound with the serum. The shaman barked something.

"What did he say, Henri?"

"He say you a bad-medicine man. A witch. Maybe he right."

"I've come only to heal thee and help thee." He waited amiably but no one came, and indeed the Blackfeet shrank back, lashed away by the staccato shouting of the shaman. Suddenly they were alone.

"Very well, then," he said. "Mister Clement, show me the carbuncle."

"Youse got them a little fired up, doc."

"It takes time. Let's see your abscess."

"Hyar," Beau said, pulling up a green calico shirt-sleeve. He bared a small boil near his right elbow. The doctor examined it cursorily.

"It hasn't come to a head. No pus in it. Best to just keep it clean, plenty of soap and water, and wait. Often they go away."

"I hear you're lackin' a guide," the man said, utterly disinterested in Sitgreaves's verdict. "I reckon I could git you to Owen's." He rolled down his sleeve perfunctorily.

"There are lots of men to guide us, Mister Clement. But none who would abide by our conditions."

"I reckon I heerd about that from old Victoria. Old Skye, he's not willin' to risk his neck anymore, so he quit you. Me, I been thinkin' on it and I'd do it for a price. You understand it ain't natural, goin' unarmed like you want."

"We didn't ask Mister Skye, or thee, to go unarmed, Mister Clement. But to obey the Sixth Commandment."

Beau squinted. "And what be that?"

"Thou shalt not kill. We take it seriously. Even in matters of self-defense. And war."

"Youse jist waltz whar yoah going and trust it'll come out right?"

Sitgreaves smiled. "No. We trust Providence will deliver us if we discover the Divine Will—the Divine Light we call it."

"Might work back in Phillydelphia. I reckon these savages ain't heerd of this whiteman's Providence."

"He's here, Mister Clement, and he's got no color."

"No wonder ol' Skye got shut of you. I'd be drunk

as a skunk too if'n I got into the bind you got him into. But I reckon I can git you to Owen's. For a price, you know. I don't lose my scalp cheap." He laughed at his little joke, yellowed teeth poking through his thick beard. "Call me Beau. I'll call you Bill. And if you can fork up five hunnert dollars cash-money, we got us a deal."

"What would the deal be—Beau?"

"I reckon I can slip youse amongst and between them savages to Owen's Post without me cutting off a topknot."

"Cutting off a topknot?"

"Scalpin'. You kill one, you scalp him."

Sitgreaves studied the man closer. He seemed rougher, dirtier, less kempt than Skye. And better armed. The doctor spotted a Green River knife at his belt, a boot knife, a revolver in a battered holster; no doubt the man had a rifle in his gear. But there was something else, something he couldn't put his finger on, that troubled him. Years of medical practice had given him a rare insight into the character of the mortals he dealt with, and the man before him evoked a certain wariness although he could not fathom just what set the tocsins sounding.

"We haven't five hundred dollars. If thee'd take less, a hundred maybe, we'd consider it in Meeting—Beau."

"A hundred ain't much. You got more, I reckon."

"What we have will go for our support at John Owen's post."

Clement looked relieved. "You gonna vote or something? You and them others?"

"No, not vote. We'll seek the illumination we need, the counsel of the Divine Light. Tell me—what would thee do if we were imperiled by tribesmen? Would thee abide?"

"Whatever you say, Bill. Ya say, don't shoot them red devils, and I'll just set my piece down and let youse palaver." He squinted sharply at the doctor. "Depends some on what ya got in that wagon back in the post thar. Ya got a lot of stuff they want, gold and all, and they'd likely jump ya.''

"Gold?" Sitgreaves was surprised. "No, not a lot. Mostly the tools we'll need for farming—tools and seed, writing materials for our work, my medical kit.''

"They'd butcher ye for them Percherons, I reckon.''

"We don't think so. We have a stallion and mares for breeding. They'll become a farm herd. Did thee enjoy the sight of them out here, so far from any other?''

"I reckon you got plenty o' things in the wagons they'd cotton to," Beau said. "Even if you ain't sayin' much.''

"Help me pack up my things, Mister Clement, and I'll take thee to meet the Friends.''

The mountaineer dismantled the tent while Sitgreaves collected the rest, and they trudged back to the fort in the long afternoon light. Off in a corner of the yard the Skye women worked awls through leather before their lodge. The erstwhile guide was nowhere in sight but Sitgreaves knew the unfortunate man lay stupefied within. At least he had waited until he got here, the doctor thought wryly.

Sitgreaves gathered his colleagues and Abby from the corners of the post and presented Beauregard Clement to them, knowing they would find the man less pleasing than Skye. Still, clothing didn't make the man—as any Friend knew—and perhaps this one would be their salvation. The Friends studied the mountaineer quietly, assessing, even as Clement peered eagerly at each of them, reading whatever he needed to know in their demeanor.

"This gentleman is Beauregard Clement, from Missouri and Arkansas, but a man of the wilds for many years," Doctor Sitgreaves began. "He tells me he knows the country and could lead us to Owen's Post— say, that reminds me, Mister Clement. Skye told us that there'd be only one pass that'd permit our wagon and carriage through. Would thee know which?''

"I rightly do, rightly do.''

"Good. Mister Clement has offered to take us to Owen's Post—perhaps for a hundred dollars in cash, though it's not settled—and while he's no more inclined to our views than any other man of the wilds, he's ready to abide by our needs.'' He turned to Clement. "Thee do understand that we are firm on this, sir? That a tragic event, a skirmish, a fight, a chance shot, might ruin our purposes here, destroy the trust we seek to build, set at least one tribe against us? Do thee surely grasp that, and will thee surely abide by it, even if events seem perilous?''

"I reckon I could. Yas, youse can count on ol' Beau.''

Sitgreaves wondered how truthful the man was. Something whispered in him to beware. "This is a sacred thing to us, sir. Will thee swear to it before Almighty God?''

"I shore do. Youse can rest easy. I ain't about to plug no redskin. Afore the Almighty.''

Victoria had joined them, Sitgreaves realized, peering sharply at Clement, her gaze traveling to his weapons and then off to his gear, where a shining rifle rested in a saddle sheath.

"Goddam, you got a Sharps breechloader,'' she exclaimed.

Clement smiled easily. "Nice hunting rifle, ol' gal.''

"Killing sonofabitch,'' she said. "Skye, he wants one but ain't got the cash. Cost a heap.''

"Lots of robes, lots of robes,'' Clement agreed.

"You traded a heap for it. You some man with a bow, too, I see. That quiver, it's goddam Siksika, and the arrows, they all marked different. Some Dakotah, some Absaroka. Some Assiniboin.''

"You got a fine eye, ma'am. As any wife of Skye would.'' Clement smiled amiably. "I trade a lot.''

''Goddam,'' she muttered.

Doctor Sitgreaves flinched. He dreaded her presence when she used the name of Divine Providence in vain. He turned to his colleagues. ''Have thee any questions to ask Mister Clement?''

''Are thee a believer?'' asked Diogenes Fall. ''Have thee a faith that steers thee, a compass for the helmsman of thy soul?''

''Raised up a Baptist by my ma and pa, and still say my prayers afore I roll into my robes.''

Diogenes Fall smiled. *''Pax vobiscum,''* he said.

There were no more questions. Abby looked hesitant. His son and Freeman Price stared passively.

''Very well, then, Mister Clement. We must leave thee for a while and seek out the necessary guidance. But before dark I'll have a decision for thee. We will engage thee or not, as the Light shines.''

''You got some secret way o' knowin' inside a man?''

''Nay, we are blind. But the Inner Light gives us wisdom, Mister Clement. And we are given to see what many men don't perceive.''

Clement hitched up his leggins nervously. ''It ain't proper, getting a peek at a man like that. Only I got nothin' to worry about. Youse got my word and that's that.''

''Very well then, Mister Clement.'' The doctor steered his group toward Denig's house where they would meet in the parlor as they had in the past.

''Sonofabitch,'' said Victoria, and the doctor winced.

Within the cool, brown parlor, the Friends settled themselves quietly on settees and armchairs. This had become a familiar ritual to the Denigs, and they had always slipped into other parts of the house. This, like most Meetings of Friends, would be largely silent as each of them turned inward, hoping through meditation to reach the inner illumination taught by George Fox, the founder of the sect in the seventeenth century. If any of them, inspired by the Holy Spirit, wished to speak, he or she would do so for the edification and instruction of the others.

Doctor Sitgreaves knew that each, without being bidden, would seek in his own heart the wisdom of Divine Providence as regards the man named Beauregard Clement, who waited out in the yard. The doctor silently cleared away the rubbish of his own thinking, his ill-formed impressions of the man, and waited in childlike simplicity for some inkling of the Divine Will for them. The others were doing the same.

Abby sat rigidly, her gaze upon a portrait of Denig but her spirit, the doctor knew, far removed from the world. His son Artemus sat with eyes closed, awaiting the wisdom beyond mortal knowing. Freeman Price seemed engulfed by a golden world beyond the ken of man; indeed, Price reached his own pathways by thinking on Paradise, with a golden throne and alabaster streets. Only Diogenes Fall seemed excited, brimming with something or other. The doctor knew he ought not even to be examining his colleagues and family, but ought to lose himself in the tenderness and wisdom of the Divine, and so he, too, shut his eyes.

Nothing came to him. The silence of God offered him no clue, drew aside no veils. But that was enough. Even in the silence the Inner Light shone.

Across the gloomy parlor his son rose to speak, and faces quietly turned to him. "I don't trust this man. We'd be fools to go with him." The youth's harshness sometimes grated on the doctor, but he ascribed it to being young. Surely the Inner Light shone in him no matter the tone of voice.

Doctor Sitgreaves felt satisfied that there would soon be a divine, impermeable unity among them.

His dear Abby stood, her face composed into a portrait of surrender. "We must not be in a hurry, for our days and weeks are but smoke to the Divine Will." She sat again, her skirts and petticoats rustling in the quiet.

She, too, then. It was almost settled.

No one spoke. Time ticked by. Then Freeman Price said, "I am with thee."

"It cannot be!" exclaimed Diogenes Fall.

Startled, the doctor waited for the old classics scholar to explain himself. Fall's shrewd wisdom had been an asset from the beginning, as if Providence had turned the man's classical education, garnered at Yale College, and used it to underline, enhance, the Inner Light. How often the Inner Spirit had expressed itself in Latin at these Meetings! *Dei gratia!* By the grace of God. If ever there was doubt, they always yielded to his light, which burnt hotter and brighter than the light of the others.

The gaunt scholar rose, his face ruddy with months of outdoor living. "Time is of the essence!" he said. "We must hasten. We must be about our business. We must not waste a second. Our work is precious. Our purposes are luminous and sublime. We must set aside doubt and fear. Does anyone here doubt, even for a moment, that we will arrive safely? That we will have the Divine Presence with us every step? That if we delay, we are afraid of where the Spirit may take us? *Vincit que se vincit.* He conquers who conquers himself!"

Something crabbed at Doctor Sitgreaves. Four Friends had been led by the Light to turn down Clement. One Friend eloquently argued for the man and claimed his Light was the true one. That rarely happened in Meetings, where the holy silence seemed to draw them together until they were of one mind in harmony with the Divine. Could Fall have confused his own conceits with the Divine Will? Doubt flooded the doctor and yet he felt helpless to mend the trouble.

"Amen," he said. He eyed Fall sharply. "Are thee sure?" he asked in all earnestness. "Very sure?"

Fall looked insulted, and the doctor pressed no further. But the others looked troubled too, wavering in the uncertain Light.

They filed out and into the bright yard where Beauregard Clement lounged, hawking up brown spit.

"Would a hundred fifty dollars suit thee?" the doctor asked.

Something brightened in the mountaineer's face. "It's a mite cheap—got ya a bargain, ya do—but I'll do 'er."

"Thee will agree to bring us no scandal?"

"Scandal?"

"Thee will abide by the Commandment?"

"Oh, har, I reckon I can do 'er."

"Very well then. We'll engage thee, Mister Clement, and place our fate with thee. Providence will guide our every step but thee will care for us, and bring us meat, and see to it that a good wagon trail is open to us. And thee will translate carefully. I didn't ask thee: what tongues do thee speak?"

"Aw, none, except the sign language. Don't much like to deal with the red devils."

"I thought thee were a trader."

"Oh, I do 'er, all right. The signs, my hands, they be all I need to git along."

"It seems odd," said the doctor. "Very well, then."

He pulled a long glove-leather wallet from his black frock coat and withdrew greenbacks, all tens. "A hundred now. The rest when we arrive. Are thee satisfied?"

"That'll do 'er."

"We wish to begin at once. We can make a few miles today. These summer days are long."

"Now?" Clement looked startled.

"Within the hour. We must harness and pack."

Clement smiled, baring those stained yellow teeth again. "Reckon I can do 'er," he said.

Chapter 21

The lodge stank so much of stale whiskey and urine that Victoria hated to be in it. But neither did she roll up the lodge cover to permit the cleansing breeze to purge the lodge, lest the whole fort see the shame within. Mister Skye lay in the gloom, greasy in his filthy robe, emerging from his stupor now and then long enough to guzzle from his crockery jug or teeter to the latrine, which lay in a noisome corner of the post.

She hated this part of being Mister Skye's woman. She always had. All the rest filled her bony breast to overflowing, but not this. They laughed at him when he lay like this, a roaring clown, weak and dirty and helpless. The engagés walked by and snickered and whispered. She loathed the fort and dreamed of the time they could escape into the sweet land, which knew no palisades. He'd been off to his other world for days, and she knew he'd run out of whiskey. She'd helped it along, furtively pouring most of it into the dust outside the lodge. She could never stop him from his trips but she'd learned how to make them shorter.

And she'd watched over them all, as she always did when he left them. She sat fiercely before the lodge, her weapons always handy, no matter that it was pitched, this time, in the very yard of Fort Benton and no harm would befall them. Maybe no harm. One never knew. So she sat crossly, day after day, repairing his clothes, resoling moccasins, looking after little Dirk to give Mary a few moments of freedom.

Behind her, Skye rolled, sat up, roared like the bull moose, laughed at some bawdy thought wobbling through his saturated brain, and stood. She heard a great splashing and knew he hadn't made it to the whitemen's place for that. The air round the Skye lodge stank, and she wondered how long Denig would tolerate him this time. She refused to turn and look, letting her thin back speak to him. She heard a vast burp, the sound of his belly bubbling, and then silence again. In moments like this she liked to think of her man clear-eyed and keen of mind, riding the great horse across a high meadow under a bowl of sun, filled with his roaring joy. She'd needed that vision more and more through the years during times like these.

At least, she thought, he'd held off this journey to the other side until he'd gotten his clients here safely. Often he didn't. The need pounced on him in the middle of his journeys, leaving her and Mary to make do, comfort the clients, carry on. This she did, knowing secretly she guided better than he did, though the whitemen didn't trust her skills as much.

Jawbone shrieked. For days he'd paced back and forth in his tiny prison, mad with rage, ready to murder Skye. The horse hated these trips of Skye's, and she feared for her life whenever she bridled him to lead him to water, or brought him some of the post's expensive hay. Jawbone kept his vigil, screaming his alarms even as she kept hers. The awful shrieking annoyed the engagés, ruined their sleep, offended them, until they stared dourly at the animal, wishing him dead and fed to the fish. But no one approached. Jawbone curled back his lips, clacked his teeth, flattened his ears, and promised destruction to anyone other than Victoria or Mary who came within twenty feet.

She turned to see what he shrieked at and discovered Doctor Sitgreaves and that one called Clement talking earnestly while the doctor stowed away his medical bag and a tent in their great wagon. She knew approximately what they were talking about. The Friends had found a guide at last. Sure enough, in a few minutes Sitgreaves was introducing Clement to the rest of the Friends, and then the Friends disappeared inside the Denigs' house. Clement eyed the yard furtively, focusing on the Skye lodge and Victoria, and then sidled back to the wagon, peering into it, poking and probing it, studying its underside, its wheels and hubs, looking for something.

She watched narrowly, and knew Mary watched too, and yet the one called Clement—who reminded her of a beaver because of his protruding front teeth—never clambered into the wagon or opened casks and crates and trunks. Still, she could see he wanted to, and was deterred only by her own gaze across the empty yard. A while later they emerged from Denig's—they'd had one of their Meetings, she knew, because of the way they conducted themselves—and after a brief negotiation they all sprang to action. They'd struck an agreement and they were going to leave at once. The Sitgreaves boy, Artemus, began harnessing the Percherons even while the rest scurried to their quarters, and Doctor Sitgreaves paced toward the company office to settle accounts with Denig.

She sighed, grateful the Skyes were no longer a part of it. When her man came back—maybe tonight—they'd leave this post and slide through this Siksika country until they got down to the Elk River, the Yellowstone, and the land of her own people. The thought filled her with eagerness.

She didn't think much of Beauregard Clement and some instinct told her the man was less than honorable, but that was no concern of hers. The Friends had made their own Big Medicine in the Denigs' parlor and had the protection of their whiteman's God, and that was that. She grunted, wondering about all those things which she couldn't explain, and which tore at her from a dozen directions, making her mind crazy.

A while later the Friends gathered in the yard. The afternoon sun threw long shadows into the compound, but on this summer day they could still make eight or ten miles. They looked eager to bring their medicine and friendship to the Peoples. Clement had saddled up his horse and loaded his packhorses, and was waiting patiently while the Friends said good-bye to the Denigs, Malcolm Clarke, and others.

Then at last the party rattled through the yawning gates of Fort Benton, out upon the levee beside the Missouri River. Clement led them, just as Skye had done; the black carriage drawn by the Percheron stallion came next, with the doctor driving and Abby beside him; and behind, the boy, Artemus, cracked his whip over the great mares drawing the covered wagon. Beside him sat Freeman Price. Diogenes Fall had chosen to walk a while.

In a moment they were gone, leaving only golden dust, the smell of fresh manure, and a silence behind them. Denig glanced dourly at her and the lodge, and vanished in his office. Gone, then. The Friends had hired someone else. She felt oddly sad about it. Even ashamed. This was the first time they'd failed to take a party the entire distance, and something incomplete and wrong hovered in the silence. She found herself hoping that man, Clement, would take good care of the Friends—and suddenly knew he wouldn't. But it was not her business. In fact, the Friends had been as eager to discharge the Skyes as the Skyes had been to conclude the agreement, and what the Friends did now, and the decisions they made, weren't her concern. And yet it was. Her mind crossly dismissed her worries but her spirit, rising from the sacred place, whispered alarm, fear—and caring.

She arose and stretched, driving the stiffness from her muscles. Something stirred within her. She clambered through the oval lodge door and found him snoring on his back, exhaling rotten fumes. She booted him hard with her moccasin, right in the ribs. He growled. She kicked him again, trying to hurt him. He roared. Then his bleary eyes opened and slowly collected his world, and her.

"Ah," he muttered.

"We go now. Get up."

He stared at her, and then rolled over.

She kicked his backside. He was sober. He hadn't had any more of the spirit water because she'd poured away the last of it at dawn. "Get up," she snapped, and booted him again, feeling his soft thigh take the jolt of her toes.

"Thirsty. Get me a jug."

"Goddam, you had two jugs. We go now. Get your ass up."

"Head pounding."

"Good."

She intended to kick him again, harder, but he rolled suddenly and sat up, exuding a foul odor along with a rank breath.

"All right," he said, groping around for his hat. He clamped it down, and she knew he was up. Outside, Jawbone shrieked and snorted, hearing the muttering of his lost master.

"He mad at me?"

"He kill you this time."

"Where are we?"

"Fort Benton. In the yard. I can't stand it anymore."

Skye stood, scratched his various parts and yawned.

"I get water," she said. "Or maybe I just throw you in the river. Sonofabitch, I can't stand to get near you."

Skye grinned. She handed him a ball of yellow soap she'd bought in the trading room. He took it, slipped on his camp moccasins, and wandered into the yard, staring at its solemn emptiness. She knew he'd wander toward the lavatory, a place with washbowls and pitchers, in the engagés' barracks.

"Where's the Friends?" he asked, registering at last that the wagon and carriage and Percherons were gone.

"They hire a new guide and go. Little time ago."

"Found some bloody devil to do it, eh?"

"Man named Clement. He come in outa the mountains, traded a few robes and plews, and then sniff around them Friends."

"Don't know him."

"He got a funny name. Beauregard. He got beaver-teeth, yellow, and a beard, and dirty buckskins."

Skye frowned.

"You know him? He says he knows you. I didn't like the sonofabitch none."

"I can't rightly remember," Skye said. "I knew so bloody many. But that name—it'll come to me soon if he's been around the bend a time or two here."

"He's gonna steal from them Friends."

Mister Skye ignored her and rumbled off toward the barracks with that rolling sailor gait that always fascinated her. She felt her heart lift, having her man back, and began crushing coffee beans and dropping them in a blackened pot she would take to the kitchen and put on the cast-iron stove there. They wouldn't let her build a fire in the yard.

He returned sooner than she expected, smelling sweet, his face scraped clean, a sharpness in his eye.

"I got coffee coming. You look good. You even smell good."

Beside her, Mary stood, ready to thrust his son into

his massive arms and enjoy an evening as a family once again.

"I know him," he rumbled. "That Clement."

As they rode into a dying sun, Beauregard Clement wondered what he had gotten into. Here he was, escorting five pilgrims who hadn't a firearm among them and who would decline to use them in any case. Normally, a party of five or six well-armed and savvy men would discourage most red devils. But these people seemed to invite trouble traveling as if they were on a Sunday picnic.

What if they encountered Bug's Boys? It could put him under. He alone was no match even for a small hunting party. A pack of them devils could swipe everything these Quaker pukes possessed, including the Percherons. And everything in Beau's bags too, including them greenbacks that ol' Sitgreaves had peeled off the wad. If trouble came, he could ditch them in a flash, but that was the only option he had. As for the rest, he couldn't do nothing until a week or so, and a hundred miles or so, had passed. He wanted the business to happen far from Fort Benton and at a place where he could work over the site carefully, make it look like red devils done it.

But perhaps he could cut a deal with the Indians—let them do it and split the stuff. He might roam ahead, find them, and lead the devils to them Quakers. Then the whole hoedown would be real, not faked. And if he played his cards right he could do his own dealing, get shut of them skins, and get everything anyway, along with a few robes.

They angered him and he really didn't know why. They just did. They were stupid and trusting, like baby pigs or puppies, arousing sympathy when they deserved none. Imagine the dumb of it, coming here unheeled, surrounded by coyotes. They had to work at it to be that dumb. But that didn't explain his rage either. He hated them, and what would happen would be *all their fault*. They were as stupid and trusting as a cow being led to the throat cutter, as dumb as a hen around a man with an axe. He felt a contempt for them high-toned types, well-dressed types, educated and fancy types—the damned doctor couldn't even do some medicine on the savages, scared them off.

And that was another thing: helping the Injuns. These pukes was abolitionists and nigger-lovers too, so that it made a man puke to think about it. Pukes, all of them. Deserving what they'd get. Trying to wreck the world. Tear apart Arkansas and Missouri with their preachy talk. They didn't know right from wrong nohow.

He considered doing it right then and there, scarcely ten miles upstream from Benton—making the whole thing look like a bad encounter with the savages. But he contained himself. No sense ever throwing suspicion on himself. He'd survived by being careful, and he'd continue. He'd shoot that puke doctor first, just for doctoring Injuns. Then, while the woman screamed, he'd shoot the son—the only one burly enough to cause trouble. Then he'd shoot the other two, clerk-types, and finally the woman. And not a weapon among them to stop him, except their sad stares. Goddam, he'd do it for the South if nothing else.

He called a halt after ten or twelve miles of travel along a river trace, in a cottonwooded flat across from the confluence of a nameless creek. But the mosquitoes were so thick that he turned them up to the bluffs, and after half a mile of travel across gulchy prairie he halted them again in a shallow coulee that sloped gently toward the river. A fresh breeze kept the mosquitoes at bay. He hadn't hunted and didn't intend to. They could supply him with vittles. He slid off his jaded stallion, clambered stiffly up a rise, and surveyed the sweeping country in the dusk, finding no movement.

"I reckon we'll be safe enough here," he said. "You

standin' guard tonight, keepin' them draft horses from being stole?''

"Mister Skye's horse always stood guard,'' said Sitgreaves.

Beau grunted. He didn't know what good it would do to have unarmed puke Quakers standing guard. They wouldn't know if a hoss was getting stole, and couldn't do nothing about it except wake him up, and by then the horses would be good and stole.

"Picket them in the coulee, not up above,'' he said roughly.

He'd let 'em all sleep in the coulee. He would roll out his blanket up above where he could git if he had to. He would picket his own horses and mules maybe a quarter-mile from them others, too.

Except to unload his pack animals and hobble them, he did nothing, preferring to watch them make camp. The boy, Artemus, did most of it, erecting two wall tents, picketing the three Percherons on good grass, and unloading supplies from the sagging wagon. One of the men—Price, he thought—collected firewood from the river bottoms while the woman dug into canisters and crates full of staples bought at Benton.

He discerned a quietness about them, an established order in which they did their appointed tasks without a word and without the fear one usually found in pilgrims, who thought an Injun lurked behind every clump of sagebrush.

"Mr. Clement, would thee join us for supper? We have many things to discuss,'' said Sitgreaves.

"I was fixin' to. Long as you ain't payin' me much, you can supply vittles. I hunt meat—that's extry.''

Sitgreaves paused, stared, and smiled. "That wasn't in the agreement, but we may accommodate thee.''

Beau had never heard a big word like that, but it didn't matter none. The pukes could use all the fancy words they wanted and still end up where they would end up.

"Mrs. Sitgreaves will have griddlecakes directly," the doctor added.

Clement eased himself to the clay on a slope that gave him a fine view. He settled his Sharps beside him—never did it leave his hands if he could help it—and watched idly, picking at his teeth with a stem of buffalo grass.

The doctor settled his portmanteau in one of the wall tents and then joined Clement. "We haven't provisions to last the whole trip. We were expecting thee to make meat—a buffalo now and then, Mister Clement."

"Don't like to be around buffler. Lots of Injuns stalking them and we'd get us into a jackpot. Naw. How come you to be without a weapon? You got some objection to makin' meat, too?"

"Our son—Junius—brought a rifle to hunt with. We lost him and the rifle."

"Lost him?"

"Killed by Blackfeet while shooting buffalo, Mister Clement. We've grieved, Abby and I, every day since."

That baffled Beau. "Youse took a hard lesson, but ya still ain't armed. Youse got money enough to buy a score o' rifles and revolvers at Benton. Youse taken a lesson and still—"

"We could have, I imagine. But we've set our trust in Divine Providence—and thee."

"Leavin' me to guard the hosses, leavin' me to fetch meat, leavin' me to keep from getting my hair—your hair—lifted. I should of charged double."

"None of us knows the first thing about hunting, Mister Clement. A rifle would have gained us nothing. And as for guarding the stock, why, we came to an agreement, I trust . . ."

"But this hyar's plumb crazy." Beau felt a rage rise in him. "Leavin' it to me. How'm I gonna get shut-eye? I got to watch all night for them thievin' red niggers."

"We are better armed than thee may suppose, sir.

And the Indians'll learn gentler ways in time. Thee ought not to see them in that light, but as brothers and sisters. Oh, we treasure our drays, and we know they're a temptation, but we'd rather track them back to their village—as Mister Skye did when we asked him—and make peace with them. We wish to establish something, and that is that we're friends.''

The doctor fixed him with such an amiable smile and such goodwill in those bright eyes of his, that all Beau could do was curse privately.

''I heerd Skye nearly cashed in, goin' into the village without youse owning a toadsticker.''

''It was a close thing,'' the doctor admitted. ''I'm sure it's why he decided to leave our service. I hope thee will also make that choice if thee can't abide by our terms.''

''Oh, I reckon I'll get youse through. Only ya got to obey me when things ain't going right. I got to hide youse.''

''We don't need hiding, Mister Clement. If thee encounter Blackfeet, bring them to us. We'll parley with them. Thee will translate, I trust. We're counting on thee for that.''

''I have griddlecakes for thee,'' said Abigail. Clement noted a stack of them steaming fragrantly on a camp table and several more browning on a black skillet over a well-made fire. She was a right attractive woman, slender and alive, and the knowledge confounded him. Edgily, he stood, dusted grass and dirt off his britches, and helped himself, wishing he'd had a squaw or two over the years.

They ate silently as dusk stained away the brightness of the day. He hadn't had griddlecakes like that for years, and he relished them. They finished, contented and filled, and slid into that sweetness of the evening when people draw close and share things barely spoken by day.

"We must seem strange to thee, Mister Clement," said the older one, Diogenes Fall.

"I reckon youse got your ways and I got mine."

"The Friends have no creed, you know. No clergymen, either. What we do is listen quietly, and in the deepness of the soul we try to hear the voice of God."

"Youse trying to get religion into me?"

"Nay," said Fall. "But we'd like thee to know of our dream. It's a poor world when no one cares about injustice or poverty, and no one lends a hand to someone in need, wouldn't thee say?"

Before Clement could respond, Fall pressed on. "Among the Friends around this fire, thee sees men and a woman who wish to give a voice to redmen when they are pushed aside, abused, robbed by unfeeling whites."

"Sounds plumb—" Beau was going to say *traitorous* but didn't.

"We see it as charity. We'll induce them to lay down their arms, plow and sow and reap, learn to listen to God. Doctor Sitgreaves here will bring advanced medicine to them—he's always been at the forefront. Admirable, wouldn't thee say?"

It didn't seem admirable at all to Beau Clement. In fact, they seemed crazy as loons.

"It's called love," said the other, Freeman Price.

Clement grunted. They weren't gonna weaken him with fancy talk. He could drive arrows into them all right here, if he was of a mind.

Chapter 22

Barnaby Skye knew he'd slept late into the morning. Through the smoke hole, the sky looked cobalt and the shadows on the lodge cover had retreated. Outside the thin membrane that shielded his family from the world he heard the bustle of engagés pressing robes into bales.

The Skye lodge smelled sweet. Victoria and Mary had moved it bodily from its former site, and now it stood farther back in the yard. They had cut a mountain of sagebrush and rubbed his robes with it to celebrate his return to them. They'd hung a great sachet of it from the lodgepoles, where its sharp fragrance pummeled everything within the lodge, including Mister Skye's sour-smelling flesh.

Often, after one of his drunks, he had himself a good sweat, Indian-style, in a sweat lodge of bent willows tied at the apex and covered loosely with robes. There he would sit naked, pouring water that Victoria supplied him over fire-heated rock until he could barely stand the blast of steam that opened his pores and sweated the poisons out. But he couldn't do that here, in Fort Benton.

He peered up from his robe, at peace with the world. He knew his women and Jawbone hated these times, that he disgusted them, that he burdened them and his clients whenever it happened. And yet he felt unrepentant. This was how he lived his bloody life, and they would bloody well get used to it. Still, having crawled out of the jug at last, he found himself enjoying the morning, the cool air, the scented lodge, and the patient love of his women. In a moment he would restore his friendship with Jawbone, who would bite him as a sign of displeasure and then permit himself to be groomed. It would end with him snorting and shrieking and playing and nipping and making an ass of himself. But Skye would not have a mannerly horse, and everything about his obnoxious roan was exactly as he wanted it.

His lovely ladies were out in the yard somewhere or at the mess tables. Here in the heart of Fort Benton, they didn't cook or gather wood, and had more leisure to visit with other women, mostly the wives of squawmen like himself. And they dallied for hours in the company store where they were privileged to wander behind the counter, examining every imaginable trade item, and running up a tab that made Skye groan. But they deserved it all and more, and their patience with him could not be repaid at any price.

They'd leave sometime today—it didn't matter when because they weren't shepherding clients. They'd ford the Missouri and head south toward Victoria's people and summer with them high in the foothills of Absaroka, where the mountain streams ran sweet and icy, and the grass grew thick, and buffler and deer multiplied. He loved that country of the Crows more than the country around Fort Laramie where he based himself for business reasons, and took every opportunity to linger there in the roots of the Beartooth Mountains.

They should leave at night, he thought, remembering that a large portion of the Blackfeet nation camped around the post these trading days. Plenty of Blackfeet warriors, such as his old enemy Moon Hides the Sun, would gladly scalp him and kill his women and destroy Jawbone if they could. Around the post a neutrality kept hostile tribes from falling upon each other, and a village of Cree—Blackfeet called them the Lying People—camped eastward of the post, unharmed by the larger villages of the Piegans and Bloods west of the post. He and his family were safe here—but a few miles away they wouldn't be. He did have one advantage: the villages were all located north of the Missouri, either close to the fort or back on fresh grass along the Teton River a few miles away. He and his family would be splashing south across the ford immediately in front of the post and into a flat wilderness punctuated by buttes.

"Mister Skye, ye old coot. Are ye up?"

That was Edwin Denig's voice. How quickly the fort got wind of everything, including the end of his drunk.

"Aye, more or less." Skye clambered out of his robes, clamped his battered top hat down, slid into his camp moccasins, and emerged into brilliant light, blinking.

Denig looked him over, wry amusement across his usually dour Scots face, and beckoned him toward his office. Skye followed, seeing nothing of his family. Inside, Denig poured him a cupful of anciently boiled stale coffee which the guide downed in a gulp.

"It's no business of mine, but your clients left yesterday afternoon with a guide who's always been a question mark."

"Clement."

"That's the one. A loner. Brings in robes and skins, trades a little. Possibly steals a lot. I tried to urge some caution on Doctor Sitgreaves, without effect. I'm not comfortable with it."

"Out of my hands, mate. We're heading south."

"Ye know anything about Clement?"

"I do. He trapped through the last years of the beaver. A loner. He partnered up a few times and always came into a post or a rendezvous alone, with a story about his partner going under. He never sent his partner's share back east to a widow or relatives, like most of the coons would. No one trusted him much and the part-nering stopped. And the beaver trade gave out. I didn't know he was still in the mountains."

"He is," said Denig. "Comes in here once in a while to trade a few robes—and pick up a few gewgaws. He makes his way by trading for robes, I guess. Always alone. But he seemed all-fired eager to latch onto the Quakers, and a lot of my engagés noticed him peering and poking around the wagon and heard him asking a lot of questions."

"Fixing to rob them, I'm afraid, mate."

"Or worse?" Denig let it hang in the air.

"Edwin, I am not engaged. We're on our way south. Sitgreaves, for all his gentleness, is a hard man who knows how the stick floats."

"And totally unarmed and unwilling to use arms to defend himself."

"I don't think we can change that, mate. If it worries you, send a brigade after him and let them keep an eye out."

Denig leaned back in his battered oak chair. "There's more, Mister Skye. We got word that a big party of Piegans, all warriors, took off a while ago, heading upriver."

Skye stared, saying nothing. Denig was working him toward something. But he wasn't going to do it. He was free and clear; the accounts with the Quakers were set-tled.

"Squawmen told us. Their wives talk some. Git the news. Git the village gossip. Also got wind of it at the trading window. About a dozen of them led by the old

Blood shaman, Walks at Night. Another in there was Diving Otter. Know him?''

Skye shook his head.

''Big burly warrior with plenty of coups. He had a toothache. Sitgreaves put him under and pulled the bad tooth. Scared the crowd half out of their wits, and old Walks at Night was muttering and rumbling. Then Sitgreaves tried to vaccinate for the pox, did it to a breed boy, and the whole bunch fled. Clement was watching.''

''What do you mean, put him under?''

''Anesthesia. Painkiller.''

''Never heard of it. If a sawbones is going to cut, you just drink spirits.''

''They put ye under now.''

Skye felt himself being sucked into a whirlpool, and resisted. ''Maybe they just want more doctoring, Edwin.''

''Maybe they want to kill a witch. A bad-medicine man. Or keep him from giving his medicine to the Flatheads. They know where he's going and what he's going to do for a lot of tribes. He told them often enough. And they don't like it.''

''They never harmed Father De Smet when he came through. In fact De Smet preached to every enemy the Blackfeet have.''

Denig shrugged. ''De Smet didn't put a warrior to sleep or steal pain from the warrior or steal his spirit or scratch the arm of anyone and rub a disease into the wound.''

''What're you saying, Edwin?''

''I'm remembering the Whitmans.''

Barnaby Skye lifted his hat and settled it again. Who could not remember the Whitmans? In 1836 Dr. Marcus Whitman and his lovely blond wife Narcissa had come west with the resupply to the rendezvous, along with another couple, Henry and Eliza Spalding. They were missionaries en route to the Oregon country on behalf of the Presbyterian and Congregational churches. The women were the first to cross the continent, and were a source of wonder and joy at the rendezvous, where mountain men suddenly turned decorous, even shy, in their presence. They were especially smitten by comely Narcissa, whose glory was a head of golden hair with auburn tints. Mountain men and tribesmen alike gaped. The two missionary couples continued to Fort Vancouver and enjoyed the hospitality of Hudson's Bay Company, and eventually each couple founded a mission farm, the Spaldings at Lapwai, and the Whitmans at Waiilatpu, near Fort Walla Walla.

There the Whitmans farmed, taught agriculture, supported the Cayuse Indians, taught their religious beliefs, adopted or raised several half-breed children, including the girls of Jim Bridger and Joe Meek, and helped destitute immigrants during the great migration to Oregon. But that huge migration and later a measles epidemic that killed a number of the vulnerable Cayuse who had no resistance to whiteman's diseases, turned the Cayuse people against Doctor Whitman and affectionate Narcissa. Doctor Whitman worked himself to exhaustion caring for ill red and whitemen, but a half-breed egged the Cayuse Indians into striking at the missionaries in 1847. They killed Doctor Whitman with hatchet blows to the head and shot Narcissa to death, along with others. Even now, in 1853, the horror of it reverberated through all whitemen in the west.

"I remember," said Skye. He felt trapped.

"Perhaps the fate of the Quakers is in your hands, Mister Skye."

"I don't want it to be," Skye said, knowing that it was, and that he would go, and that Victoria and Mary would probably wail.

Much to Mister Skye's surprise, Victoria and Mary didn't object. On the contrary, their faces lit up when he told them he wanted to shepherd the Quakers the rest of the way.

"We got to do it," said Victoria. "Quitting half-way—it's no good. Them Quakers are lambs. We got to keep the wolves away."

Mary nodded. "I don't like that Beauregard. I didn't trust him and I think maybe he's going to do something bad. Then we'd all feel like we didn't do what we could."

Skye nodded, wondering how they'd take the rest of the news: "Big party of Piegans and Bloods rode out this morning—upriver. Maybe a dozen, maybe more. Led by that medicine man, Walks at Night. And the one Sitgreaves doctored, Diving Otter."

Victoria paused, her gaze narrowing inward. "Medicine," she muttered.

That's all she said, but Mister Skye knew what was passing through her mind. Maybe Doctor Sitgreaves had done something to offend the spirits. Maybe he was a witch, making bad medicine. Maybe the Piegan shaman, Walks at Night, was right. Maybe they would kill a witch.

"Say it, Victoria."

"Sonofabitch!" she bellowed.

The doctor's little death—his anesthesia—had created a sensation among the tribesmen, and they had as many notions about it as there were tribesmen thinking about it. Denig had told him that some were calling it spirit-robbing. Others wanted to steal Sitgreaves's ether inhaler so they could have the power to put someone to sleep. Others were certain Doctor Sitgreaves had made an alliance with under-earth spirits, or under-water spirits since he had poured a liquid into a sponge. It didn't matter what they all thought. Probably the dozen or so Blackfeet that had trotted out that morning had a dozen different opinions about Sitgreaves, but they all shared one opinion of what to do with him.

"What do you think, Mister Skye?" Victoria's sharp questioning required a sharp answer.

"No spirit stuff, Victoria. He used a new way to deaden pain to take out a tooth. And he did it to make Diving Otter comfortable, keep him from suffering. His whole life—every day he has left—has been given to the Indians. All of you. Those people live only to help you, see that justice is done, bring you good things, teach you. His only satisfaction is the knowledge that he's helping. That's love."

Victoria grunted uncertainly. Then, "All right, goddam it."

Wordlessly, she and Mary began dismantling the lodge. Skye caught the mules and ponies and bridled them, then lowered packsaddles onto their scarred backs.

He rubbed down Jawbone, who screeched like a steamboat whistle and danced around so much in his tiny pen that Skye had trouble saddling him.

He reprovisioned at the trading room, buying paper cartridges for his Hall-North carbine, coffee beans, sugar, a new green flannel shirt. That, and the tab his women had run up, cost a hundred dollars. Fodder for Jawbone and the saddle and pack animals ran thirty more. A summer's income shot, and he still owed Bullock a lot. He completed the paperwork in Denig's office and had Denig debit Skye's account with Bullock at Fort Laramie. They'd have to live on almost nothing until they found another client next summer.

"Well, Barnaby. Ye'll be risking your neck again."

"We couldn't abandon them, mate."

"I wish the pilgrims wouldn't come out here, but the world's changing. We'll see a lot of them this summer, I hear. Scientists. Princes. The army. Governor Stevens is on his way."

"These are different, Edwin. They're not in it for themselves. Trying to protect the redmen."

"It's a mad mission."

"A noble one, mate. Coming all the way from the east to help redmen. Futile, I think. The tribes are doomed. When the buffler are gone—the tribes'll be gone. They won't start farming. It's all fading, the old world, the gone beaver world."

"I reckon the fur companies are hastening the day. We sell them the arms to shoot the buffalo to end their free life. I cain't say as I miss any sleep about it, though."

"The Friends do. They see it. That's why they didn't set up around a fur post. They figure Owen's is more of a farm, even if he trades for furs some. It takes something powerful strange to inspire them to push out here. I got so I admire it. Victoria and Mary admire it. Sitgreaves, there's a type of man I've never seen before, and I bloody well know a saint when I see one."

"If he lives," said Denig dourly. "They're crazy, you know."

"If he lives and we live," Skye replied. "I don't know why we're risking our necks."

"I talked ye into it."

"No you didn't, mate. None of us trust Clement. My women had been worrying it around."

"Will of God, maybe. Git ye gone, Mister Skye, before I do something foolish, like shake your hand."

Mister Skye stepped into blinding light.

They forded the Missouri in the afternoon, the sunlight on the pulsing river so intense it brought tears to their squinting eyes. The green water had not yet ebbed to its autumnal low, making passage hard for the burdened animals. Only Jawbone enjoyed the water, whickering and snorting, glad to be uncaged and going somewhere.

Blackfeet, mostly women and children, watched solemnly as their ancient enemies braved the river. The departure of the Skyes was well observed along a full mile of the flat. The ford angled toward the south bluff, which rose steeply from the river. A trail there led them uphill, and then down again into an ancient bed of the Missouri where Shonkin Creek now ran.

The Skyes paused, letting the sweet menace of the wild permeate them again after the hubbub of the fur post. On leaving a post they always paused, renewing their understanding of the silences of nature, the swift subtle rhythms. In the Shonkin bottoms they had entered the real world again. The post could as well have been a hundred miles away. They waited quietly, wishing to know if they had been followed. No one came.

They rode across the valley and up its south slope, leaving travois marks, signs of passage. When they reached the crest of the bluff they peered out upon a broken plain interrupted by odd buttes. A giant flat-topped one rose to the south. Far to the south, a raptor circled. Nothing else moved except the wind.

Carefully, they back-trailed to Shonkin Creek and turned westward in the water, splashing toward Armageddon. The travois poles bounced over wet rock, stirred up brown mud, and left no lasting mark.

They left the creek after half a mile of slippery passage, at a place where they could ascend the bluff and parallel the Missouri across a broken country laced with great coulees. The ruse might confuse followers for an hour or two—unless a solitary Piegan hunter had seen them. One could never know.

They spread out now, with Victoria scouting ahead as she usually did, the cat's whisker who saw before being seen. Somewhere up the Missouri and on its opposite bank, Clement was guiding the Friends along an old travois trail that had barely seen wagon wheels. And somewhere nearby, also on that far side, a party of Blackfeet stalked them.

Dusk caught the Skyes far southwest of Fort Benton, but they didn't stop except to water the animals and themselves. In speed lay the safety of the wilderness. A moonless dark night sagged over them, making travel harder, forcing them to retreat from bluffs and dead ends time and time again. Their passage took them through a land of giant shoulders and muscled necks, where the river cut its way around the Highwood Mountains to the south. But Barnaby, Victoria, and Mary Skye never paused, and when Dirk grew restless in her lap, Mary slipped a bit of jerky to the boy.

They cut across a great oxbow of the river, negotiating a mile-wide rocky headland, hurrying ever westward. Skye wanted to pull ahead of Clement and the Friends, ahead of the Blackfeet following them. But whenever they paused at some overlook to peer toward the inky bottoms of the river, they saw nothing. Whoever slept or rode or ran in the river valley lay veiled by darkness.

They rode again, up and down, snaking two miles to get ahead one mile, while the big dipper spilled around Polaris. At last they struck a valley with a sizable creek, and Skye thought it must be the Highwood, roiling out of the mountains. They cut downstream, avoiding dense copses of cottonwoods, aware that this was a favorite camping site of the Blackfeet. He didn't feel at all tired, and beneath him Jawbone seemed positively charged with energy after his long incarceration. But he knew that was an illusion. The stumbling push through the night had drained them, left them less alert. They'd come over thirty tortuous miles, and had to be far ahead of the Friends and their wagon.

They crept out upon the wooded flat at the confluence of the Highwood and the Missouri very late, just when a morning moon rose to illumine the far shore and the bluffs beyond, a prophet of the sun making straight the ways of the world. The river ran sullenly between shrouded banks. Far across the oily waters they heard horses whickering, and then two of their own responded, whinnying out into the void.

Chapter 23

Ever since leaving Fort Benton, Abigail Sitgreaves's spirits had sagged. For as long as the Skyes had shepherded them west she had buoyed herself along, even through the death of Junius. Something about the Skyes imbued her with courage.

She hadn't wanted to come on this trip; and giving up her comfortable home and sheltered life in Philadelphia had wrenched her spirit and made her lament the prison of wifehood. She'd never had any choice but to come, and so had tried to make the best of it. She'd gathered her courage and wits together each morning after yet another miserable night on a hard cot, either too cold or too hot or oppressed by insects or danger.

And yet, until now, the mere presence of Barnaby Skye—she hadn't even learned his given name until a few days before—had been reassuring, and his Indian wives had turned out to be a delight, sisters in hardship sharing their ways with her. But now the Friends were in the hands of Beauregard Clement, and she found him disturbing. Rough, yes, but something worse beneath.

She found him sinister without having any reason to think it.

She arose when the sky had barely begun to brighten. A morning moon glowed half empty over the shoulders of the prairie. She couldn't stand it inside her wall tent with William Penn even a moment more. He had become the source of her hardship and dread, and she wrestled with a deepening anger toward him, an anger that included the death of Junius—who wouldn't have died if . . . She put that thought aside, ashamed.

She had intended to walk in her robe down the coulee to the river bottoms and perform her ablutions there, but even as she stepped out into the chill air she saw Clement standing on the ridge above like a prehistoric reptile, that shining rifle of his cradled in his arms. Something in her shrank, and she withdrew into her tent and finished dressing, not wanting to go outside again until the others were up.

When she nerved herself to step out again she found him standing a few yards away, startlingly close, awaiting her presence.

"Better not go down there. Injuns passing in the night. Fresh tracks. I been scoutin' some."

She nodded slightly, not wishing to speak to him.

"We ain't goin' back down to the river. We're cuttin' straight for Sun River up here on the plains. About forty miles. We got to anyway to git around the great falls. We got to git moving. That's a piece for wagons, even with the draft horses."

She wanted to wash but couldn't without water. At least there was a copse of junipers where she could find some privacy.

She started for it but he stopped her. "When I say git moving, I mean git moving."

She wondered what he meant, and finally realized he meant for her to arouse the rest. "Thee are the captain," she said tartly, and continued on her way.

When she returned, the camp had been dismantled.

She realized they would be leaving without breakfast. There was no fire. Clement stood above, on the ridge, eyeing the universe nervously. They were waiting for her. William Penn sat in the carriage, unshaven, holding the lines to the big stallion; Artemus sat on the wagon bench, ready to drive. The others were choosing to walk, which they often did to begin the day with a constitutional. She slid to her seat in the buggy, feeling it creak beneath her.

Above, Clement mounted his shaggy horse, dragged a picket line of packhorses with him, and they were off, rolling out upon a vast, broken, dry land.

"That was fast," she said.

"He is worried about hostile Indians."

"Thee do not seem to be."

He fixed her with that sinless gaze and smiled. "What is there to fear? Our intentions are plain upon our faces and in our words."

The response didn't satisfy her now. Good intentions didn't ensure safety. Especially when dealing with people so different, so—primal. She glanced at him wearily, suddenly seeing not an adult at all but a perpetual child. He was like a five-year-old boy standing curbside, waving blithely at a conquering enemy army, unaware of the darkness around him. She sank heavily into the quilted seat feeling vulnerable and afraid.

"Thee are unhappy," he said.

She didn't reply.

"I wish he'd take us straight to them instead of sliding around them like this. Thee shouldn't regret anything, Abby. We will renew the world, the two of us. Let thy light shine and banish thy melancholy, for it offends Providence."

She took it for a rebuke. She found him insensitive, and closed her eyes as they drove westward into a blooming morning. The horizons slid some unfathomable distance away and a frightening emptiness engulfed them, making her desperate for the safe, familiar world of Philadelphia. Or even the fathomable world of Fort Benton. For the first time in her life she found herself disliking William Penn. Or at least admitting to something within her soul she'd never dared examine before.

"Please say nothing more." Her response startled herself more than it startled William Penn.

He acquiesced, although even his silence made her feel guilty. He peered eagerly about him, exclaiming at every sight, every circling hawk, every bounding white-rumped antelope, every vista opening upon a sharply defined horizon seen through air without smoke or haze.

The sun burnt down, and she drew her bonnet forward against the glare. The carriage creaked, the wheels hissed over virgin clay, the iron rims scything sagebrush. The horse sweat, foamed about the tail, and soured the air, listlessly dragging its burden even farther from her home. And with each step she felt less safe, and grew more distressed, even angry, with William Penn Sitgreaves. She'd married a child: It came upon her as she sat beside him. An innocent. A fool who'd subject a woman to brutal danger, discomfort, loss of privacy, terrible food she could barely choke down, and—the things redmen and whitemen did to women when there was nothing, nothing, to stop them.

And for what? A dream she'd never shared. He'd taken her for granted. Where had his love fled? He'd never asked her if she'd wanted to come here. He'd simply presumed she did. He'd never thought she might not; never offered her the option of staying in Philadelphia; never recognized she might have feelings about this trip, have a will of her own. She realized, suddenly, that his love for her was conditional; she had to be his servant, his helpmeet, his yielding companion. What if she resisted? What if she demanded to go back to Fort Benton and the next keelboat or steamboat home? What if she insisted on it? Would he love her—truly love her as a separate person, not just a part of himself, if she did?

Sadly, she knew the answer. Her child-man would not understand, and would be hurt and astonished that his own wife might not share his grand dream of healing the world.

Bitterly she watched the desert wastes unfold their emptiness. It was as if this sudden burst of insight on this particular empty prairie had severed the two of them. A prairie divorce, immutable, unchangeable, for eternity. The man beside her had become a stranger. The creed that had shaped her from childhood had failed her: it had become her prison. Worse, she didn't trust any of it. It seemed as treacherous to her soul as these empty plains were to her body.

Around noon, Beauregard Clement steered sharply south and led them into a surprising gash in the prairie none of them had suspected was there. One moment they had been toiling across dusty flats, the wheels of their carriage and wagon churning up powdered clay and spitting it at the sun; the next moment they reached the lip of a valley where a mythic plow had cut a furrow into the skin of the world, and they descended down a steep slope that pushed the carriage and wagon into dray, and onto a narrow flat that wound between tawny bluffs. At its head a cold spring flowed lustily, and around the spring grew majestic willows and cotton-woods, providing shade.

"I reckon youse can rest hyar. Water them plow horses and stay cool for a while," he said.

Gratefully, they slaked their own thirst with the slightly alkaline water, and settled into the thick grass. Innumerable deer and antelope had come here, leaving signs of their visits in the wet clay around the spring-fed pool. But they saw no moccasin prints.

Clement stared at them fiercely, studying them as if to memorize their faces. "I'm going to scout around some," he said. "I've a notion they's Injuns around. Youse wait hyar. Don't move for nothin'. Stay hid. Ain't a soul gonna see youse down hyar if youse mind to stay put.''

''Thee are the captain,'' said William Penn.

''Bug's Boys around.''

''If thee finds them, bring them to us, Mister Clement. We wish to make our purposes known to them.''

Clement grunted. ''I'll decide that.''

''Thee will not embarrass us, I trust, Mister Clement.''

Clement glared, and then rode down the cleft in the prairie, which probably debouched into the Missouri many miles away.

She watched him go, leading his two packhorses, until he rounded a bend and vanished. Something tugged at her, tickling her mind but not quite revealing itself.

''William Penn, I don't like him.''

He smiled. ''Enjoy this Eden, Abby. We've a haven here and a place to restore ourselves and our horses. We must be getting close to the great falls of the Missouri.''

''He took his packhorses with him! He's not coming back,'' she said, an unreasoning fear lancing her.

''What of it? Thee should rest, or find us a bite to eat.''

Fear swept through her, followed by anger. ''I am not your slave,'' she retorted, deliberately avoiding the reverential Friends way of addressing each other.

''Let us have a Meeting,'' he replied.

''Let's leave right now, William Penn. Right now! We don't need him. He's going to hurt us, I just know it.''

He found her hand and tugged her toward the others, like a dog on a leash, she thought. She pulled free and fled through the canopied shade, away from the spring, away from the Friends, away from her terror.

It was only a matter of time before that bunch of red devils backtracked, picking up the wheel sign they'd lost, and came a-howlin'. But Beau wanted to know how much time. He rode down the gulch half a mile, his new Sharps across his lap, and then picketed his packhorses in some brush. He reined his good saddler up the steep bluff, feeling the animal claw clay, and then out upon the prairie again, his destination a hog-back a quarter of a mile distant that would give him a view.

A few minutes later he dismounted just under its crest and crabbed up the last yards until he could peer out upon their back trail, the indelible mark of wagons. From his kit he extracted a prized possession, a pow-erful spyglass he'd stolen, and with this he scanned the country clear back toward Fort Benton. He couldn't see the fort but he could see the great bottoms where it sat in the distance.

Then he focused on a faint blur of dust a few miles off, the circle of prairie in his lens bobbing until the glass picked up the rhythmic trot of horses and riders, twelve or fifteen. He didn't bother to count. The red devils were five or six miles back. He had an hour at most. It irked him. He didn't want to risk anything so close to Fort Benton, but now he was being pushed into it. Still, he thought, it might just work out fine. He could pin it all on the Piegans.

He stumbled down the slope to his horse, clambered up as it sidled away from him, and raced back toward the pukes. The more he thought about the approaching Piegans—or whoever they were—the more he liked the whole deal. He hit the bottoms and turned the horse back toward the spring, kicking it into a jarring gallop. He rarely galloped the horse, having bought it for its fast walk.

He found the pukes lounging in the grass, except for the woman. She'd gone somewhere. It didn't matter.

"You," he said to the boy. "Git the harness off them Percherons and bridle them."

Artemus stared, then clambered to his feet. Beau watched him go.

"The rest of youse. Git your bags. Valises. Trunks, Git!"

Doctor Sitgreaves stood up. "Perhaps thee should tell us what thee are about, Mister Clement."

"Just do it."

But the doctor wouldn't be hurried. "Have we guests coming? Shall we get our gifts and tobacco?"

"Just do it." Beau's voice cut through the resistance, and he watched these puke Quakers begin to dig their things out of the wagon. Let them get their own bags out. It'd save time. Whatever they had worth having, it'd be in those bags, he knew. He'd poked and probed around the wagon enough to know that it contained nothing he cared about. It'd be in the bags: coin, greenbacks, letters of credit. Not jewelry. These here pukes didn't have a bit of it. He cursed softly while Sitgreaves, Price, and Fall slowly poked around, lifting pieces out.

Too slowly. He slid his hand down to the old Dragoon at his hip and lifted the heavy revolver. "You. Sitgreaves."

William Penn turned and stared into the bore of the weapon, his face spasming slightly. Then Fall and Price caught on as well.

"Thee disappoints me, Mister Clement."

"Shut up. One more word and—I'll shoot. Take off your frock coat."

Slowly, the doctor pulled his black coat off, an odd sadness in his bright eyes.

"Toss it slow and easy."

The doctor did, letting it land near Beau's feet.

"Empty your pockets," Beau said as he dug swiftly through the frock coat, finding the wallet in a breast pocket.

Carefully, Sitgreaves emptied his pockets. They didn't contain much. A penknife, a few coins.

The boy had figured it out and was edging away.

"Youse. Git here." Beau lifted the bore of the revolver and aimed straight at the boy's chest. Artemus hesitated. It was a long shot.

"Thee must obey," said Sitgreaves tautly.

Artemus nodded and walked slowly forward, straight into the bore of the revolver.

"Take off them boots. You. You too, Sitgreaves."

Slowly they both settled to the ground and began unlacing the boots. Beau waved the other two away from the valises.

"Lie down, and take off them shoes."

Both stared at him. He lifted the revolver and pointed it squarely at Fall. The man muttered and wilted. Nothing but sheep, all of them Quakers, he thought. Both of them eased into the grass and began unhooking and unlacing.

Beau darted toward the valises and turned them upside down, checking swiftly for false bottoms and hidden compartments. He found a sheaf of banknotes in one. Nothing in the rest. Just clothing. Not a thing he wanted. It didn't matter. The real wealth of this outfit grazed on a picket line.

He ransacked every bag, tossing clothing out, a few books, junk. It didn't matter. Gold he was after, and by now he knew Sitgreaves hadn't brought any. He'd used letters of credit on his bank. He paged through a book, something in a strange language, and pitched it into the pond.

"Memento mori," muttered Fall.

"What's that mean?"

"Remember that you must die."

"Shut up."

He felt like killing the old fool. But he didn't. He didn't want bullet holes in them. Let arrows and war clubs and scalping knives get the blame. He collected shoes, tossing them into the pond, where they spashed and sank, sending ripples outward. Time was wasting.

"Where's the woman?"

"Surely thee will not—"

"Shut up. I ask a question and youse answer."

"She—went for a walk."

He peered sharply about, not seeing her. He didn't have time to find her.

He sheathed his Dragoon Colt and trotted to his saddle horse to get the bow and quiver. Then he realized they were on his packhorse. He stopped, surveyed them all. He could make it look like Indian work anyway with his hatchet. Or he could shoot them. Or he could leave. Every one of them pukes would be tied to a tree in an hour or two, and the dying would go slow. That'd be best, if it happened. If Sitgreaves didn't talk his way out of it with that golden tongue of his. But Sitgreaves knew not a word of Blackfeet.

Beau didn't like it, leaving witnesses behind. He never did that. On the other hand, he'd spent a half hour already and needed another half hour to get clear of the Piegans.

"Pukes," he said, swinging up on the saddler. "Goddam pukes, nigger-loving pukes."

They stared. He grinned at the barefoot bunch. "This ain't nothing compared to what's coming," he yelled.

He rode toward the picketed Percherons, pulled up the picket pins, and led them off. They tugged on their lines, not wanting to move so fast, and that annoyed him. He yanked savagely and felt them yield. What he didn't need now was some slow horses fighting him every step. He had to get them to the river and swim them across before the red niggers caught him.

Not that they would, he thought. They didn't come after the pukes for that. He grinned suddenly. Naw, they wouldn't come after him, not with a bunch of bad-medicine barefoot pukes to torture all day and all night.

He spotted the woman hiding back in the brush. Puke woman didn't even know how to flatten herself to the ground.

"Puke," he said to her. She tempted him, but he

ignored the temptation. The Piegans'd fix her, too. She was crying. ''You ain't seen nothing yet,'' he said.

He trotted around a bend, the Percherons lumbering behind him, faster now. At the place where he'd stashed his packhorses he swiftly strung the horses onto two picket lines. He'd whip them if he had to. He peered irritably at the ridges, knowing he'd be long gone, across the wide Missouri before the Piegans showed up.

It'd been the easiest one he'd ever tried. Not a weapon to stop him. But not perfect, leaving witnesses for the Injuns to kill off. He debated coming back in the middle of the night, just to make sure the Piegans were having fun with the pukes. He was good at loosing arrows at people around a campfire.

Chapter 24

Numbly they watched Beau Clement vanish around a bend in the coulee, leading the Percherons. Robbed and abandoned. Doctor Sitgreaves surveyed the wreckage, wondering what to do next.

Freeman Price turned on Diogenes Fall. "Divine Light, was it? Clement the one? Thee wouldn't know the Divine Light if it blinded thee."

"It's all ordained! We must be tested," Fall said. "Thee lack understanding."

"Thee insisted on Clement," Price continued. "All the rest of us saw the true light. Thee spoke thy own will."

"Take that back, Price."

"Now what're we going to do? Stuck here! Thee got us into this, and thee can get us out." Freeman Price glared.

It appalled Doctor Sitgreaves, this un-Friendly conduct. Bickering. Blame. "This is no time for that," he said. "Put things in order, and we'll seek guidance after that."

Angrily, the Friends gathered tumbled clothing and sorted it. In a few moments everything had been restored to the proper valise or trunk and returned to the wagon. As they worked, the doctor considered matters. Except for the Percherons and some cash, they were in good shape. The farm implements, the seed, the medical and surgical paraphernalia, their clothing—all of it remained. Clement hadn't touched the important things. All they needed was horses or mules, or even oxen. And that wouldn't be challenging with Fort Benton a day or two back.

Privately he raged at Diogenes Fall. Arrogant fool. Confusing his own pettifogging notions with the Divine Light. The overeducated idiot had been dictating to them all and calling it Providence. The doctor resolved to put a stop to it: this enterprise was his own; his funds underwrote it; his medicine would cement relations with the tribes. Everything, from purchasing fares on the steamboat to outfitting them all, had been his own doing. He decided they'd have to ignore the old fool in Meeting. One robbery, one Clement, was all they could stand. One Fall too, he added maliciously.

Abby returned, something malevolent in her face. "Now we'll go back," she said.

"Nay, Abby. We'll buy horses at Fort Benton and go on."

"Not with me."

"Thee are coming."

"I'm going back. Thee never asked me whether I wished to come. Now I'll tell thee."

"It was the Inner Light telling us to come!"

"Telling thee to come, not me."

"Abby, we'll discuss this at some other time," he said, dismayed at this outburst.

"No, we'll discuss it now. I'm going back to Philadelphia. Thee can do whatever thee wish."

"But thee are my wife. I—urge thee to remember it."

"Urge all thee want. The next keelboat downriver I'll be on."

"But what—are thee well, Abby?"

"My eyes are opened. I see thee."

"Let us have a Meeting, Abby. We'll all find the comfort we seek."

"I've had my own Meeting, thank thee. I'm not thy handmaid, not thy servant, not thy humble wife who does what she's told and goes where she must."

"But—Abby!" William Penn Sitgreaves was appalled. "Thee are resisting everything the Friends—"

"Explain it to Lucretia Mott. See if she agrees. Besides, the Friends have no creed. Thee has said it a thousand times."

"Lucretia? What has she to do with this?"

"Emancipation! Of women! From men!"

"Emancipation?"

"Abolition. Of female slavery. Did thee ever ask me if I wished to come? Have I a will? Have I wishes? Thee never thought of it. I'm walking back to Fort Benton right now and employ the Skyes to take me back."

"With what?"

"With this wedding ring."

He sighed. Female difficulties. "I'll go with thee. The rest can guard our possessions."

"Guard! With what?"

From beside the wagon, Diogenes Fall broke in: "Divine Providence. The possession of Friends. *Magna est veritas, et prevalebit.*"

"Thee are a learned fool," she said, and stalked off.

Hastily, William Penn Sitgreaves ran after her and caught up as she labored up the slope. He was astonished by all this, but certain it would pass. Abby had her little moods. Often in the past, now that he thought about it, he'd sensed a mocking tone just beneath the Friends civility. Lucretia Mott had obviously poisoned her mind, and he'd have to deal with the poisons.

"I can't prevent thee from following, but I don't wish to talk with thee," she said.

"Bickering," he said by way of reproach. "And we've come to set an example for others."

"I'll bicker if I choose."

They reached the crest of the bluff and peered out upon the prairies again—and something else. Riding toward them, straight along the wagon tracks, was a party of Indians. They came at a fast walk, bronzed tribesmen of a sort he couldn't determine, but they carried fearsome weapons, feather-bedecked lances, war clubs, bows with arrows nocked in them. A terror swept him, a sense of his own impending doom.

"Oh!" she cried. "It's too late! William Penn, they'll kill us. And when I die, blame yourself. Thee've killed Junius and now me. And Artemus. Thy own flesh and blood." She sobbed then.

Rattled beyond thought, he turned to run toward the wagon and suddenly realized they had no place to hide. He grabbed her, intending to pull her to him, but she shrieked at him, beat on his chest, and yanked free.

"Let me die emancipated!" she hissed.

On they came, looming larger, their ululating voices, their cruel faces visible to William Penn, their war-trained corded bodies, their wild-eyed ponies, their coup feathers, their deadly engines of death. He felt his gorge rise, knowing the yawning grave, knowing . . .

They yanked their ponies to a halt, ten, fifteen, in a semicircle around them, boiling up dust and terror in the shadowless light. *Diving Otter!* The one whose tooth he'd pulled stood in his stirrups, mocking at the doctor. And the other one, the shaman, half-concealed in a buffalo-horn headdress, a huge medicine bundle bounding off his scrawny chest. And others he'd seen in the crowd when he'd anesthetized Diving Otter.

Then he understood. He'd offended their medicine somehow. He'd violated some taboo. He'd put Diving Otter to sleep, the blackest magic. They would kill him to purify the People. He'd read enough about these Plains tribes to know that. They lived by dream and spirit, finding helpers and enemies in animals, even in stones and hills. They'd kill him, butcher them all. Kill the Friends who'd come to help them, heal them, be their voice among whitemen. Kill him! The thought of his own imminent death galvanized something inside of him. He felt an odd ripple of excitement, almost exhilaration.

They laughed cruelly, spoke in a tongue he didn't understand, pointed fingers at them, and finally drove the doctor and his wife before them down the bluff and into the green vale below. Behind him, a dozen lances probed, their points deadly and sinister, forcing them toward the wagon and carriage where Artemus gaped, and Fall and Price stumbled backward, their gaze upon the cruel lances and arrows.

William Penn waited for the end. Everything left him, his wits, his intelligence, and he stood meekly. Abby wept. Her accusations burned in him; he'd brought his own family and himself to this. And his friends as well.

The Blackfeet leapt lithely from their ponies and tied them to the willows and cottonwoods. They herded all the Friends to a place in the grass and motioned for them to sit there. Price looked ashen. Fall looked outraged. Artemus looked sullen. The doctor wondered if prayer might help. But he was too rattled to pray, and he was doomed anyway. And he suddenly doubted whether God existed.

Still they lived, second by second. He wished wildly that Clement would return and rescue them. And then he realized, with a dark flash of insight, that Clement knew these warriors were coming; he had robbed them and fled, knowing what these warriors were going to do. The thought was unbearable to William Penn.

"Morituri te salutamus," Fall snarled.

"Oh, shut up," Abby snapped. "What does that mean?"

Fall laughed wickedly. "We, about to die, salute thee."

The warriors spread out. One stayed up on the bluffs, a vedette. The rest congregated around the wagon while Diving Otter clambered inside and began pawing through trunks and valises. Gradually, he passed certain items out, black leather cases, a small portable cabinet full of little drawers—and Doctor Sitgreaves realized Diving Otter was pulling out the entire surgery, everything he'd seen at the time he'd come to have his tooth extracted.

Bad-medicine things, then. All these would be cast in a heap and tabooed. They'd shake rattles at them, jangle hawk bells, beat drums, dance around them, and destroy them all.

Sure enough. Gently, the warriors carried his surgical case to a place in the grass. Then his medicine chest, full of herbs, roots, chemicals, acids, powders, extracts—things gathered from all over the world to bring to the Bitterroot Valley. Then came the case full of carboys, the bag with his instruments, forceps, catheters, lancets, catgut, needles, scalpels. Then came the porcelain flask filled with ether he had made from sulfuric acid and alcohol. And the black case that protected and pinioned the ether inhaler. As if to signal the importance of these, Diving Otter himself carried them toward the pile, clinging to them as if they were the sacraments of a heathen god.

Sitgreaves wished he could talk, say something, anything. "Do thee speak English?" he croaked.

They turned, stared, laughed. Nothing. Why had he been so slow to learn the sign language? He might bargain, make peace with his fingers and hands. But he hadn't. And not a soul among the savages could understand him.

Sure enough, the tribesmen settled themselves into a circle, sitting cross-legged in the grass. Two of them produced drums, actually rawhide stretched taut over wooden hoops. and began a slow, murderous heartbeat. It was coming, he knew; they'd make medicine to destroy the bad-medicine things heaped there—and then kill them all.

The shaman—Walks at Night, Sitgreaves remembered—stood solemnly and motioned the doctor forward. William Penn Sitgreaves stood, shakily, and trembled forward toward his execution.

A great weariness suffused Mister Skye as they stood on the timbered bank of the Missouri, trying to fathom what lay across the water. His body had not yet sweated away the poisons of his long drunk, and now they taxed him. A sleepless night driving across rough terrain hadn't helped either.

He turned to Victoria. "You got any notions about those horses?"

"Siksika."

"Might have been Quaker horses."

"We came too far. They aren't this far yet."

"Piegans. I reckon we're well upstream from Sitgreaves, and the Piegans must be, too. Maybe they're just out hunting."

"Haw," she said.

"Want to cross? We still got darkness for cover."

She shook her head. He was too tired to debate the matter, and deferred to her. Wordlessly, she steered her little mare toward a grassy area back from the river and dismounted. Skye and Mary followed. She intended to rest and to give the horses a brief respite as well. Not a bad idea, he thought, sliding wearily off Jawbone. They wouldn't cross now; they'd wait for bright sunlight to show them what was across the water.

He pulled his pad saddle off Jawbone and roughed up the wet hair with his fingers. The evil horse snorted and butted him, and then turned to eating. Mosquitoes swarmed around them and the horses, but he felt too tired to slap them off.

His son had turned crabby after the sleepless night, fussing and whimpering. Hunger probably. Mosquitoes certainly. Crossly, Mary washed Dirk's face and gave him jerky to chew on.

"Mister Skye," she said softly. "I want to go away from here. Why do we do this?"

"Denig asked me."

"We got no business with the Friends anymore."

"Hate to see them hurt."

"We're in Siksika lands. They kill us fast. Me and Dirk. You and Victoria and Jawbone. I don't like it here. Let's go south, back to Absaroka. Or back to my people."

Victoria listened, reading his thoughts as she always did. He glanced at her and Mary and saw two women as tired as he, and a sullen child. They were afraid; they all were afraid, prowling this land of their enemies. They'd worked hard for the Friends, making meat, scouting, cooking. He owed his wives something, happy times with their people, Crows and Snakes. Still . . .

Somewhere across the river were some vulnerable people depending on an old mountaineer Skye thought might be a cutthroat; and a party of Blackfeet was prowling around. He peered across to the far bank, obscure in the half-light, not knowing what to do. He hated times like this.

"We're all tired," he said. He lifted his top hat and ran stubby fingers through his matted hair. Mary peered at him, her brown eyes pleading. Victoria's agate eyes watched alertly. They deferred to him usually—it was Indian custom—but not always.

"I promised Denig." He had always kept his word.

Still they stared. His women had been as tired as this many times, and had suffered ordeals beyond description—but always for a good reason, for the sake of his clients or their own safety. But this time they had no reason. Except a promise.

"You stay here. Back from the river. Out of sight.

Maybe back up the creek a piece.'' They knew what he was about to say, and frowned. ''I'll cross and do some prowling. I'm thinkin' that if I can get a look at the camp, and if the Friends are all right, and Clement's taking care, and the Piegans aren't around, then we'll cut south. I figure that's what I have to do to keep my word to Denig.''

''Maybe the Piegans kill you. All alone. Tired as hell, goddam booze in you still.''

''Take care of my boy.''

''We maybe never see you again.''

That was the thing that hung over them year after year, the ace of spades waiting to trump them. Impulsively he hugged the old woman and felt her tears wet his shirt. He hugged Mary, who squeezed fiercely. And then he lifted Dirk up and clamped him. The boy squirmed and fussed.

He saddled Jawbone again, checked his possibles, his paper cartridges for the carbine, the revolver at his waist. Jawbone snorted, whirled his head back, and nipped Skye hard across the forearm. Skye punched back, and the horse squealed.

He headed for the river, not looking back because he couldn't manage to. The bluffs above blossomed gold as the dawn sun smote them, but the bottoms remained obscure. Jawbone clacked his teeth and minced down into the turbulent water, taking tentative steps forward while the water socked and pummeled his legs and then his belly. The bottom fell out from the far-side channel, and water swallowed Jawbone. It boiled up into Skye's lap. The horse almost overturned but then its rhythmic swimming took hold and a moment later it struck hard bottom on the other side of the channel. After a few minutes of travel across mucky shallows, Jawbone lunged up a grassy bank and shook violently, spraying water everywhere.

Skye reined the horse to a stop, letting river water

sluice away while he listened and watched, absorbing the place and its dangers. A half hour earlier they'd heard horses over here but now he found nothing.

He steered Jawbone downstream, toward where the Friends must be, zigzagging first to see whether he could cut any wagon tracks. He found none. But half a mile downstream he found a campsite, a place riddled with the prints of unshod hooves. There'd been no fire, but he made out places where Indians had slept. Around fifteen. They'd left not long ago, backtracking downstream. The Piegans. They'd overshot in the dark, missed Clement and the Friends, and were now hunting the wheel tracks. It alarmed him. There wasn't much he could do alone against a party that large.

He followed cautiously, not knowing how far ahead the Piegans were or what sort of mood they were in. He pulled his Hall-North from its saddle sheath and carried it in his lap, steering Jawbone with his knees. Thus he proceeded through a moody silence, hearing no birds because of the passage of the Piegans ahead. Maybe they were returning to Fort Benton but he doubted it.

The bottoms seemed preternaturally quiet, the way nature is when predators prowl, and it made him jumpy. He arrived at a deep vee in the bluffs where some large coulee debouched, and crossed a dry watercourse. Still no wagon tracks.

He paused there, trying to make his weary mind work. If the Piegans had missed the Friends in the night, it was likely that Clement had left the Missouri bottoms somewhere downstream and topped out on the prairie.

Wearily, he turned Jawbone up the dry coulee, northward he judged. He'd top out a couple of miles ahead and then see if he could cut some wagon tracks up there. Thus he proceeded through the morning, surprised that the coulee continued beyond the bluffs, a shallow trough piercing into the prairie. Now and then he rode up to its rim and squinted out upon a sea of brown grass seeing nothing.

Then, a few miles further, he saw a rolling dust cloud in the east.

Chapter 25

Nothing in all of Doctor Sitgreaves's gentle life had prepared him for this terror. He felt as helpless as a twig in a waterfall. The very Indians he'd come to help now sat in a circle staring at him, and God only knew what sort of bloody savagery lay behind their bright eyes Everything he'd read—and doubted back in the genteel east—tormented him now, especially their fiendish skill at torturing their victims.

Was this to be the end? Would they die in agony, lashed to some tree? Would Abby be subject to that, and more? Would his last living son, Artemus, be cruelly butchered, mutilated, scalped? A sudden grief shook him. He sobbed. These brutes were simply playing with the Friends, as a cat toys with a mouse.

That frightful shaman stood in the center of the savages, sinister in his barbarous regalia, staring imperiously at the doctor. Walks at Night opened the case containing the ether inhaler, and withdrew the instrument. Reverently, the shaman lifted the glass-bowled pipe high, arching his back, crying to something above.

Then he addressed the earth beneath him in his nasal voice, and then he offered the pipe in each of the cardinal directions, chanting something or other.

The ritual resembled the peace-pipe ceremony, but it didn't matter. This time, these Piegans were exorcising the witch-medicine of the doctor. The thought set Sitgreaves's heart to rattling unbearably fast. He was the witch.

Then the shaman beckoned to Sitgreaves, who found himself shambling forward. The shaman pointed at the glass dome and at the flask of ether. The doctor hesitated. The shaman jabbed a finger at him, and stroked the pipe reverently. They wanted him to load the apparatus.

Trembling, almost unable to do what was required, he removed the stopper from the flask, smelling at once the heady tang of the volatile ether; then he removed the sponge from the glass bowl of the inhaler and poured a generous amount of the fluid into the sponge. Then he stuffed the sponge back into its bowl, capped it with the vented stopper, and stopped up his flask of ether as well.

The shaman took the pipe reverently, lifted it again to the heavens as if offering a gift, and handed it to Doctor Sitgreaves's erstwhile patient, Diving Otter—the only one among them who'd breathed in the ether. The warrior handled the pipe as if he were holding a sacramental wafer—and sucked mightily, exhaled and sucked again, and a third time. He smiled and passed the pipe to the savage on his left, who repeated the ritual.

Diving Otter giggled. The one next to him completed the ritual, and giggled. Doctor Sitgreaves gaped. Thus the pipe went the round, ending at last with the shaman, who solemnly sucked and laughed, just like the rest. Gently, he handed the ether apparatus to Sitgreaves and beckoned him to recharge it, which the doctor hastily did, adding an extra dollop for good measure. Could it be? He handed it to Diving Otter, who chortled and emitted peculiar savage grunts. The warrior sucked mightily, once, twice, thrice, and keeled over, a beatific smile on his face. The next one tenderly rescued the apparatus, and rendered himself insensible. And thus it went around the circle, each Piegan whickering and grunting and giggling himself into oblivion, the shaman last. He whirled and capsized, nearly breaking the fragile device, but the doctor snatched it from him just as Walks at Night crashed to earth and lay inert.

Doctor Sitgreaves wept. And laughed. Before him, like a circle of corpses, lay stupefied Piegans. It reminded him suddenly of something he'd come across in his medical reading. Long before medicine had made use of sulfuric ether as an anesthetic, its properties were well known. Young rakes and ladies in the larger cities had entertained themselves with ether-sniffing parties, marked by hilarity and ultimate insensibility. Like nitrous oxide, or laughing gas, which Humphry Davy had discovered in 1795, ether induced giddy good humor before it stupefied.

Was this what these warriors wanted? Had Diving Otter described something so titillating that the rest had to try it? It had to be something like that. Before him, a gaggle of warriors sprawled like corpses, each an eager participant in a new religion. Nearby, that old fool Diogenes Fall tittered nervously. Doctor Sitgreaves scarcely saw the humor in it; he'd been too near death to enjoy this.

An awful thought occurred to him: what if one or another of these Piegans overdosed himself—and died? Anxiously, he surveyed them all, one by one, looking for the vital signs. Not satisfied, he began to check pulses, crawling from one to another half hysterically. They all lived.

He stood at last, feeling some semblance of calm. His pulse had settled down. He peered about the peaceful grove. Indian ponies dozed on their tethers. Up on the crest of a far ridge, the Piegan vedette still patrolled. Not that his warnings could arouse the slumbering warriors, the doctor thought. It'd be a while, a half hour maybe, before any of them stirred. He felt the last of his terror slide away as he discovered himself to be safe, at least for the moment. Was it only a respite, a prelude to a slaughter, once the Piegans revived? Were these the noble red heathen he'd come west to defend, to doctor, to teach?

The rest of the Friends stirred, peering about in amazement, as if rescued from the guillotine just as the terrible blade rumbled down.

"Cogito, ergo sum," said Fall wryly.

Abby's weeping abated. She stood, dusted off her gray skirts, and peered at the assorted open-mouthed bodies. The rest stirred, each too shaken to say anything or find any amusement in the turn of events. Ether had slain the attacking army.

Abby stared sharply at them all and walked back toward the slope, her intention plain.

"Abby! Where are thee going?" the doctor cried.

"Philadelphia."

"But Abigail. We've escaped. We're whole. We're justified. We're out of harm's way. Divine Providence has smiled! Everything we believe in is proven here, now! See these savages, rendered harmless! We've made friends! We've kept the commandment!"

She turned and met his gaze with her own. "Divine Providence, is it! Is it the Divine Will that these creatures should be rendered senseless? Is that Providence? Drunk, senseless, stupefied on ether? Give me none of your scandalous religion, William Penn Sitgreaves. Give me none of it!"

He gaped at her, unable to grasp that she had rejected the beliefs that had nurtured her. "Abby! We're safe now!" he cried, plaintively.

"I'm sick of being vulnerable. Give me strong men with guns in this wilderness. We've a right to defend our persons by any means. A duty! I'm sick of this. I'm sick of terror. What hope have thee, with fourteen stupefied Blackfeet who may kill us all when they wake up? With the horses stolen? With our good Mister Skye and his wives gone—because your stupid demands drove them off? What are thee going to do, William Penn—turn thyself into a guide and take us through trackless wastes none of us knows, past violent Indians who never heard of the Ten Commandments?"

Her withering contempt reached him, and he had no answer to most of it. "I'll go with thee to Fort Benton. We'll find a guide and draft animals."

"Thee'll find a guide and draft animals. I won't. I'm going down the river."

Artemus said, "I'm going with her. Before the whole Sitgreaves family is killed."

"But son—thee are a part of this great work."

"I wasn't asked."

"But the Inner Light—"

"I wasn't asked. Thee never bothered. It was all thy purpose, thy vision, not mine."

"But Artemus . . . it's a long walk to Fort Benton."

"It's the way to Philadelphia. I'll escort Mother there."

"Thee must seek guidance first—"

But Artemus joined Abby, and they toiled up the slope of the coulee. Sitgreaves watched them vanish over the lip of the bluff, engulfed by a helplessness he'd rarely known. His world was falling apart: his family, his faith, his mission, his sense of who he was. Even his deepest belief. Was he a Friend? And around the circle of sleeping Piegans, some began thrashing and twisting, a sign that they would soon revive—and decide the fate of the remaining Friends. Doctor Sitgreaves strode to the middle of the circle, where the inhaler lay along with the flask, and restored them to their cases, and to the wagon. Then he waited.

* * *

Through all of Barnaby Skye's years in the mountains, the sight he was witnessing never failed to send a fear coiling through him. The drifting dust concealed the number of fast-moving riders but not their purposeful trajectory toward a known object. Scores of his trapping friends had been caught by such parties, alone and beyond help, beyond even the comfort of knowing their death would be noted and reported back east. No single man, not even equipped as he was with a new breechloader, could hope to confront a party of warriors and live to tell about it. The sole option was escape. That or saving a bullet for himself, the ultimate kindness.

He studied the distant whirl carefully, squinting against a blinding sun, his eyes barely protected by the rim of his silk top hat. But he had to see, even if he had to convulse the muscles around his eyes into slits. Plainly the riders followed a track, never deviating in their westward progress. He could see no other movement across the glaring prairie, no buggy and wagon, no horses. Neither could he see a refuge that might harbor the Friends. Unless the very trench he'd been following was their refuge a mile or two ahead.

Gently he eased down into the gulch and clambered up on Jawbone. The roan seemed well aware of something ahead, and stood with his ears laid back and his jaw working against his upper teeth. There, below the lip of the prairie, Skye's world had shrunk to a valley scarcely fifty yards wide, vanishing around a bend a couple of hundred yards ahead. An avenue of escape, or an avenue to take him straight toward the Friends and Clement, if indeed they were up a way. A vulnerable place where any warrior lurking on its lip would have an easy shot at him.

He sweated freely, feeling the old terror rise through him, finding the choices an agony. He could cut and run. He could see about the Friends. Maybe he and Clement, with his new breech-loading Sharps, could do what needed doing. He never did decide, but some visceral thing in him heeled Jawbone, and they edged forward on wire-taut nerves, pausing at each bend of the snaking gully, listening where eyes could not see. Thus they progressed through silence two hundred, three hundred yards.

Then it all happened. Jawbone shrieked and began pitching. A horse just around the next bend whinnied. Two or three others whinnied. A rider hove into sight, his rifle leveled at his shoulder. Skye kicked Jawbone and the horse lunged just as the rifle crashed and a ball buzzed by. The other man—a whiteman—kicked his horse while digging for a cartridge and opening the breech. The breech . . . Clement! A gaggle of horses hove into view, packhorses, big horses, Percherons. Jawbone pitched, denying Skye his own shot, and Clement loped past. Clement turned in his saddle and shot backward, a wild effort. Jawbone snarled, and lunged at the passing Percherons. Puzzled, Skye held his fire, letting Clement escape to the south. The sick, shaken feeling he knew so well came upon him. Once again, death had whipped by. One day it wouldn't whip by. He felt his gorge rise and held in the vomit.

Skye calmed down Jawbone, running a hand under his mane. Clement had shot at him. By accident? Clement had the Percherons. Was he taking them to pasture? Were the Friends just ahead? Was Clement running from the Blackfeet—ditching the Friends? Leaving them to their fate?

He had no answers. He sat Jawbone, watching his back trail, afraid that Clement would try something. The dust in the gulch hung there. His heart hammered. He wondered whether the war party—if that's what it was—had heard the shots down in this place. Most of all he wondered what to do. Go after Clement—who could easily ambush him? Get the bloody hell out himself? Go defend the Friends with his breech-loading carbine?

He could discipline his gut no longer and tumbled

off his horse, nauseated. His belly convulsed; a quaking overtook him and he coughed up bile, splattering his carbine, terrified that Clement would shoot him while he was on all fours. He stood and wiped the slime from his mouth. Jawbone snapped his teeth. Skye mounted and rode toward the Friends.

He edged quietly through a sunny silence for another half hour or so and then rounded a bend and beheld a bright green glade, astonishing in the browned prairie. At the same moment a dozen Indian ponies whickered, and Jawbone shrieked. A Blackfeet sentry up on the yonder ridge fired an old fusil into the sky. Mister Skye turned Jawbone, prepared to bolt around and bend out of the line of fire. He'd been too late. The Piegans had gotten to the Friends first.

"Mister Skye, Mister Skye!"

Sitgreaves's voice, faint in the breeze.

Skye stopped, eyeing the ridges sharply. He eased off Jawbone, carbine in hand, and edged around the bend, keeping low. Cottonwoods blocked his view. But beyond, through the brush and leaves, he saw bodies, all sorts of brown bodies sprawled on the ground. And Sitgreaves standing among them. Could it be? Had the Friends slaughtered a whole party of Piegans?

Up on the ridge, the sentry was riding his pony down toward the verdant hollow at an easy pace. Skye meant to keep an eye on him. Cautiously, fearing snakes, Skye mounted his unruly horse and eased into view, feeling naked, waiting for the crash of a rifle or the twang of a bow, and the blow to his person. He sweated, his nausea still upon him, and then steered Jawbone into the glade where a dozen or more warriors sprawled near a small pool beneath a spring.

"My goodness. Mister Skye! Thee of all people!"

Skye saw the doctor, Price and Fall. Mrs. Sitgreaves and the son were missing.

"Divine Providence," said Price.

The Piegan sentry rode in, his old fusil carefully held

across his lap. The rest of them seemed to be dead or dying. A few moaned softly, or twitched.

"I bloody well don't fathom this, mate. Are they sick?"

"Ether, Mister Skye."

"Ether?"

"An anesthetic."

"And what's that, Sitgreaves? Tell me, and bloody fast." He remembered that Denig had said something about this.

"It puts them to sleep. Permits painless surgery."

Skye studied the corpses. They were obviously about to croak, the ones still thrashing. "Did you ether them?"

"They inhaled it themselves. Insisted on it."

Skye knew death throes when he saw them. He glared at the sole living Piegan, who smiled like an imbecile. He studied the Indian ponies malevolently. He noted the trade muskets, bows, arrows, lances, hatchets, war clubs, tumbled down among the corpses. War, then. Some damn medical hocus-pocus. "Where's the woman?" he asked harshly.

"I've lost her."

"I knew it. They killed her. And you got your revenge."

"No, not at all Mister Skye. She and Artemus—they left. Walking to Fort Benton. They—we had a controversy."

"A controversy, a *controversy*. That's what you call it, you bloody Friends. And now you've poisoned an army of Piegans, three or four lodges of them."

Sitgreaves eyed him brightly, that maddening, boyish innocence back in his face. "Nay, Mister Skye. They'll all come around soon. They sampled it just as they sample whitemen's spirits, and had a fine old time of it. The inhaler's like a pipe. They suck the gas, begin to feel a certain, ah, levity, and then slip into a deep sleep."

Skye didn't believe a word. "Where'd Clement go?"

"He robbed us. Took off suddenly. I'm sure he saw these Blackfeet coming, and did his dirty work while he could."

"I ran into him."

"If thee would, Mister Skye. Go get my wife and son. They couldn't be half a mile off. And then I'll tell thee everything. About that scoundrel Clement. About these friendly Blackfeet. About my ether inhaler. Try it, try a whiff. Thy ladies will enjoy a whiff too. It brings on fits of humor. And Mister Skye—would thee accept employment again—on thy own terms? We've some difficulties here, but thee've been sent by Divine Providence to make things right."

"I'll think on it," Skye muttered, kneeing Jawbone.

Once he'd gained the top of the bluff he spotted them at once, small dots in the east. He set Jawbone into an easy canter and caught up with them.

"Mister Skye!" exclaimed Abby.

Artemus said nothing, raking Skye with a hostile gaze.

"The doctor wishes ye'd come back for some talk, ma'am."

"Let's go on, Mother."

Skye understood the sullen youth. "I reckon we can talk some. Maybe things'll change, lad. If things don't change, the Skyes could escort you back to the fort. Safer than walking alone. The Blackfeet—they don't quite add up to what you imagine."

"What William Penn imagines," said Abby. "I harbor no illusions."

"I suppose he wants to employ you again. Now that Clement flew his true colors."

"He does. But it won't be on the former terms, ma'am, if we accept."

"And what did William Penn say to that?"

Skye laughed. "He proposed it. Come along, and if you don't patch things up, my ladies and I'll take you back. We'd be going that way anyway. Put you on our packhorse.''

She sighed. "I'll listen. Mind thee, I'm not changing my mind . . . Fort Benton's such a long walk.''

They turned and he escorted them back, keeping Jawbone well away from them. The roan was acting edgy lately.

"How'd he kill all the Blackfeet?''

"They're not dead, Mister Skye.''

"He ethered them. Admitted it to me. And they looked dead or dying to me. Saw it with my own eyes.''

"Nay, Mister Skye. Thee'll see. It's a great blessing. It takes the pain from surgery. From childbirth. Diving Otter—he's the one who received it—he must have told the rest that—well, he liked it.''

"They're going to come around—as good as new?''

"Like the end of a drunk, Mister Skye.''

She angered him.

They crossed the brown plains to the lip of the bluffs, and peered down into that leafy green vale where the wagon stood helpless, and the useless carriage.

Below, two of the Blackfeet were no longer corpses. They sat up, staring around them.

"Oh, Mister Skye,'' Abby said, and he caught a sob in her voice. He turned, and found her weeping. "I just want to go home.''

Chapter 26

Beauregard Clement ran his horse and his lumbering string of horses a mile or so along the coulee, not daring to stop until he'd put plenty of distance between himself and Skye. The unexpected sight of Mister Skye had rattled him. Skye was the last person he'd expected to encounter. Skye was drunk at Fort Benton.

He'd shot at Skye, thinking he'd shot at a stray Injun until he saw the top hat and made some sense of that frantic moment. Skye changed everything. Clement stopped beside some cottonwoods to puzzle things out and let the sweated horses blow. The big Percherons were slowing him down. He wished he'd killed Skye, but it'd happened too fast, and Sky was shooting at him. Maybe he should go back and do the job.

Anger crabbed at him. He didn't know why Skye was sniffing around but he knew Skye could wreck it all. Skye alone could hold off the Piegans and rescue the pukes. He hoped the Piegans had jumped the pukes before Skye got there. Dead men told no tales, he thought. But he couldn't count on that now.

He clambered down from his gaunt horse and walked to loosen his stiff legs. Then he clambered up the bluff of the coulee, his Sharps in hand, to take a look at the world out on the plains. From that vantage point he saw nothing but rolling grassland shimmering under the sun.

He wiped sweat from his brow and settled his broad-brimmed beaver over his head again. If the Quaker pukes lived, then Skye would learn about the robbery. If the pukes had been butchered by Piegans, then he was safe. It didn't matter that Skye had seen him with the three Percherons. He could explain that—running for his life when the Piegans jumped them. Simple as that.

But he didn't know.

And not knowing affected everything. If the pukes were dead his secret was safe. He could walk into any fur post and not worry. If the pukes were alive—he was a wanted man again.

He clambered down the bluff, stirring up a rattler, sweating like a pig in the brutal heat, not knowing what to do. He could cut and run with the Percherons. Sell them in Salt Lake City. They'd fetch plenty anywhere settlers had rooted down. But he wouldn't know. He could come back to the northern mountains and live as he had—if he knew. Or he could assume Skye knew, the world knew, and head south, down Santy Fe way, or Taos, drink aguardiente and flirt with the chiquitas, prey on peons for a living. It was a big world and news like this wouldn't travel a thousand mountain miles.

But he wished he knew.

He settled in the browned-off grass while his horses cooled down, sitting against a rock with his Sharps across his lap. He comforted himself with what he did know: Bug's Boys would have gotten to the pukes before Skye did. He'd seen them back at Benton, fire in their eyes, after the puke doctor had scared them witless. Bad medicine. Bug's Boys believed in that stuff.

But he wasn't sure of it. He sighed, knowing what he would have to do. He had to cache his horses and sneak back there and see. He had to find out where Skye's squaws were, where the Piegans were, where Skye was. But most of all, he had to make sure the Quakers were dead. He wished now he'd shot them instead of trusting that Bug's Boys would cover his tracks. He wished he could kill them all—Skye and his squaws, and the pukes. But he knew better than to tangle with the Skye family.

He considered the most daring plan: ride straight up the coulee right now, in broad daylight, and have a look. Cache the horses right here. He didn't want to hang around until dark. The more he thought about it the better he liked it. He liked to get things over and done with. Feeling some better, he climbed into his battered Santa Fe saddle and turned the sweat-caked sorrel north, riding soft-footed, his Sharps at the ready, steering his horse with his knees. Nothing stirred. The sun pummeled him viciously, sucking moisture out of him. Periodically he steered the horse up the bluff to study the plains above, and saw nothing.

He passed the place where he and Skye had fired wild shots and headed onward toward the pukes, his nerves screaming. But he had every advantage. Skye wouldn't expect him. A half mile from the spring he tied his horse to a juniper and stalked forward, his Sharps in hand. He moved like a wraith, so soft a passage that not even the magpies objected. He'd done that often, like a catamount, soundless, approaching within twenty or thirty yards of deer and bear, somehow invisible to them.

He snaked smoothly around the last shoulder and beheld the trees masking his prey. He had to be even more careful the last few yards, avoiding sticks. But in a few moments he was able to peer through a screen of foliage, and what he espied startled him.

He couldn't fathom it. There lay a dozen or so dead Piegans, sprawled across the earth. Two sat up, looking

wounded though he could see no blood. For that matter
he could see no blood on the corpses either. Skye was
on foot, and beyond him Jawbone glared at the world,
his ears laid back. The Quaker pukes lived. The entire
lot of them stood talking with Skye.

Clement couldn't imagine it. He stared, thunder-
struck. He wheeled his Sharps around and aimed at
Skye—and then lowered the weapon. He didn't know
where Skye's women were but he knew they could
butcher him fast. He grasped, too, that the robbery was
no longer a secret, and if he wanted to make it a secret
again he'd have to kill all the pukes and Skye and probably Skye's women. Puzzled, he watched one of the
Piegans stand and stretch. One of the corpses stirred,
and Clement wondered whether the rest would too. He
wondered what had stricken them.

Several of the Piegan ponies were staring straight at
him, and he knew his scent had reached them and that
sooner or later Skye would notice. Baffled, Clement
eased backward a few yards, ready to retreat to his horse
at the slightest sign of trouble. He needed time to make
sense of all this.

Another of the Injuns stirred. They were alive, then.
Soon they'd all be up. But right now Skye was the only
armed man in the camp. Unless his squaws were
around. But Clement hadn't seen them. It struck him
that he could get out of this if he acted fast; the chance
wouldn't come again. Kill Skye, then shoot the pukes
and stupefied Piegans at his leisure and ride away free.
He'd make it look like a battle, put a few arrows into
the pukes.

Excited, Clement stalked forward again, found a log
for a bench rest and set his Sharps on it, and focused
down the barrel until the blade lined up on Skye's back.
Easy. He squeezed, and the Sharps carbine boomed.
Skye took the ball below the shoulder blade and tumbled forward. He stumbled, then sagged to earth. His
carbine flew; his top hat rolled away. A great red stain

blossomed on his shirt. He flopped on the ground like a dying trout, rumbling and sobbing.

Clement laughed. A lead pill would take grizzlies as well as rabbits. All his life he'd remember this. He cackled, some crazy spastic humor erupting in him.

Clement chortled and reloaded, watching the puke Quakers stare, stunned, paralyzed, as the big man toppled to the earth. Clement slithered through the brush and out into the open. Now it'd be like shooting rabbits. The woman screamed, and the scream lingered in the wooded vale, echoing from the bluffs until the whole world screamed back at him. Let her. He'd silence her after he shot the two live Injuns, who were running for their weapons.

Another scream shattered the air, a deafening shriek, and the next thing Clement knew, a gray blur of horse thundered at him, ears back, teeth clacking, yellow eyes hellish. Jawbone. Clement swung his carbine around and shot, too fast. Too late. Jawbone smashed into him and the blow broke bones, snapped Clement's neck, knocked air out of him. Clement felt himself hit the earth violently, his head slamming into rock. He couldn't breathe. He couldn't move. Above him the horse reared, and its forehooves whipped down, crushing Clement's chest and belly. Clement felt ribs snap and his back crack. He felt a white numbness in his feet. Nothing moved. The numbness turned into red pain and he groaned. Jawbone's vicious teeth clamped his ear and ripped it off, bit his nose and cheek and tore his face open. Blood blinded him. The horse whirled and his rear hooves cracked his pelvis, snapped a thighbone. Clement felt his body jerk and spasm, and saw white fire in the sky. Jawbone's shriek deafened him, until he could hear nothing more.

The sky turned black, and the frenzied horse vanished down the coulee in the night.

* * *

William Penn Sitgreaves grabbed Skye's carbine, scarcely knowing why. Abby was screaming, Jawbone shrieking and galloping toward the brush below, the two sensate Picgans running toward their ponies. The other Friends, paralyzed, gaped at Skye, groaning on the ground, and at the brush where powder smoke lifted faintly.

"Run, Abby!" he cried. "Take cover."

Abby didn't. Not until Artemus dragged her, screaming, into the wagon.

Another shot erupted from the brush, and Jawbone shrieked. A man did too, somewhere back there. The Indian horses squealed and snorted, and yanked back on their pickets, breaking them. The two Piegans leapt upon their ponies and began herding the rest.

There were no more shots. One or two of the dazed Piegans on the ground peered up at the world.

Doctor Sitgreaves ran to the wagon for his bag. "Artemus—take this and use it," he said, thrusting Skye's carbine at the youth. The boy took it and began at once seeing how it worked.

Sitgreaves found his bag and raced to Skye, who lay sprawled on his stomach, his mouth in the dirt. Swiftly, the doctor slit apart Skye's calico shirt, examining the wounds. The small entrance wound in the upper right back bled little, but the exit wound gouted blood. Skye lived, at least for the moment.

Sitgreaves grabbed his stethoscope and placed the trumpet firmly over Skye's heart from the back. He found a weak beat, irregular and spastic. Like his breathing: gasping and irregular and whistling strangely. Vital signs unstable. Skye coughed suddenly, a racking sound that sounded like he was choking. A frothy pink collected around Skye's lips. The ball had torn through the bronchi, and fluids were being pumped up the trachea.

The right lung had collapsed. Fluids were collecting in it. Gently, he turned Skye onto his back. The ball had pierced through muscle, apparently shattered the second rib entered the pulmo dexter in the upper lobe, the lobus ventrocranialis, and exited just above the second rib below Skye's shoulder, carrying debris with it. A fatal shot unless Skye survived the shock that traumatized him, then survived the flooding of the lung, the collapsed lung, and infection. Sitgreaves turned Skye, elevating his left side to keep blood out of the good lung, and stuffed his frock coat under that side to keep it high.

Skye shuddered, spasmed, and slid into a comatose quiet. Sitgreaves listened through the stethoscope, heard nothing, swiftly compressed the chest with his hands, and then hammered a fist sharply over Skye's heart. He listened again and found a feeble, tentative pulse. He listened for eternities while Skye's heart stuttered, faltered, paused for long agonizing moments, and then suddenly slid into a soft rapid beat. Good.

Sitgreaves peered around him at last. The wooded glade seemed peaceful. Several more Piegans were recovering, and peered about them. Artemus had vanished in the direction of the brush. The last he'd seen of Price and Fall, they'd flattened themselves to the earth near the spring.

He didn't dare move Skye. The larger chest wound pulsed blood slowly, and what didn't drain into the lung slid red down Skye's chest. He tweezered bits of bone out of the hole, and then tied off some small bleeders. He sutured the ragged edges of flesh together with silk thread, having a bad time of it. He wanted to close that larger hole at once, but the flesh around the exit hole was so shredded he had trouble drawing it together. He paused frequently to listen to the thread of pulse and the terrible gurgling and whistling. But Skye's faltering heart stumbled on, and his left lung wheezed oxygen into his blood.

Fearfully, he turned Skye onto his right side and then cleaned the entrance wound in Skye's back. He'd leave

that one open a while to drain the lung. He found some
clean dressing in his bag and plastered it over the wound
to absorb the blood dribbling from the lung. The cloth
turned crimson instantly. He turned Skye onto his back
again and checked the vital signs. Skye coughed and
muttered, opened his eyes and closed them. Sitgreaves
saw awareness in them. A terrible gurgling sound accompanied every gasp.

For a while more he worked over Skye, doing what
he could which wasn't much. Bright lung blood leaked
from Skye's back into the soaked pad, surging out with
each spastic breath. But it slowed as the lung hemorrhage slowed. The doctor prepared a saline solution,
lowered Skye's britches, and injected it with his big
metal syringe into Skye's rectum, just as he had done
for Jawbone. Skye's pulse still raced and his breathing
came in short irregular gasps. Keeping Skye alive had
absorbed Sitgreaves so much that he was scarcely aware
of the rest. Most of the Piegans were up now, staring
at the doctor as he worked. None said a word. He suddenly realized he was trying to save the life of their
enemy. But none of them hindered him, not even Walks
at Night, the shaman, who watched the doctor impassively.

He wondered what Skye was doing here. Everything
had happened before the Friends and Skye had come to
any understanding. Denig had sent Skye; the doctor
surmised that. But why? The Blackfeet? Something
about Clement? He wondered why they weren't curious, weren't excited, and then he spotted the body
sprawled below the spring. Clement. Scalped. Broken
to pulp, grotesque and bloody, Jawbone's work. Some
of the Piegans had dragged him out of the brush. One
of them was brandishing Clement's Sharps, exclaiming
over it.

Where was Artemus, Artemus and Skye's carbine?
The doctor waited uneasily, unable to leave Skye. This
would be a long vigil through the night and the next

day. If Skye survived a night, the doctor would move him into the wagon.

The day dragged silently, ebbing on the breath of Mister Skye. Artemus returned, walking up the coulee dragging a picket line with the Percherons on it. With him was Diving Otter in possession of Clement's horses. A big coup for Diving Otter, Sitgreaves thought. The sight of the Percherons gladdened him. The Piegans crowded around Diving Otter and the horses, exclaiming as Diving Otter opened Clement's packs and began handing out treasures to his friends. A quiver with various kinds of arrows in it seemed to excite them.

"Thee has the Percherons, Artemus," said Sitgreaves.

The youth peered back stonily.

"Thee has done well, and given heart to thy mother."

"Will he live?"

"I don't know."

"He'd better."

Sitgreaves didn't know what to make of that.

The boy watered the great animals and inspected them, finding no injury. The Piegans studied the giant horses thoughtfully, saying nothing. None of them could speak to the Friends anyway. Skye had finger-talked a bit before he was shot, but now the Friends and the Piegans were separated by a silent gulf.

The Piegans surrounded their shaman and began discussing matters, pointing now and then at the Friends, the wagon, the Percherons, and Skye. It seemed to the doctor that their controversy grew heated at times although they seemed to heed the words of the shaman, who had resumed wearing his buffalo-horn headdress. Then the group of warriors flew apart, some trotting toward the Percherons, others toward the wagon, and one or two straight toward him—and Skye. A sudden fear caught him.

"No!" yelled Artemus. The youth lifted Skye's carbine and pointed it squarely at the shaman, Walks at

Night. He pulled the hammer back to full cock with a loud click.

"Artemus!" cried the doctor.

The warriors paused. Some of them swung bows with nocked arrows toward the youth but Artemus didn't waver.

"He'll die first!"

"Steady, mate," muttered Skye.

Sitgreaves stared downward, and saw Skye awake and alert.

"Don't weaken, lad," rasped Skye. "They want the horses and the ether machine—and me."

The Piegans paused, thoughtful. The moment stretched taut but Artemus never wavered. The shaman stared, stood very quiet, said nothing. Wills clashed, and death lay in the balance. Sitgreaves was aware of half a dozen drawn bows aimed at his son. And more aimed at himself.

Skye turned toward the doctor. "Say Denig, mate," he whispered. "Just say Denig. Say Culbertson. Say American Fur."

"Denig," croaked the doctor loudly. "Denig! Culbertson! American Fur! Denig! Denig!"

"Stand up, mate," Skye whispered. "Stand back-to-back with Artemus."

Sitgreaves didn't know whether he could do that, not with those arrows and lances poised to slaughter him. He closed his eyes, found the necessary iron within, and stood slowly, eyeing the warriors. Then he stepped behind Artemus, turned, and faced them, terror rippling through him. He was protecting his son with his body, only his body.

He could not see the shaman but he heard movement and felt Artemus twisting, following with Skye's carbine. Then, like hailstones melting, the Piegans lowered their weapons and mounted their ponies, following the shaman. Soundlessly they rode up the slope into the sky, and out upon the universe. One minute they threatened murder; the next they vanished.

Not a bird caroled. Even the breeze lay ensnared. Sitgreaves watched the retreat but his tortured body didn't ease. Artemus grimly followed the shaman with the carbine until the shaman rode into the sky, and even then he didn't lower the weapon.

Sitgreaves glanced at Skye, but the guide had slid back into oblivion again. He prepared more saline solution, his only recourse against hemorrhage.

Slowly Price and Fall emerged from the brush near the spring where they'd flattened themselves.

Fall stalked stiffly toward Artemus. "Some Friend are thee!" he snarled. "With murder in thee. Threatening them."

Artemus sighed. "Maybe I'm not a Friend."

"I can see that! Thee almost killed us."

"And where were thee, Diogenes? Hiding in the grass. Trusting in Divine Providence, I presume?" asked the doctor.

"Doing what the Inner Light instructed," Fall retorted.

"Artemus saved thy life. And mine. And Abigail's."

"I was ready to be taken up," Fall announced.

Sitgreaves didn't feel like arguing. Fall always got in the last word anyway, usually reinforced by Latin and conceit. "We'll be here a day or two while I look after Skye. He can't be moved. If thee would, thee might see to Clement."

"Clement's not my business. Let that boy do it."

Doctor Sitgreaves knew, suddenly, that his entire mission lay shattered. Abby and Artemus wanted to go back. The long journey had demolished the Way in them both. Fall's arrogance would only make the work miserable, and there'd be spats.

"I'll do it," said Artemus wearily. He thrust the Hall-North carbine into the doctor's hands and walked to the wagon for a shovel. The doctor hefted the shining weapon, feeling its deadly weight, its sinister power—and its comfort.

From the earth, Skye peered up at him. "If I'm going under, don't wait," he whispered. "Take the carbine, mate."

"Thee aren't going under."

"Can't breathe."

"Thy right lung's collapsed. I have to keep the wound open to drain it. Keep it drained and thee've a chance."

"Look after my women. And Jawbone."

"Jawbone saved us, Mister Skye."

The guide nodded. Tears had collected in his eyes.

Chapter 27

Victoria heard Jawbone long before she saw him. Mister Skye's horse raced up the valley of the Big River, shrieking and bleating. The sound sent a chill through her. She and Mary stared at each other, and then she ran through the timber to the riverbank and beheld him on the opposite side, pacing wildly, his flanks soaked black—and no one in Mister Skye's saddle.

All her winters with Mister Skye she'd feared that this might happen. But now it was happening. Something terrible had stricken her man, and there was Jawbone across the water, pacing insanely.

"I'm coming," she cried.

The horse stood with his forelegs in the water, waiting.

Victoria hurried back to the concealed lodge and found Mary in tears, saddling the horses.

"You stay!" she told Mary. "Something bad. If I don't come back, go to my people. Save the boy. He's the child of Mister Skye!"

"But I can shoot—"

"Stay! Maybe the Siksika killed him—and us too."
Mary nodded unhappily.

Victoria decided to take her bow and quiver. She rejected her long rifle. Silence was the friend of small women. Swiftly, she gathered the things she needed and climbed onto her bay pony even as Mary began dismantling the lodge and breaking camp. She turned her mare toward the river and urged it through brush until she reached the shore. On the far side Jawbone stood in the water, nickering at the sight of her. She kicked the mare into the cold stream, which tugged at her legs, and when they hit the deep channel the mare slid deep and swam rhythmically toward Jawbone while Victoria clung to the mane and felt the icy water numb her. Then the mare splashed out in great leaps, shuddered the water off, and followed Jawbone, who screamed at them and bolted off.

For several miles Jawbone led them, pacing himself, sometimes cantering, sometimes trotting, but never pausing. He turned unexpectedly up a dry coulee that led to the prairies above, and there the horse followed a shallow scoop ever northward.

Victoria rode easily but still the little mare had trouble keeping up, and her withers and shoulders blackened with sweat. Still Jawbone led them, his shrill screaming urging them on. They came at last to a large bend, and beyond that a dense woods which lay entirely in the coulee under the plains. And there Jawbone suddenly stopped, and stood stock-still. There probably was water ahead and near it she would see what she dreaded to see. She slid stiffly off the pony, feeling her age, and nocked an arrow in her bow. Then she padded after Jawbone, who walked delicately through the woods, somehow missing sticks and making not the slightest sound. A great medicine horse, she thought, whenever she beheld Jawbone doing something wondrous.

She would die, perhaps. But not before she had killed

some of the Siksika! How she hated them. If they'd
killed her man, some would die for it. Then she'd die
this hot sunny day, die the same day as her man died,
and they would go to the Beyond Land together. That
would be good, going to the Spirit Land together. She
feared the pain of dying, but not the dying.

She followed Jawbone, as careful as the horse to glide
silently through the shadows. Ahead, through foliage,
she caught glimpses of people in an open grassy park.
The Friends! She slid closer, studying the place. The
wagon hulked to one side, the carriage nearby. Closest
to her was the youth, Artemus, shoveling—a grave. A
terror swept through her. And beyond, near the wagon,
the doctor, Sitgreaves, sat beside Mister Skye, who lay
bloodied and shirtless on the earth. She fiercely held
back her tears and watched. Where were the Piegans?
Where was that guide, Clement?

Too late, then. Her man dead and the boy was digging the hole in the breast of the Earth Mother for him.
A hollowness emptied her of all feeling. She watched,
unable to bring herself to go hear the story. She stared
at her man, sprawled awkwardly on the earth, his top
hat off to one side, unmoving. So it had come to this.
On this day her man had died, and for no reason at all.
These crazy people weren't paying him; he had no reason to come except that he cared about them and had
promised Denig he would. That's how death overtook
Skye, not for a good cause but for nothing, like a blind
stroke of fate, bad medicine, bolting out of the heavens.
Fire Horse.

She nerved herself for the badness to come, gathered
Jawbone's rope rein, and stepped out upon the grassy
flat. At once the youth dropped his shovel and lifted
Skye's carbine. Then, slowly, he lowered it. Beyond the
youth another body lay inert. Clement! Scalped! Siksika, then.

Doctor Sitgreaves stood hastily as she and Jawbone
approached. Beyond, the other Friends stared. Mrs. Sit-

greaves was nowhere in sight. Was she dead, too? Victoria stared down at her man, bloodstained, gray beneath his ruddy flesh—and found him staring back at her, his eyes alert.

"Goddam," she said, her own eyes filling. Then she sobbed, and felt helpless.

"I'm glad thee came, Mrs. Skye."

She felt the warm arm of this Quaker man around her shoulder, and she sagged into him, unable to speak.

"He gonna die," she said at last.

"Maybe not. It depends on things. Whether his lung fills with fluids. I'm keeping the entrance hole open to drain it. We'll know tomorrow."

She pulled free of the man and slid to her knees beside Skye, wanting to see his breath, to feel life in him. His eyes had closed and he seemed oblivious of her. She thought he'd just died, but then she sensed the gentle rise of his chest, along with a faint gurgling. His lips were splattered with foam and blood. He lived, but for how long? Again tears came, sliding down her weathered face. She touched him, almost afraid that it'd hurt him more. But he didn't notice. The chest wound had been sewn shut but still gurgled with every gasp of her man's lungs. She desperately wished the doctor would seal it better. Flies congregated around the torn flesh.

Jawbone minced forward, as if afraid, and shoved his speckled ugly snout close to Skye's face, sniffing. He caught Skye's breath, lifted his head and whickered. It startled her. From then on, the horse stood sentry over Skye.

"Siksika," she hissed, noting the prints of unshod hooves everywhere. Still, things puzzled her. Why did the Friends live? Why were the Percherons untouched?

"Nay," said the doctor gently. "They were here, but they didn't do this. Clement did it. And Jawbone killed Clement."

"Clement? Him?"

Patiently, the doctor explained as much as the Friends knew: Clement had robbed them and fled just before the Piegans from Fort Benton arrived. The Piegans had sampled the little-sleep pipe. That was when Clement shot Skye . . .

She listened to the story, astonished. The little-sleep pipe. They'd come for that, for the medicine-magic of the whiteman. But Clement came back and shot Mister Skye. Clement's purposes were murky to her but it didn't matter: Clement was dead. Nothing mattered but Skye.

She settled into her own vigil beside him, alarmed at every faint shift of breath, every cough and spasm, every long agonizing pause. Around her, the Friends resumed their work. Artemus heaped earth over Clement. The two wall tents went up. Abigail Sitgreaves, tear-stained and shaken, emerged from the wagon and began kneading dough silently. Day faded into amber twilight but Victoria never moved. She held Skye's hand, sending fierce messages to her man with her fingers; sat and waited as the stars blossomed. The Friends offered her biscuits and water but she wanted none. Often before, she'd sat beside Skye, keeping vigil while he slept away a drunk. But now she sat beside Skye while he wrestled with death.

Once in the evening he coughed, and terrible gurgling sounds rose from him, and he seemed breathless and troubled. Sitgreaves pulled the poultice from Skye's back and rocked him back and forth until the back wound drained the collected fluids in the lung. After that Skye's chest labored less.

"Victoria," he whispered. "Where's Mary and Dirk?"

"They safe. They hiding from Siksika. I told her to run, run with Dirk to my people if—things are bad."

He didn't reply, and she didn't know whether he'd heard her.

The evening grew chill, and Mrs. Sitgreaves brought

a shawl to Victoria, which warmed her shoulders. But she didn't move. The Friends slipped into their tents and the gloomy night closed around her. She pulled a blanket over Skye, and then another. Cold might kill him, she thought. Cold was the enemy of life.

She did not move through the night. Once his hand clamped hers and then released, and she was frightened. But he breathed again. Her ears told her more than her eyes. She heard the terrible rasp of his breath, the long uneven pauses, the gurgle of some sinister fluid bubbling deep within his chest. Sometime in the night, Sitgreaves appeared, half-dressed, with a candle lantern. He placed the trumpet of his stethoscope on Skye's chest and listened.

"Maybe he'll make it," the doctor said. "Keep holding his hand. Let him know you're here."

"Don't bury me here," Skye whispered. "Bury me at Fort Benton. Someone'll remember me there."

In the silent dawn, William Penn Sitgreaves examined Mister Skye and found the right lung clear. The internal bleeding had stopped. He sutured the hole in Skye's back as best he could, using silk thread to draw the reluctant, angry flesh together. He could do nothing for the ruined lung. He dreaded to move Skye for fear of loosening the clots that checked the bleeding, and finally decided not to move him at all. Instead, he waited for Abby to dress and then tried to erect his own wall tent around Skye to keep sun and wind off him— but Jawbone loomed over him, threatening to kill him. So he stopped. Only when Victoria drew Jawbone back could he complete the task.

Through all this Skye dozed, almost unaware of the world except when the curved surgical needle darted through his inflamed flesh, and then he groaned. Victoria lifted Skye's head and managed to pour a little water into him. But Skye had acquired a raging fever, and in his lucid moments he peered up at them through fever-bright eyes sunk into blackened hollows. Still, in spite of the raging heat of his body, Skye's heartbeat and breathing sounded better.

Sitgreaves turned to Victoria. "We can only wait. If thee would like to bring Mary now, I think the time is right. I don't think anything will happen for the next day."

She stared at Skye in the filtered light of the tent, reluctant to leave him. "Goddam," she muttered. "I should stay here."

"May as well get her," whispered Skye.

It always startled them when he spoke.

She turned to Sitgreaves, a stern look in her eyes, and then slipped out into the early sun. He noticed she rode Jawbone and left her bay mare.

He stepped outside and found the Friends waiting quietly for news. "He's feverish," the doctor said.

The Friends stared silently. They all had separated somehow, driven into their own private worlds, no longer bound to one another. He knew as he surveyed them that they needed reconciling. Some decisions had to be made. In this obscure grove beside a cold spring in an anonymous land, everything had come to a head. His dream, the great enterprise to which he'd dedicated the rest of his life, hung in the balance. What they decided here would decide the future, would confirm all his planning and his dream—or destroy it.

They were waiting for him to begin. He knew the preference of all of them except Freeman Price.

"Shall we have a meeting?"

"No!" said Abby. "We will discuss this without a Meeting."

Perhaps that was best, the doctor thought. Diogenes Fall had a way of confusing his own will with the promptings of the Divine Will, and proclaiming that his Inner Light shone brighter and truer than anyone else's. Still . . . the ingrained beliefs of a lifetime would not yield so easily.

"We may each follow his conscience," he said, leaving it up to them.

"I'm going back to Philadelphia," Abby said. "And that's that."

"I'm taking her back," said Artemus.

"We've no guides. I think I'll work for the redmen from the east, where I can accomplish something," said Freeman Price.

"I see them in a different light," said Fall. "I've been shown that there are better uses for my time than supporting these savages. I'll go east with the others. *Nisi Dominus, frustra.*"

"What does that mean?"

"Except the Lord build the house, they labor in vain that build it."

"Thee surprise me."

Fall laughed unkindly.

He turned to his wife. "I wish to speak with thee privately, Abigail."

Wordlessly she followed him out of earshot of the others.

"Would thee come to the Bitterroot for a limited time—two years, Abby?"

"No."

"Would thee wait for me in Philadelphia for two years? Wait as my beloved wife?"

Her face clouded, and she didn't answer.

"I love thee even more than the day we repeated our promises," he said. "I confess I gave thee no consideration when I asked thee to come to this hard place. And I would make known to thee the heaviness of my sorrow. Thee and Artemus are the treasures of my life. Thee came this far, unquestioning, lifting my soul. What other woman would have? If thee would wait—I'll return to thee, my work done as the Light compels me. I'll practice my surgery, gather what I need to know about the native peoples, fashion some plans for their well-being—and then return to thy bosom. Two years, Abby? Long years, but only two?''

She sobbed brokenly. Some bitter thing had broken inside of her; he could see that. "I'll wait two years for thee," she said.

Unaccustomed tears came to him then. He had scarcely dared to hope. Her coldness had shut him out of her soul, and he sensed she had good reason though he could scarcely admit it to himself.

He took her arm and walked softly over virgin grass until they could compose themselves.

"It is something my Light compels me to do," he said.

She laughed between her sniffling, and he thought he'd offended her again. But she simply clutched his arm.

"I'll miss thee," he said.

She laughed again, not altogether kindly, he thought. "Do what thee must," she said crisply. "And you'll find me at Walnut Street."

"Abby—do thee love me?"

"For better or worse."

It wasn't the best of answers, he thought sadly.

When they were composed, they swung back toward the others who stood about, waiting.

"I must get Skye to Fort Benton," he said. "He'll be a month on his back. And it'll be another before he can travel much. If he lives, of course. And it'll be a few days before I dare to move him. I'm hoping one or both of his ladies will take me to the Bitterroot."

"Thee'll find a way, I'm sure."

Back at the camp they found the black stallion harnessed to the carriage and valises piled in its boot. The Friends weren't intending to wait, not even for breakfast. They could make it to Benton before dark if they hurried.

Things had whipped along much too fast to suit him, but he understood their haste. It shook him that in moments he'd be alone here, alone with a desperately wounded man until the Skye women returned.

Artemus approached and thrust Skye's carbine at the doctor. "We can make it by dark if we leave now," he said coldly. "The sooner we return, the better chance we have of catching a fur company boat."

"Son—Artemus—"

The youth turned to him, not unkindly. "Thee must do what is given thee, Father. It's a good work. I'm proud of thee. I only wish thee'd asked—asked—" The youth reddened, struggling to say things that he couldn't say very well.

"Go safely, Artemus! Help thy mother! Keep thy faith!"

The boy turned away, mostly to conceal what lay upon his face, the doctor knew.

"I'll return by and by," the doctor cried.

"Fare thee well, Sitgreaves," called Fall. He was sitting impatiently in the carriage, the lines in his hand.

Beside him, Freeman Price nodded and waved cheerfully. Artemus sat alertly in the back seat. They all seemed to be popping to escape. William Penn could see that. Escape to the comfort of the east, to safety.

There was yet one place not filled on the quilted leather seats of the carriage. Before him, Abby stood, her face ravaged by more than she could conceal within herself. She'd dried her tears, though. The reality of this moment had stricken her as terribly as it had stricken him.

"I may never see thee again," he said.

"Thee must do what thee will. I'd be disappointed if thee didn't," she said. "Thee'll come home. Thee'll walk through the door someday."

Neither could speak. But he suddenly knew she loved him a little, no matter his strange pursuits.

He set the carbine on the grass and hugged her. She clutched him fiercely, and as fiercely pulled free and walked stiffly to the carriage and settled herself there, her face averted.

Old Fall slapped the lines over the rump of the dray, and the Percheron lifted into a swift trot, swinging the carriage around and through the grove. It pulled the loaded carriage up the sharp slope easily, and at the rim they all seemed to pause and look back. The black Percheron whinnied. The Percheron mares, down below, whinnied back. Sitgreaves thought Abby and Artemus waved, but he couldn't be sure. And then they disappeared. He stared at the place where they had been and saw only the sky.

He pulled his gaze away from that spot and back to the forlorn camp with its sagging wagon and sagging tent.

He picked up Skye's carbine almost mindlessly, and knew at once why, and sat down on a log to wait.

Chapter 28

Barnaby Skye whirled in and out of darkness. He was aware, one feverish night, that Doctor Sitgreaves was applying cold compresses to bring the fire of his body down. He dreamed of England and his parents. He could scarcely move. He hadn't the strength to breathe, much less turn over in his blankets. Each breath hurt, though not badly if he lay still. But the smallest movement sent tongues of flame through him—especially the coughing, which tortured his wounded lung.

He knew that Sitgreaves doctored him, and Sitgreaves's tent kept hot sun off him, and chill wind. Once a sharp shower deluged the place, and water seeped in and wet his blankets. Victoria and Mary were there, sat beside him for long periods, and fed him hot broth. They held his hand. Sometimes they brought Dirk in to see him, and the boy smiled dutifully. He was his mother's child, though, and seemed glad when Mary let him scamper away.

Mostly he slept. He had no sense of healing or gaining strength, though days came and went, light and dark. He asked for laudanum once, but Sitgreaves refused.

"Thee are too close," he said tersely.

Too close to going under. He grew aware of the world outside his tent, and things puzzled him. Once or twice a day Jawbone poked his ugly snout into the tent and whickered softly. He knew his family was here. But what of the Friends?

"They all went back east," Sitgreaves explained.

"You alone, mate?"

"That's right. I'll carry on."

"To the Bitterroot? Without them?"

"For two years. I'll do just what I intended. Bring medicine to the tribes, record their ways, listen to them, form an idea of their life that I may use in the east to protect them."

"Alone?"

Sitgreaves smiled gently. "They found these wilds too alarming. The hardships too much."

"Not even—Mrs. Sitgreaves?"

"She especially wanted to return. They took the carriage and hoped to go back on a fur company keelboat."

Skye closed his eyes a minute. Talking tired him. "How long have I been here?"

"This is the eighth day."

"What are your plans?"

"To wait until I can safely move thee back to Benton. Thee'll need many weeks at Benton before thee can travel."

"How soon could you take me there in the wagon?"

"Thee're very weak, Mister Skye. The wagon lacks springs. I don't want to risk tearing apart—"

"Don't want to go there," he said. They were safe enough right here. That shower would have erased the tracks, wiped away all signs of passage to this off-trail place. They were camped in an odd crack in the prairie, far from any Indian trail.

"It'd be best for you to go. They can care for thee."

"Victoria's making meat?" he asked.

"She says she hunts the coulee. There's seeps the deer come to. She never rides out on the prairie. She's a splendid huntress, Mister Skye. We always have meat hanging."

Skye nodded, and shifted his weight. His flesh itched whenever he lay on it too long.

"If I just stay put, mate, am I out of danger?"

"No. There's the danger of a blood clot breaking loose and reaching your heart."

"I put it wrong. Is there anything more you can do for me here?"

Sitgreaves hesitated. "If thy lung fills up, I could drain it. If the fever returns—"

"Middle of August," Skye said. "You've got to go."

"I must find a guide at Fort Benton, Mister Skye."

"I reckon Victoria'd take you. She's better'n me anyway. Mary'll be here to help me."

"I hesitate to go with only—"

"She'll get you there. We need the fee. Owe a lot."

Sitgreaves pondered. "It'd have to be a letter of credit. Clement took my cash, The Piegans . . . We never got it back. But if a letter—"

"Fine, fine," said Skye.

For two more days Doctor Sitgreaves tarried. He prepared small packets of powders and instructed Mary in their use. He left a vial of laudanum. He talked endlessly with Victoria in the evenings after she returned from her daily prowling. Skye couldn't make out what was being said, but he registered her explosive muttering. The doctor checked Skye frequently, poked his chest with the stethoscope and listened for long periods. Skye felt no better, though his appetite had grown and he could sit up against a backrest to eat. It maddened him that he couldn't see beyond the canvas walls of the tent. He wanted nothing more than to see grass and trees and sun.

More and more, Mister Skye puzzled over the riddle of Doctor Sitgreaves. One noon, when the doctor crawled into the tent for a routine check on his patient, Skye belayed him.

"You mind telling me what happened, mate?"

Sitgreaves looked rueful. "I fear I was too taken up in dreams to notice how others felt about it. Abby, especially. She never wanted to come, and I'd never asked her. Artemus too. It'd never occurred to me, Mister Skye! We gather in our Meetings not to impose our wills, but to submit them. At least most of us do. Some of us abuse our ways. Perhaps I do also. I was utterly blind to my own wife's feelings."

"But you're going on, mate. All alone. Not a Friend with you. You're not even sure if John Owen wants you."

"Ah, Mister Skye. The first tribesman I heal, the first suffering I alleviate, the first glimmer of understanding of what these redmen will need—why, sir, all these years of preparation will not be in vain."

"But alone? Even two years?"

He sighed. "Abby'll wait. She doesn't disapprove; she only wants to stay among her comforts. It'll be hard for her. And more so for me."

"But why, mate?"

"I felt the Light, sir. Thee'd have to be a Friend to know what I mean. The Light! The white thundering Light! It fills thee, it transforms thee, it guides thee, it assures thee through doubt. It fills me, sir, every particle of me. Not a preacher or a priest said a word or taught me a thing. This was direct—direct from the Source! What can one weak mortal do but obey and rejoice?"

Skye almost envied the man, but still doubted. "The Light didn't touch the others, mate."

"Yes it did. They chose not to heed it. That's always the choice of mortals, Mister Skye. I suppose more formal religions would label it sin."

"You sayin' the ones that turned back sinned?"

Sitgreaves looked shocked. "I'm sorry. Thee has well rebuked me. Not sin, but fear. So many fear to heed the Light within them."

"And what's the result, mate? It won't change the world none. Won't make whitemen any kinder to the redmen. Won't keep 'em from killing off the buffler and driving the redmen into the earth."

Sitgreaves stared dreamily into some horizon. "I can't stop history. But I can heal one person. I can give one thoughtless person reason to pause. I am one, Mister Skye, but even alone, I can make my limited world a little finer."

"I wish you success, Doctor. Ye heal all ye touch, including me. They'll not forget you. The tribes never forgot Father De Smet. He brought them some caring, some instruction, some baptism, and a little talk about loving their neighbors. I'll miss you, Doctor Sitgreaves. I'd of gone under, but that's not why. You're one of a kind. I've never met the like of you. Most come into the west to get something for themselves. You came to give—to heal and protect strangers. That bloody well says it all. I got you this far without firing a shot; Victoria'll get you the rest of the way. She thinks you're crazy, thinks all whitemen are crazy. But she loves you, too."

Sitgreaves's face was radiant. "I count thee a friend, in both senses, Mister Skye. Perhaps thee'll escort me back when the time comes to return to my dear Abby and Artemus."

"Glad to, mate."

Later that afternoon, Victoria crawled into the tent, looking cross. "I got lots of meat hanging," she said angrily. She always sounded angry when they were about to part. "I got to take that crazy goddam doctor to Owen's in the morning. Just me and him and them big horses. I'll damn well shoot if I feel like it. No crazy man's going to keep me from—"

"You want my carbine?"

"Naw. But maybe the revolver. You keep the breech-loader. Shoot the hell outa the Siksika. You get well. See that Mary feeds you."

"Mary takes good care of me."

Something malicious rose in the woman's face. "Don't bust anything open," she muttered. "I'll come back and maybe you'll be well enough to go."

"Victoria—no. Don't come back this way, past all the Blackfeet. From Owen's place go on down to your Kicked-in-the-Bellies and hole up with your people, and we'll come when I can. I figure to hole up here a while. A good enough hideyhole."

"Maybe I never see you again. I get into trouble. You and Mary and the boy, you get into trouble."

"Maybe not," he said quietly. "We've had lots of days to think about that, haven't we?"

"Sonofabitch!" she snapped, but it was agreement. And tears collected on her weathered cheeks as she gently held him close.

Victoria had never guided a crazy man before. She knew he was crazy because of the childlike innocence she saw in his face. Crazy people deserved the utmost respect because the spirits had touched them and made them special. That was known to all the tribes, and all the tribes honored the mad. Doctor Sitgreaves had that quality, all right. And no one but a mad person would go on such a long journey to help strange people.

They made good time. The Percheron mares had regained their strength during the long pause at the spring, and now pulled the wagon effortlessly. Doctor Sitgreaves drove. Victoria scouted ahead, hunted, and drifted back now and then to see how the crazy man was doing. He was doing fine.

How odd it was to guide just one man, and a mad one at that, without Mister Skye. But he certainly gave her no trouble. They reached Sun River and he crossed carefully, struggling with a soft bottom at one point. They proceeded up the Big River, the Missouri, with the great spine of the Rocky Mountains ever closer. Giant shoulders rose from either side of the river, but the bottoms still afforded them passage. She kept a sharp eye out for the Siksika—how the name curdled on her tongue—and saw signs of recent passage. An entire village had crossed to the south bank at a place where the buffalo swam.

Each night they made a silent camp. She had nothing to say to a crazy man, and he didn't press her. He made his bed in the half-empty wagon and she on the ground, except one night when it gusted cold, with a hint of winter in the August air. That night he set up one of his wall tents, and she slept comfortably beneath the chattering canvas.

They made a good crossing of the Dearborn in a place where travois poles and ponies had worn a path to a hard-bottomed ford. That river would take her to a pass that would bring her to the Blackfoot River on the western side, and the Blackfoot River would take her almost to the Bitterroot Valley. And yet she dreaded that choice. The Blackfoot ran through dense forest and was a favorite route of her enemies. She rejected it.

From then on, as they toiled up the Missouri in a southwesterly direction, she worried about passes. She had to take his wagon over the forested spine of the Rockies, and had no idea which pass Mister Skye had had in mind. No wagon had ever gone there before; no road existed. Soon the river would pierce a choking canyon walled by towering cliffs. She could not take a wagon there. She could not even go by horse or on foot. Long before, the white captains, Lewis and Clark, had called the place the Gates of the Mountains.

They left the Missouri and followed along a small creek Mister Skye called the Little Prickly Pear. All about them the arid mountains catapulted upward, but so far, at least, there was passage for the wagon. Even so, it took a terrible punishment, plunging over creeks, banging over yellow rock, skidding down steep grades. Doctor Sitgreaves kept a gentle hand on the lines and kept the jarring wagon from catastrophe. They pierced through dry hills and onto an arid flat filled with the sign of recent passage. And yet she saw no one. Their luck held, but she dreaded the moment they would suddenly confront a party of Piegan horse stealers. Nervously, she eyed the wagon tracks that told of their passage. And the giant hoofprints of the Percherons, a thing that would excite any sharp-eyed tracker.

She abandoned the Little Prickly Pear and cut south, as Mister Skye had done once, and found the unnamed creek that would lead them toward a low and almost treeless pass she remembered. Forest was the enemy of a wagon. There'd be a creek on the west slope, and it would lead to the Little Blackfoot, and that would take them to the Deer Lodge Valley and the Clark Fork. From there they could traverse level ground—more or less—clear to the Bitterroot. She hadn't chosen this route; the route had chosen her, hemming them according to the logic of the mountains. She despised this barren prickly-pear valley, and felt its dark spirits upon her.

All that day they ascended toward the continental divide along that nameless creek. Now and then Sitgreaves was forced to detour up huge coulees, and once he and Victoria had to shovel a way down a cutbank. The steady uphill travel wore down even the mighty Percherons, and he was forced to rest them frequently. They fought for each mile.

High on the east slope they came to a ford of the creek, a place where the faint trace dropped steeply to the rocky creek bed and twisted upward again, all in a hairpin curve. She splashed across and ascended the far slope, ever alert for unwanted company, and turned back just in time to see the wagon rock down the approach, twist just before the creek, lurch, and jolt to a halt, the front wheels in the water and the mares standing in the flow. Sitgreaves clambered out, peered underneath, and stood helplessly. She rode down there, not liking the place because it hid both their past and future.

"Broken axle," he said.

She waded into the water and peered under the wagon. The front axle had snapped, and the small front wheels tilted at crazy angles, water spilling through their spokes. Wordlessly she unhooked the traces and drove the mares to the far side.

She loosened the wagonsheet while he watched silently.

"We can take some. You decide what you want," she said crossly. The crazy man didn't know what to do.

"Take some?"

"Pack. We got two big mares. We got a wagonsheet. I can make a good pack from that and the harness. You ride the other. I can make some stirrups for you."

"Oh. What would thee suggest I keep?"

He annoyed her. He'd turned into a boy. "Goddammit, how should I know. Maybe your medicine things. Your clothing. Maybe a little coffee and sugar. Maybe your things to make the little signs on paper. Maybe that's all we can take."

"Not the farming things," he said. "We can't take the plow or the scythe or the hoe and rake . . ."

"We can take what you want most. What're you going to do in the Bitterroot?"

"I see," he said. That galvanized him at last. He climbed into the rear of the wagon and began thumping around in there, while she eyed the ridges suspiciously and began organizing what she'd need to make a pack load. One by one, he carried his medical things out. They didn't bulk large. Then his two personal valises. Then a field desk with his writing things. Forlornly he examined his implements and seed, coming to grips

with loss. He lifted out the two wall tents, neatly bundled with their collapsible poles.

"What're them for?" she asked.

"Why, Mrs. Skye, it wouldn't be proper—"

She snorted. "You're too fat for me."

A faint smile crinkled the corners of his eyes.

"Take one, dammit," she said. "If you got room."

It took them most of that day to sort out what Doctor
Sitgreaves wanted to take, fashion a pack frame that
employed pieces of the wagon and the surcingle of the
harness along with the wagonsheet, and load it all. Victoria manufactured two crude stirrups from the traces
and anchored the long leather loops to the surcingle of
the mare the doctor would ride. He seemed perfectly
amiable about the whole thing. Most whitemen grieved
when they were forced to abandon possessions, but not
this one. They were able to salvage his entire medical
equipment, some clothing, his field desk, a bedroll,
some kitchen and mess things, and some sugar and coffee.

She itched to escape that dangerous place. She shoved
him up on the nervous mare and stuck his boots into
the leather loops that would make bareback riding bear-
able for the portly man. And then they rode off with
the doctor leading the pack mare on a line. Both mares
seemed uncomfortable with the unfamiliar loads on their
backs, but came along. They topped the barren divide
at dusk, seeing layer on layer of purple mountain ranges
before them, and through the twilight she steered them
down as far as Dog Creek—the name came back to her.
And well off the path, behind a mountain shoulder, she
made camp.

She had no meat to cook, and made no fire. Some
fear crabbed at her.

"We ain't eating tonight," she said.

"I will endure."

"It's too damn bad about the wagon."

"I came into the world possessing nothing, and will leave it the same way."

They had scarcely talked in all their days of travel, but she sensed he wanted to now.

"You gonna be alone," she said. "No wife to care for you."

"It saddens me. I miss them. Each day, I've been hardening myself to it."

"Two winters—that's a long time."

"I'm afraid it'll be more than two years, Mrs. Skye. I'll never see them again."

"Sonofabitch! Are you sick?"

"No, quite hale. But I won't return to them. I'll spin out my days here in the mountains."

"You crazy."

He was staring hesitantly at her in the solemn dark. The stars glittered everywhere. Freshets of icy air coiled off the peaks, chilling her. "Ordeal sometimes strips away the delusions, the comfortable falsehoods with which we cushion our lives, Mrs. Skye. I didn't know it would. I didn't expect it. I found myself—my soul, rather—naked in the midst of our ordeals. And I saw Abby's soul naked as well."

"Don't you look at my spirit naked," Victoria snarled.

He laughed. "Thee wears thy spirit plain to view, Mrs. Skye. The Friends sometimes don't. Many other whitemen don't. I didn't."

"What do you mean?"

"I now see myself as Abby sees me. I was a curious child, eager to know how everything works. And a tender one. I nursed wounded birds and kept turtles, and never dreamed the world was a harder place. I still am a curious child, and I still don't know how hard the world is."

"That's how your woman sees you?"

"Yes, and Artemus also. And now I peer through a glass darkly. There was always—forgive me for burden-

ing thee with this—something in Abby's union with me
I didn't want to see. I suppose I'm saying she mocked,
and I pretended she didn't. All these years, just under
the surface, she—mocked. And Artemus scorned me.
For all the false years. Only Junius, that bright open
lad, only Junius—''

She heard his voice break, and heard him fight back
the choking. ''I'll be buried in the Bitterroot Valley
someday, madam. I've no home to return to.''

Chapter 29

They camped beside the Clark Fork in an austere valley with little game. They were on the Pacific slope now; this water would eventually tumble into the Columbia. It made Philadelphia seem all the farther away for Doctor Sitgreaves.

Riding the Percheron mare hadn't been as bad as he feared. Her broad back supported his bulk well, and the stirrups Victoria had fashioned were a comfort.

They made camp silently, dragging the bulky pack off the other Percheron and picketing the two mares on good bunchgrass. She had chosen a bench in a small coulee well back from the river trace, where their fire would not be seen.

"You get firewood and make camp. I'm going hunting. Maybe deer come to water now."

She eyed the twilight hopefully.

"I wish thee luck," he said heartily, since they lacked meat.

She glared at him and rode west, downstream, on her bay mare, her old long rifle across her small lap.

She didn't approve of him, he knew. But who did? Not his family. Not the Friends who'd abandoned him. Maybe not himself. He supposed that if he did enough for the Indians he might make up for his other failings. He'd only recently discovered that his enthusiasms didn't endear him to others. Obsessions, he should call them. Obsessed people shut out the needs of others. Obsessed people never wondered what their spouses thought.

He sighed, knowing it was too late to remake himself. He thought the die had been cast in his childhood, maybe even before he was born, and all that remained was to live out his life according to the nature he found himself the possessor of at age fifty.

He watched Victoria vanish into the twilight, as lithe and silent as a stalking puma, and then set about his familiar routine, feeling his stomach gnaw at him. Not many times in his life had he wanted for food. He unrolled the wall tent they'd salvaged from the wagon and assembled the clever collapsible poles in the amber last light of a late August day. It'd turned chilly at night, and the tent was welcome.

That's when he found himself not alone. Astonished, he peered up at twelve, no, fourteen Indians who were watching him silently. They were on foot, and had ghosted in so quietly he had no inkling of their presence until they were upon him. A swift terror laced through his gut, but he overcame that. He'd come to help them, and meant them no harm. He smiled.

"Welcome," he said. "And who are thee?"

None replied. These weren't the tall Blackfeet he'd seen before. These were shorter, stockier, bandy-legged ones, lightly clad even in the chill evening. They wore less plumage than the proud Blackfeet, but were well armed with lances, clubs, bows and arrows. They weren't painted, and he took that for a good omen.

He knew the peace sign, at least, and raised his hand. It evoked no response. He walked to his pack, hunting for a tobacco twist for a peace gift, and found he had none; the gifts had been jettisoned.

"Would thee speak English?"

None would. He wished Victoria might translate for him.

Almost as he thought it, he heard the distant boom of her rifle. Meat, then. The Indians heard it as well, and it excited them into swift action. Several of them ran to the Percherons and pulled up the picket pins, exclaiming at their great size.

"No!" cried the doctor. "Thee mustn't. Those will carry my surgery."

They ignored him and hastily bridled the mares. The horses stood so tall, and these Indians were so short, that the riders had to be hoisted up by the rest.

"I'm going to Owen's Post. John Owen, the trader. Do thee know him? These mares will carry my surgery!"

He lumbered toward them, intending to grab the reins and take possession of his own, but a warrior lowered his lance and barred the way.

The rest pawed through the pack, upending medical chests, surgical tools, carboys and flasks, tins of ointment, vials of powder.

"But these are dangerous to thee!" he cried to one who was fondling the blue bottle of laudanum. "An overdose will kill thee!"

The Indian uncapped the bottle, sniffed, and capped it again.

Others examined scalpels and clamps, exclaiming at their treasure. Some pulled his clothing from his valises, but it proved to be too large for them. Others discovered his sugar and coffee, skillet, pot, and spoons.

"But thee don't understand! I've come to help thee!" he cried, frantic. "These things have no value to thee—but with them I can heal, spare thee pain . . ."

They either didn't understand or ignored him. One

found his field desk and pulled out paper, nib pens, and ink bottle. He uncorked the ink and poked his finger in, then smeared its blackness over his chest and arms, making great chevrons. Others joined him, blacking their cheeks and ribs until all the ink had vanished.

Oh, where was Victoria?

Swiftly, in the deepening gloom, they sawed the pack sheeting into smaller squares and made bundles for all the loot, one per man. The heavier things they hoisted up to the riders on the Percherons.

And then, as silently as they had emerged in the twilight, they vanished off to the east, carrying everything except the clothing they'd rejected. He stared helplessly, obscurely glad he was alive, yet appalled at the plunder. Now he had nothing but himself.

He did not know who they were. Perhaps Bannocks or Snakes. They had spared his life, perhaps because he was unarmed and obviously harmless. The paradox of being robbed by those he'd come to help didn't bother him much. They were ignorant of his intentions, and were only doing what their own culture had fostered in them. Thus he arrived not at forgiveness, but understanding. What was there to forgive? Especially if predatory white trappers had treated them harshly? Surely that had to be it: these warriors were simply taking revenge. That was what he had come all this way to find out about. He sighed, knowing that this, too, had been Divine Providence at work. He would be a lonely David in a world of Sampsons. Eventually, he'd become one of them: sit at their campfires, hear their drums, share their hatreds, and turn his back upon the comfortable world he'd come from.

Victoria returned with a doe hanging loosely over her mare, and paused in the dark, staring at the looted campsite.

"Sonofabitch! What people?"

"I don't know."

"How many? They painted?"

"I didn't count. A dozen. No, not painted. On foot."

"Horse-stealer party. Take everything almost."

"It's just as well. They needed it worse than I do."

"You crazy goddam bastard. Why ain't you mad?"

"They were simply getting revenge, Mrs. Skye."

"Revenge? They stole everything you got. They stole the mares. They stole the medicine. Did you fight? I bet not. You just smiled."

"We don't believe in—"

"That's the trouble," she snapped.

"It was their culture."

"It was your stuff. How you gonna make medicine?"

"I'll have more shipped. Meanwhile I can live with them. Learn their ways. Make myself one of them."

"You get new stuff, they'll take that too. They don't respect no one like you."

"They'll learn about me. They respected Father De Smet, didn't they?" He had her there, he knew. The Jesuit had traveled safely among all the tribes, teaching, helping, taking their messages and needs to the officials back east.

She glared at him. "He was a friend, yes. But he didn't approve of their ways. He tried to teach them the whiteman things. Your religion. He got mad if they stole from him. He didn't try to make himself one of them."

"I see little difference."

"Well, I do. Him, the blackrobe, he didn't hate nothing about where he came from. He brings the words in the sacred book. He teaches peace, quit the fighting. He says, learn how to plow and plant. He says he got the true faith and whites got lots of good things to teach the peoples here. But you, you think all the whiteman back there are no damn good, and the peoples out here got the better ways. If we got better ways, how come you're here?"

"I can't explain it to thee! It's too subtle for thee!"

But she wasn't listening. She let the doe slide to the grass and picketed her little bay mare. Then, before doing anything else, she nocked an arrow in her bow and walked a great circle around the camping site. She didn't return until the night had thickened.

"We gotta move," she said.

She retrieved the slain doe and the mare while he picked up his scattered clothing, and then she led him straight across the river. He waded behind her horse, splashing across a sandy bottom while the icy water lifted to his thighs, tugging at him. On the south bank she turned her mare downstream and he walked behind, feeling water boil in his shoes and leak away. They camped a mile or so distant, just when he began to raise blisters on his heels.

Fiercely, she dressed her doe and cooked thin strips of loin over a fire that could have fit in a hat.

"You got a long walk," she said gently. "Maybe you can ride my mare some. Not all the time. I'll get you to the Bitterroot somehow."

He detected a kindness in her voice that hadn't been there an hour earlier.

They made good time, taking turns riding Victoria's mare. The little horse turned surly when carrying Sitgreaves's great weight, but it didn't matter. Walking had always been easy for Victoria, and she glided along, sometimes beside him as he rode, other times scouting ahead on foot.

She was used to probing far and wide, seeing what dangers loomed in every direction, but now she couldn't, and had to trust her instincts. She did keep them as far from the river trace as she could, even though it made the going much harder. And sometimes, when she felt uneasy, she hid him in a copse of trees and probed ahead.

He had fashioned a bundle from his spare clothing and hung it on the end of a stick, which he carried over his shoulder when he walked and in his lap when he rode. They had only her buffalo robe for the chill nights, but he armored himself with several layers of his clothing, and they managed. She carried her bow and quiver with her, but the rest of her gear stayed on the mare, adding to the weight it carried. She would have preferred that Doctor Sitgreaves walk always, but his heels had blistered and a spell on the mare now and then helped him.

They made better time than if he had been driving the wagon over these trackless lands. With the wagon, their progress had been continually stymied by obstacles: ditches, creeks, cutbanks, boulders, belts of trees, patches of sagebrush, steep banks—all of which had to be negotiated somehow. Too, they'd had to rest the draft horses and care for them constantly, checking for harness sores. Walking was easier and faster, and left no wagon tracks through grass and clay behind them to signal their passage. So this wasn't so bad, she told herself.

They lacked food much of the time, and she was hard put to find anything. But it was a prime season for roots like the camas, and greens, and she made tasteless meals of them along with anything she could kill, including small creatures. They had no eating utensils, and only her Green River knife to cut things up. But they managed. It was hard to find large game while hunting on foot. But they survived, and he never complained. Not about the lack of food, nor his aching feet, nor the increasing cold.

In fact, she had come to marvel at him even if he was crazy. She had come to see this dignified man with the bright eyes and childlike face in terms of negative virtues. He never complained. He never lamented all that he had lost or his current condition. He never grew angry with her or even short-tempered. He never scorned her or looked down at her as so many white people did. He never argued or questioned her judgment or imagined that he knew better what to do. He never was lazy, waiting for her to do the camp chores.

He never made idle talk, diverting her from her heavy task of keeping them safe and fed. She knew his feet tortured him, but he never insisted on riding the mare too long. In the evenings he removed his battered shoes and washed and rubbed his feet, but never sulked or whined, as many would have done. She knew he was sometimes sick, feverish, but he hid it from her.

She came to like him for all those things. She saw courage and dignity in him. In spite of the obvious aches in his body, he found ways to ease their life together. He gathered firewood, cleaned the ground where they would sleep of every stick and pebble and lump to ease their rest, and cared for the mare, making sure she was not galled by all her chafing burdens. She saw in his countenance an acceptance of life as it was, a kindliness toward her that counted for a lot on the trail together, and best of all, an unfaltering will. He never wondered whether he should continue, or whether to give up and go east, or whether he'd made a mistake. He wished to go to Owen's Fort in the Bitterroot Valley, and that was that. As the weary days slogged by her affection turned to admiration. He had traits as strong as Mister Skye's, even if they were radically different. He was a man. He was hard, though he seemed soft. He had set himself a task and somehow he would achieve it, even if he had little more than the clothes on his back. She realized she was in the company of someone grand, a chief, a headman, a great one of his people.

But she still thought he was crazy.

One night they reached Hellgate, the place where the Blackfoot River tumbled through a gorge and emptied into the Clark Fork. Whitemen called it that because it was the place where the Siksika poured through to raid the Salish people. French trappers had named it la Porte de L'Enfer, and the Americans had picked it up. They were at the northern extremity of the Bitterroot Valley, and not far from Owen's Post, but this was a dangerous place. Chief Victor's Flatheads lived to the south around

Owen's Post. Chief Alexander's Kalispels lived to the north in the valley of the great lake. And the Kootenai lived at the northern end of that long lake. Often, these peoples and the Siksika met right here. She led Sitgreaves far back in a crease in the mountains rather than risk a night on this great Blackfoot road.

"Two days now, and we'll be at Owen's Post."

"We're that close?"

"Them mountains, they the Bitterroots." She pointed southwest at a vast linear range of jagged blue peaks, some of them whited by early snow, all of them backlit by a dying sun. "Damn nice valley."

She watched carefully to see his response. They had emerged from an intimate valley of the Clark Fork, and out upon a verdant flat surrounded by pine-clad slopes that now lay before him. Once Mister Skye had told her about the people of the Black Book, who had wandered the earth en route to the Promised Land, a land of milk and honey promised them by the One Above. She eyed this doctor who was so full of the wisdom of the One Above, and wondered if he was seeing the Promised Land.

He stood, saying nothing, his bright eyes surveying the wide place, and the mysterious valley, his destined home, running off toward the south.

"Sonofabitch. You don't say nothing."

"It's hard to talk about birth. Harder to talk about death."

"You mean Junius?"

"I mean future and past."

"What you gonna do there?"

"Why, find out if I'm welcome. I never heard from Owen. See what sort of quarters there might be. See whether I can earn my keep—give labor or service of some sort. Send word back east some way—I'd like to send a letter with thee, letting my family know of my arrival . . ." He paused, his face downcast a moment.

"A letter with thee ordering a new surgery and pharmacy."

She wondered if in that moment he had decided not to contact his family. It seemed like it.

"If there are no suitable quarters, I'll build some. Perhaps hire some Flatheads to help me."

"How you gonna pay?"

He fixed her with his gaze. "With medicine. With teaching. There's much healing I can do with a kitchen knife, with a needle and thread, with herbs. Much of my ability to heal lies in my head, not in the things they took."

"How you gonna live alone?"

"That will be hardest. That's the death and the life. I must make new friends and let other—friends—go. And I'll have my work. Learn several languages. If Owen has paper, I'll begin my journal."

"How you gonna eat?"

"We'll see what I can arrange with John Owen and his—Nancy? Is that her name?"

"That's the name he gave her. Like I'm Victoria. You gonna have a new wife?"

"I—haven't thought about it."

"Goddam, you need a wife. Them Salish make good ones."

"I'll consider it."

"You ever going back?"

This time she saw a hurt in his face as he hesitated. "I don't know. Maybe, if I fail here."

"You got big medicine."

"I might fail. I might be too soft, too foolish. I might be unwise. I might not have listened to Providence. I might starve for company. A talk with a colleague. A glass of wine. A Meeting."

"Maybe your people, they come here after you make a place."

"No—not ever."

"You can't live alone. You gotta have someone."

"I've lived alone for many years without knowing it."

"Maybe Owen sells, or goes away, and his post dies."

"One lives day by day. Nothing is ever easy or guaranteed."

She eyed him contemplatively in the blue-stained light. At bottom he remained a mystery to her. She could not fathom his reasons for coming.

"How come you gonna write stuff against your people?"

"Only if I must, and only if they treat thee—thy people—as they've treated other people of color." He smiled at some recollection. "I will be a voice crying in the wilderness."

"We Absaroka got contraries. Everything they do is backwards, wrong way. If they say high, they mean low. If you say stop, they go. Like you, maybe?"

The doctor shook his head. "No, Victoria. Not like your contraries. Every Friend seeks to be a prophet, hearing the Divine and rebuking the world."

"Sonofabitch," she muttered. He was crazy after all.

Chapter 30

The sight of Owen's Post, which he first saw from across a lush meadow, enraptured Doctor Sitgreaves. The old St. Mary's Mission, founded by the Jesuits a decade before, lay in an exquisite place, with the wild peaks of the Bitterroots, tipped with snow, vaulting in the west, and the formidable Sapphire Mountains rising to the east. In between lay a verdant, mild valley, bisected by the Bitterroot River, which wound between tall-grass meadows and copses of aspen. The sketchy descriptions of the place he'd read back in Philadelphia didn't begin to do justice to it.

Father De Smet and Father Anthony Ravalli had raised a log chapel there, which became the nucleus of a mission and farm where everything needful was grown. But the mission had failed, and in 1850 the Jesuits had sold it to John Owen, a former army sutler who, with his brother Frank, added buildings, built a stockade, and began the trading post. It was said back east that Owen, a small rotund fellow with a florid face and a black goatee, brought a wagonload of books, being highly educated, and was a merry soul as well. That had been one of the things that had drawn the doctor to this place.

And yet, his startled eyes beheld the unexpected as well. Beside the post were canvas tents pitched in an orderly row. And bustling around these tents were blue-shirted soldiers. It flabbergasted him. United States soldiers here! But unmistakably, a large number of them were camped across the meadow, and their pack mules grazed on picket lines near by. A sadness struck him: soldiers here in a peaceful valley. He felt an excitement and loathing sweep through him. But there was no help for it. He silently trudged across the meadow at the bottom of the wild mountains, Victoria riding beside him. An odd thing struck him: the post seemed unused. He saw no domestic animals, no signs of grazing, no gardens, no lodges of visiting tribes.

He walked past blue-clad soldiers who howdied him and examined his tattered clothing and the bundle he carried on a stick over his shoulder, and made his way into the stockaded compound, with Victoria following silently. There at last he found Owen himself, easily identifiable, and along with him a tall, saturnine army lieutenant who watched him approach with curiosity.

"Thee are John Owen," he said, aware that the trader and the captain were taking his measure. "I am William Sitgreaves."

The mention of his name evoked no recognition in the trader.

"This is my guide, Victoria Skye."

A faint light lit in Owen's face. "What can we do for you, Sitgreaves?"

"I wrote thee about coming here with my party. Didn't thee receive—"

"Sorry, no. We closed the place last fall. Just returned two days ago. Blackfeet drove us out. Stole our horses, killed a man, made it impossible to do business.

But now with the army setting up a cantonment here, we'll try it again. What did you say your name was?''

"Sitgreaves. William Penn Sitgreaves. I'm a physician. I came—'' He suddenly found himself unable to explain it all, especially with that lieutenant eyeing him.

"Doctor Sitgreaves, this is Rufus Saxton, in command of these troops.''

The officer shook hands with Sitgreaves and ignored Victoria.

"A doctor, are you? A regular physician and surgeon?''

"Philadelphia School of Medicine, sir. I came to practice among the tribes here—''

"Where's your kit?''

"Ah, commandeered by tribesmen, sir.''

"A regular doctor, are you?''

Sitgreaves nodded.

"I've a sick list. Five men. Two with the ague, one with a broken arm—kicked by a pack mule. Other two ailing, one with diarrhea, the other, I don't know. You'll take care of them.''

"I haven't much—''

"We've a field surgery, but no one knows how to use it.''

Doctor Sitgreaves pondered that. "Would thee tell me, sir, what thee are doing here?''

"You a Quaker?''

"A Friend, yes. Founder of the Indian Aid Society.''

Saxton frowned. "We're en route to Fort Benton to meet Governor Stevens. Came from Washington Territory. We'll start talks with the Blackfeet—putting the devils on a reservation, you know—and then escort Stevens out to the coast.''

"Sonofabitch,'' said Victoria.

Saxton frowned. Owen laughed.

"There'll be a depot near here. Cantonment Stevens,'' the lieutenant added. "Now, what was your business, Doctor?''

"I came, at first with a party of Friends and my family, to be of service to the tribes, practice medicine, be a voice for them . . ." He decided to say no more.

"Here?" asked Owen.

"I had explained it all in a letter . . ."

Owen stroked his black goatee. "Might be an attraction. Draw some business. But you're here alone."

"The others—turned back. I lost a son."

"Goddam Siksika," said Victoria.

This time, the officer smiled. "Well, sir. I'll get the field surgery and you can begin. I can't have a sick list."

Doctor Sitgreaves found himself following the officer out of the stockade toward a mound of equipment in the care of a blue-shirted corporal. The surgery turned out to be an oaken cabinet of a size to fit on a mule. Within, he found a splendid array of surgical instruments, steel with polished wood grips, a variety of powders and herbs in rugged brass vials, poultices and dressings of every descriptions, and medical devices, including catheters, lances, and a stethoscope.

"We've not discussed my fee," he said softly.

"Fee? I can requisition your service. This is army country, Sitgreaves. All Indian country is."

"I would accept the surgery, sir."

"It's not mine to give you."

"I'd welcome half, then."

"I told you I won't."

"I don't know that I wish to treat thy men." That went against his very soul. He would help anyone at any time, if he could. But he hoped to negotiate something out of this.

"Look here, Sitgreaves," Saxton said unpleasantly, "I can requisition your service. I can take you bodily back to Fort Benton and keep you in my custody as long as I choose. There's no civilian rule here, and you'd better get used to that."

"Thee would even compel me to go against my conscience?"

"Doctor, I'll compel you to perform any service the army needs."

"Thee are mindful of my liberties, I see. Very well," he said. "Let's be about it."

He set and splinted a tricky spiral fracture of the ulna and gave the man some laudanum; treated the ones with ague with quinine he got by boiling Peruvian cinchona bark; put the weathered soldier with dysentery in isolation, fearing a communicable disease, and gave him paregoric. The other, with a bilious fever, he could do little for. He dosed the man with a tincture of aconite and applied cold compresses. And all the while he worked, he mulled over his astonishing circumstance, doctoring soldiers whose mission would oppress the very tribes he wished to help.

He yearned to pilfer small amounts of everything, and a few instruments that could tide him over until he got new supplies. But his own rectitude prevented it. He left instructions about further dosages with a private who was acting as orderly, and drifted back to the compound.

He found his cheery host in the kitchen of the log house, along with Victoria. They were being served elk steaks by a tiny Indian woman.

"Nancy, this is Doctor Sitgreaves," Owen said. "Join us, please. And if you would, Doctor, tell us your story. I have some of it from Mrs. Skye."

He did.

Owen peered through the open shutters at Mount St. Mary, bolting upward in the west. "Glad to have a man about. Educated one at that. I've the best library in five hundred miles. I'll be wanting help here and there. You can man the store when I'm away. It's not a safe place, Sitgreaves, even with the army around. I can't ask you to help defend—not with your beliefs. But sure, stay and share the luck. Only one thing—don't rile up the army."

"I'll try not to, Mister Owen."

"I like your ideas, Doc. They ain't practical, but that's no account. It'll be a draw. They'll come for doctoring and trade."

"I feared as much."

He needed to be alone, and wandered through the old place, admiring Father Ravalli's gristmill, barns, and fields. Soon the fields would be plowed and productive again; there'd be cattle and sheep and swine and poultry; the grapevines would be pruned and fruitful, the fruit orchards groomed and yielding. Soon the Salish and Shoshones and Kootenai and all the rest would return and trade and tell him their dreams and woes. Soon he'd spend a winter's eve sharing thoughts and books and authors with the former army sutler, sharing good talk beside a glowing hearth. Soon, Divine Providence willing, he'd be writing his reports and dispatching them to Friends back east, truly a voice crying in the wilderness. Soon, he'd be delivering brown babies, helping with difficult births. Soon he'd be teaching midwives, showing tribesmen how to sow and reap. And soon, too, he'd be burying the dead, comforting the bereaved. Life would go on. He'd be a part of it in this demiparadise, the most exquisite place he'd ever seen. A contentment came upon him. He'd lost everything, his dear family, his possessions, his self-esteem. And won everything back.

He found Victoria sitting her mare and waiting for him.

"Are you happy?" she asked doubtfully.

"Very."

"I gotta go."

"I know. I want to thank thee. Thy wisdom and skills, they got us through. Thee are a most remarkable woman, Mrs. Skye. I love thee dearly."

The weathered old lady slid off the bony mare, weeping, and hugged him.

"Sonofabitch!" she muttered. "I didn't know leaving you would be this hard."

Barnaby Skye dozed away the summer days in his lodge, pitched in an obscure crease in the empty prairie, beside a cold spring. The weakness lay upon him. He could scarcely sit up for more than a few minutes. Travel of any sort was beyond him. He knew eventually he and Mary and Dirk would be discovered, and by Blackfeet too. The very thought brought anguish. He'd be helpless in their hands.

Mary had cared for him from the moment Victoria and Doctor Sitgreaves had departed. She'd kept his left side higher than his right to keep fluids out of his good lung. She'd changed the doctor's dressings, cleaning the suppuration from the entry and exit wounds. She'd pressed her ear to his right chest and listened for long periods, and once, frowning, she'd pulled the poultice off, cut Sitgreaves's sutures, and slid a hawk quill into his injured lung, piercing through new flesh which hurt like the devil even though she had been gentle. Then she'd helped him turn over, and held him up while an odious fluid pulsed slowly from the chest wound. Then she'd packed an herb she'd ground into a powder into the wound, stitched and poulticed it again. He didn't know what herb; Indian women had so many. It had hurt like hell.

But mostly she hunted food, taking the child with her. She usually came back without meat, but often with roots and berries. She wasn't the huntress Victoria was, especially with her bow and arrows. She didn't dare risk the noise of a shot. The food gathering went badly, he knew. She vanished for longer periods, roaming farther down the coulee toward the Missouri, often returning weary and half desperate.

He grew desperate himself, wildly hungry and unable

to do anything about it. One evening she came back with nothing but some lobes of prickly pear.

"Mister Skye, I can't find anything else," she said.

Dirk had grown fussy for lack of food.

"We'll have to go to the Missouri bottoms. Can you rig a travois for me?"

"Many people go there."

"Back some. Back up this coulee a half a mile. Is there a place?"

"I don't know whitemen's miles."

"Back maybe twenty flights of an arrow. Back from the trail along the river. Still up the bluffs—on top."

She frowned. "Mister Skye, this is the revenge of Fire Horse. His spirit gets even. He tries to kill you."

"I feel bloody bad about it. I made a mistake."

"It is Fire Horse. Maybe I will talk to the spirit."

"Later, Mary. Let's go. We'll leave at dark."

But she shook her head. She vanished from the lodge, and a while later he smelled smoke. He didn't like that; it gave away their hiding place. Then he smelled sage on the smoke, and sweet grass, and he knew she was making medicine. He heard her chanting out there, a low singsong in her Snake tongue. Somewhere in the middle of it Jawbone whickered. She sang some more, her voice too low for him to catch her song.

Jawbone poked his head into the lodge, as he did every little while, and eyed Skye malevolently. Then he vanished. Mary finished her song in the dusk. He felt desperately hungry. Dirk complained and wept.

She appeared in the lodge door at last, in lavender twilight. "I tell Fire Horse you sorry, you feel bad, you honor him as great medicine horse like Jawbone," she said simply.

"I do feel bad about it. Felt bad from the moment I pulled the trigger."

"I think Fire Horse forgives. I see him galloping across the sky."

After that she broke camp, working in the velvet

night. She rigged a travois to one of the pack mules, using lodgepoles. She dismantled the lodge and abandoned the rest of the lodgepoles. They'd leave too much sign, plowing earth as they dragged behind one of the mules. She folded the lodge cover and lashed it to the travois poles as a litter to carry him. Then she helped him into it. The small effort started his heart pounding, and sucked his strength from him, and hurt. He clung to his carbine as if it were a healing wand.

Through the night Mary led her party down the crack in the prairie to the place she knew. Jawbone walked freely beside the travois, limping slightly though the flesh of his shoulder had healed over. Skye bounced and hurt, and his heart raced. Sometime after midnight, he thought, she pulled to the left and took them around a thicket of willow trees and brush to a level bench below the prairie and above the coulee bottom.

"We close to the big river now," she said.

She unloaded him there and picketed one pack mule. The other, with the travois, she took into the darkness and was gone a while. He knew she was making pole tracks down to the river; in the morning she'd brush away the ones that turned aside to this place. His stomach complained, along with his entire body.

And there, in the next weeks, they prospered. She made a hut of their lodge cover. She slew does in the lush bottoms. He gained strength swiftly, and began walking a bit. His chest always hurt, and he had no wind, but he felt life and power unfolding in him, as if Fire Horse had forgiven him; not only forgiven, but offered him strength. Maybe there was something to it, he thought.

One day she raced to the lodge in terror and picked up her old flintlock. "They come!" she whispered.

He lifted his carbine and lowered it, knowing he could not bear the recoil in his right shoulder. "Who?" he asked.

"Siksika village."

He was tempted to find an overlook and watch the great caravan, the warriors in splendid array, the massed horses dragging travois and lodges, the women and children and dogs. But he had seen many such villages in transit. Instead, he and Mary found the mules and her pony and held their muzzles, ready to clamp hands over their nostrils at the first sign of whinnying. But the village passed, heading upriver.

"Mary—let's go. I can ride some. Tonight. I can't stand it one more day here. It's getting cold. Like to reach Victoria's village before it blows."

They left that night. Mary packed the lodge cover on a mule and abandoned the two lodgepoles. They'd use no travois, leave no mark of passage other than a few hoofprints. He clambered onto Jawbone unaided, proud he'd managed it. His medicine horse whickered happily. It felt fine, bloody fine, to be on board. Jawbone pranced and danced. Skye lifted his old topper, something joyous in the motion, and settled it down upon his gray-streaked hair. They walked the horses easily down to the Missouri, ghosts in the night, and headed downstream to a buffalo crossing he knew, a good ford, especially now that the water ran low. They crossed, and the crossing was like putting an alien world behind them.

They headed south toward a pass that coiled between the Highwoods and the Belts. It would take them to the Judith Basin. This was still Blackfeet country, but by traveling nights they'd slide through. He'd find buffler in the Judith country, and he craved the meat. He wanted tongue and hump and boudins, dripping with grease. He wanted to stuff it into him until he burst. It was some powerful meat, mountain men always said; gave a man strength, buffalo did. He yearned for buffalo strength.

He wondered how Victoria had fared with Doctor Sitgreaves. They'd be at the Bitterroot by now. Probably she was heading home, a wraith gliding unseen across a wild land. He'd see her soon in the lodges of her family, in the Absaroka village of Many Coups, her cousin. They'd likely be makin' meat on Big Timber Creek at the foot of the Crazies this time of year.

He'd delivered his client once again. In all his years of guiding, he'd never had most of them turn back as the Friends did, but he felt sure that Sitgreaves was now at old St. Mary's, the place he'd set out for. Nothing would stop that gentle man with the determined mind and the will of steel. Not the loss of a beloved son, not the retreat of his wife.

Skye had come to like that man. Better yet, he'd come to respect him. He'd come to respect them all, strange as their views seemed to him. What other group sought the well-being of others, and sacrificed themselves to be friends of all the world's hurting and hopeless ones?

"Mary," he said to the woman ghosting along on her pony beside him with his sleepy son in her lap. "What do you think of those Friends? Of Doctor Sitgreaves?"

"He is a big man. Big medicine. Big power from the One Above. There's no one like him. Not redman, not whiteman. They strange people, Mister Skye, but the strange ones make the world a better place, I think."

"They bloody well do at that," he said. He lifted his black top hat into the black sky as a salute to a gentle doctor far away, and rode on through the bright starlit night, filled with the gladness of being alive, being himself, and being with Mary and Dirk, heading for a rendezvous with Victoria.

AUTHOR'S NOTE

The *Skye's West* books are not historical novels, but they don't stray far from history. My fictional characters and events play out against a background of real people and events.

Most of the fur company people in the story were real persons, including Alec Culbertson, his Blood wife Natawista, Malcolm Clarke, and Edwin Denig. Denig and his Assiniboin wife, Deer Little Woman, were actually at Fort Union at the time of the story, but I moved them to Fort Benton for story purposes.

John Owen, the former army sutler who bought St. Mary's Mission in the Bitterroot from the Jesuits, is another real person, along with his wife Nancy and brother Frank. Their circumstances are accurately described in the story. The depredations of the Blackfeet drove them out in 1852, and they returned with Lieutenant Rufus Saxton and his troops in September 1853. For the next twenty years, that post would be a major factor in the settlement of what is now Montana.

The *Robert Campbell* really did bring those illustrious passengers up the river that year. As early as the 1850s, over two decades before the Battle of the Little Bighorn, the Smithsonian was collecting fossils from the Dakota badlands in the heart of the Sioux country.

THE DRAGON REBORN

sequel to *The Great Hunt*

Book Three of *The Wheel of Time*

by

Robert Jordan

Praise for *Eye of the World*

"A powerful vision of good and evil...fascinating people moving through a rich and interesting world."   —Orson Scott Card

"Richly detailed...fully realized, complex adventure."
                                              —*Library Journal*

"A combination of Robin Hood and Stephen King that is hard to resist...Jordan makes the reader care about these characters as though they were old friends."   —*Milwaukee Sentinel*

Praise for *The Great Hunt*

"Jordan can spin as rich a world and as event-filled a tale as [Tolkien]...will not be easy to put down."   —*ALA Booklist*

"Worth re-reading a time or two."   —*Locus*

"This is good stuff...Splendidly characterized and cleverly plotted...The Great Hunt is a good book which will always be a good book. I shall certainly [line up] for the third volume."
                                                    —*Interzone*

The Dragon Reborn
coming in hardcover in August, 1991